Beacon

in the

Medieval

Darkness

Published by At Last Communications

Printed in the United States of America
ISBN-13: 978-0-9842768-2-0
ISBN-10: 0-9842768-2-3
Library of Congress Control Number: 2015908714

THE CAROLINGIAN CHRONICLES, VOL. 2

Beacon

in the

Medieval

Darkness

ACACIA OAK

At Last Communications 2015

Dedication

In appreciation of those who learn from the past and constantly seek new ways of examining old problems...

Janice C. Swab, Irene Kokkala, Carol C. Banks, Sara Lary, Heidi L. Kar and all the rest. You know who you are.

"To have another language is to possess a second soul."

"Right action is better than knowledge; but in order to do what is right, we must know what is right."
Charlemagne

Chapter 1

PLANS & COUNTER PLANS

"Hildegard's not there? What are you saying, Roland? No one's at Lord Baden's manor? Where are Hilde's mother and father, her brother – Gerold?" Charlemagne stumbled against Samson's side. "You didn't find anyone?" He held to Samson's pommel. The big horse hovered close, sensing his master's worry. King Charlemagne's eyes bulged with fear; his face was pasty white. He was as near to panic as Roland could remember.

As if in response, the heavens pelted rain on the little gathering. A mere three hundred yards from King Charlemagne's mobile court, the men huddled around Roland, Charlemagne's Peer and one of his most trusted advisers. Roland shook the water off his mantle and, as softly as he could, answered his sovereign.

"We found nothing more, Sire. Ogier, I and our escort scoured the Baden manor and the surrounding countryside. I assure you. We spent several nights in the hay loft, hoping someone would return home. By the abandoned feel of the place, no one was near the manor for a week or ten days before our arrival." Charlemagne paced, his foot coverings black with mud. The soil, drenched by two days of storms and decimated by hundreds of animal hooves, was a thick, soupy mix underfoot. The more Roland explained, the faster the King walked, the more rapidly he rubbed his hand together, the more agitated he became.

"There's nothing to do but mount a search for them. The neighbors, though far-flung, have no knowledge of the Badens' whereabouts. In fact, several were surprised no one was at the manor. We searched far and wide, Sire. No one has any information about the Count's family."

"Aye! A search, of a certainty!" The King grasped Roland's suggestion eagerly. "But where do we look? What direction do we go? This is like a journey into darkness. I despair before we begin." Charlemagne beckoned for Roland to follow and led the way to his sleeping tent. Once inside, he paced from the tent door to his sleeping linens along the wall and back again. Roland, unsure how to proceed, signed with relief as Oliver, the logical Peer, entered the tent.

"Good morrow to you, Sire, and to you Roland. You two, come with me and walk along the river. This promises to be the last day of sun, if the clouds in the distance fulfill their promise."

"Are you mad, man? I must find Hildegard! There's nothing more important. And, somehow, taking a walk fails to interest me." Sarcasm was thick in the King's voice.

"My reason for the walk, Sire... I have a plan for finding Lady Hildegard and her family. If they were spirited away, I want no one to overhear my suggestions." Oliver explained. The King stopped pacing to stare at Oliver.

"You have a plan?" He asked, holding his breath. At Oliver's nod, the King's face brightened. "Tell me."

Oliver turned his steps toward the river as he explained. He believed the Badens traveled to Septimania. He thought they left of their own choice. There was nothing out of order at the manor, no evidence of struggle or attack. Neither buildings, gardens or orchards were

2

damaged. Roland's description of the manor suggested that all disappeared into thin air.

"Something frightened them into leaving their home." Charlemagne stared at him intently.

"Aye, just so." Roland agreed, nodding.

"Why Septimania?" Charlemagne asked.

Oliver reminded the King that the Baden and Hautgard families were good friends. Hildegard was the Hautgard's guest when the King checked on their safety a year ago. In fact that was when he met Hildegard as a young woman. And Septimania was across the realm. Few Frankish people travelled there and the Hautgard manor lay isolated, not easy to find. It was a perfect location for being unseen.

"If one flees from danger, a safe haven is the preferred destination." Roland injected.

"Aye." Charlemagne answered. "It does seem well-reasoned. But why, Oliver? Why flee in secret, it seems?" Oliver, not looking at the King, shook his head slowly.

"I suspect they fled to protect Hildegard, Sire. Mayhap, the Count believed her in danger." The King saw the deep concern etched on Oliver's face. He caught his breath and fumbled for a bench, sitting down heavily. All his strength, considerable for his six-foot, 5 inch frame, seemed to leach from his body.

"Dear God. This is worse, far worse than I thought." He mumbled.

Oliver shook his head slightly at Roland. He had no idea if the Count's fears were realistic, if Hildegard were the one in danger. But he could think of no other reason for the Baden family to leave their home. He hesitated a moment, then asked the King a question.

"How many people knew of your…infatuation, your love for Hildegard, Sire?" He asked.

Charlemagne startled and stood to protest but seeing Oliver's face, he stopped. He shook his head. He knew Hildegard was the soul of discretion. In fact, he complained to her. She spoke to him casually, never for more than three of four minutes. She avoided being alone with him…even in the midst of a gathering. She did nothing to bring attention to her regard for him. But I? He thought. I was not nearly as careful as Hilde." He admitted.

"In fact, I often complained of the little attention she gave me. But I think few suspected our feelings." His last sentence faded into the silence. His hand went unbidden to his mouth. "Oh, God! My wife, Desiderata, speculated when we were still married. She complained to the Queen Mother, demanded Ma-Mam send Hilde away!" All the color drained from the king's face; his hands shook as he held them out, beseeching his friends.

"Who would harm Hilde, though, based on nothing more than rumor and innuendo?"

"Many." Oliver answered. "Many would judge her, harm her, seek to destroy her. Minds skewed through wrong interpretation of court tradition; colored by a biased interpretation of church teachings; or made jealous by her rapid rise would easily condemn her. And, once those judgments are made, condemnation and retribution follow." He shook his head and urged them not to dwell on fears but commit themselves to search for the Baden family. Now, the King stood.

"Let's begin this moment! What do you propose, Oliver? I can ready myself in no time. Let's hurry…"

"Nay, Sire, you cannot come." Oliver stepped toward Roland. "I'll leave for Septimania this morning. Roland. Will you counsel me on the terrain, suggest the best route?"

"You jest, surely!" King Charlemagne's voice erupted. "I must come; Hildegard is my life! She will look for rescue."

"You cannot." Oliver replied. "To protect her, few can know of your relationship, Sire. If anyone suspects their destination, your presence in the search surely places them in increased danger. Nay, Sire; you cannot go."

"But I must protect…? Charlemagne grew even more distraught.

Oliver shook his head. It was impossible. The King had a battle with Lombardy looming over him. And the Pope wrote often of his own fears, seeking the King's protection. Three birds arrived from him last week. Those challenges, though, were nothing compared to the Saxon threat. The Saxon tribes were on the move again. It seemed Charlemagne must soon confront a Saxon army as well as a Lombard one.

"Aye. You're right. Oliver will take up the search, Roland. If I know our Peer, he already has spies on the road west, looking for signs of the Baden's journey." He hugged Oliver's shoulders. "Thank you from the depths of my heart." Oliver grasped the King's shoulders in return.

"When I bring the Badens home, that is the time for thanks." He looked at the two men. "God speed to each of you. Stay alive until I can return and defeat Desiderius' forces for you."

Oliver grinned at them, mounted his horse, and waved his two companions forward.

King Charlemagne watched the three men as far as he could. His life's happiness rested on their shoulders. He turned back to Roland standing beside him.

"My friend, the weather grows worse. Summon our commanders. We need not worry about King Desiderius now, nor about his threat to Pope Hadrian. Hadrian must protect his city, deflect the Lombard king somehow. We must attend to the Saxons. If we delay, dislodging them will take additional effort and more loss of life. We give them no quarter this time. Their defeat must be complete." Remembering Oliver's words about Hilde's dangers, Charlemagne turned to Roland.

"Tell me, do you know Desiderata's fate? After she severed our marriage and left my court, did she return home? Is she in Pavia; do you know?" Roland startled at the quick change in subjects, but he knew the King meant to close the discussion about a march to Rome.

Roland assured the King that he had no reports of Desiderata in Pavia. His spies did locate her brother, Adelchis, about two fortnights after he left the Frankish court. Rumor had it that his sojourn home was slow because of some sickness contracted before he left their court.

Some twenty days previous, a spy reported seeing Adelchis in Pavia with his father, Desiderius. But no one could located Desiderata. Roland suspected that she would surface after the Pope annulled her marriage to King Charlemagne. Then, she could seek another marriage with hopes of comfort and glory.

Oliver suspected Desiderius sent his daughter somewhere else in Italy. "I know nothing of Desiderata's fate, Sire. But, make no mistake. She wrecked Desiderius' best chance of getting your realm. We must not underestimate his anger or his thirst for revenge. His threat to us remains…now and in the future."

"Aye, we will defeat him yet, but not this season. We march toward Aachen. Oliver will find Hilde and, soon, all will be well. Mayhap, those warm, mineral waters will soothe my worries and my impatience." Charlemagne paused, considering his next words.

"What think you of a siege of Pavia?"

"Let's watch the Saxon commanders. If all remains quiet, we may be free to invade Lombardy early in the spring. With even less ice and snow than last year, the Lombards are already caught in the mountains. In the spring, we'll be less than a week's journey from them." He rubbed his temples, looking to the south in the direction Oliver moved.

"Ahh, Roland; I fear the fighting will never end."

"Mayhap not, Sire. The battle seems ever before us. But we fight not just an enemy. We fight for your dreams – your dreams of a better life for our people."

Roland noted the King's worried frown, the grim lines around his moth. He prayed Oliver would find Hildegard and her parents and bring them safely to Aachen. A great rejoicing would sweep the court and, of a certainty, return light to King Charlemagne's eyes.

***

The long days, marching toward Aachen and watching for Oliver's return, added furrows to Roland's brow and weight to his shoulders. But God was with them, and the army finally camped in Aachen, resting from the sheer length of their summer campaign. It was now well into autumn. The huge trees looked learner, forlorn without their leaves. Small rodents, even squirrels, seldom appeared before mid-morning. And the birds, buffeted by the rising wind, flew in short bursts, never aloft for long.

As the court journeyed, more than two-thirds of the army left for home. The soldiers made preparations for the winter, to hunt and protect their families, to rest and grow strong for another battle season. The rest of the army and court settled in Achen. But these show days increased the king's disquiet.

He became even more frantic about Oliver's mission and Hildegard's safety. Mayhap, it was the warm waters of Aachen which healed his weariness and turned his thoughts, once more, to his beloved. Or it was the time of rest, too soon to plan for next year's battles, which concentrated his thoughts. Whatever the case, his worry for Hildegard increased daily, his impatience arising even before their mid-day meal.

***

Last night, instead of bedding down, Roland left camp to scout the road ahead, cognizant of the need to watch for enemies - Lombardy spies or possible scouts for some other stealthy invader. Blinking to refocus his tired eyes, he spied the head of a horse just below a distant hill. Its rider leaned close to his mount, seeming one with the animal. The horse turned its head toward the rider and stopped. It wobbled as its nose almost touched the ground. At a slight movement from the rider, it walked slowly forward. Both rider and horse drooped. Even though it was morning, they appeared exhausted.

Mayhap, they're hurt or wounded, Roland thought. A smudge of purple peeked from under the rider's saddle. *That's King Charlemagne's color! Who holds the King's colors?* Noticing the backward tilt of the rider's head, Roland stared intently, straining to identify anything else familiar.

"Can it be Oliver?" Roland blurted out. His heart jumped at the thought. Overcoming his natural caution, he snapped his reins. His horse bolted toward the slowly-moving rider. The rider's head came up; his back straightened.

"It is Oliver. Thank God, he's safe!"

Roland touched his horse's neck; the animal lengthened

its strides. Realizing Oliver saw and recognized him, Roland lifted his hand and waved. The two friends bore down on each other, meeting a few moments later, reaching for each other's shoulders, giving fierce bear-hugs.

"I feared my eyes deceived me!" Roland shouted happily, swiping his long, black hair from his eyes. "Our forward scouts began watching the woodland trail, as well as this road, for you - ever since the last moon's turn. Where were you? Found a cave of naked women, did you; unable to tear yourself away?" He beamed at Oliver with a twinkle in his eye. Oliver laughed aloud.

"No jokes, no jokes, my friend." Oliver chuckled. "It hurts every time I laugh." He grimaced, pressing his side as he leaned into a pain. "Nay, no cave; I assure you. And did I find a cave of naked women, what would I do? Exactly as you, I would give them clothing and rescue them."

Oliver's chestnut hair was a warm contrast to Roland's dark locks. But, whereas Roland was well-clothed and hearty, Oliver was clearly ill: his coloring pale, his hair dry as straw; his eyes weary and red-rimmed. His clothing, torn and stained, suggested hardship and want. He ran his hand through his unruly, tangled hair.

"Aye, you would...for certain!" Roland laughed, riding his horse around Oliver, slapping his friend gingerly on the back. "You're late in returning. Are you badly hurt, my friend?" His voice was grave as he dismounted, holding the bridle of Oliver's horse for him to do the same. Roland quickly put a hand under Oliver's arm to steady him. Oliver's hair looked gray, highlighted with road dust. Although his broad shoulders gave the immediate impression of strength, his slender frame trembled as he dismounted. He groaned as his right foot touched the ground.

"I'm almost recovered." Oliver answered, pausing to catch his breath. "A band of outlaws overtook and beat me. They gloried in the blood-letting, threatened my life anew when I had no food. One raised his sword at Streak. My smart horse raced off when they pulled me from my saddle; and, though they chased him, their nags couldn't catch him. He came back to me...about the time I realized the outlaws left me to die." Oliver took a long drink from the flagon Roland offered. "I'm happy to see you, old friend."

"Here, sit on this tree trunk," Roland suggested, pointing to a log near-by. "We'll rest here before we turn for the court. You look like you've seen the halls of Hades itself, if you don't object to the truth." He rummaged in his bag and held his hand out to Oliver. "Come, eat a traveling stick. How about an apple, some nuts? I have both in my bag." He again felt around in his traveling pouch, pulling out the fruit first.

"Many thanks, Roland," Oliver answered, smiling. "I'm better...truly. Seeing you, I can forget these bruises. I was so weary coming up the hill, I didn't focus. Why are you out here in the cold?"

A vast expanse of forest stretched back and forward on both sides of the road. The trees' lush, summer foliage - all black-green against the brilliant blue of the sky - was now a memory. The hints of color Oliver remembered from the start of his journey had disappeared, replaced by dull, brown leaves muddling the ground. The vast expanse of birch, aspen, oak, and maple raised empty limbs into the sky, heralding the winter's rapid approach. Oliver moved carefully, his legs stiff, sometimes trembling.

"I feared I might never stand upright again, too long in the saddle." He pressed Roland's arm. "Is there to be war? I heard nothing but tales of Saxon rebellion as I traveled. Do they invade our lands?" Roland shook his head affirmatively.

"Aye. They're marching, though who can guess the reason. This is not the time to begin battle. We wait for spring and our next campaign against them." He stopped. "What news of Hildegard, Oliver? Where is she? Did you find her and her family?" His brow wrinkled; he held his breath, fearing the worse.

"She's on her way here." Oliver explained, smiling through his weariness. "Ogier, Bertram, and I escorted her and her family from the Hautgard manor. Those first weeks of our search, we missed them by a week or so. They left the manor, moving in stealth toward Septimania, just as I thought. Journeying there, we found them eager to return with us. I traveled toward Aachen as quickly as possible. Thanks for sending the messenger." He smiled.

"As we speak, Hildegard travels toward us, disguised as a young squire to my two men." Oliver grinned at Roland. "Her disguise is quite convincing and she is handy at building fires and roasting rabbit. Her parents and Gerold follow some two days behind." Roland laughed out loud, relief and thankfulness coloring his enthusiasm.

"This is good news, Oliver, most especially for our sovereign."

"Aye, I hope it will invigorate him. God knows he needs some good news; the pontiff's expectations and Desiderius' threats never seem to end." Oliver noted. Roland nodded.

"I am overcome, though, to hear of yet another rebellion by the Saxons and just as you welcome me home. I always hope for peace." For the past four years, Oliver had been the only peacemaker within the Frankish court, first counseling King Pepin and, now, his son. Indeed, he often alienated the battle planners, the commanders - the King particularly - with his pleas for caution and compromise.

"Peace, my friend? I think neither you nor I will ever see it." Roland answered quietly. "But to change the subject...why do you travel ahead of your companions? Are you scouting the roads for the King as you return?"

"Aye, something like that." Oliver laughed and, then, sobered. "People in the inns know me; I didn't want to draw attention to our 'squire.' Bertram and Ogier will, I hope, not attract the interest I would. My coming alone seemed the best course. But I don't recommend traveling without companions, Roland. I've had frightening times, close calls. And, then, this last attack..." Roland noted, again, Oliver's weariness.

"Come, come to camp," Roland urged. "Charlemagne will be glad of your return. He missed your steady counsel." At that, Oliver laughed.

"Charlemagne doesn't need me, Roland; he has you." Oliver replied.

"Aye." Roland agreed. "But, sometimes, I am more shortsighted than I want to admit." He mounted his horse. "The King promised a comfortable stop for this winter's Christmastide. Everyone is happy to be in Aachen. Of a certainty, this is Charlemagne's favorite place and one of the warmest manors!"

"Let's hurry then." Oliver replied. The two men turned their horses east, riding side-by-side, each relieved the other one was close by. Just as dusk promised nightfall, Roland gestured to the right. They crested a little hill.

On the other side, just below them, rode the King. Seeing Oliver and Roland, he waved and lightly touched his horse. Samson quickened his steps. Charlemagne wheeled the huge horse beside Oliver.

"What news?" He asked, his eyes wide with worry; his hands moving up and down the reins.

"Hildegard's on her way to Aachen, Sire." Oliver reported, bowing slowly from the waist. "My men are some two days behind me, riding slowly with no urgency...all the better to shield the lady." He glanced at the King's face and hurried to add: "She's fine, Charlemagne, a bit weary of traveling but in fine spirits. And healthy," he added. "A little heavy in the belly she is, Sire, so hug her carefully." Charlemagne did not try to hide his delighted grin.

"Come, come to the fire and tell me everything!" The King demanded. Then, seeing the weary set of Oliver's body, he looked at him closely. "Are you ill, my friend?"

"Nay, Sire, only very weary." Oliver replied. The three men, bound by love and duty, turned their horses down the hill and cantered toward the ruddy glow of the Aachen manor below.

Two days after Oliver's return, Hildegard and her two guardians met Rinaldo as he patrolled some half-league from Aachen. He rushed them to the manor, urging the weary party to quicken their steps.

"Are you hungry, my lady?" He asked Hildegard. "Forgive me. I thought you would wish to see our King first, before you eat, I mean." He added.

"I do, indeed, wish to see him first, Rinaldo, before anything else." Hildegard assured him. Rinaldo helped her dismount and called to Charlemagne as he ushered her into the front hall of the Aachen manor.

"Sire, she's come! The Lady Hildegard is here!" He watched Hilde pause just a minute as she stepped inside. He heard a great sigh and listened as King Charlemagne ran down the corridor toward the door.

"Ahh, my love! At last, you're here with me, where you belong."

"I'm so happy to see you, Charley." Hildegard said before she burst into tears. Rinaldo did a quick jig and turned to the cook rooms. He planned to bring a banquet back for his king and the soon-to-be queen. He ran through the manor, calling to one and all.

"The Lady comes! Our Lady Hildegard is home!"

***

Hearing the shouts and happy noises from outside, Abbot Fulrad rolled his piece of parchment. He frowned. Why in the world was there merry-making now? Usually, at this time of day, all was peaceful: the day's last meal was some time away; children helped gather wood and secure livestock; hearth fires smoked from the addition of more fuel, court workers rested from the early morning's labors.

"Who comes to the court?" He asked out loud. "Yet another free-loader here to beg, no doubt." He shook his head, then stood still, the better to hear.

"The Lady returns!" A voice shouted.

"God be praised. The King's prayers be answered!" Another screamed.

"Can it be?" Fulrad grabbed his mantle and flung it over his shoulders, rushing from his office beside the chapel. "God's hand must be in this, if she returns." He hurried down the corridor, waving people aside as he bolted forward. "I must have prayers of thanksgiving tonight...even before our meal." He turned as Rinaldo half-ran down the corridor.

"Wait! Stop!" The Abbot reached for Rinaldo's arm. "Is it she? Has our Lady returned?"

"Aye!" Rinaldo replied, smiling broadly as he turned back to the Abbot. "She arrived minutes ago, Abbot."

"Where, where is she...at the front of the manor? I

must welcome her immediately!" Fulrad's smile spread from ear to ear.

"She's very weary, as you can imagine. The trip nearly exhausted her." Rinaldo reported. "I believe she's is already in her sleeping chamber, Sir."

"But I must see her!" Abbot Fulrad cried. "Her return is... a blessing, a true blessing to this court."

"Aye!" Rinaldo agreed. "But she needs to rest. As the sun rises in the east, she will, of a certainty, greet everyone as we break our fast. She journeyed far this day... a long and frantic ride. The Lady Hildegard will bid everyone 'Good Morrow' in the morn, Sir." He nodded to the Abbot and quickened his steps.

"The Lady Hil...Hildegard!" Abbot Fulrad stopped dead still; others in the corridor parted behind him and moved on. "Hildegard! It is she?" His face paled; his mouth tightened. "Hildegard! I thought it the Lady Desiderata who returns. Nay! Nay, not Hildegard!"

Chapter 2

LOVE AND WAR

Charlemagne made no effort to restrain himself. He folded Hildegard in his arms, there in front of everyone, and held her tight. He looked down at her dear face looking toward him and kissed her deeply. He felt tears welling in his eyes as he tried to quieten her.

"Don't cry, my darling." He begged. "You're finally home; we won't be separated again. I vow to you." He reached down to kiss her again, a gentle kiss meant to convey his thankfulness for her. As he pulled her yet closer, he felt her stomach press against him. He jumped back.

"I haven't hurt you, Hilde, have I?" He questioned. "I didn't mean, I squeezed you but…have I hurt your belly?" His hand trembled as he carefully, and very slowly, ran it over her rounded stomach.

"Nay, you do no harm, my dear." Hildegard answered, laughing with delight. "I really am quite strong, not nearly as fragile as you assume. Come, give me a bear hug! The babe and I deserve the best you can do!"

With that said, she hugged him strongly around the waist, doing her best to control the tears which rolled down her cheeks. "It's been so long, I scarcely know you." She teased.

"You must learn all you don't know," Charlemagne answered, "for I will never let you go! Ohh, Hilde! Welcome home, my love."

Hilde's homecoming was all she dreamed. Charlemagne did not leave her side. Everyone left at court, many of the commanders, and all the manor workers came to bid her welcome. Finally, seeing her weariness and the pale cast of her face, Charlemagne called a halt to the greetings, picked her up, and carried her to their bedchamber. There, he fed her delicacies from the manor's food stores, rubbed her feet and wrapped them in heated linens, and generally retrieved anything she wanted. Hildegard, finally finished with the long journey from Septimania, was content to lie quietly, to gaze at the man she adored, and to recount the story of her family's stealthy journey from home.

"It was exhausting." She admitted to Charlemagne. "Difficult for all of us, but it seemed the only choice we had. As soon as you left, in the taverns and inns, Gerald heard travelers ask about me: where I was, how long before I returned to court, if you were coming to visit. He went incognito to two of these inns one evening and felt we were in danger...or, at least, that I might be. The people most interested in me, he said, seemed to be drifters - men with no traveling bags or non-descript men eager for work. He feared they hoped to profit from knowing my location or, even, to whisk me away. His face pale and creased, he paced and talked, planning as he worried. And, of a certainty, my parents packed as soon as he paused for breath. We fled to Count Hautgard, believing Septimania the safest destination. We wore old clothing, slept in our cart, and moved through the woods...beside the road... but always out of sight."

"It was to be a great adventure but Gerold and Father were so uneasy." She sighed. "It's a great relief to be with you, my dear. Life is frightening out there. Poppa and Gerold will defend me with their lives, of a certainty.

But what would they do if overwhelmed by soldiers or worse, those who seem to roam from place to place?"

"You're safe now, sweetling. I'll not risk you again. Oh, Hilde, my life is barren without you." Charlemagne answered. "For now, remember: you're the love of my life. I shall love and adore you forever." Hilde smiled, touched his face gently, and whispered.

"I feel the same, Charley; but I need to sleep now. I am so very weary." With that, she curled her arm around his big one, laid her head on his shoulder and slept. The King smiled gently, extricated his arm and covered her with sleeping linens. He pinched out the candle, put more wood in the firepit, climbed in bed with his love and held her throughout the night. In the morning, he declared it was the most exciting night of his life. His Hilde was home at last!

***

Nothing would do. Charlemagne was adamant. The wedding must take place as soon as possible.

"I care nothing for guests, for the terrible weather, for anyone who might be inconvenienced by this ceremony." He declared to Abbot Fulrad. "Days, weeks, months pass; we still wait for the pope's dispensation. My second marriage must be dissolved. Why can his Holiness not hurry? As soon as my messenger returns from Rome, Hilde and I marry…the very next day, if possible. I'll not be dissuaded. Plans move forward, as of today. Spread the word, Fulrad. I'll wed my bride as soon as possible." King Charlemagne came to a halting stop.

"Good God! I must speak with my mother." He exclaimed. Fulrad turned in his tracks, his face drawn, his eyes startled.

"With Queen Bertrada…?" He asked, staring into the

18

King's face.

"I must, Abbot. She needs to make peace with my marriage. I will marry the mother of my child! There will be no discussion. She must adjust to reality."

"Is this a propitious time, my son?" The Abbot asked.

"There is no propitious time. My mother damns any undertaking she doesn't conjure up herself. I will declare my love for Hildegard, convince Ma-mam of my complete devotion. She needs time to accept my choice. Her dreams of influence and manipulation end today." Charlemagne's voice firmed as he spoke; his breathing quickened. Consciously, he unflexed his fists and smiled at the Abbot.

"God go with you, son." Abbot Fulrad muttered. "Mayhap, HIS strength is equal to this task."

"Aye, we must both believe so, Abbot. I have need of HIS strength." Charlemagne turned away. As he left, the Abbot's face turned grim. He slapped his right hand against his thigh, his face drawn in anger.

"If only Queen Bertrada can talk some sense into him! He must not marry this woman! His first wife, Himiltrude, the Queen Mother sent away. He's not responsible for that. "

"This second wife, Desiderata, was the princess of Lombardy. She brought allegiances and influence to him. Even though his mother arranged the marriage, still, he married of his own, free will. It was a sham of a marriage but that's his bed to lie in. The Pope did not approve of this second marriage and he probably won't countenance this third one. What will I say to him? Ohhh, he must not marry a third woman! This is not the Christian way! What can I do?" He moaned, consciously not cursing as he increased his pace down the corridor.

***

"Ma-Mam," Charlemagne began. "Good day to you. I must check in with Theodoric but wish to greet you first. And I have happy news," he declared.

"Do you?" the Queen Mother responded, lazily moving her eyes from the yarn she worked. "Where have you been? I thought you evaluating the siege engines; yet, I could not find you in the manor or the army camp." She eyed him critically. "You abandon your mother."

"Forgive me. Much demands my attention; not the least is my concern for our planned siege. But there is good news. Hildegard of Swabia returns to court." He looked directly into his mother's face.

"But, why?" Queen Bertrada asked. "She contributed little when she was here...except to feed rumors, of a certainty."

"In that belief, you are one hundred percent wrong." Charlemagne said succinctly. "Her efforts for the good of our people were always quite extraordinary, though I know you and most of the court ladies care nothing for that." The Queen Mother stared into his face, raising her eyebrow at his defense of a mere maid-in-waiting.

"I have no interest in maids," she replied dismissively, "their good works or their usefulness to the court." She paused, watching the King closely. "We do need to talk about...your plans...your marital interests, I mean to say. Such a topic is far more reaching than maids-in-waiting and their travels." She waited for a response, primed to attack any rejection he made against another marriage.

"I have no interest in maids-in-waiting, just as I have no interest in marital matters." Charlemagne declared. "Not ever again! I already chose my next...and last... wife." Queen Bertrada's back stiffened; she turned to voice an objection. Her son ignored her and continued speaking.

"The decision is made. Hildegard of Swabia and I marry immediately." He smiled at his mother, his prim mouth daring her to object. The jaws in his face flexed. But, as usual, Queen Bertrada did not notice his reactions. She sprang from the bench, stretched to her full height and began screaming objections to her son.

"You jest, surely!" She screeched. "No marital interests? Dear God, how did I birth such a fool? Have you no concern for the future of your realm? You will not marry a mere maid, don't be an ass! "

"Enough!" The King commanded. "Don't speak another word! I forbid it. I will not listen to your objections – not a single one! Do you understand me?"

"But you must!" The Queen Mother insisted. "Of a certainty, you are not serious. Marry Hildegard of Swabia? Ha! This is a joke; I demand that you send her away. I will not allow it." She glared at him. "She is unacceptable; the choice is absurd!"

"I absolutely will not send her away. Never." Charlemagne answered his mother, his voice low and cold. "Nor will I listen to your objections, to your harping, to your 'holier than God' attitude. Raise your voice, stamp your foot, stare me down! Nothing you say matters. I take no advice from you, not ever again."

"Do you hear me?" He asked, looking directly into his mother's face.

"But, I want to..." The Queen Mother spoke but the King's voice cut her off.

"There, there's the crux of it," he quickly responded. "Your wants are no longer my concern. I now concentrate on my wants—no one else's. I don't want or need your opinion. From today forward, I make my own decisions—now and hereafter." He held his hand out, silencing the Queen Mother.

"Here are the facts," he said as he began ticking off points on his fingers. "Hildegard is pregnant with my child." He delighted at his mother'sshocked expression and, then, stepped back from the calculating face she turned to him. "She loves me; I love her. As soon as my messenger arrives in Rome, the Pope will annul my marriage to Desiderata. With his order, she can go to another man unspoilt. So be it. I hold no regrets with her choice. When the annulment comes, Hildegard and I shall marry." He relaxed his face, knowing the Queen saw his confidence.

"If Hilde is content with this progression of events, God be praised. HE knows I misled her, treated her cruelly, and failed to acknowledge my love for her openly and proudly." He stood straighter. "I will never make that mistake again. Speak no more of this, Ma-Mam. I will hear nothing from your lips." As the Queen stepped forward, King Charlemagne pointed at her.

"Your single-minded plan for me - wedded to Desiderata - wasted a year of my life and, of a certainty, hastened my conflict with her father. By the grace of God, your machinations did not destroy this court. But I give you no more chances." He glared at her, anger rising yet again at her meddling. "And I take no further advice from you, Ma-mam...not a single word."

"I must go," Charlemagne continued, "there are many duties." He gazed soberly at her and left. His mother's dismissive attitude toward Hildegard, her implication that Hildegard was but a nuisance fed his anger. The tight set of his mouth and his unblinking eyes showed the control he exerted on his temper.

Truth be told, his mother's need to control, her unfair judgments, her constant criticism undermined his belief in himself. And, in turn, he did not protect Hildegard's reputation. He felt embarrassed for her. Her love for him and her steady devotion - constant even during his ill-conceived marriage - earned her respect, not dismissal. His mother, in her great ignorance and hateful arrogance, deemed Hilde nothing!

Hildegard's loving regard and belief in his dreams - such a contrast to his ice-maiden wife and to his intense, controlling mother - delighted his heart, and gave him the courage to believe in himself. Long before his mind understood her value, he pledged his heart to Hilde. *Such a pledge was premature, for a married suitor.* H acknowledged. *But, soon, she will be my wife. The only impediment is the Pope's annulment. Heaven grant that it comes soon.*

"Anyone at the court who does not accept Hildegard is welcome to leave," the King decided. "In fact, there are several, my mother included, whom I would happily escort on their way."

Charlemagne called for a new tent from Eggihard. He laid small limbs and dried leaves on the ground, covering them with oriental carpets.

"Your feet should be neither wet nor cold, Hilde," he explained to his beloved as she examined her tent. "Take this parchment." He handed her several sheets. "Draw the furniture you would like. I shall send to Tours, to a particular woodcarver, and direct him to make the pieces - just as you sketch them out." Hildegard looked with delight into the King's face, giving him a huge smile. She started to speak; but he prevented it by kissing her deeply.

"Nay, nay," the King said when he caught his breath. "It's my pleasure to present you with gifts. I don't vow a gift every day. But you will never doubt my love for you, my dear Hilde, never again."

Hildegard settled into the routine of the mobile court: preparing for winter even as the siege of the Lombard city of Pavia began. The siege required much hunting for the court and the troops. Food for the soldiers and for the animals which accompanied them was a constant concern. Tents and clothing needed constant repair. The ice and snow made constant fires and layers of clothing necessary for one and all.

Because soldiers could not return home to help their families survive the winter, they were short-tempered and fraught with worry. As a result, previous companions argued among themselves; those who did not get along together found additional reasons to disrupt and criticize. Little resentments escalated into fist fights and personal items disappeared from tents. As men wagered on the duration of the siege, impatience with the constant cold, the increasing snow, and constantly frozen drinking water frayed everyone's temper.

Although Hilde's personal happiness blossomed, she worried about possible battles and feared the threats of reprisal from the Lombards. She quieted her fears in dreams of her child, content in the knowledge that Charlemagne and his court were eager to welcome either a boy or a girl. *Of a certainty*, she told herself, *a boy would be best; but a girl will be loved and valued as well.* She overheard court members comment on the King's deep love for her and felt reassured again and again.

Abbot Fulrad, startled at Charlemagne's renewed attitude, noted the King's new-found enthusiasm and appreciation of life's endless possibilities. With Hildegard's return, the King reclaimed his dreams, and in doing, moved his soul far beyond the petty distractions that previously so hampered him. Once he ceased trying to please everyone, he became confident of his own choices. Charlemagne slowly began, not only to revive his goals for his people, but to organize plans and develop methods which would lead to the realization of these dreams.

Although he admitted it to himself but kept it hidden from others, Charlemagne's overwhelming need was to acknowledge the woman he loved to everyone. Hildegard's steadfast love for him, in the face of overwhelming discouragement, embarrassed him. She was so loyal, he was so much less so. He would shout his commitment to the heavens, to all the world! It was time to decrease his mother's influence and, incidentally, her presence.

"Ma-Mam," the King greeted his mother. "I fear the constant strain of our mobile court is undermining your health." He pulled her into a comforting embrace and patted her back. Queen Bertrada, surprised at his concern, smiled. It is so gratifying, she thought, that my boy worries for my well-being.

"I will admit," she smiled brightly at him; "this last trek almost depleted my spirit, Charley. And when you were so ill you could not travel with the returning army, I feared for your life. I wish never to know if you are ill or injured...until you obtain a total recovery." Charlemagne nodded solemnly, urging her to continue talking, afraid that if he said a word, he would show his ultimate intention. Thinking his nod reflected his acceptance of her concern, the Queen Mother looked him over critically.

"You seem thinner to me," she observed. "Why do you refuse to eat the foods I serve on your plate, Charlemagne? That stubbornness, you see, ruins your appetite. I'll bet you eat little more than meat on most days. Listen to me and follow my directions, for your own sake!" Charlemagne uttered a soft, muted sound, willing she hear it as his acceptance of her words.

"And during our battles with the Saxons, how did the court function, Ma-Mam? I want to know your thoughts so I can identify specific shortcomings to the seneschal. Egginhard is eager to improve and expand all the comforts the court requires…as long as I can afford them, of a certainty," the King added. His mother smiled widely. She never worried about the cost of the court, relying on Charlemagne to confiscate the goods the court needed or to obtain more support from the nobles.

"If the common people must go without, so that our court is splendid, so that we may continue to be proud of the comforts we offer visitors and members alike, that is only appropriate," the Queen stated. "I daresay the milk-maids, the dog handlers, those who plant the crops, they often expect more than is seemly for their stations." She checked her braid, making certain that it curled just so, as it supported her small crown.

"Nay, Ma-Mam," Charlemagne objected. He would not let such comments go unanswered. "Nay, you have the wrong of it. In fact, out servants often suffer from their own goodness. When a noble or a guest demands some special tidbit, another blanket, warming of stones for their linens, another hand to clothe the children, our workers give their time and energy willingly. They do, in fact, give too much. I am convinced of it," the King replied. "Nay, I have no quarrel with those who keep the court functioning."

"I worry that you're not as comfortable as you would like, that the constant moving throughout the realm wears on your nerves and increases your concerns. For example, doesn't all this moving affect the durability of your jewelry or the freshness of your gowns." Charlem-agne saw his mother ponder his words. "Oh, you under-stand me! Everyday comforts must be replaced sooner because of the constant travel." He watched his mother carefully from under half-lowered lids,

"The mobile court is always difficult, son," Queen Bertrada replied. "I so wish you would establish a permanent court." Her eyes sparkled. "A permanent court would relieve us of many of these concerns."

"I daresay it would," the King replied. "But, Poppa always urged me to be out among the people. It builds connections, this traveling. The people like to see me moving through the realm." He paused, as if thinking. "But, as for you, Ma-Mam, I have a solution. I have three small castles which are occupied only as we occasionally pass a night or two in them. You must choose one of them for your own!"

Queen Bertrada's eyes flashed; her mouth fell open; a huge smile decorated her face. For years, she yearned for a court over which she could preside with even more authority. Having a castle, she could acquire the very best in tapestries, carved furniture, and elegant clothing.

"I'd like nothing better!" She assured Charlemagne. "That would be heaven for me, a place to call my own!"

"Why, then, it shall be done!" The King replied, deliberately frowning as he spoke. "Forgive me, Ma-Mam. I had no idea you were so wistful for a permanent castle. Choose from the one in Aachen, Poiters, or Lyons. Any of them may be yours!"

"Oh!" Queen Bertrada was breathless. "I should very much like the one in Lyons!" She squealed with glee. "It is very near the abbey there. I often thought the abbey would make a perfect retreat for me...after your father died." She looked quickly into the King's face. "But you needed me with you."

"Then Lyons shall, as of this day, be your home, Ma-Mam," Charlemagne replied. "On our journey for this year's Yuletide, mayhap we shall winter there. You will have time to refurbish it, all to your specifications. Then, as the rest of us begin our spring circuit, you may wave goodbye to us gladly." He smiled widely into the

Queen's eyes.

"What a joy that will be." the Queen replied, caught up in the moment. "I shall look forward ..." Her voice trailed away. "I'm not to make the spring circuit with the court?" She asked, her eyes widening in horror.

"Of a certainty, Ma-Mam, you will not have that duty again." Charlemagne replied. "It is the rest of us who must continue to travel around the realm. You will be safely ensconced in your own castle!" Kissing her quickly, the King hurried from the chamber. Outside, he yearned to laugh aloud; but he controlled himself and raced from the manor. He did not want to hear his mother's wail of anger when she realized how he duped her.

***

"Charley, I would speak with you." His sister, Gisela, said some three days after the conversation with the queen mother. "It's rather important. Abbot Fulrad, please excuse us." The Abbot bowed deeply, relieved to move himself from the King's presence. *He is going to keel over*, Fulrad thought, *with all this passion and excitement! He must learn that sacred ceremonies must not be rushed.* He shook his head in regret. *Charlemagne listens to no one about this marriage; mayhap, Gisela can influence him.*

"Gisela, come!" Charlemagne urged. "I need your clear-eyed thinking; help me remove these court ...and church...obstacles from my marriage ceremony. Surely, it's not necessary for a wedding to be so complicated!"

"Most weddings take months of planning, brother." Gisela replied. "But I come to beg you for patience. I do have an excellent reason for requesting it of you." She took Charlemagne's hand in hers, led him to a seat by the firepit, and nodded toward it.

"Please sit. Sit and listen." The King, with a greatly

exaggerated sigh, sat; folded his hands in his lap; and looked up at her.

"I will give you five minutes." He growled. "Then, I must be up, driving my court to make preparations." Gisela smiled warmly at him and hugged his neck. He motioned to a near-bench and moved as if to move it closer.

"Nay, Charley. I prefer to stand just now." Gisela said. "I don't wish to ruin your plans for an immediate wedding. But, you must wait a bit longer."

The king's head swiveled around to stare at her. He opened his mouth to object as Gisela put her hands over his mouth.

"Listen to me, Charley. You must think of Hildegard. She IS pregnant, very pregnant. The baby may come at any time." She stopped and caught her brother's eyes. "Do you understand me, Charley? Her time is very near. This is not the most propitious time for a wedding. Think of it. You will have a manor filled to overflowing with guests - lords and counts from all over the realm flooding to this manor; overrunning Aachen in the dead of winter; carousing and gobbling up the resources of all the townspeople. Nay, Charley, you *must* re-consider!"

"Is Hildegard in pain?" Charlemagne asked, a frown on his forehead, a cloud passing across his eyes. "This weariness, does it indicate a problem…with the birthing, I mean?"

"Nay! Nay!" Gisela hurried to convince him. "Nay, I'm not suggesting anything is wrong, just that her labor may begin any moment. In such a case, the wedding must be postponed, anyway. A woman just delivered of a babe cannot deal with a wedding, dancing, and hours of merry-making, brother. It is beyond her endurance. Please! Think of Hildegard."

"I did not imagine it was time for the babe to be born, Gisela." Charlemagne replied thoughtfully, counting on his fingers. He looked at his sister, his eyes wide with understanding. "Aye! She is near the end of her ninth month!"

"Exactly." Gisela responded. She sat beside her brother, placing her hand on his arm. "You must postpone the ceremony until your babe is born."

"But, then, the wedding must occur in the darkest, coldest time of the year! Many will not be able to fight the cold, make their way through the ice and snow. Who will celebrate with us?"

"The court, of a certainty, will celebrate with you... as always. Your Peers, your commanders, your soldiers will be here. As for those who come to carouse, to relieve their boredom, even to get away from home, we'rebetter off without them. Charley, there will be much food, aye and drink saved, if the wedding occurs later." She saw her brother consider her words. "But the more important argument is about Hilde. She cannot expend her strength for a wedding now. The baby's birth is too close."

"Aye, I understand." King Charlemagne replied. "I see." He caught Gisela's eyes, holding her hands captive in his right hand. "...the babe? Its birth can be any time? You mean, I may be a father, what...within the next fortnight?"

"Aye! The midwife thinks she has not five days left." Charlemagne stood.

"My dear love! Then, I must go to her immediately. I cannot leave her alone...not for a moment."

"Nay, nay. Don't rush out of here and frighten her. You must be quiet and serene, all the better to affect her mood. She must stay as placid as possible."

The King sat abruptly on the bench alongside his sister. He rubbed his temples.

"I scarce know what to do." He admitted. "My excitement threatens to overwhelm my good sense." He smiled at Gisela. She laughed at the goofy look on his face, at his joyous anticipation of his babe's birth.

"You will be fine," Gisela soothed. "You may still encourage plans for your wedding. Just don't set your heart on a certain day, alright?"

"Nay, I will not." King Charlemagne promised. "I will think only of Hildegard, of helping her rebuild her strength after the journey here." He turned toward the chamber door. "I will go to her now, Gisela, and ask if she has need of anything."

"Aye." Gisela replied. "Do so quietly, can you?"

Chapter 3

HOPES AND DREAMS

Charlemagne was a pest for the next two days – underfoot and begging Hildegard for anything he might do. He read from the Greek masters to her, even corralling a young poet to recite his poetry. He brought her tarts and sweet rolls from the cooks, full-bodied wine from Fulrad, wreaths and decorations from the maids-in-waiting. But, as luck would have it, the third day he announced he was going hunting. The meat larder in the cook tent held less than its usual capacity. The King left the manor with a sizeable hunting party, remembering to caution Gisela before he departed.

"Send a squire immediately, if Hildegard needs me." He told her. "I would hold her hand during the pain, if she'll let me."

"I think she would not ask that of you, brother. Have no fear; we will take good care of her." She reassured him.

***

Hilde stood in the middle of the court tents, pointing to show Jocelyn where the wreaths should be placed. She reached toward the blank space beside the Queen Mother's tent and doubled over in pain. Slowly, she eased her body down, oblivious of the dust beneath her. *I wonder if the rabbit stew last night was too heavy for me. I did eat a goodly portion of it.* She remembered. As she began to think the pain would not return, another stab clutched her side.

"Ohhh," Hildegard sighed. She took a deep breath. Almost immediately, Jocelyn was at her side, urging her to stand, to lean against her. Hilde felt her body slide toward her friend.

"Thank goodness you're here, Jocelyn." Hilde said. Jocelyn was a sister of Maria, Hilde's best friend. The three girls came to the Frankish court together as maids in waiting. Hilde and Jocelyn were both serious young women, interested in bettering the lives of the Frankish people. But Maria? She was a 'flibidy jibit,' her mind on only men, romance, and merry-making. Jocelyn was serious and capable. Hildegard trusted her completely.Hilde braced herself, her eyes wide, her forehead glistening, as she realized she was in labor.

"Jocelyn, my time has come." She stammered.

"Aye. There was no doubt in my mind when I saw your face at the first contraction. Come, lean on me. We must get you to the birthing chamber. Rest easy. All is prepared. I sent Basina for the midwife and the healer as soon as I saw you grimace." She smiled at Hilde, hoping to reassure her. Jocelyn, herself, was terrified but knew she must not let Hilde see her fear. *That will surely do her no good.* She thought. As she steadied Hildegard, Jocelyn saw a commotion below them. Oliver jumped across the deep ruts in the ground and hurried to her.

"Come, Jocelyn. Let me take your place. I'll carry Lady Hildegard to the midwife, if you will but step away. Come, she doesn't need to walk there herself, I think." Jocelyn stepped back as Oliver slid his arm around Hildegard's waist.

"Relax, my Lady." He said. "I'm going to carry you

across to the birthing tent." Hilde's pale face turned to him; she mouthed a silent 'thank you' as she felt Oliver pick her up. He turned to Jocelyn.

"Go, quickly. Find Gisela. Tell her to intercept the King on his return. Of a certainty, someone watching these Yuletide preparations already left to carry him the news. He'll burst in here like a raging boar. She can meet him and walk him to the birthing tent, take him in hand – so to speak." Jocelyn nodded and hurried to the noble women's 'day tent.'

Hildegard held her breath, imagining Oliver's progress toward the midwife's tent. He carried her gently. Actually, he hummed a lullaby. Hildegard smile.

"Oliver, I must summon you to put this babe to sleep." She said, watching Oliver's startled face. "You have very soothing humming."

"Forgive me, my Lady. I sometimes hum when I'm nervous." Oliver answered before he thought.

"I'll bet you're not nearly as nervous as I." Hildegard replied. "But, all will be well. I'm sure of it."

"...of a certainty, my Lady." Oliver replied, speeding up his steps. As he turned to the birthing chamber tent flap, he wondered how he would open it. Just then, Jocelyn held the flap open wide and urged him inside. Oliver placed Hildegard on the sleeping bench and almost sprinted to the door.

"Thanks, Sir Oliver!" Jocelyn cried out. "I think he means to leave this chamber, Hilde, as soon as possible." Smiling to herself, she removed Hilde's garments and pulled a linen shift over her head.

"Rest here, Hilde. I'm going for additional linens. Lady Rothaide will be here soon." She hesitated.

"Hurry, Jocelyn." Hildegard answered. "I want you beside me when the babe enters the world." She lay back, trying to absorb the pain as the midwife advised her yesterday. Jocelyn squeezed Hilde's hand.

"On second thought, the Lady and midwife are coming, I'm sure. I'll wait for them." *You have hours of pain ahead, Hilde.* But she did not speak the words aloud. As she stepped into the corridor, Klara, a maid-in-waiting,hurried to her side. .

"What can I do, Lady Jocelyn? I heard the Queen's labor..."

"Aye, Klara. It begins. Please find Lady Rothaid; she's on her way here. Ask her if you can do anything to help. And Midwife Inglunde should arrive at any... Oh, here she is now!"

"Right away, Jocelyn." Klara replied as she half-ran toward the court ladies, gathering to sew, talk and wait.

In less time than it takes to peel an orange, women from the court filled the birthing tent. Hilde closed her eyes and turned on her side towards the wall. It was impossible to answer all their questions. As quickly as she finished replying to one query, there were three more directed at her. One of them, she thought, I answered three separate times. The midwife buzzed around the women: spreading soft linen on her 'birthing bench,' as she called it. It was, indeed, a bench where a woman could sit. A hole carved out of the middle and three small logs on each side gave the woman in labor a place to sit and to rest her arms.

Tis more likely, I'll grab that top log and hold to it. Hilde thought as another pain wracked the bottom of her belly. She took a deep breath and blew the air from her mouth to keep from keening aloud. *I cannot believe the pain is so cutting. How can a small babe make such a powerful force?*

Hildegard heard Queen Mother Bertrada enter her chamber. She knew it was her future mother-in-law because the skirts of the women swished the floor stones as they curtsied. Sure enough, the Queen's voice blared forth.

"So, her time has come, has it?" She asked no one in particular. "I don't envy her the hours from now until dawn. It's likely she'll regret whatever pleasure made this babe." No one in the chamber said a word, though a murmur of shock from the maids-in-waiting echoed in Hildegard's ears. "But, never mind." The Queen added. "This babe, this son I fervently pray, will bring honor to his father and, likely, to his mother as well." She looked around the room, wondering at the number of people pressed inside. At that moment, Gisela opened the door. Her indrawn breath reverberated above the women's heads.

"What are all of you in here?" She asked the women. "Please, leave Hildegard in peace. She must concentrate on the birthing. You will distract her thoughts and undermine her strength." Gisela walked resolutely forward, forcing the countesses and ladies to move before her. But they did not move toward the outside, merely parted for her to pass and closed the space in behind her.

"Are you deaf?" Queen Bertrada asked, her voice loud and hard. "You heard Gisela. Vacate this space! She and I and Midwife Inglunde are the only ones allowed in here...on my orders." Gisela moved to her mother's side. "The rest of you leave this chamber." The women and maids herded toward the door, all-of-a-sudden eager to obey, afraid of the consequences if they did not.

"Thank you, Ma-Mam." Gisela murmured. "I have a boon to ask. Only you can fill it. We are unable to locate Healer Dagaric. Do you think you can find him and hurry him here?" Gisela smiled sweetly at her mother, rubbing her hands together as if they itched intolerably.

"The mid-wife has much faith in his herbs, Ma-Mam. She fears Hildegard will labor for many hours yet."

"I daresay she will." The Queen Mother agreed. "Aye, I know where he 'concocts potions,' as he describes it. Tis more likely he is drinking potions.

I shall bring him here immediately."

"Take your time, now. If he needs to retrieve potions or salves from his stores, accompany him there and, then, move him along." Gisela said.

"Of a certainty," Queen Bertrada nodded her head as she strode across the tent and jerked back the flap.

"You may have a little peace now." Gisela whispered to Hilde. "Try to breathe into the pain and rest between." Hilde blinked her eyes in understanding as another contraction began building. In a few moments, Healer Dagaric ran into the birthing chamber. He withdrew several small flagons from a well-used traveling bag. Sniffing each one, he mumbled to himself, then turned to Gisela.

"I have several potions I can give her," he began, "but not until labor is well along. For now, she must work, suffer, and work some more. I do apologize but this pain. Women must bear it alone." Gisela nodded her head.

She knew there was little the healers or midwives did for a woman in labor. There was fear that herbs would stop the labor process itself or dull the mother into unconsciousness, so Hildegard must bear it as best she could.

"Did you see Queen Bertrada?" Gisela asked Dagaric. She'd sent Queen Bertrada to find the healer because she wanted her out of the chamber. Her acid comments and focus on the pain could do Hildegard no good.

"She already searches for swaddling clothes." Healer Dagaric frowned. "We are some long hours away from needing those."

"Aye, but if it keeps her away from here, more's the

good." Gisela replied. "I only hope the pain is not beyond Hilde's strength to endure."

"If that were the case, little lady; none of us would be here." The healer spoke softly, squeezing Gisela's arm in sympathy. "I, myself, will stay to wipe her brow and have ready soothing herbs, once the child is born. She needs, most of all, to know we're here." He went to the tent door and beckoned to someone outside. A young man came in, carrying a beat-up wooden barrel. The barrel's ends were stretched with animal hide.

"Play gently." The healer directed. The young man looked around, spied a dark corner on the other side of the room, and backed away. Within a few moments, the soft thump of hands on hide rolled through the chamber. Very quietly, his voice hummed and crooned to the music of his hands. Healer Dagaric nodded and smiled.

"This music will help our little mother." He assured Gisela. She helped the midwife build up the fire, placed stones around the pit, and asked her maid to drop the stones in a flagon of water when they were hot. The maid, attending her first birth, began gathering extra stones in order to have a ready supply of stones warming the water.

True to his word, the healer bathed Hildegard's forehead, neck, and arms with cool water. Midwife Inglunde occasionally whispered encouraging words to the laboring woman, gave her short sips of water between contractions, and continuously urged her to breathe deeply.

"When you feel the contraction at its hardest," she advised, "breathe slowly out through your mouth. Heed me, little one; breathe slowly. Think only of your breath; breathe beyond the pain." Hildegard tried to follow her directions but found herself losing focus. She reached toward Gisela.

"I cannot keep...the breath in my mind, G'sela." She

complained. "I feel so t..tired."

"Aye, you are doing hard work, Hilde. Here, let me count for you. At the count of one, begin breathing in. At my count of six, breathe out. Now, try it as I count." Hildegard did as Gisela suggested and, soon, developed a rhythm which corresponded to the labor pains. As the hours stretched out, she breathed automatically, thinking little of what she did or of anything happening around her.

"You must not allow her to sleep." Midwife Inglunde cautioned the healer and Gisela. "She must be awake to help push the babe out...when the time comes."

"And when will that time be?" Gisela asked, frightened at Hildegard's weakening strength.

"I cannot tell you when," the midwife replied. "She is a woman; she wants this babe. In any event, she will push. She cannot do otherwise. She herself is likely to tell us when she must push."

"And if she does not know?" Gisela asked.

"Then, the babe will tell her." Midwife Ingunde replied.

Despite all her efforts, Gisela began to doze. She startled and stood, glancing over at Hildegard. She had her eyes closed but was breathing in time to the drum which whispered from the corner. All of a sudden she jerked; her eyes flew open.

"Ohhhh!" Hildegard exclaimed. "That was a bad one!" She slumped back on the bolster behind her back but, immediately, sat upright. "Gisela! It's much worse!" Inglunde hurried over to Hildegard and placed her hand on Hilde's belly.

"Aye, it's time for you to push, Lady Hildegard." She encouraged. "Here, hold my hand and squeeze as much as you can." She saw Hilde's face pale, her eyes squeeze together, her breath come in a great gasp. A small trickle of blood dripped from Hildegard's mouth.

"Quickly, quickly, bring the clamp twig!" She called. The healer picked up three two-inch pieces of small limbs cut from a tree. He hurried to Hildegard.

"Open your mouth, Lady Hildegard. I will place this twig between your teeth. When the next pain comes, bear down with all your might." It took a moment for Hildegard to understand him; but, then, she opened her mouth. Healer Dagaric placed a twig between her teeth and, before he could move, Hilde gave a muffled moan, clamping down on the twig.

"Exactly so!" The healer encouraged her. "Now, one more push. Inglunde sees a bit of your baby's head. One more push. Now....!" Hildegard grimaced, moaned and pushed.

"Aye! Aye!" The midwife shouted. "Here it comes!"

***

King Charlemagne rushed into the birthing chamber. His eyes bulged, his breath came in small gasps. He ran to Hildegard's sleeping bench and took her small hands in his huge ones.

"Hilde? Hilde? How are you feeling? The messenger came to say you were in labor. I rode as quickly as Samson could bring me. My dear, please forgive me for leaving you!" Hildegard opened her eyes and smiled.

"You are forgiven, my dear." She answered quietly. "What do you think of our son? Isn't he beautiful?" She yawned and kissed the King's hand. "He looks just like his father." She smiled, a far-away, pleased look on her face.

"Beautiful like his father, hum?" Charlemagne chuckled. "Rest, my love. We'll discuss my son's beauty when you wake. He's a fine, little man! I cannot describe my delight!" He bent over to kiss his exhausted wife, and watched her eyes close slowly. Then, he turned to Gisela to take a second look at his first-born son, the longed-for heir to his realm.

The babe had his father's fair hair but his eyes were dark like his mother's. He gazed steadily into Charlemagne's face, seeming to wait for a word. The King bent over him and kissed both his cheeks, then his little upturned nose. The baby watched his father stand erect and gave a small frown. Then, he sighed and closed his eyes.

"Of a certainty, he is not afraid of a big man." The healer chuckled. "He's a fine boy, Sire. You should rightly be proud of him. His journey did take hours; but, as soon as we cleaned him and his mother nursed him, he felt all was right with the world."

"He is a fine, strong babe, is he not?" King Charlemagne beamed. "I cannot tell you my relief - that he and Hilde are well. She is healthy, is she not, healer? She is so eager to sleep I cannot determine her state for myself."

"She earned her rest this day." Healer Dagaric stated succinctly. "Your battles with the Saxons, Sire, pale in comparison to the fight she just waged. Thank God she is strong. And the child is perfect – a blessed birth for the court to celebrate!"

"Aye! Aye! Celebrate we shall! The rafters will ring with my toasts and my singing." Charlemagne declared. "But all must wait until Hilde can celebrate with us. Right now, she needs recovery from battle fatigue!" The healer laughed with the King as Gisela stood watching them.

"Why must every effort, every struggle be described as a battle?" She muttered to herself. "Does everyone think nothing is of value if not won by physical strength and against great odds?"

"Oftentimes, that's the truth of it, Lady." The midwife

commented, nodding to Gisela.

"Aye." Gisela acknowledged. "But other triumphs – wisdom acquired, a beautiful painting rendered, a book written or even copied for sharing – pale in comparison to the battle. But war is man's primary occupation. He never tires of its imagery, its challenges, or its perceived glories."

"Perceived glories only, my lady; all us women know that." Midwife Inglunde declared.

***

Walking so slowly he scarcely moved, Abbot Fulrad headed toward the library. King Charlemagne was there, accepting ongratulations from members of the court. Of a certainty, the Peers and the king celebrated before breaking tonight's fast. Now, commanders, nobles and their ladies, high-ranking townspeople, and favorite soldiers came to share this happy birth with their sovereign. Fulrad's absence, his avoidance of the merry-making, would be quickly noted and earn him questioning from the king. He must make himself go! The Abbot plastered a smile on his face and picked up a silver cup as he left his chamber.

"The babe is here; it is a male child and the longed-for heir. There is no hope for a reconciliation with Desiderata; the King's marriage ceremony will soon be upon us all."

Chapter 4

Inside Dangers

As time for the year's annual assembly arrived, Charlemagne led his troops south. Every count, lord, churchman, and independent landowner in attendance agreed this year's first battle was to be against the Saxon invaders. Charlemagne knew such would be their choice so his battle plans already were in place. He did not object to lingering, though. Every day of rest was important for Hildegard. Already, she walked, looked after their child, and re-gained her strength.

The King waited for soldiers to return to his army. Oliver, Theo, and Roland recruited in all directions; their cries for soldiers swelled the size of the force. In another few days, the army moved north toward Strassberg to begin the campaign against the Saxons.

But, before the first battle, Charlemagne and Hildegard planned to say their wedding vows, here not so far from Serbia so that Hilde's family could join in the festive and long awaited ceremony.

The wedding was quite a splendid affair. Hildegard did not want fanfare and tumult. She already had a child, after all. But the King, delirious in his happiness, continued to add celebrations to the important day. As soon as the date was chosen, he opened his wine cellar to the court, replenishing it as the greedy nobles---and their wives—drank. Even as the carts arrived with more wine, the King laughed and happily urged everyone to imbibe the spirits.

Hildegard's family, journeying from Swabia, confirmed that three of Hildegard's friends accompanied them: Hildegard's favorite herbalist, a specific dog trainer, and a certain kitchen maid. Hildegard laughed gaily when Charlemagne told her he summoned them. He received extra, loving attention for the next three days.

"Charlemagne," Hildegard said to him one evening. "I have a boon to ask of you. I would like for us to wear the same color in wedding attire when we marry." She explained her thought. "We are, after all, one now and should present a united look. Do you object?" She asked.

"Nay. I think it a positive notion. You have a particular color in mind, do you not?" He asked, praying she would not choose pink or orange. He smiled wryly and received a questioning smile from Hildegard. "I agree with whatever color you choose, my love," he added. "Your wish is my command, particularly on our wedding day."

"I wish for us both to wear emerald green, Charlemagne," Hildegard ventured. "It's a strong color, reminds everyone of growing things, of new beginnings, of fresh starts. I would embroider green jasper onto my belt and mantle, the same for your tunic."

"Aye," the king replied, "green jasper for faith, as we take our vows. Perfect! And I wish one large, red jasper nestled in your breasts that all may see my pledge of love," he directed. He frowned and looked at Hilde apologetically. "I fear we cannot find orange blossoms, my dear. They would never transport in this cold."

"Fear not," Hildegard replied. "Your love wafting over me is precious enough; orange blossoms would be a repetition! I would prefer an herb bouquet, in any

44

case." Charlemagne chuckled to himself. I am blessed, he thought, not for the first time. *My bride who is already fertile wishes for luck and fertility again with an herbal bouquet! What joy God gives me.*

"We shall have a wedding to delight your heart, my love," he assured Hildegard. "No other woman is more beautiful or more beloved than you. This wedding, I do now declare, is to be filled with bright, brilliant colors... all the better to reflect the happiness and joy of the day. Announce to your friends. Tell them to make good use of bright purples, reds, blues, greens, and yellows. We shall have no one dressed in dark brown or black, no gray either." Then, Charlemagne laughed. "Some of the nobles will be appalled," he joked. "They will need to acquire new mantles! So many of them, prefer dark colors. I'll not allow those at this most joyous wedding!" And so, the preparations began.

***

"I know people must sit as they enjoy the wedding feast." The King told Roland. "But the dancing must be continuous! I shall dance many, many times with my bride. We might even begin every set that's played!" At Roland's dropped mouth, Charlemagne laughed heartily.

"Say nothing, Roland," he beamed. "I have seen you dance for hours with your current lady-love. Isn't it said that dancing is the music of romance?" At Roland's nod, the King smiled. "So I thought! I must romance my Hildegard as often as possible!" He, then, sent messengers throughout the kingdom, inviting all musicians to hurry to the castle for the nuptials, to come early--all the better to hone their skills for the day of the wedding.

Never was a wedding so happily planned, so willingly organized. Couriers raced to the far reaches of the realm, inviting all the nobles, even the realm's minor officials. Hildegard had met many of the King's subjects in the court's previous journey around the realm. In those circuits, she charmed them all with her friendliness and easy manner. And, now, with her gracious nature and loving personality, she endeared herself to those in the court who previously knew her little. Everyone was excited and happy about this marriage.

Many in the court made special preparations. The maids-in-waiting announced they would decorate the castle in colors of red and green. They wished to highlight the green of Charlemagne's and Hilde's garments. And they added red to enliven the atmosphere, they said, to reflect the excitement and laughter this wedding brought to the court.

Jocelyn recruited Adam, Oliver's squire, to climb the spruce trees and knock down cones. These she threaded with gold-embroidered silk cloth, creating fanciful flowers—all with brown centers. Maria persuaded the manor children to offer games, rough-and-tumble play, and refreshments for those children who would accompany their parents to the nuptials. Gisela ran errands for Hildegard, repeatedly referring to the needs of her 'sister.' She even won over the reluctant matrons who previously had the King in mind for their own daughters.

Roland organized sedate riding jaunts, helping to extend meal times for the heavily-overworked cooks and bakers. They, poor things, boiled, roasted, baked, and cooked from early morning to late night.

"What do you on these rides, Roland?" Oliver queried. "Mayhap I should come along with you."

"I do anything I can think of, Oliver, to entertain the guests. We have rides to search for animal tracks; that's for the children." He explained. "The countesses want to gather cattails, my friend." Roland continued. "The fuzz covering the seed is now dry and soft. The ladies use it to line their headdresses. Its warmth is welcome to the head and ears." Roland opened his hands, clearly puzzled. "That's what they told me, Oliver. The young women—no longer children but not grown—having seen Jocelyn's flower creations, all want to take cones home."

"...and the non-noble women, the maids and servants who have come, the nuns?" He asked. "They just want to see the castle, the stables, the river—anything connected to the court's daily activities." Roland pretended exhaustion to Oliver. "It's been interesting, though: I must admit that."

"Anything involving a pretty young woman is interesting to you, Roland," Oliver laughed, envying Roland the time he spent with Jocelyn. "I admire your enthusiasm, but who's entertaining the men? It seems you have no time for them." Roland looked sheepish and ducked his head; but when he raised his eyes, they were laughing.

"I have no idea. The women come to me, asking for entertainment. What's a Peer to do?" Roland sobered. "Rinaldo organizes hunting parties for the men. They seem particularly blood-thirsty to me, Oliver."

"No doubt they are eager for the King's hunting forests," Oliver replied. "After all, they are sure to find game on lands set aside for the King, though the large animals are not so plentiful now, in the winter." Roland nodded his agreement and answered.

"They all dream of bear, Roland, though what they would do with one—especially the lads—I can't imagine!" Roland turned toward the stables.

"If you wish an interesting afternoon, Oliver, join me! I daresay all the ladies will be enthusiastic about having another man around. And my charges are more charming than the hunters!" Roland winked at Oliver, bidding him farewell.

Just as the Peers joined wholeheartedly in entertaining the wedding guests, so did the castle workers. Everyone in the court was positively touched by Hildegard's gracious ways. It was their pleasure to give back in their care of the wedding guests. The cooks, serving and scullery maids, bakers, even the herbalists, lent their skills in planning, organizing, preparing, and serving well-prepared, succulent food. They cooked, baked, roasted, boiled and decorated for days, all with good hearts and growing excitement. Parties of hunters departed the manor every day, bagging deer, squirrel, rabbit and an occasional elk for the banquet tables.

Though the winter weather promised to prevent many well-wishers from journeying to the wedding, grandiose preparations continued. No one would tolerate the King nor his bride being embarrassed or criticized for any lack of entertainment or refreshment.

***

King Charlemagne came upon Hildegard in the library, crying in the corner. His heart stopped; his voice rose as he hurried to her side.

"Hilde? What in the world is the matter? Please, dear, don't weep like this. What is the trouble?" He pulled her into his arms and kissed her gently. Then, he turned her face toward his, his eyes wide with despair. "What? Tell me."

"It's my wedding dress, Charley. It's missing! Countess Robard and I looked everywhere. She was sewing the last embroidery, only last night. And, now, it's disappeared from her storage trunk. What shall I do? There's no time to make another garment." Her stricken face looked into his, tears welling in her eyes."

"How can a dress just disappear?" The King asked. "It makes no sense."

"I don't know." Hildegard replied. "I can only report that we cannot locate it. It was sooo beautiful, Charley. I couldn't wait to wear it for you." The tears coursed down her cheeks as she sat slowly on a nearby bench. "Who would do this? Answer that." She rubbed a spot on her tunic and looked into Charlemagne's face. "Someone has deliberately moved or hidden my dress. Or we would have found it." Charlemagne had to admit that seemed the case. Countess Robard was the soul of care.

"Aye," he said. "She is well-organized, always in command of her responsibilities. It is inconceivable she would misplace a needle, much less a wedding dress. But, at this time, there's no help for it. We must find you another dress, one suitable for a wedding." Hildegard shook her head in worry.

"But where?"

"Ahh!" The King's eyes snapped. "Gisela has a green dress! It may not exactly match my tunic; but so be it. You'll have to shorten it; but she will be delighted for you to use it, Hilde. Don't worry. You and I shall go to her now, this minute." He dabbed at Hildegard's eyes, urged her to splash water on her face, and hurried her out the door.

"This is not the dress you imagined, my love." Charlemagne spoke soothingly. "But nothing can diminish your beauty anyhow. This attire will be fine. Worry no more. And don't cry. It does break my heart."

***

The happy day finally arrived. Charlemagne and Hildegard stood in the door of the Church together. Hildegard's heart warmed as she looked into the eyes of her court family. No one looks unhappy or disappointed or troubled, she thought to herself. *All are smiling. This happiness is the foundation on which Charlemagne and I will build our lives together.*

"We are united in heart and life," the King announced to the wedding guests. "We, therefore, walk together down the aisle, secure in our love for each other and grateful to you for sharing our joy in this long-awaited celebration!" He kissed Hildegard's hand, smiled into her face, and waved as the well-wishers burst into applause.

As Charlemagne decreed, the Church shimmered with gowns, breeches, mantles, and tunics in a rainbow of colors. No pastel or soft colors appeared. Instead, a sea of bright purples, lush reds, rich greens, vibrant blues, sunny yellows, and brilliant oranges flashed in the candlelight. Even the men outdid themselves, wearing greens, blues, and reds with pride. Charlemagne nodded, pleased, as he looked around the Church.

Some of the counts were absolutely gaudy, wearing reds and oranges, blues, red and yellows all mixed together! But, seeing Roland, the King could understand the young women's adoration of him. He sparkled in a tunic of purple, embroidered with lilac threads over breeches of soft tan. Around his shoulders was a mantle of lilac, bordered by purple, and set with winking rubies.

Oliver, resplendent in a vibrant-hued blue mantle, over breeches of forest green and a tunic of light, yellow-green beamed first at Charlemagne and, then, at Hildegard. His mantle's edge boasted embroideries of yellow-green and blue with green jasper gems around its hem. Rinaldo was startling in red breeches, softened by a blue tunic and mantle.

Abbot Fulrad beamed as Charlemagne and Hildegard walked into the chancel. He welcomed them with hugs and quick kisses on the cheeks. His purple vestments, rather than the traditional black, enlivened his delighted face and set off the green of Charlemagne's and Hildegard's mantles.

Gisela's rose-pink gown was striking, not nearly so full-skirted as those of the other women, unique in its elegant drape around her tall figure. The lavender mantle around her shoulders highlighted her face. A large, mother-of-pearl brooch matched the earrings dangling from her ears and captured the soft sheen of red and lavender in her clothing. Oliver escorted Gisela, his bright blue and green garments blending with Gisela's vivid gown. They were as startling as an unexpected field of tulips, bright and unique in their finery. Gisela looked a princess. Oliver was no less a prince this day. He glanced behind to smile at Hildegard's family. Oliver found Hildegard's brother, Gerold, as fine a companion as did Roland and looked forward to deepening their friendship.

Hildegard's father wore deep blue breeches with a matching mantle, embroidered in green threads. His accompanying tunic of chartreuse was a startling color; but set off his coloring perfectly. The Duchess of Swabia wore a blood red gown, bordered with birds and flowers in black and gold embroidery. Her mantle in gold also boasted black ermine around the neck and gold embroidery along the edges. Her headdress, in contrast, ballooned with red, gold, and black silk — all held in place by gold beads and, again, red jasper gems.

The Queen Mother, beaming at everyone - as if she personally made all the preparations for this union - glided down the aisle on Roland's arm. They were almost twins. Both were dressed in deep purple, Roland's lilac mantle matching exactly the color of Queen Bertrada's silk gown. Her lavender-tinged, gray mantle was bordered by purple bands. Her headdress was short, a small crown draped in the silk colors of her clothing. She and Roland talked together, both nodding at on-lookers as they passed the aisles.

King Charlemagne was nothing, if not elegant. Across his broad shoulders, his emerald mantle boasted a line of black ermine, so black that it almost looked blue. Green jasper gems were embroidered along the mantle's edges, set into flowers with petals of sapphires. His tunic reflected the same pattern, though it was a deep, reddish-rust color, as were his breeches. His face, though, outshone any clothing—so resonant, calm, and joyful did he look.

Hildegard's emerald gown was bordered by an edge of black ermine. That same fur edged the deep cut of her bodice. She wore a necklace of green jasper, repeated in the belt which cinched her waist. Her hair, curling and shining in the candlelight, cascaded below her shoulders. As was customary for a bride, it lay unbound, rich in its deep, black color, seeming to absorb the light, glittering as Hildegard walked down the aisle. And, there, in the hollow between her breasts lay the King's red jasper, winking constantly back at every guest.

Amid the applause which greeted them, King Charlemagne and Lady Hildegard of Swabia entered the Church. To their right, a choir of young girls hummed softly, quietly singing a Germanic folk tune, one of the King's favorites. He and his bride walked slowly down the aisle together, smiling and nodding to well-wishers on each side. As the couple approached the altar, Jenna stepped forward and handed little Charles to Charlemagne. The King bent down, kissed his little son, and, then, kissed Hildegard's cheek. He paused to wipe away a tear and smiled at Hildegard. His bride kissed her infant son, glowing as she smiled at Abbot Fulrad.

"Dearly beloved," the Abbot intoned. "We are gathered to unite this man and this woman into holy matrimony. If anyone has reason to object to this union, let him speak nor or remain forever silent." The congregation waited, all secure in the knowledge that this was not a marriage anyone dared question. Queen Bertrada was uneasy beside Roland; but he placed an arm on her shoulder and steadied her.

"Get on with it, Fulrad." The King was heard to say as Hildegard shook her head in amusement.

"Do you, Charlemagne, King of the Franks, take this woman Hildegard, Lady of Swabia, to be your lawfully wedded wife...to love her, honor her, protect and keep her in sickness and in health?" The Abbot asked.

"Aye!" The King answered loudly, "and I do vow to obey her as well, though you did not require that of me, Abbot," he added. Hildegard laughed aloud, as did the rest of those who heard the King's reply. Abbot Fulrad turned to Hildegard, his own eyes moist as he smiled into her face.

"And do you, Hildegard, Lady of Swabia, take this man, Charlemagne, King of the Franks, for your wedded husband—to have and to hold, to love and protect from this time forth?"

"Aye, I do," Hildegard replied. As soon as the words were from her mouth, the King kissed her gently on the cheek. Then, he knelt.

"A prayer of thanks, Abbot," the King said, raising his voice so all would hear his words. "...a prayer of thanks for the blessing that the Lord God bestows upon me—the gift of this wife!" As the Abbot lifted his head from the prayer, King Charlemagne of the Franks and his dearly

loved wife, Hildegard, both kissed their son, Charles—
the heir of the Frankish realm.

Chapter 5

BATTLES TO COME

Little more than three days after the wedding, the Frankish army moved toward Saxon lands. Already, three small settings on the outlying borders of the Frankish realm suffered a Saxon onslaught.

King Charlemagne, hoping to surprise his enemy with an unexpected appearance, began the army's march at dawn each day. Soldiers and court members, cooks and camp followers, broke their fasts astride horses or in carts. Of a certainty, the Saxons knew the King would come. But, Charlemagne hoped his army would arrive before the Saxons posted scouts to watch for them. On the first morning of battle, tThe King kissed his new bride farewell and took his leave.

"The court will march until late afternoon, Hilde." He said to her. "And, then, camp in the crook of the Wels River. We must see if the spring rains' mud is deep there. It may be hard sloughing the next few days."

"I'll look for you late in the night, dear one." Hildegard replied. "A brief respite for the men and horses may be a positive break. When you confront the Saxons, there will be constant battle. Aye?"

"We fight as long as there is light. Aye. But, hopefully, with this large mass of men, our battle will not be overlong." He smiled, trying to dispel her worry. Hildegard's face paled as he talked. Her hands worried the embroidery along the hem of her tunic. "Don't worry, my dear. I'll see you before the moon is high in the heavens."

***

Hildegard readied her young son for sleep. She held little Charles against her shoulder and slipped her back against the tent flap to move outside. The air was muggy. It felt just as steamy as it had at mid-day when she washed her headdresses and noticed the clouds of mosquitoes hovering in the shallows of the river.

"It's much too hot for this time of year. We've only just seen the last of ice and snow." Hildegard murmured to herself. "I hate to think of the heat August and September will bring." She laid the lad on soft linens and waved a piece of cloth back and forth over his body, trying to cool him so he would sleep.

"I know you feel hot, Charles," she murmured softly to him. "Here, I'll fan you with this linen. You must sleep now. Tomorrow, Jocelyn comes to take you on a walk beside the river. It will be much cooler there." The lad, his eyes closing slowly and then jerking awake, fussed low in his throat and tried to roll over. Hilde rubbed his back and fanned, rubbed his back and fanned as she hummed softly. Soon, little Charles was asleep, though he frowned and fidgeted.

"It's so hot," she murmured again, continuing to fan the sleeping child. After long moments, Hilde stood and popped back into the tent. She splashed water on her face, sprinkling it on neck and arms. She pushed a stray curl off her forehead and realized her hair clung to her head. "Lord, Lord, what kind of weather is this?" She pushed her damp hair behind her ears and left the tent. Moments later, she checked on her son again. He finally slept softly, though his little face was flushed. At a slight sound behind her, she turned. Charlemagne dismounted from his horse.

"Hilde, your hair is wet. Have you been for a swim in the river? I wish you'd waited for me. We never swim together anymore." He said, his voice softening in his love for his wife. "Could we have a swim now, do you think?"

"Nay, Charley," Hildegard replied. Waving a dismissive hand, she added, "I was not waiting for you. Excuse me husband, I do not mean to be abrupt. I feel slightly weak in my stomach, even light-headed. The heat in the tent is fearsome." She smiled at him and pointed to little Charles. "I brought Charles out here; mayhap there will be a breeze in the night. Inside, the tent is suffocating!" The King drew back the tent flap and stuck his head inside.

"Aye, you are much better off out here," he agreed, withdrawing his head from the tent. "The tent is as hot as a Christmas fire. Lie there by the babe. It makes me peaceful when he is sleeping beside us. I will linger a while here with the two of you. Any stray breeze will cool us, I hope." He evaluated the location of the linens. "Let's move your linens a little this way. You will have a more level bed and more chance of a breeze. Here, I'll move the boy."

The King rested Charles on his chest, as he pulled the sides of the linen sleeping pallet. The little boy was clearly not happy to be moved. His face crumpled as he stuck his fists straight up, ready to cry. Quickly, the King planted a kiss atop his head and stroked his cheek. Little Charles relaxed and snuggled against his father's chest. Charlemagne placed a straw-stuffed square of linen under Hildegard's head as she lay down. He lay little Charles beside her and began fanning them both. The linen, draped over his huge arm, filled with air as he moved it back and forth. Hildegard felt cool quickly. Removing his overtunic and foot-coverings, Charlemagne knelt to lie on the make-shift bed. At that moment, the just-vacated tent burst into flames.

Charlemagne jumped up, checked on his sleeping family, and ran to the tent. Spying the flames devouring the tent, two soldiers grabbed buckets and rushed to the river. But Charlemagne could already see any effort would be useless. The tent burned hotly, its total destruction imminent. He heard a stumble and, standing on tiptoe, saw a dark flutter move away from the back of his tent.

"Wait there!" The King called as he raced around the tent to waylay the runner. The heavily clothed man never hesitated. He ran quickly over the ground, obviously aware of the most expeditious route toward the river. Men, bringing sloshing water buckets and soldiers forming a line to the river, blocked the runner's route. He ran around them as Charlemagne dashed after him. Attracting Peers and soldiers who joined him, the King raced after the runner in the distance, stumbled and lost his stride.

All of a sudden, he stopped. *What am I doing? He might double around and try to hurt Hilde and our son.* Charlemagne turned in mid-stride and raced back toward the oak tree. As he sped toward his tent, Queen Bertrada came out of her own tent near-by and called his name.

"Charley, what's the trouble?" She called.

"See to Hildegard and Charles, Ma-Mam," Charlemagne shouted. "They sleep under the old oak." As he turned, fire and smoke burst into the air. The tent collapsed.

Theodoric sprang from his horse and raced to the King. "We stopped ayoung man along the river road," he reported. "He's young, too young to be wandering about. Ganelon and Janlur are restraining him; he threatens everyone this side of Mecca. Sire, we know him not." Charlemagne sat heavily on the ground.

"Post additional guards," the King directed, "and secure the entire camp. See if anyone is missing! Search every tent. Account for every court member. I come to question this boy."

As the King stood, his mother stared into his face. Her mouth opened and closed, as if she could scarcely breathe. Charlemagne noticed the stiff set of her mouth. The pursed lips and frown warned the King of her temper. She, glancing at the smoking tent and seeing Charlemagne's frantic run, quickly judged his lack of care. The Queen stopped almost against his chest, aiming her critical barrage at his face. The King sighed; he had more important duties than hearing his mother rant about dangers in the camp.

"You see, do you not, this threat to your family? You eat roast with your soldiers and share war stories as a thief or assassin threatens your wife and son! There is no reason for a tent to burst into flames," the Queen Mother pointed out. "Hildegard had no fire lit, nor was she burning candles. Who is at fault here?" She shook her fingers at Charlemagne. "Your son and heir could easily be hurt or kidnapped. Explain this carelessness among the guards! Your little son is in danger!" The Queen fumed.

"Ma-Mam, please." Charlemagne answered. "Tell me something I don't know. Help me. Identify the mind behind this attack! Tell me who runs from my tent." He raised his hands in question. "Any imbecile can see there's danger; but from where, from who? Can you answer those questions?" Charlemagne shook his head and slowly released his fists.

"All you do is scream what I already know. Your hysteria weakens my mind. Why are you so quick to point blame? What would you have me do—run amok through the camp looking for a guilty face or choose three people at random and bury arrows in their entrails?" He pulled his dagger from his boot.

"Stop, Ma-Mam, stop! You are no help! Go back to your tent. I have no time for this, not now!" So saying the King half-ran toward the river, leaving his mother with her mouth open, ready to rail at him should he turn.

"Any idiot can see camp security is compromised." He slowed to a walk, again frightened for his wife and son. "I can't think something might happen to my Hilde. I will not consider it!" He whispered to himself. "Always, we move through our land with no concern, with no thought of danger. But no more! Enemies come in marauding groups, among friends and acquaintances and, now, entirely alone. How could I be so stupid? Both Saxons and Lombards seek to harm my family. I might have lost both Hilde and our son."

King Charlemagne sped beside the river bank, hurrying to the guards who held the unknown prisoner. Several of them surrounded a man in rich clothing. Why...he is but a lad, the King thought, looking at the young man slouching insolently within a ring of Peers.

"Who is this boy, Ganelon?" the King called, as he spotted Ganelon, Roland and Oliver. Thank God, Oliver has returned, the King thought. "Is he one of our young squires or a guardsman's son? I don't recognize him." He looked over at the young man once more but did not remember his face.

"Welcome home, Oliver." he whispered to his Peer.

"Thank you, Sire. I'm happy to be back," Oliver answered.

"Nay, Sire, none of us recognize him." Ganelon replied. "A guard at the east of the camp stopped him. The boy jerked his bridle and rode hard, away from the camp. He did not honor a command to halt. Morris hailed the boy as he rode into camp and, again, commanded him to stop. When the lad charged on, a member of the guard followed and outran him. We're ready to question him, Sire; he is disarmed and bound."

"I shall question him first," King Charlemagne declared. "A boy, you say?" He asked. "What age boy? ... surely old enough to know tent burning is a crime?" The King asked Ganelon, expecting no answer.

"Aye, old enough, I'd say," Ganelon replied. "The guards report he's a fine rider, controlled the animal like a master, until Parton finally ran him down. ...a beautiful animal, Sire, well-fed and cared for." Two guardsmen stood as Charlemagne and Ganelon approached. They flanked a young man dressed in embroidered pants and a richly decorated tunic. They turned him toward the King.

"Nay, not here," Charlemagne shouted, "we need light. Take him to the cook's tent." The king knew the cook's great fire always burned. This close to dawn, the cooks were up, preparing bread for tomorrow's first meal. "I must get my sword, if I need to separate a neck from a head." He bristled, fearful anew for the lives of his wife and son.

A few moments later, Charlemagne joined Ganelon, Oliver, Roland, Fulrad, Roderick, and Jason in the cook tent. The guardsmen brought in a boy, twelve years or so by the look of him, in rich clothing with a gold clasp securing his mantle. He sweated profusely, his hair wet. Charlemagne, upon seeing his cloak, immediately understood its value. The mantle was black as night, perfect clothing to mask movement.

"Who are you?" the King questioned, "and what business do you have in this camp—besides burning tents, I mean?" For once, Charlemagne controlled his temper. The fright he suffered in thinking of Hilde's and little Charles' danger took all the fire out of him. No longer the hot-headed warrior, he vowed to get information from this lad. *Maybe, probing will get answers demands will not.*

"Have you a fondness for fire? Mayhap you like to see the rush of light and heat?" The lad said nothing. "Answer me, boy; I'm waiting." Charlemagne said. The youth looked at the men gathered in the tent. Not a single one of them wore distinctive clothing. The boy made the mistake of assuming they were all common foot soldiers. He sneered at them.

"What business is it of yours—if I am here or why?" He snarled. "You've no right to question a lord about his own business. How would you like to escort me home …a silver cup for your trouble? My father would likely add to that, if you tell him of the bravery of my assault. You wouldn't have caught me, had I not wished to be caught," he boasted.

"Tell me, which of you would recognize the King? I wish to see his face…before I plan my next adventure."

"He be big," Charlemagne answered, "more so than me. He does move slowly as a result. After the wine of the night, he sleeps in a soldier's tent, moves his linens to confuse his enemies. No one knows where he is abed 'til he wakes. He rises in the dark, breaks his fast before the sky is light." The Peers, startled by the King's charade, worked fiercely to cover their astonishment. Charlemagne continued.

"Don't see, though, what business you have with him. You done burnt his tent. He'll be mighty angered about it." He shook his head. "My friends here and I, we'll lay low for the day. His temper is famous all over... the heat of it. Many will be scorched by his anger this day. Anger you earned, by the way."

"Ha!" the boy answered. "What's a little tent anyway? It's easy for him to get another. No, he'll be angry I made it into this camp. My success, my brilliance will fire his temper!"

"So, this represents some kind of challenge for you," Charlemagne answered, "some kind of game? What do you seek: to look good in your friends' eyes, to impress your father, to make a reputation with your lord?"

"...with my lord?" The young man barked. "Do you know who I am? You don't recognize my signet? I am the Lord Morston of Lombardy, nephew to King Desiderius." His chest puffed up. "I have befriended Queen Gerbegna and her sons, the rightful heirs to King Carloman's realm. You think I need to earn a reputation? ...hardly that. Nay, I'm avenging King Carloman and the wrong done his family. And I must get back to it." He apparently believed he wasted his time here, talking. Fidgeting with his hat, he backed toward the door. Oliver moved to the door and held up his hand.

"You won't be leaving just yet, lad," Oliver said. "Methinks we might join your efforts... that is, if you're willing to tell grown men what to do." Oliver's voice took on a whining tone.

"Oh, I'm not the only one eager to right wrongs. When my uncle hears of my success, he will champion my efforts." The young Lord Morston's eyes narrowed and grew cunning. "It'll go better with him if I have men of my own. Aye, it might be useful to have some of you along with me. But there are too many of you here," he noted, frowning. "Which ones of you want a part in this plan?" He looked at each man in turn.

"We must all join you, Sir." Roland answered for the men. "That way, there'll be no suspicion among the King's soldiers when we leave. Companions come and go together as they please."

The young man stood undecided, no longer eager to leave the tent but unable to guarantee wages to seven men. I mustn't seem weak or inexperienced to them, he told himself. He gave a quick response.

"We shall leave together," he affirmed. "You must call me Lord Morston. As soon as my father dies, I'll be making the decisions for our manor. It must happen soon; my uncle assures me. Your presence will convince my uncle not to work against me, as he has against my father."

"I've heard this name," the King responded. "It's said Lord Morston is an upright man, one loyal to King Charlemagne. You and your uncle oppose the King and your father?"

"Of a certainty," little Lord Morston answered. "When King Carloman died and his family hurried to Lombardy, my uncle became Queen Gebnega's protector. He's much smitten with her and forgets our mission — to take the empire for her sons. He'll remember it when I return. His duty is to conquer and, then, to kill King Charlemagne." The King took a step toward the bragging boy.

"I expect you think it your duty as well," Charlemagne said, as he searched the boy's face. "I'm the King and am much saddened by your words." He held his hand in front of the boy's face, showing his signet ring. "Do you recognize the ring of Frankland?"

"Oh, God, I am undone," young Lord Morston cried. "You've tricked me! I'm doomed." Before any of the Peers could move, he ran to the back bench, grabbed a cooking knife, and fell on it. Bright, red blood gushed from his belly. He shuddered and died. Charlemagne and his

Peers stood in silence, looking down at the very young culprit lying in a ring of his own blood.

"Another misguided one gone to hell," King Charlemagne said. "Wrap his body, just as it is; take it to the first gate at Strasburg. Leave it there. Someone will find him and see the manner of his death." Charlemagne posted additional guards over his camp.

***

"What do you make of these attacks?" Oliver asked Roland the following morning. "There seem more threats in the last few months than I ever remember."

"Aye. I counted them this morning after breaking my fast. The one against the lad, mayhap against both the boy and the Queen. I know others call it happenstance, but I worried when Hildegard's dress disappeared. I construe that as a threat, don't you think?" Roland nodded, his face solemn. "Now, we have this young, untested lord violating the safety of our camp. I do worry, Roland. It doesn't seem normal, somehow."

"Not to me either, my friend. Let's remain on guard, watching at all times." Roland answered.

Chapter 6

Long and Protracted Battle

After a long, grueling march through spring mud slicks, across freshly rising rivers, and around mudslides from crags above, King Charlemagne's army drew near to Saxon lands. He located his court some two leagues from a semi-permanent Saxon camp, while the Frankish army camped another league behind the enemy. Although Charlemagne hoped for conquest, this battle was just one in the continuing conflict between the Franks and the Saxons.

As his father and grandfather before him, King Charlemagne demandedthe Saxons embrace Christianity and renounce their heathen ways. After two days of fighting, the Saxons surrendered and threw down their weapons.

They declared their allegiance to Charlemagne and their acceptance of his faith. But surrender was an abdication of their ancestral beliefs and religion. So, while the peace held for a little while, there was always another war looming. Nevertheless, Charlemagne delighted, both in his victory and in the limited time necessary to obtain it.

"Now," he said to Roland. "Now, finally, we can confront Desiderius. Only Pope Hadrian's threat of excommunication saved the Holy City from Lombardy's last threat. The Lombard king will not back down so quickly again. He does want Rome, Roland. We must stop him."

"What do you propose, Sire?" Roland asked, already weary at the prospect of marching into Italy. "Will the Lombard king move on Rome again, do you think?"

"I trust him not." Charlemagne shook his head. "All winter I sent couriers between him and Pope Hadrian, trying to get them to reach some type of accommodation. All my efforts failed. Now, there is nothing to do but defeat Desiderius. How I wish some accident would befall him! With that, his ambitions--not shared by all of Lombardy--would end. These constant challenges would be unnecessary." He shook his head, wishing his father were here to offer advice.

"But this is useless dreaming, Roland. Summon the commanders to my tent; we move from this Saxon battle to an outright war. The sooner we go, the sooner we can return to our Frankish realm."

"We must cross the Alps, my friends," King Charlemagne told his commanders. He saw their puzzled looks, the doubt in their eyes, the subtle resistance in their shoulders. "There is no choice. Desiderius continues, month after month, year after year, to threaten Pope Hadrian. His lust for power drives him to Rome. He hopes to overwhelm the pointiff, assume most of his power and, then, rule us all. Like grandfather Martel and my father before me, we defend the Church. With the Saxons once again defeated and no visible foe attacking, now is the time to march against the Lombards."

"Is there no hope for resolution without a fight?" Abbot Fulrad asked plaintively, his brow furrowed.

"I know no other way." Theodoric replied. "Charlemagne tried, again and again, to make peace. Desiderius accepts nothing; he refuses to give up his dream of ruling a greater realm, Lombardy and Frankland joined as one."

"Aye." Fulrad nodded. "Power is a great stimulant; once it is tasted, most men will not, willingly, surrender it."

"Bring me any suggestions you have, any plans, for getting our army over the Alps." Charlemagne directed them. "Remember, the *clusae* fortifications protect the Lombards well. We must deal with that strength as well as the deep mountain passes and the towering peaks. We march immediately. We'll cross the mountains, rest and strengthen ourselves, and invade Lombardy by mid-summer. Come but one day from now with your suggestions – both possible routes for invasion and means to cross the mountains. Need we carry pickaxes, climbing ropes and goats for our hauling?"

As the men filed into his tent for their next meeting, Charlemagne could see no one had an answer for his march into Italy. Roland and Theo argued as they came inside; Rinaldo and Oliver shook their heads at Ganelon's words. And Count Janlur, the most gregarious of them all, stood alone, studying the various maps of Italy.

"Has anyone a viable suggestion?" The King greeted them. "Can no one recommend a route through the Alps?" The men silently shook their heads. Theo held out his hands in supplication.

"You tell us." Ganelon challenged the king. "I see no way to cross into Lombardy in stealth. The very time it will take us will make our march known many days before we arrive."

"Then, it appears you must accept my plan." Charlemagne replied, his eyes glinting. "I have a route. You will not like it. But like it or not, this is our best chance for surprising the Lombard Army. Come to the table; let me show you my proposal. It's easier to see on the map itself."

"It is a circular route, back-tracking our steps, moving

slowly in many of the passes; but it is possible. Watch here. We go down Val Sangone, down to Giaveno, and turn up to arrive at Avigliana. You see? Going this way, we come up *behind* the Lombards. At that point, our great advantage is the element of surprise."

He heard the collective intake of breath as his commanders followed his finger's movement. In his own mind's eye, he saw the deep crevasses, the tremendous heights, and the sheer angles his army would confront. But, because of the difficulty of the route, mayhap no archers would fire down on them. *Let's hope no one knows we are moving,* he thought. Hearing no reaction from his commanders, the King continued.

"It might be worthwhile to send a small coterie of soldiers to approach the Lombards to the east of Pavia. We can deliberately show ourselves and, then, scatter into the nearby forests. The approach of our second contingent, from their rear, will never be suspected."

As the King predicted, the Lombards were unaware of the second army's approach. Their rear attack sent the enemy flying; their soldiers fell back immediately, right to the walls of Pavia – the Lombard stronghold. Thus began the late summer siege of Pavia, a siege that continued as the months went by.

***

The long siege of Pavia, the lack of activity, the isolation of the camp took its toll on Hildegard. The threat implied in the burning of her tent haunted her dreams, mayhap contributed to the death of her newly-birthed infant daughter. Charlemagne was delirious at Adelheid's birth, overcome with joy at having a little daughter. Despite Abbot Fulrad's pleas for him to guard his safety, he often spent nights in a row in the tent with Hildegard, lit-

69

tle Charles and little Adelheid. Then, one morning the infant did not respond to her mother and would not nurse. In another day, she died.

Cherishing little Charles even more, Charlemagne spent hours with his l

son, but not so Hildegard. She could not overcome her sadness, nor move on with her life. The loss of her infant daughter, a disaster neither she nor Charlemagne had any reason to expect, shook the foundation of their shared lives.

For King Charlemagne, who believed hard times and sorrows were punishments from God, the baby's death was particularly grievous. He knew he was sinful, often admitted his sins to Abbott Fulrad. But, look as he would, he could not find a stain on Hildegard. If a difficult birth or a sickly body had condemned his little child to death, mayhap he would feel her loss less keenly. But her joyous, positive interaction with everyone in the court, if only for a few months, made the loss of her difficult to accept and much more sorrowful.

Worried for his queen's health, the King became more solicitous of her. He hunted much less often, freeing more time for her and little Charles. He came to know the rudimentary plot arrangements for herb gardens, just as he studied and evaluated plans for his orchards. His frequent offers of a 'stroll' to Hildegard after the evening meal required he decrease the time he and his Peers engaged in 'useful' thinking. He enjoyed poetry readings, debates on points of religion, informed arguments during his beloved 'philosophical' discussions - an activity promoted to increase the rational abilities of his court. But, now, he ceased participating in those activities to give his time unsparingly to Hildegard. The court seneschal called Charlemagne a 'magician,' as he constantly searched for any method which would enliven or lighten Hildegard's burdens. The entire court worried about her.

For her part, the Queen searched for ways to distract herself from her child's death. She expanded her interests in Charlemagne's affairs, studied the seneschal's records-- about court foodstuffs, procurements needed when they journeyed around the realm, herbs acquired for cooking and healing.

Even during the months of the siege of Pavia, passing churchmen, nuns, and minor nobles still stopped to swear allegiance. Hildegard welcomed each one, learned of events throughout the realm and endeared herself to one and all. Her gracious spirit won her friends among the nobility and, then, among the peasants. Reports of her sympathy and concern for the common people sped through the kingdom. But no matter how much she accomplished, Hildegarde's sorrow over Adelheid's death seemed to haunt her. The King was frantic about her state.

"Adeleid's death brought Hilde to her knees," King Charlemagne sighed. "She sleeps seldom and grieves constantly, all the hours she's awake. Can I find nothing to assuage this sorrow, to bring her back to us? Sadness hangs on her as if her very skin." He shook his head, dismounting before a rough, forest hut. Seeing it two weeks previous, Hilldegard insisted on sleeping in the hut when they re-located. Their camp had become a mud hole during the long siege of Pavia..

I dread going inside. Hildegard's killing herself with sadness. Her eyes have become permanent pools of blood, red and somber. How can the woman grieve so deeply?

"Hilde," Charlemagne whispered his wife's name. She rose from the hearth and stood before him. "Follow me, my love." He implored, rubbing her cold hands in his large, warm ones. "Come for a walk with me in the wood. A walk will do you good. You've not seen the sun in days."

Hildegard gave a small shrug from stooped shoulders; the tear tracks on her face seemed almost permanent. Charlemagne couldn't remember her face without the wetness.

"I don't want to come, dear," she replied. "The sun will never shine for me again. I've lost my precious, sweet babe. How's it possible to think about the sun?" Hildegard was a young bride and a young mother, barely fourteen when little Charles was born. With Adelheid's pregnancy, she birthed two children in less than twenty-two months, seemingly with no ill effects. Her first child, Little Charles, had been a strong and healthy infant. She saw no reason to worry about the dangers of childbirth or the early deaths of Frankish children. But Adelheid's brief life changed that. The harshness of Frankish life struck down its children, just as the constant battles took its men.

After little Adelheid died, King Charlemagne remembered many infants' deaths, even still-born sisters from his own childhood. He chastised himself bitterly for not anticipating a possible loss and making an effort to prepare his wife for it. But it's late to think of that now, he thought. Gently, he pulled and led her outside.

"You must be brave, my dear. You have a son to care for. Charles is growing withdrawn. He barely talks to my Peers and refuses to play with the counts' children. He needs his mother; you must think of him." Hildegard gave no indication she even heard his words. "Please, Hilde," the King begged. "We all need you."

Charlemagne felt he would have more success fighting against Oliver, Roland and Ganelon, all three. His exhaustion was constant; his heart heavy as he searched for ways to help his wife. What have I done to earn this re-appearing sadness, so much worse when the sorrow lies in death? He asked himself, yet again. *My firstborn, Pippin, came deformed; now, this precious baby girl is lost!*

"I must hold Hildegard together," he muttered, returning his thoughts to the present. "I must help her put this despair behind her." *Little Adelheid looked so much like Poppa! And they both died of some unknown malady. I only hope the two are together now, separated from this world's suffering.* "An infant and a king...both cut down before their time." King Pepin had been a demanding father, harsh and unrelenting in his expectations and slow to show approval, but Charlemagne missed his steady presence.

"Let's walk toward that little copse, Hilde," the king suggested. "The oak and maple leaves are beginning to color. Come, come with me." Earlier in the week, Charlemagne discovered and noted a lovely, lush spot surrounded by huge oak trees. He hoped to raise the Queen's spirits with the beauty of the place and tempt her palate with pickled pigeon eggs, a gift from Caliph Omar during his recent visit.

He, also, wanted her opinion about the 'elefant,' the beast Omar and other sheiks described to him. Charlemagne so longed for one of the beasts, as his very own. He wished it to lead his army into battle! How fearsome it would be. His enemies would scatter like leaves.

But for now, he led Hildegard to his newly-discovered trysting spot. As they broke their fast yesterday night, she actually laughed at the antics of an itinerant troubadour. The man mimicked barnyard animals, setting everyone in the tent chuckling. As Hildegard walked slowly with him, he recalled the light patter of yesterday night's entertainment. Finally, he saw a smile cross her face. Charlemagne spread his blue mantle for Hildegard, urging her to sit comfortably on the thick grass.

"Rest here, my dear," he said. "I found this quiet, beautiful spot to impress you. See again the beauties of my empire."

"This spot does have great beauty, Charley," Hildegard nodded. "But you must agree. Is not this beautiful place God's work, on loan for our enjoyment, mayhap?" Hildegard always delighted in giving a response Charlemagne did not anticipate. Her unexpected lightness moved the King. He bent down to kiss her lips, ignoring the deep sadness in her red-rimmed eyes. As Charlemagne sat back, Hildegard put her hands around his neck and kissed him once again. Before he knew what he did, Charlemagne was sitting beside her on his cloak, kissing every inch of her face.

"Charley, I've missed you," she murmured.

The King's heart jumped. He kissed her again and again. He knew she adored him. The feeling made her confident that all he did was good for her. And he never disappointed her in his sexual performance. Long ago, he adjusted to her intense, wholly focused love-making.

Hildegard did not moan and thrash about; she seldom asked for any particular stimulation; she just shut out any distraction. In her passion, she did not hear the guard marching about the tent or her child crying. She did not complain of a numb arm when he lay on it, nor of an awkward position as they fed each other's hunger. She gave her entire being to the sensations of the moment, only moving to increase the sweetness of her body's reactions. She didn't shout out; she didn't murmur sweet words; she just concentrated. So, when Charlemagne felt the urgency in his wife's kiss, he knew her long mourning for Adelheid was over.

She's finally garnered some acceptance. Her buoyant heart is turning a corner, is reaching out to me, ready for surcease from its sorrow. I know my passionate response is far too speedy for Hilde, Charlemange thought. *My patience in waiting for her to come back to me, of her own choice, has been especially difficult. And the waiting did not hone my sexual control one bit!*

He rolled onto his side, the better to hold this precious girl who loved him with her entire being. She grew into womanhood with him and became her own person after their marriage. *This makes her even more lovely and desirable. Her clinging, her need for me opens my heart completely to her. I must hasten her healing. All of the court needs our little queen. Everyone adores her. He quivered and expelled his breath, turning back to his wife.*

His immediate, physical need satisfied, Charlemagne pulled his thoughts away from the world's view of his queen and concentrated on her body. He moved his hand slowly over both breasts, lingering only a moment on the erect nipples of each one. Traveling down the middle of her body, he slid his hand—as gently as he could—between the very top of her thighs, pressing that soft mound with special care. As soon as his hand appeared, Hildegard's body pushed against it, already shuddering, moving with a rhythm which waited for just this moment. He felt the trembling in Hildegard's muscles, held her close to his body and moved in tandem with her. With a small moan, her passion was spent. She clung to Charlemagne's neck, weeping silently.

"Oh, Charley, I have missed you so!" she sobbed, as the will to live reasserted itself. "You are the world to me; your dear arms and strong mouth a refuge. I must help our people as you help me, my dear." She sighed, relaxing in the King's arms.

***

The next morning Hildegard set out to help the people even more. She asked everyone in the court and the court workers, as well, what she might do for the people of Frankland. It was difficult for her to acquire knowledge of their needs; her rank and inability to see many of them limited her awareness.

"Even if the people are frank with me, could I understand their speech? The dialects vary all around the realm. Some of them, I have no idea what they say," she admitted to Gisela, the King's only sister. "I've found those who ask the most are those who want the most. Many quiet, humble people wait for a thing to be offered, too self-effacing or too meek to make a request themselves. Someone must be aware of their needs as well." Gisela, who was a nun, visited from her abbey.

"I must heal myself, Gisela," Hildegard continued. "Peasant women lose their babes every day. I have no luxury to sit around and grieve. It is both weak and selfish."

As events proved, it was her own practical, good sense which finally healed Hildegard's heart. Recovering, she sought advice, talked to all manner of people, and spent hours alone, thinking. She sought to identify the problems which plagued the realm and, finally, named them: too little learning, constant poverty, marauding bands of outlaws, disease and illness. Once she identified the challenges, she sought solutions.

"I'm determined to be a good queen." Hildegard said to herself. "I can't go to battle and don't wish it. But there are battles other than with the sword or the knife. My battles against ignorance and want may be the most difficult of all. But I must do some good for the people."

She did not know to whom she should speak. "I know the most pressing problems but which one is the most dire? Who really knows the people in the realm? I followed Charlemagne's urgings to seek several opinions but which one has named the biggest need? Mayhap, asking Oliver will bring some clarity. I hope he doesn't laugh at my questions or think me a naïve dreamer." She screwed up her courage. "He often advises Charlemagne; surely, he can help me." She reassured herself, hoping for the best. She sent for Oliver, asking him to meet her in the tent which housed Charlemagne's scrolls.

Before each year's visit around the realm, King Charlemagne borrowed scrolls and codices from the monasteries or nunneries to examine during his circuit. Often, as Hilde rose for morning prayers, she found the king reading from this collection. As like as not, he was at it all night. Here, in the midst of wisdom, she, too, hoped to find some answers. There was a light scratch at the tent flap.

"Come in, Oliver." Oliver entered the room, carrying a sheaf of parchment, two quill pens, and a container of ink. "What have you there?" Hildegard asked. "It looks as if you are here to write a missive. Helping Charlemagne with church doctrine, mayhap?" she smiled, though she was startled by the expectation which the writing materials implied.

"You gave no reason for your summons, my Lady," Oliver explained. "I wanted to be prepared to respond to any command." He bowed his head to her.

"Oh, Oliver!" Hildegard laughed. "Be at ease. I just want to talk, to ask your advice and your opinion. Charlemagne and I wish to improve the daily lives of the people. He gave me leave to identify immediate needs and describe solutions. I know you can help me."

Oliver shook his head, preparing to deny he could aid her. "What do you want to know, Queen Hildegard?" he asked. "I'm not sure I understand."

How can the man not get beyond my title and speak with me — one person to another? Hilde thought.

"Might I ask you a question or two? We can talk starting from your answers." Plunging ahead, Hildegard began. "If you wished to make Kurt's or Taut's mothers happy, what would you do for those two lads?" She knew Oliver worried about the welfare of his squires. Here was a place to begin.

"Oh! I would find more food for their families, no doubt!" Oliver answered without hesitation. "Even though I bring them fruit, nuts and any sweet cakes I can get from the cook tent, they are always talking about food...and looking for it." Oliver chuckled. "Their parents do all they can. They were enthusiastic when we asked if the boys wished to become squires. It wasn't for the advancement alone. They knew the boys would have more to eat, here at court."

"Usually, squires are chosen from the sons of nobles; you know the process. But I was so disturbed with the laziness of Count Rogston's boys I decided to seek squires from outside the court nobility. It opened my eyes, my Lady." Oliver paused for a moment, then shook his head.

"In asking around and talking to people, I found at least one-half of the country people are hungry...not all the time, of course, but more often than I ever realized."

"And the villagers are not?" Hildegard inquired.

"Not as often, my lady," Oliver replied. "Most of the villagers till the fields together and, then, share the harvest. There seems always to be one peasant woman who has ten methods for cooking or preserving apples. Another one knows how to make bread dough stretch, by adding small pieces of tender leaves, for example. The miller grinds acorns and shares them with his neighbors. But there's no such sharing outside the small villages.

The babies, especially, are at risk and women older than thirty years; both are often lost, especially in the coldest time. The babies...er...the babes...born after Christmastide..." Oliver's voice became very soft. He dropped his eyes. "...most of the new babes are dead before Easter."

"Merciful Lord, Oliver, is the hunger this bad?" the Queen asked, her voice shrill and trembling.

"Aye, my Queen. I don't exaggerate. Hunger and cold are ever challenges. And, of course, the constant war's no help. When there's fighting, there no men to help gather the harvest...if the battles are late in the year, I mean."

Hildegard was numb. She knew the financial edge on which the court lived, of course, as it crossed and recrossed the realm. Their court lived off the land as often as it could; but more than half its stores came from the nobles. *What if there were no nobles to supplement our resources?*

"Then, I need ask no other questions, Oliver. Food will be my most immediate concern—a lot more food." The following morning, Hildegard summoned Abbot Fulrad, the court priest, who shared her concern for the people of the realm.

"Abbot," Hildegard began. "The King wishes to increase food productionin the realm. He feels the monasteries should lead this effort. One moment, let me continue." Hildegard responded as the Abbot stepped forward, as if to speak. "The monks have cultivated garden plots within the monasteries' walls for years. They must be knowledgeable about soil richness, crops which flourish or wither in specific regions and climates, crop yield and seed production as well. Isn't it true that Tours monastery produces a bounty of red plums while people know Ingelheim for its pears?" The Abbot's eyebrows rose as he nodded at Hildegard's question.

"Aye, my Queen, this is true. In fact, Ingelheim is famous throughout the realm for its pears." How does she know this? Fulrad wondered.

"Then, this knowledge must be shared with local peasants," Hildegard replied decisively. "Any knowledge the monks have of soil enrichers should, also, be described." She stopped at Fulrad's blank expression. "Come, Abbot Fulrad, you and I both understand feeding the soil to increase crop yield. In Serbia, my brother's farms use manure to restore the soil. This cannot be a unique practice to his court only. Every farm produces manure, Abbot Fulrad." The Queen's impatience showed in her face.

"Aye, my Queen. Of a certainty, I believe you make a strong point!" Understanding broke across the Abbot's face. "We can do it, my lady. Of a certainty, the monks will gladly share such knowledge. And, mayhap, we can learn from the peasant farmers as well."

"I hope so," Queen Hildegard responded. "The realm needs to produce a much greater quantity of food, much more for the people. We must learn from each other - peasant, noble, farmer, and cook alike." She spoke carefully, trying not to show her exasperation. What small ideas has the Abbot had all these years? She asked herself. *Why has he not identified better ways to feed the people?* Abbot Fulrad smiled but spoke eagerly.

"My lady, let us begin this afternoon. I leave for Tours in two days' time. If you would, identify a peasant from each nearby village to accompany me, the monks can instruct them. Or would you come with me?" The Abbot's voice rose in his enthusiasm. "The soil and clime are much like this area; the peasants with me will benefit from discussion about crops as we journey back and forth to Tours. Let's begin this sharing now, all of us together. Spring planting will soon be upon us. I daresay the brothers at Tours will provide seeds — to spread their fine crops, you see. We can use their pride to give impetus to your idea." Abbot Fulrad was excited. He imagined healthy crops all over the realm.

"I cannot accompany you, Abbot." Hildegard said. "I have two or three men who will gladly come to learn from you and your brothers. Share your enthusiasm with them and all will be well."

***

Having obtained Fulrad's support and enthusiasm, Hildegard approached King Charlemagne with an idea of her own.

"Why not have designated farmers plant two crops together in the same field?" She suggested to Charlemagne as they put on their bed clothes. "What about planting corn and, then, some weeks later, planting beans between the corn stalks? The bean vines could climb the corn stalks."

Charlemagne stared at his wife. He couldn't believe her suggestion.

"Hilde, what inspiration! Aye!" He shouted. "It might work! Where did you get this idea?" He stood and walked around the sleeping bench. "I'm no farmer but it sounds reasonable. Farmers surely grow more than one crop at the same time. Why not grow them together?"

"This is MY idea, Charlemagne." Hildegard's voice was firm, her hands balled into fists. "And I want to test it. I want a plot of earth of my own to plant and tend. Mayhap, I can interest Sircine's son in hoeing for me. She sometimes brings him to wait as she works in the kitchen. He's a big boy and could help with my planting." Hilde tapped her foot slowly. "When the court moves toward another destination, I'll turn my plot over to a local peasant child. With a little instruction about watering and weeding, the child and its family may produce some sort of crop."

"Aye, we'll do it!" Charlemagne replied, laughing. "Mayhap, some of our lazy countesses will be led by their queen's interest in crop production!" 'Plot farming' spread along the route which the King's court followed. At every move, Hildegard cajoled a village child to care for her planted crop and wished the family good health. Seeing the queen's efforts, others encouraged children to tend a little plot of earth. Very slowly, a number of court members learned about the difficulties and vagrancies of farming. And some of those efforts produced a little more food...for children along the court's circuitous route.

Farmers and monks, lords and ladies compared the yields of their fields. The most important result of this activity was the enthusiasm, the sharing of information, the appreciation of common techniques the 'plot tenders' gave to each other. They developed a new, co-operative spirit among nobles and peasants, among ladies and farmers, and among all the children.

***

"We shall continue this talk next week." Queen Hildegard said, dismissing her group of farming advisers. They really suggest odd things, she mused. *One of those who tends grapes wanted to plant grapes with corn...so the grapes will climb upward. He couldn't answer the man who asked what happens to the grapevines when the corn stalks are removed!* Hildegard chuckled to herself.

"These farming advisers describe their methods and equipment well. Their suggestions are always clear to me and they are always respectful. But I know the farmers themselves will never listen to my words. They can't believe the Queen would know such things. How do I share ideas? How do I get the planting lore from one place to another?" Hildegard was flush with valuable farming knowledge – diagrams of plot layouts, drawings of various tools and their uses, harvesting and preserving methods. But she needed to get the knowledge to the people. She startled from her thoughts as little Charles ran into the room. His face was pale and sweaty; his right hand held out in front of him.

"Ma-mam, I have an OWW!" he announced. "I need you to make it better." He ran to Hildegard and grabbed her legs. "Ma-mam, it hurts." He whispered. Hildegard looked at little Charles' hand, unfolding his fingers from their fist. There were thin, bloody lines across the inside of his hand. *His palm is lacerated! He must have dragged it over some very rough stones.*

"Oh, my dear boy, you are so brave," she exclaimed. "This kind of hurt would have me in tears!" Hildegard praised him.

"I fell beside the swords. They cut my hand." Charles explained. "It hurts but I'm not crying." He hiccupped and, then, held up soft strips of linen. "See? They're for my hand; the healer gave them to me."

"You have some tiny cuts, Charles. Did your hand hit the tips of the swords; were they lying on the ground near where you fell?" His mother asked. She wrapped the linen around his hand, ripped the edges and tied them. "Don't get the strips wet. Try not to use your hand for the rest of the day." Hildegard kissed her brave son and sent him to the cook tent for a sweet cake.

"A cake'll make my hand better," he assured his mother as he and the tent guard raced each other to the cooks.

"That's it! The healers are the ones, of a certainty!" Hildegard exclaimed under her breath. "They are the best ones to introduce the new farming methods...and be the first to use the seeds from afar. Everyone respects the healers." In addition to sharing and exchanging agricultural lore, the healers exchanged herbal remedies and folk medicines. New farming methods would be a natural part of the information they passed on.

***

"You have a wonder of a wife, Charlemagne," Abbot Fulrad said. "Every village I enter is abuzz with praise for Queen Hildegard. They wonder how she looks and, incidentally, if you treat her well. Why not take her on your rides through the countryside? She's a valuable asset to your realm. The people ask after her everywhere. They're all touched that she works for the whole realm, not just the nobility."

"She IS a wonder," Charlemagne agreed. "I'll take your suggestion and have her ride with me. She will be delighted to spend more time on her horse." Hildegard accompanied Charlemagne the next day as he rode in a two-league semi-circle around their camp.

Since no one could predict when the siege of Pavia would end, Charlemagne decided to travel about, moving through the rural areas of Lombardy. Soon or late, Desiderius must surrender. He could not defeat the Frankish army. In the meantime, King Charlemagne used the time to win friends, to talk with peasants, to honor small land-owners with a visit. The people responded with enthusiasm; and within weeks, his visits became an expectation instead of a surprise.

Though many villagers were wary of meeting the King face to face, every single person in the village came out to gaze at Hildegard. Very soon Charlemagne understood. *If I planned my battles with so little understanding, he* thought, my soldiers would be wasted. *I would lose each battle.* He confided to Roland.

"The people come to see Hildegard. They gravitate toward her. Although they are deferential to me; they remain sullen. And, why not? I invade their homeland, camp outside their King's city, and refuse to leave their lands. Still, they stretch to catch Hilde's eye, to touch her garment, to hear her greetings. Some even hope she will speak directly to them." He nodded at the throng around them. *Look at those delighted faces…and look at my wife!* Hildegard held one infant while balancing a two-year-old on her lap. She smiled into every face and complimented the hair, the eyes, the smile of each child she saw.

"She do be a queen," an old peasant woman said. "I can see none of those 'high airs' in her. She not be like Desiderius' women -- the wife and daughters. She be the first kindly queen I ever saw….in all my years."

Chapter 7

LOVE AND FRIENDSHIP

Returning to camp from the last, small village, King Charlemagne left his exhausted Queen to her ladies and moved to his tent to study the military reports of the day. There was no change in the stalemate. Desiderius still hid within Pavia; Charlemagne's army camped outside. This must end soon, Charlemagne thought.

Without his conscious control, his thoughts returned to the day he spent with his wife. *I could learn much compassion from her.* King Charlemagne realized. He remembered her eagerly talking to the peasant mothers, her delight in the weed blossoms two little girls gave her, and her praise of the young boys' play battle. *She is easy to emulate.* Charlemagne's mouth dropped open at his thoughts. He felt surprise at his own insight. *I just need to feel for my people, to understand their struggles and their needs. I'll emulate Hildegard's concern, her worry for my people.*

As the King thought of his wife's good heart, and, then, of his father's wise advice, Hildegard sought to help and comfort one of her own.

***

No stranger to sorrow herself, Hildegard watched Jocelyn as the court women gathered to play board games. They think these games engage me, she thought; but nothing removes Adelheid from my mind. She sighed, a deep, mournful sound of loss and hopelessness. Hearing the sigh, Jocelyn looked up. She smiled, unsure how to comfort the Queen. Hildegard beckoned to her.

If I cannot recover myself, mayhap I can comfort Jocelyn. For weeks she has barely smiled. And, even then, she stares toward some distant, vague spot – surely a place unreachable from here. Hilde felt Jocelyn rise and turned on her brightest smile. Jocelyn curtseyed at her feet.

"I told you, Jocelyn." Hildegard spoke more sharply than she intended. "You are not to bow or curtsy to me. We are friends. This deference doesn't please me and is unnecessary." She patted Jocelyn's shoulder to blunt her cool tone. In her own ears, he sounded blunt and impatient.

"You did, Queen Hildegard." Jocelyn affirmed softly. "But I would not have the on-lookers--she nodded her head toward the watching women — call me disrespectful. Besides, if I don't curtsy, Hilde," she added in yet a lower voice, "they will lecture me for poor courtesies and criticize you for a woeful lack of discipline." Jocelyn flashed a bit of a smile. "This is best, for both of us."

"How distressing!" Hildegard answered, though she kept her voice muted. "Why do people expect me to have no friends of my own? Heaven knows, the King has his Peers and no one utters a single criticism of him." She frowned, disgusted again at the severe rules of the court, especially for its women. She smiled apologetically at Jocelyn and took her arm.

"Walk with me. Let the old sows think what they will." Hilde felt Jocelyn's held-in laughter and smiled sweetly. "I appreciate your concern for my reputation; but if I am to make change, I must do as I see fit. And, now, I must speak to my favorite maid-in-waiting."

"As the Queen wishes," Jocelyn replied demurely,

though her eyes twinkled as she looked at the Queen.

"I would know your heartache, Jocelyn." Hildegard spoke forthrightly. She held her hand up to deflect Jocelyn's protest. "Nay, don't deny it. We are good friends; I sense your moods and like not the sadness of your spirit. If I can help you, please let me."

"No one can help." Jocelyn rubbed a tear from the corner of her eye. Hildegard's concern disarmed and touched her. "You are the only one who can see into my heart." She admitted, her eyes filling.

"And, thus, you must talk to me. We're friends." Hildegard assured her. "Speak. I shall share your burden and look for a solution as well."

"I'm confused, your majes... Hilde." Jocelyn admitted as the two of them strolled around the women's day chamber. "For the last fortnight, two men vie against each other, seeking my attention. Neither of them makes plans with me but they both seek me out." She stopped speaking. "Oh, Hilde, mayhap I misconstrue their intentions."

"Describe their actions. Likely 'tis I am better equipped than you to determine their intentions."

"And I may misconstrue," Jocelyn repeated. "I must not jump to conclusions...about either of them."

"Let me be the judge." the Queen suggested. "Describe their behavior, if you will."

"Both of them appear, with no warning." Jocelyn replied, smiling. "I speak true. I look up and one or both are walking toward me. They may bring me a drink, a piece of fruit, a sweet delight or not. Their behavior does not seem planned, not in their appearance or in their actions." She sighed and picked at a loose thread in the embroidered rose on her bodice. "The reason I question their motives is my own confusion, Hilde. They both seem to enjoy my company, like to talk and joke with me, and are always teasing. I do grow weary, Hilde, of the teasing." She shrugged, gazing toward the open windows. "They seem so engaged with me; but neither of them hints at special feelings or, even, at a personal interest in me."

"It's clear: both of these men want to be around you." Hildegard tried to decipher Jocelyn's description. "Has either of them asked you to do join them for a special activity: to go riding, to dance at the next court event, to meet in the garden or to gather nuts together? Or do both seem to come upon you by accident?"

"It's hard to explain, Hilde. They seem to have no plans to see me. They act surprised when I appear. But they must be seeking me out because they have no reason to be where I am." She rubbed her hands together briskly.

"Let me give you an example. Yesterday night, I left the banquet room before the poetry reading. I usually enjoy it, Hilde; but just then, I felt hot and tired, a little queasy in my stomach. So, I left the banquet hall and the food smells, to read in the library. It was only moments before the taller man came in, pretended to be surprised to find me there, and asked if he might read beside me. I agreed, of a certainty, and returned to my parchment. I could feel his eyes on me as I read; I felt uncomfortable." She admitted. "So, I stood to get a drink. Seeing me rise, he hurried to the table to pour a drink for me and, then, one for himself. I did not even ask for a flagon. It was very strange."

"It could be coincidence." Hilde replied. "Or you gave some indication of your thirst — licking your lips, mayhap, or a glance at the water flagon which you do not remember. Did he do anything else?"

"Aye," Jocelyn confirmed. "He wondered if I would

like to talk, so we exchanged views on your 'plot farming,' on the purple-hued headdresses which the Roman women wear in the Holy City, and on the perfect-sized family."

"Truly?" Hildegard raised an eyebrow. "And did you agree on the size of a family?" She asked, trying not to laugh. "What divergent topics you discuss." Jocelyn was all seriousness; she nodded her head.

"Aye. The subjects had no connection, one to another; but the conversation was pleasant. And we agreed four children was the perfect number." She seemed happy to identify the conversation topics but blushed when she gave the number of children. Hildegard, watching Jocelyn closely, saw the quick smiles, the sad frowns, and the slight tremor of her lips.

"Did the conversation make you happy, Jocelyn?" She asked.

"Happy?" Jocelyn repeated. "Oh, I don't think so. I mean, the subjects were so disconnected, I could make little sense of it." She dropped her eyes to the floor and continued. "But it *was* nice to have this man's attention, to see him listen to my words intently, as if there were nothing else so important."

"I understand your feeling." Hildegard searched for the right thing to respond. "We all want attention from someone. Sometime, the attention is the crux of it, not the words' being said or, even, the person's actions."

"Mayhap," Jocelyn replied. "But the conversation itself frustrated me, Hilde. It seemed to have so little purpose and, thus, so little meaning. I mean, when my husband and I talked." She dropped her head. "You know we lost him near to two years ago." Jocelyn straightened her shoulders and looked into Hildegard's face. "He and I, we always had so much to say to each other. Sometimes, my words would overrun his. Ha! I guess every interaction is different though...among friends or among those who make our hearts jump."

"Aye. Our reactions differ one to the other." Hildegard agreed. "Can you give me an example of a conversation with the other man at court?" She asked. Oh, I do wish I knew who she's talking about, Hildegard thought to herself. *But, for some reason, she doesn't want to identify him.*

"Aye," Jocelyn responded. "There have been several." She stopped to think. Jocelyn seemed to lose herself in her thoughts: her eyes glazed over; the worry lines in her forehead disappeared; and a small smile lit up her face. "I was playing with the new litter of puppies. There's one I particularly like and I have the habit of kissing his little head. He always tries to lick my cheek." She giggled. "He's a dear puppy, Hilde." She looked over at Hilde and, then, realized Hildegard waited for a description of the encounter.

"Anyway, just as I planted a kiss on my pup's head, this second man walked into the stable."

"'I've been wondering when you would come to see the puppies.' He said to me."

"'I visit them every day.' I told him." Jocelyn continued her story.

"'Aye, I know,' he answered. So," Jocelyn looked into Hilde's face, "I asked him if he liked animals." Jocelyn shook her head, her smile wide.

"'Aye,' he answered. 'I trust them more than I do people.'"

"I must have looked startled," Jocelyn admitted, "because he nodded at me and, then, looking so serious, asked a question. 'What do you think of animals, Jocelyn?'"

"I didn't even think, Hilde. I told him I much preferred

being with animals than with people, too." She sighed and smoothed her tunic. "Why did I say such a thing, Hilde? It was a stupid comment."

"Nay," Hildegard replied. "I see nothing stupid about it. If you like animals more than people, so be it. You are doing no harm." She shook her head. "There are days I would surely join you in such a preference!" The Queen laughed aloud. "So, what happened after that? Did he accept your words, smile in support, or bid you farewell?" Hildegard hated to probe. She disliked asking leading questions; but Jocelyn offered little about her reactions to either of the encounters.

Hilde's questions were not trite; she wanted to evaluate Jocelyn's reaction to her questions. *Did the man leave on hearing Jocelyn's preference for animals? What was his comment?* Jocelyn bristled, irritated at Hildegard's question or at her laugh.

"He accepted my words and the conversation moved on from there. We talked for a long time."

"About what?" Hilde asked innocently.

"About animals, for certain - about the animals we like, the ones we don't understand, the ones which intimidate us. Ha!" Jocelyn laughed. "We even talked about the animals we would 'improve!' She pointed at Hildegard. "Can you guess what he said about a pig, Hilde?" She didn't stop for the Queen to respond. "He said we needed to change the pig's feet, to give him big feet like a duck; so he could walk on water or mud at his pleasure!" Jocelyn laughed, her smile stretching from ear to ear. "Don't you think that's clever?"

"It's certainly different," Hilde agreed. "And you liked this man's conversation...in a way you didn't like the other one, I mean?" Jocelyn stopped laughing and looked into Hilde's serious face, struggling to see the meaning behind the question.

"Aye," she replied. "I did like this conversation better. It was more fun; that's a certainty." Hildegard nodded. There is nothing in either conversation to provide information, she thought to herself. *The only importance is in Jocelyn's reactions. She just likes the second man better and,* Hildegard realized-- just as the thought hit her brain--*she likes the subject of the second conversation.* Hildegard nodded to herself. *This second man knows Jocelyn well. He chose a subject she loves, animals, and made his comments funny for her, encouraging her to laugh.*

She felt Jocelyn waiting – her face watching Hildegard, her lips slightly parted, a little smile around her mouth. Hilde turned her eyes to Jocelyn's face and framed a question.

"Which of these two men do you prefer, Jocelyn?" She wanted to know.

"Oh, Hilde! I don't know," Jocelyn replied, her voice mournful. "I asked myself the same question. I don't even know if it's important. Why should I care about either of them? I mean, it's not like they're important to my life...or anything."

"But, don't you see," Hilde began, "one of them may become important to your life. The way you are acting, the conflict you feel, the frustration trying to understand, what do those things tell you, my friend?" Jocelyn looked at her, rubbed her forehead, and shrugged.

"They don't tell me anything," Jocelyn stubbornly answered. "Nothing."

"Oh, but they do." Hilde insisted. "I don't understand your reasons for not wanting to admit it, but all this tells me something."

"And, just what is that?" Jocelyn challenged her. Hildegard sat on a near-by bench and pulled Jocelyn down beside her. She put her arm on Jocelyn's shoulder and hugged her close.

"It tells me you want one of these men to feel you're special, Jocelyn; you would like to be special to him." She felt Jocelyn shift her body. "There is no reason to be embarrassed or defensive about it." Hilde spoke into the silence. "It's time you were interested in someone. You've been a widow for two years now. It's marrying time for you. That's what we women do, you know. And why shouldn't it be?" She asked her friend. Jocelyn stood up, walked to the hearth and turned to face Hilde – her eyes wide, her face glowing.

"Hilde? Can it be possible? I don't dare think I might have the good fortune to attract the man I adore!" She admitted. "How can I let him know how I feel?" Hildegard smiled, trying to be encouraging.

"Let me think on it. I need to analyze your words. Soon, you must name the men to me." She saw the shake of Jocelyn's head. "I will never betray your confidence, Jocelyn. But if I know the men and see them with you, my judgment will be better served. You can be certain I will not lead you wrongly."

"I know," Jocelyn answered reluctantly. "You'll think better for me than I will for myself. I trust you, Hilde. But I am so unsure about all this." Both women startled as a fast-riding noble rode passed the window.

"He must be here to see the King." Jocelyn said softly.

***

"Sire, a messenger from King Desiderius just rode up." Oliver said, holding a parchment out to the King. "It is a declaration of surrender. The messenger says King Desiderius surrendered to Theo." Charlemagne looked into Oliver's face.

"It's signed in Desiderius' own hand?" He asked, afraid to believe the siege might, finally, be over. Oliver handed the parchment to Charlemagne. "Aye, it is," the King confirmed, as he looked at the unrolled parchment.

"It came under his own banner, delivered by his captain of arms." Oliver confirmed. "Desiderius wishes to meet with you one day hence when the sun is highest in the sky."

"Where shall we meet? Does he wish me to come into the city? Why does he presume to choose the time or the meeting place?" Charlemagne asked. "He's the one defeated."

"He always wishes to command, Sire; you know that. Aye, he names the place - in front of Pavia's gate, between the city and our forward troops." Oliver replied.

"Accept his request." Charlemagne clapped Oliver on the back. "I will not quibble over choosing a surrender spot! It's over, Oliver! Thank God, the siege is over."

"Thank God." Oliver echoed the King's words.

"Aye!" Charlemagne said, allowing relief and enthusiasm into his voice. "We must move out of here, Oliver, quickly! The Saxons invaded Hesse weeks ago. They must be stopped." He frowned then and held up his hand. "Nay, wait. We cannot march yet, I fear. With this surrender, we have new laws to implement, overseers to choose. As with other peoples we conquered, I will allow Lombardy nobles to rule their realm. They must swear allegiance to me and accept the rules of governance. Direct Fulrad to make all necessary preparations for Desiderius' surrender." He frowned.

"We must not linger here a moment longer than necessity demands. The Saxons threaten us again; we must march."

"What are your terms, Sire?" Oliver asked.

"Complete surrender," Charlemagne replied. "Desiderius will be stripped of his crown, his lands, and any valuable possessions. Be certain to take his sword. As of tomorrow, we exile him to the monastery at Corbie. His wife must enter a nunnery." The King looked directly into Oliver's face.

"I do not relish imprisoning his son, Oliver," he admitted. "I love Adelchis. Must we punish the son for the flaws—the immense ego—of his father? What a fine Peer Adelchis would have made." Oliver said nothing. The King raked his hand through his long hair and spoke regretfully.

"Arrest him, too," he directed. "We will send him to the monastery at Tours, separate the father and son. To be merciful, I will spare Desiderius' miserable life. Doing that, I can spare Adelchis' life and get little criticism. How I wish I could free him." Charlemagne shook his head. "But Ganelon must conduct him to Tours personally."

Charlemagne hung his head, wearied by the decisions he must make to protect his realm. *Adelchis would be loyal to me; I am certain; but neither of us has that luxury.* As it turned out, Charlemagne's soldiers did not find Adelchis. He somehow fled Pavia before his father's surrender and went into hiding. After Desiderius formally surrendered his realm to King Charlemagne the following day, the Frankish commanders met in the King's battle tent. Charlemagne nodded at Oliver, Roland, Ganelon, Theodoric, and Rinaldo.

"Although it will be weeks before we leave here, we must make battle plans for responding to this Saxon threat. I weary of this constant conflict. This time the Saxons **will** stay conquered. They must all be baptized. Each of them has one choice: accept the Christ or die. I shall make it clear." Oliver noticed a spring in the king's step.

"At long last, we can leave the Lombard realm. Make all preparations for our departure." Charlemagne nodded at his friend.

"I shall, Sire," Oliver answered. As he turned to leave, Charlemagne delayed him with a hand on his arm.

"Summon Fulrad. He must implement the governance he and I discussed. Anticipating this very victory over Pavia, Fulrad and I established a governing structure for Lombardy alone. Fulrad will begin the transition to our laws as soon as possible and remains here to judge their effectiveness. Secretly, some of the Lombard dukes already pledged their allegiance to me. We will ask them to repeat their vows in public. Do you have any idea how many of them resent Desiderius, Oliver?"

"Nay, I do not, Sire." Oliver answered. "But I did hear sarcasm in some noble's words of him, even as their companions praised him. Lombardy ever has factions working against each other, as I remember. I only hope their allegiance to you is more certain than their loyalty to Desiderius." Charlemagne shrugged.

"We trust none of them, my friend. Their vacillation gives us all the more reason to strengthen the army." Firmly changing the subject, Charlemagne continued.

"I shall reside in the palace for a few weeks; then, we march for home. Let the Lombard nobles see me sit their throne; that should discourage internal unrest for a pace."

King Charlemagne remained in Lombardy for many days, laboring to institute a governing structure and choosing individuals to hold various administrative positions.

"I'm reluctant to absorb Lombardy into the Frankish realm," the King admitted to Oliver. "Already, there is widespread hatred of us. I cannot imagine the tales Desiderius whispered. We must show these people we are not the monsters which he painted us."

***

King Charlemagne knew he had months to plan his attack on the Saxons. His soldiers were weary. They besieged Pavia for more than a year and, now, the men and their commanders both begged to return to their families. They completely missed last year's growing season, the autumn harvest, and the Frankish winter which sorely tested all its creatures.

As Charlemagne accepted Desiderius' surrender, he was mindful of the rapid pace of the days. He heard the men's worries, their concern for their families, the state of the growing crops, preparations needed for the coming winter. Men stood in line to speak to commanders about leaving. Charlemagne knew he must not ask them to fight yet again. Any lesson to the Saxons must come next summer.

Weeks after Desiderus' surrender, the army moved through Lombardy. Charlemagne's strength--just in the number of his soldiers--was obvious. He re-established support for his rule. The size of the remaining army and their loyalty to him deterred any dream a Lombard noble might have of becoming the next Lombard king.

"Let us give thanks." Charlemagne breathed. "We move toward home." He knelt to pray.

Chapter 8

COMPETING PEERS

The autumn winds of 774 blew especially cold. The King, his court, and his troops longed for home. They moved slowly but methodically north from Lombardy, foraging as they marched. But, no matter how many directives and beheadings Charlemagne instituted to control his troops' looting, there were always men who profited from their service. They stole anything of value — trinkets, food, jewelry, women--from the Lombard lands the army marched through. The Frankish army left a wide swatch of destruction behind.

Before breaking camp, the soldiers and camp followers slaughtered the animals still with them - brood cows, sows, chicken and ducks. No one wished to stop to butcher or roast meat as they journeyed homeward. Scores of children gathered last year's acorns to crush and mix with diced, dried plums and bits of apple. As an alternative, the mixture, combined with hog lard and sweetened with honey, formed 'traveling sticks' — protein-rich food easily eaten as they marched. The basterns (carts covered with leather for fording rivers and streams) were still heavily loaded and moved slowly. Even as the soldiers drank wine and consumed salt pork, hams and flour, they looted tools, swords, daggers, etc. from manors and homesteads destroyed along the march.

In the midst of this chaos, among the destitute women, alongside the wounded and dying, strode the priests. They walked as well, but used the time to sing praises for the holy work completed. According to them, King Charlemagne and his brave soldiers undertook this holy siege to fight pagans and enemies of the church. What nobler calling might the soldiers follow? Although returning home from battle was always more hopeful than starting out, the return journey reflected endings: death, re-evaluation, and changes.

Camp followers' allegiances changed as soldiers and protectors died or left for home. Women and small children struggled to serve, to make themselves useful to another protector. Fathers and husbands, lost to wounds and illness, were replaced and, eventually, forgotten as the surviving army and its followers marched into the Frankish realm.

Near the end of their return journey, more than one-third of King Charlemagne's soldiers were gone. They peeled away in groups as the army marched north and eastward. Although the army's composition changed, as fluid as the rivers they crossed, the King's court remained much the same on the journey.

The court moved in tandem with the army. It camped alongside the soldiers or at a short distance away, if danger came. Even during the battle season, the court moved. It sometimes visited counts' manors along the battle route but, often, provided respite for all manner of visitors: nobles living near-by, holy men and women on missions through the realm, foreign travelers and fighters passing through Frankish lands, and others on various errands. Although laughter, games, and cultural activities characterized the court's entertainments in the evenings, the primary aim of the court's constant movement was to hold the loyalty of the noble families throughout Frankland.

Because the people believed their king was the strongest man in the kingdom and because he was the people's protector, Charlemagne visited with the nobles in their manors. He greeted wives and children, emphasized his dashing military figure and had minstrels sing of his deeds. He appeared larger than life to every level of Frankish society, just as he planned. As the court followed its circuitous route, the King and his Peers promised protection. At the same time, they solicited support - military and financial - and evaluated the economic conditions of the realm.

Although the King's wife and his lady mother longed for a permanent home, his need to cement his power did not allow for such a luxury. He must be among the people, displaying his might and strength to them. The only time the court ceased its journey was in the bitter, harsh days of winter when the limited roads were impassable and during the Church's high feast days, primarily Yuletide and Easter.

***

"The region is well rid of King Desiderius, my liege." Oliver said. "Any deaths, all deaths were acceptable to him. I believe he would sacrifice his own children to replace you, to rule a combined Lombardy and Frankland."

"Aye," Charlemagne concurred, "he was indefatigable...even assured me his son continues the struggle against us." The King shook his head slowly and smiled. "You and I know better, Oliver. Adelchis' loyalty is to the Frankish court, not to that of his father's. I do hope the monastic life can temper Desiderius' love of conflict."

"As for Adelchis, do we know his whereabouts?" Oliver inquired.

"Nay, rumors and spies swear he's safe in Constaninople. I pray he finds a new life there." Charlemagne scuffed his shoe on the ground. "I did want him for a Peer." The King confessed softly.

"As did we all. Everyone in the court loves him, believes him a fine man, an energetic soldier. I do praise him myself." Oliver looked away, then turned back to the King. "Adelchis offered me romantic advice. Did I tell you about it?"

"Romantic advice...? What have you not told me, Oliver?" Oliver lifted his eyes from the ground and smiled.

"He told me to hasten my declaration...to the woman I admire." Oliver hesitated, coughed, and, then, plunged ahead. "He advised me to declare my interest to Jocelyn, as soon as I could, Sire." Charlemagne's body startled.

"Jocelyn?" He asked, surprised. "I didn't know she stole your heart."

"I shouldn't admit it, Sire; but she bewitches me. I can't deny my feelings. My only wish is to be in her presence." The King nodded. "Adelchis urged me to speak to her, to declare my affection." Oliver said as he tugged at his mantle. "I often think of his words."

The King quickly looked at his feet, all the better to hide his face from his Peer. Hell, he thought, here's a worrisome wrinkle, of a certainty. But he kept his face unmoved and thoughtful.

"Does she return your affection?" Charlemagne asked carefully. "Have you any indication of her regard?"

"Sire, I do not know. My ignorance makes me sleepless at night." He smiled slightly. "She seems happy to see me, to talk when we meet by chance." He remembered Jocelyn's gay laughter and Adelchis' enthusiasm for the match. "We ride together often. Adelchis swore her enthusiasm for grooming my horse is very positive for my cause. But, to be frank, I am overcome with doubt." He finally caught and held Charlemagne's gaze.

"How do I judge, Sire? You must know...with all your experience with women." Oliver replied slowly. Charlemagne folded his arms across his chest and answered.

"You must confess your feelings. Tell her." He said firmly. "You think this highly of her? Tell her. Aye, Adelchis is entirely right. Speak of your love and regard. Ask for her hand and... Nay, ask for permission to speak with her father. His permission must first be sought." The King nodded decisively. "Are you unwell?" He asked as Oliver's face paled.

Oliver gazed at Charlemagne vaguely, his eyes unfocused. The King reached out to steady his friend, as Oliver rode beside him. At Charlemagne's touch, Oliver shook himself and looked sheepishly into the King's eyes.

"Forgive me, Sire," he whispered, "your advice drives all words from my mind." Charlemagne guffawed, then motioned for Oliver to follow him. Once away from the marching soldiers, the King reined in Samson and motioned for Oliver to draw close. Oliver moved to Charlemagne's side, questions flitting across his face.

"I had no idea you wanted a wife." The King said. "But thinking on it, I agree that it's time. Surely, every man wants a son and should, also, long for a little daughter."

"Aye," Oliver acknowledged. "Please accept my regret, Sire, in the loss of little Adelheid." The King raised his hand as his eyes filled with tears.

"Do not speak her name, I beg you. I fear my loss of her will always overwhelm me, always." Oliver squeezed the King's arm, overcome by Charlemagne's sorrow. "But seeing my pain, you can understand the great gift the Lord bestows when HE gives a child. I tell you, Oliver, there is nothing to compare." Charlemagne peered keenly at his friend. *I hope I do well in encouraging Oliver,* he thought.

"If you love this woman, do not delay; tell her forthwith. All in the court love her; she is not without other admirers." Oliver's eyes jumped to the King's face.

"Who...?" He asked, his eyes locked on the king's.

"Oh, I name no names." King Charlemagne answered, his voice neutral. "I believe Jocelyn, of a certainty, must grow tired of the duties of a maid-in-waiting. After all, Hilde married me more than three years ago and they joined the court together."

"Then, I have your blessing, Sire?" Oliver asked.

"Always, my friend, always." The King smiled, as he turned Samson back toward his marching army. "Complications, complications," he muttered under his breath. "Why must my two best Peers love the very same woman?" His eyes looked out toward the massive trees. He prayed. "May the Lord Father help them both." He shook his head sadly. *Roland talked around asking Jocelyn to be his wife, thinking he's plenty of time to make the commitment. He had best hurry, if he not be too late already.*

'The women of the court will be devastated, Roland.' Charlemagne recalled his words to his nephew. *'Each one dreams of being on your arm or...somewhere else.'* He remembered saying, as he laughed heartily. Roland had only shaken his head, refusing to take the King's baited comment.

Thank God no one competed with me for Hilde. The next moment, Charlemagne laughed aloud. *Truly, no one would dare!* He realized. *I'm the King.*

Hildegard's dear face smiled in his thoughts. He understood, instinctively, the joy she would derive from a wedding for Jocelyn, mayhap her dearest friend. *Nay,* he corrected himself. *My sister, Gisela, is her closest friend. How blessed am I! My two, most loving friends - my wife and my sister - love and respect me. What a blessing!*

Looking for an appropriate place to speak to God, the King spied a roadside shrine up ahead. He approached it quickly, dismounted, kneeled at the make-shift altar and prayed. His soldiers, seeing him, left their mounts, kneeled on the ground and thanked God for their lives and for their safety.

***

At that very moment, the other half of the love-triangle spoke with Jocelyn herself. Roland chanced upon her brushing and grooming a spring colt and stopped to offer his help.

"Do you make friends with this colt for some ulterior motive or because you like young things?" Roland asked, a smile playing around his mouth.

"Good morrow, Sir Roland," Jocelyn curtseyed. "... both--to answer your question. I do like young things, the younger the better. But I want this colt for my own mount. Isn't she beautiful?"

"Her beauty does not guarantee she will make a good mount," Roland replied, "though you choose a colt with excellent potential. She's one of the most spirited of this spring's birthings and is very quick in taking direction." He walked over to stand beside Jocelyn, taken by the blue of her eyes and her slightly parted lips. Her headdress sat askew, her hands were dirty from the grooming, and her left cheek had a dark smudge where she, at some point, rubbed her finger over her face. *She looks adorable,* Roland thought, even as he realized he over-reacted to Jocelyn's charms.

"Oh! You noticed her before?" Jocelyn inquired, her

stomach clenching as Roland walked toward her. *Ohh, he is so beautiful! I mean, handsome.* She corrected herself. His shoulder-length hair reflected the sun's light; his lithe body moved in perfect harmony. He was the picture of a soldiery lord.

"Aye." Roland confirmed. "I was teaching our squires the art of saddling and bridling yesterday. We used her to demonstrate. By the third showing, she lowered her head at just the time for me to move the bridle over her nose. She is a quick learner." Jocelyn stepped toward the colt and slipped her arm around its neck.

"Mayhap you would train us both?" She asked without thinking. Blushing, Jocelyn continued. "She's learning to be a good mount. I would learn to ride in a tourney." She laughed as Roland's mouth dropped.

"What?" Roland asked, puzzled. "You? Ride in a tourney? Why, the Queeen would never allow it! Charlemagne, too, would deny you the choice! You know that, Jocelyn."

"Aye, I know. But I still yearn to ride at great speed and to look elegant as well. And I would learn to jump." Roland could not determine if she teased him or seriously wished these challenges. When she added 'to jump,' he saw a dimple in her smile. Jocelyn dropped her eyes to the ground.

"You tease me; do you not?"

"I do." Jocelyn admitted. "No one would ever countenance my riding across the field or jumping, for that matter. But knowing doesn't prevent my wanting to do both things." She placed a warm hand on his arm. "Don't worry, Sir Roland, I won't embarrass you with my riding antics. I just want to be a good enough rider to deserve this little filly." Slowly, she led the little colt to its mother, giving them both an apple. Roland walked beside the horse.

"I'm delighted to give you riding suggestions," he volunteered, "if you are not pretending to be a novice rider."

"Oh, I'm not," Jocelyn stressed. "It's true; I rode first at three years old...and every day since that I could! But still, I do not sit with elegance." Her eyes twinkled as she glanced up at him. "I wish to be more comfortable on my mount, better aligned with her. I surely am not now." And she smiled, a warm glow lighting her face.

"Then I must help you, by all means. I cannot allow you to repeat mistakes." Roland smiled into her eyes. "Your horse deserves an excellent horsewoman. And I am happy to guide a fellow riding enthusiast."

"I will work very hard," Jocelyn promised seriously, not noticing the soft look around Roland's eyes.

As the court moved slowly, its people enjoying autumn's arrival and the end of the battle season, Roland showed Jocelyn new riding techniques and provided directions in her colt's training. Some days, Maria, Rinaldo, or Oliver joined their lessons. But, as often as not, they were alone to improve Jocelyn's skills. Since Roland would take no payment, Jocelyn knitted him a woolen blanket for his own horse. Jocelyn's riding improved daily and, after many miles, King Charlemagne announced the end of their march.

***

As they moved into Neustria, Charlemagne dismissed the soldiers still with his army; urged them to rest, to clean and restore their weapons; and to rejoin him enthusiastically in the early spring. The King and permanent members of his court moved toward Carisiacum where they wintered and planned Yuletide celebrations.

Queen Hildegard, ecstatic to be settled in one place, eagerly summoned Jocelyn to help her choose furnishings for Gisela's bedchamber. Within a fortnight, the novice would arrive from her abbey to spend Christmas with her family. The two women searched through wall hangings and furniture to re-decorate the chamber. Jocelyn put her hand on Hilde's forearm and spoke.

"Advise me, Hilde, please. I am lost, for certain." Her dark blue eyes clouded with confusion. Her brown hair, burnished with red highlights, fell in tousled waves down her back. When unhappy, she constantly pushed her hair behind her ears. Hildegard often told Jocelyn to be thankful for her headdress because it gave her ears a rest.

But today, Hilde had not the heart to tease her friend. Jocelyn hiccupped as she appealed to the Queen, an understandable response after the copious tears she shed.

"I don't know how to act, what to say to either man." Jocelyn confided. Hildegard hugged her around the shoulders, the third hug since Jocelyn came into her chamber. Right now, the Queen had no advice to give.

"Here, taste this chamomile tea. You must stop weeping so I can think, Jocelyn. My thoughts seem frozen when I see you so unhappy. Drink your tea and give me time to puzzle over this." Hilde offered Jocelyn a honey-cake. Jocelyn shook her head and took a quick sip of tea.

"I'm honored…" Jocelyn stopped speaking as Hildegard held her hand out. "I'll be quiet." She sat on a bench before the hearth. Soon, her eyes locked on the oaken logs as small flames rose around their ends. Hildegard gazed into the flames as well but saw them not. Her mind was at work on Jocelyn's conundrum.

"Forgive my questions." Hildegard's voice broke the silence. "I need a few facts. Have Oliver and Roland spoken of their love to you, Jocelyn? Did both…or either of them…make a declaration, I mean?" She raised her eyebrow at Jocelyn, being certain the young woman heard her question.

"Not exactly." Jocelyn answered. "But he did try to speak to me. We've been here in Carascium what – a week? Three days ago, Rinaldo, Maria, Marc, and I returned from riding and wiped down our mounts. Oliver rode up. Our ride was longer than usual so the others hurried off to break their fast. Oliver and I were alone." She smiled, remembering. "Oliver stumbled over his words." After a few moments, Jocelyn roused herself and looked at Hildegard.

"Oh, I hope I'm not misconstruing things! Mayhap, Oliver's question meant something else." Hildegard remained silent, waiting for Jocelyn to continue.

"Nay. It must be what I suspect." Jocelyn muttered to herself and continued. "He asked if my father planned a visit to court anytime during Yuletide. He explained he wished to speak with Poppa about an urgent matter." She blushed at Hildegard's intense look.

"Did he mention the subject, identify the urgent concern?" Oliver's interest in Jocelyn came as no surprise to Hilde. Any man with any sense would grab Jocelyn. *Oliver is the deepest thinker of all the Peers; but he is so reticent and shy around women. Who could ever guess what the man is thinking?* She did not say any of this to Jocelyn. *Why confuse her or plant doubts in her mind?* Hilde asked herself.

"Nay. He said he wished to talk to Father 'about a subject of mutual interest to us both.' What can else can it be...other than his interest in marrying me? Would you interpret those words as anything else?" Jocelyn demanded a reply.

"I assume this is his intent." Hilde answered. "But I would wish a little more evidence of his regard for you." She sighed. Just this morning in the stable, she saw Oliver watching Jocelyn from a distance, seemingly garnering his courage to come near her. But he seldom said anything directly. Hildegard dare not assume his wish to speak with Jocelyn's father had to do with Jocelyn. *It may be something else entirely.*

"Might he be thinking of another horse for you, Jocelyn? A horse would be of 'mutual interest' to you both, would it not? I know he said he has his eye on a particular animal he knows you will like." Hildegard immediately regretted her words. Jocelyn's body sagged; her shoulders fell; her eager face lost its joy. She stared at Hildegard.

"You might be right. Aye, a horse makes sense. But he knows I love the filly Roland is helping me train. Suggest another horse? Nay. He approved of this one weeks ago." Jocelyn sighed, frustrated. She was unable to interpret the disparate pieces of the puzzle. "I don't know what to think."

"We don't know enough." Hildegard replied. "But tell me this, Jocelyn; do you wish Oliver to speak to your father? Are you ready for marriage, for a commitment?" Jocelyn held up her hand, as if to stop Hildegard's words. "Have you wished Oliver would speak of a betrothal to you? ...before now, I mean?" Hildegard repeated. Jocelyn jumped up from the bench and stalked around the bedchamber.

"I don't know, Hilde! I want to be married again. And, aye, I think it's time for me to consider someone. Don't you?" Jocelyn's eyes met Hildegard's. "You married Charlemagne at twelve years, did you not? I am two years older than you and you married two years ago, so I shouldn't postpone it any longer. It's not like I'm an untouched maiden. Mayhap Oliver worries about my first marriage... It was so brief, Hilde, I scarcely remember it."

"Nay, don't confuse different issues. I beg you." Hildegard replied. "Are you ready for marriage now? If so, is Oliver the one you have in mind? Do you dream of being his wife? Or do you just want a little romance--someone to swear you're beautiful, to bring you wine and cheese, to hang on your words?" Jocelyn gave Hilde a disgusted look and exclaimed.

"Please. Don't accuse me of being mindless! You know how irritated I get with my sister and her fawnings! I can't stand the play-acting, the effort Maria makes to get men to pander to her! She does embarrass me, the way she manipulates." Jocelyn forced herself to stop. She tried to cool her temper. She walked about the chamber slowly, breathing deeply. Hildegard, who still had no real answers to her questions, changed her tactics.

"When you're with either of these two men, do you think or wonder about the other one? Do you wish you were with the one who is not there?" Jocelyn put her hands over her ears; she walked still further from Hildegard. "Which one do you want to ask for your hand? Can you tell me that? And, then, assume you've been asked by one of them. What would your answer be?" Hildegard walked to Jocelyn and stood by her side. Jocelyn did not look at her.

"Which one would you accept...if they both asked you? And which one would *you* ask, if you could make the request first?" Hildegard said.

"You mean, if I asked the man to marry me, before he asked me?" Jocelyn's voice reflected her shock and, then, her amusement.

"Aye." Hilde confirmed. "If you were the one to ask first, which one would you choose? Or do you like them equally?" Jocelyn's face took on the look of a frightened rabbit. She rubbed her hands together, rearranged the brooch around her neck.

"I don't know." Hildegard looked into her face.

"You must know." She said. "Aye, you know. You may tell me a falsehood, Jocelyn; but don't lie to yourself. This is a choice you must make." Hilde sat on her sleeping bench. "What will your parents answer to Oliver or to Roland…if either asks for a betrothal? What man's name will you give when your mother asks for your thoughts on marriage and, then, on your preference between these two men?" Hilde took Jocelyn's hand in her own.

"You must answer this, soon or late. If it is later, you can say nothing now. But you must decide if you want this or not." Hildegard advised.

"I cannot decide." Jocelyn moaned softly.

"You must." Hildegard replied. "If these men's actions count for anything, you must. From all you tell me and from my own understanding of their words, they both appear to love you."

"Choosing is not possible!" Jocelyn answered, her voice shrill, almost desperate. "Choose between Oliver and Roland? I cannot. I love them both!"

"Then, which one do you love for a husband…and which one for a friend? You must decide that before either of them asks for your hand. Please, Jocelyn, consider your heart's feelings." Hildegard shook her head. She hated to see the normally straight-forward, reasonable Jocelyn act like a harebrain, a 'nink-com-poop.' Such behavior was entirely too much like Jocelyn's sister, Maria, for Hilde's taste or patience.

"I'll be back to talk later," Jocelyn answered as she hurried across the room and reached for the chamber door.

Chapter 9

MANY CHANGES

"Even though King Charlemagne loved literature, poetry, and philosophy and delighted in arguing with his Peers and advisers, he had little time for such activities. The immediate demands and constant oversight he must exert in implementing laws and statutes--many of which he penned himself--in naming officials; in evaluating the competence of those he named; in overseeing his fragile legal system took much of his time in the 'resting' days of winter.

Nonetheless, he sought out his wife after Oliver confessed his interest in Jocelyn.

***

"Of a certainty I have time to talk, Charley." Hildegard replied. She smiled at her husband. Her purple tunic set off her dark hair and eyes. Her pale pink breeches, embroidered in purple, and her cool periwinkle-colored headdress softened the overall effect of the dark purple as did the sparkling drape of a cluster of pearls on the bodice of her tunic. Her mantle, rich around the collar with ermine fur, lay on the sleeping bench, ready for a flip over her shoulders. King Charlemagne sighed. *She is so beautiful and just as beautiful within as without.*

"I love you so, Hilde." He pressed a kiss on her forehead. Thinking of his own happiness, he laughed. "And for that very reason, I reluctantly come to discuss a development with you." Hildegard snuggled against his chest. She would have to tip-toe to reach his chin; so she squeezed him tightly around the waist.

"A development? What a ponderous sounding statement! And why such reluctance? I can but think this will not be a pleasant conversation." She lifted her face for a kiss and received the King's mouth immediately on hers. After a breathless moment, he reluctantly pulled his lips away and cupped her chin in his hand, his unique gesture of endearment.

"Aye. Love is in the air...even if spring doesn't arrive for months! Hilde, I speak of Oliver." He looked into his wife's eyes; and, to his surprise, she nodded. "What do you know...or suspect?" He asked her quickly. After only two weeks of marriage, he realized Hilde knew more completely than he everything which took place in his court.

"I guess the court gossips are at full tilt." He squeezed her shoulder and moved away.

"Nay, not at all." Hilde answered. "I have no knowledge or gossip of Oliver among the court ladies. But someone hinted that Lord Oliver pays constant attention to one of our young maids-in-waiting. My information comes from the maid herself. Why, the very term suggests we should rejoice the maid is found - that she need 'wait' no longer." She smiled sweetly at her husband, eager for his opinion.

"Waiting, indeed! I hope one or two of them DO wait!" Charlemagne exclaimed. "From my observations, many of them do not wait one moment after their arrival at court! They are flirting, displaying their bosoms, strutting about the halls, twitching their hips before all the

men they see — the attractive and available ones and anyone else besides."

"My, my!" Hildegard replied softly. "Aren't you reac-
tive today?"

"Forgive my outburst, Hilde. I hate to watch those
who over-drink and those who over-tempt." He turned
to the hearth and gazed into the flames. "Let me begin
again." His thoughts turned to his conversation with Oliver and, remembering his Peer's turmoil, he smiled.

"Have you news from someone you trust, Charley?"
Hilde asked. Charlemagne nodded.

"I've a confession from the man who would change
Jocelyn's 'waiting' state." He smiled, please he was, for
once, privy to a secret. "Oliver spoke to me. He's quite
smitten with Jocelyn, I'm afraid."

"So, it's true. Jocelyn herself suspects his interest."
Hilde confirmed. "But she's unsure herself about it." The
King's eyes widened with this confirmation. "I think she
may, also, have another suitor…one who values her but
has yet to speak." Charlemagne stared into his wife's
face. She saw the muscle clenching in his jaw, the frown
between his eyes, the nervous pucker of his lips.

"Oh dear, my love." Hilde blurted out. "What's the
problem?"

"The problem is two of my Peers, the two best, both
love the same woman! What shall we do? I don't wish
to see either of them hurt or disappointed." His forehead wrinkled, the line between his eyes deepened. He
passed a hand over his eyes. "Which one of them will she
choose? I don't want to think about it. This is a quandary,
for certain."

"It is, indeed. But, this is a time when you do nothing,
Charley. This is not our business, anyone's business. This
decision is between these three people. It, you see, is Joc-

elyn's problem...and her decision." Hildegard walked closer to her husband.

"Has Roland told you of his interest in Jocelyn? Does he intend to ask for her hand? Do you know?"

"I do not." Charlemagne replied. "But I know he loves her. It's apparent to anyone who chances to see his face if she enters the room." He gave a slight laugh. "I'm not sure Roland realizes it yet himself. Men can be very stupid, my dear. You know that." He winked at her.

"But he has yet to speak of his feelings to Jocelyn." Hildegard told the king. "She only suspects he cares for her. Already Oliver asked for permission to speak with her father, though he did not explain his request. It can be for no other reason, can it?"

"Nay, it is for the reason you stated." King Charlemagne confirmed. "He came to me for advice."

"Did he?" Hildegard answered, laughter bubbling in her voice. "And your advice was to move quickly, hum?"

"Of a certainty. I almost lost you from dithering about." Charlemagne admitted frankly. "I don't wish that to happen to one of my dearest friends. I told him to act. But I was torn, I can tell you. I feel disloyal to Roland... in giving advice to Oliver."

"You must not," Hilde reassured him. "Oliver asked your opinion; Roland has not. You can only give your best advice. It is not meet for you to seek Roland out to advise him...not on this question. He did not seek your opinion." She sighed deeply. "We can do nothing, dear. This is their choice. Thank goodness we don't have parents involved. You've heard the saying 'in its own good time;' have you not?" Charlemagne nodded.

"Each one responds according to his time table. You must believe God's hand is in this, Charley. There will be a resolution of this question. I think it will come quickly."

"I know you're right, Hilde," the King admitted. "I just hate to see one hurt when the other will be so happy. Life is not fair."

"Nay," Hildegard responded, softly, putting her arm around his waist. "Sometimes it, of a certainty, seems anything but fair."

"Tell me," the King gazed at his wife. "Is Jocelyn worthy of either of them? I do not know her well." He added by way of apology for the question. Hildegard smiled sadly.

"Were there two of her, we would be doubly blessed," she responded. "Either of them will be lucky beyond measure. The one who does not win her will regret his loss for a lifetime."

***

"They must accept the Christ, Fulrad; I demand it." King Charlemagne declared. "I will not have heathens in my realm. It cannot be borne." He paced around the library, angry that the Saxons did not stay conquered. Just as he thought them subdued, there was another rebellion. "I should not be surprised." He admitted to the priest. "Poppa was ever battling them as well. Don't they understand we strive to save their souls?"

"I cannot explain them, Sire," Fulrad answered. "They surrender to your authority; but, as soon as your back is turned, they invade and plunder Frankland again."

"As soon as I'm called away, you mean," Charlemagne clarified. "They are sly, Fulrad. They attack as I march to Rome; they attack as I march from Rome. As soon as there is distance between us and them, the revolts begin once more. During the winter, I planned this upcoming campaign extensively. It promises to be a rout! Well might they worship their false gods, call on them for aid. I will show them Christ is the only answer. They will fail, surrender, and, thus, abandon their weak, vengeful beliefs."

"You may conquer them," the Abbot allowed; "but many will refuse to convert to Christianity or give you their oath."

"Then, they shall die." Charlemagne retorted. "Believe in my Christ or die; that is the rule of war. I wish to be upon them before they know we march, Fulrad. We'll move earlier in the season...before the ice crust melts along the river's shallows." He smiled smugly. "And marching thus, we will attract men along the way; soldiers from our previous battles will join as we move through the realm. Hopefully, those who don't fight will be unaware of our march...so early shall we move."

"This must be a journey of stealth while few people yet move about. Theweather does not invite marching." The King was eager to conquer the Saxons and keep them conquered, if he could. Although the battle would be bloody and many would die, his superior numbers guaranteed eventual success. "Call a meeting of the Peers, Fulrad," the King directed. "It's time to plan battles, hone our attacks and choose the best plan of attack."

"Excuse me, Sire. I wonder if Queen Hildegard and her ladies wouldn't be more comfortable camping here, in a safer place, than marching with the army." He watched the King's face as he broached the subject. "I mean to say...there is much danger as we move forward. What if our march is not a surprise after all? Enemies may be lying in wait for us, rather than being ignorant of our journey." Fulrad held his breath, afraid he said too much.

"Nay, I will not leave them here...unprotected. As always, Fulrad, the court is safer close to the army than trailing behind or, indeed, stopping as we move forward. Nay. I want my queen and my children as close to me as possible. These seemingly random attacks worry me."

"But, Sire. These incidents appear unconnected, just unfortunate incidents which share no common purpose." Fulrad objected.

"Mayhap." Charlemagne replied. "But I do not want to endanger my family or members of my court by allowing distance to separate us. Nay, they march with us, as always."

Although his army gathered and readied to march in four days, the King himself delayed their departure. The Queen was in labor with their third child.

***

King Charlemagne paced the library tent. He could not sit still, nor could he pass the time in idle conversation. Added to his concern for Hildegard's labor was his worry for the life of this child. We will be uneasy for months, he acknowledged to himself. *Adelheid was a perfect infant, pink and rosy. Why, she even smiled early.* He smiled himself, remembering the joy the infant girl brought to his heart. *Poppa always said I was a 'bat and win' man with women.*

'Let a woman or even a girl bat her eyes at you,' King Pepin often said to his son, 'and you let them win you over, no matter how hare-brained their schemes." The King got to his knees, praying to God to protect Hildegard in her delivery and to bless her and their child.

"And, if it be Your will, Father," he added, "please let this babe be a girl. I do so need a little daughter."

He left the library to stand outside the birthing chamber. He could hear Hilde panting. Then, with a weary sigh, he heard her whimper. At that, he rushed into the tent, upsetting all the women therein. He wiped the sweat from her face, kissed her cheek, and whispered

119

that he was near-by. Then, he fled. The Queen Mother frowned at him as he walked by; but, for once, she said not a word.

Hours later, the Queen Mother hurried to deliver the news: he had a healthy, screaming baby girl. Charlemagne went directly to his wife, thanking Hilde for this most important gift. Her eyes weary, her face pale and bloodless, she, nevertheless, smiled at his happy face and agreed little Rotrud was, indeed, 'perfect.' Only then could the King return to his linens and sleep.

The next day, he named the day of marching four days hence. If a few days rest could strengthen his wife and his baby daughter, he would attack the Saxons after Eastertide. Hildegard's and Rotrud's health and survival were worth any postponed battle.

***

Planning his destruction of the Saxons, King Charlemagne determined he would re-take Eresburg. Some years before, he established a garrison there and used it as an operational base for his army. While he fought the Lombards, the Saxons destroyed the garrison. He found it flattened.

It must be rebuilt, Charlemagne thought. *We shall begin immediately.*

"We build forts up and down the rivers." The King explained to his Peers, following the water with his finger. "With an extensive network of forts, we can, then, control river traffic. Nothing will get in and out of Saxony without our knowledge. The Saxons will, finally, be unable to provision their fighters or to move them."

"Building forts takes a long time, Sire." Rinaldo pointed out. "Is this to be the war of our lifetimes?"

"Aye, it may well come to that," Charlemagne admitted. "But we are the stronger force; we will prevail. I just cannot tell you when." He planned his battles methodically, using his already renown organizational skills.

Not only was the king a master of tactics; he understood the numbers of men needed for an assault, the kilos of flour necessary to feed his troops, the bales of hay necessary to supplement the horses' grazing, and the sizes of rivers and streams required to water his men and his animals. His famous 'pincer movement' won many a battle as he squeezed his enemies between two flanges of troops.

After the battle, came the slaughter. As the enemy soldiers surrendered on the battlefield, King Charlemagne demanded they accept Christ as their personal savior and administered an oath of loyalty. Anyone who refused died, executed by the Frankish commanders. Many times, the blood spilled after the battle was far in excess of that spilled during the fighting itself. Priests went among the wounded, exhorting them to embrace Christianity, painting Charlemagne as a savior himself. But if he were a savior, Charlemagne felt very little like it.

The battle won; the enemy bedded down; the King and Abbot Fulrad sat by the fire, assessing the events of the day.

"Look at them, Fulrad - decimated by our forces. Yet, this surrender, too, will not last." Charlemagne predicted. "Why do they resist so much? No matter how many surrenders we have, in a half-year's time we'll be fighting them once again. Where does the spirit of the Saxons come from? These battles are but sacrifices of their men. Yet, they always return to fight, sometimes twice in the same battle season."

They wish to be free, Sire." Fulrad replied, admiring such tenacity, even as he worried for their souls. "They wish to worship their own gods, to follow their historic customs, to be in charge of their own destiny. It's not hard to understand."

"Free they may be, free in a Christian nation." Charlemagne responded. "That is their only choice."

"King Charlemagne," Roland called his name as he cantered up the hill.

"Sire, there is a Saxon commander who would speak with you. He's gravely wounded or I would refuse him. But he insists. Nay, he begs to speak to the King. I don't believe he'll last through the speaking. He is bleeding profusely."

"Aye. I'll speak to him. What Christian would refuse a dying man's last request, one as simple as this?" King Charlemagne asked.

"He has no weapons, Sire; we've made certain." Oliver spoke as Charlemagne approached the prisoner-holding tents. "I can't give a reason for this request but thought asking you could do no harm."

The King followed Oliver to a near-by gulley where a wounded Saxon lay on the ground. A Frankish healer tried to give the soldier a drink; but the water spilled all over his chest.

"He can't swallow," Oliver noted. His eyes were sorrowful as he shook his head slightly at the king.

"Well-met, brave soldier," Charlemagne greeted him. "I'm Charlemagne. Speak as you will." He moved closer to the man and squatted so the dying soldier could look into his face.

"I would talk much but have no time," the soldier replied. "I'm dying. You can't kill me twice, so I say this to you. You think your destruction of the Irismul will destroy the Saxons, destroy their will. But this be not so! The great tree was our talisman, our hope — the very soul of Saxony. By your act, your lack of reverence, you have condemned us—Saxon and Frank alike--to fight forever. You destroy a living being and a symbol. By this act, you've unleashed a dragon. May your god protect you. May my god spite..." Blood bubbled from the soldier's mouth. He was forever silent.

Oliver, Roland, and Fulrad looked at the King. He paled visibly as the soldier spoke. But, as in times past, his anger surged.

"You speak blasphemy! I conquer all lands to bring them to the only GOD and to HIS son, the Christ. Your curse or your blessing means nothing to me. I do what I must." And the King left, cursing the soldier and all his comrades. The following morning, Charlemagne summoned Oliver.

"Tell me about this "Irismul," Oliver. "What was the Saxon soldier talking about yesterday?"

"I did not have time to tell you of it. When Ganelon overran the Saxons on the south edge of the battle, he stumbled onto their most sacred site. There, behind the hill was their religious center, Sire. The "Irismul" was an ancient tree, the symbol of the Saxon people. Long did it spread its leaves over that sacred land."

"Ganelon, amused by the Saxon soldiers' efforts to protect the tree, decided to destroy it. Rinaldo reported to me. He said Ganelon's blade bounced off the trunk, as if the tree could not be cut. But, Ganelon - being himself - persevered and cut the tree down, first the limbs and, then, the trunk. His men, seeing his cut bite into the tree's bark, rushed to help him. And so, the tree was quickly destroyed."

"What was the purpose of this? Did Ganelon know the regard the Saxons had for this tree?"

"Sire, I do not know. He saw them try to defend it...so

he destroyed it. Everything is about power to Ganelon, power and his will."

"We must keep him on the sidelines, Oliver. He will destroy something even more important if power is his value. Please tell Janlur to control him." King Charlemagne said.

***

That night in the battle tent, the King described his plans for the final defeat of the Saxons. "You know they will come at us again, as surely as the sun rises in the east. I weary of this constant battle. Let me outline my plan for overcoming the Saxon resistance," he told them. "We will wait and, then, massacre them. As God is my witness, the Frankish army will deliver these Saxons to the Lord's justice."

"As we already considered, we'll labor mightily in constructing fortresses along these Saxon rivers: the Lippe, the Hase, the Weser. We will lay siege to the Saxon strongholds. Our own garrisons, we supply from river barges. In the mountains, we replicate the Saxons' ambush tactics and, using their own methods, we'll destroy these rebels." The men stirred restlessly. They had little experience in on-going battle with one recalcitrant enemy.

"Is it possible to destroy them with one blow?" A newly-named commander asked. "Battles each year with the same foe, it does take the heart from the glory of the fight. Such constant strain, it's not uplifting for my soldiers."

"Are you daft, man? There is nothing uplifting about war, Captain Soisson." King Charlemagne replied drily. "It's our destiny to defeat these people. God wills it. In addition to the battles we instigate, we will deploy bands of men throughout the Saxon countryside to demand surrender and conversion of the rural Saxons. Any Saxon who refuses will die. There is no recourse. No bargains will be struck, no second chances given. To live, these Saxons will do as I require. Do you all understand me?" He looked at each man in turn. "See to it."

And so began the long, bloody, near extermination of the Saxon people in their own lands. The Frankish army engaged the Saxons repeatedly, defeating them in small and large battles. Hunkering down after a defeat, they rose completely defiant months later. Their inspired leader's name was Widukind, a soldier who led the Saxons for years against Charlemagne's rule.

***

On this day, the Frankish army defeated the Saxons and subjugated them, here at the end of the battle season. And, once again, Charlemagne turned his troops toward home. They marched only a few leagues before he received a mud-stained parchment from Pope Hadrian.

///

King Charlemagne,

Ruler of Frankland, Defender of the Faith, Loyal Servant of the Holy Church, Friend of Christ and His Angels, Minister of Pope Hadrian

My Son,

A Lombard noble, Rothgard (called the Duke of Friuli) and Duke Arechis (the Duke of Benevento) together plot an insurrection against you for the spring. Duke Rothgard, along with other Lombard nobles, conspire together and plan to destroy the Lombard people. They lust for power, taking everything from their countrymen: land, women, livestock, water craft… even children.

You must prepare for battle. Their souls have long since been lost.

Save us Charlemagne! The people and the Church are at Rothgard's mercy!

Pope Hadrian

//

Charlemagne read the Pope's missive aloud to Roland who had, only moments before, presented him with a report from his personal spies in Lombardy. King Charlemagne's cheeks flamed red.

"Is there any collaboration of this?" Charlemagne asked Roland, hoping the report exaggerated, intending to produce panic and over-reaction. Roland nodded and signaled his squire. An older man, gray at his temples, stepped from behind the squire and kneeled before the King.

"King Charlemagne, this is Michael Maccanti. He serves as my most-trusted spy, has worked with me since before I took leave of my mother's house. He begs to speak with you directly."

"Rise and speak." Charlemagne ordered.

"I ask only for mercy; I ask for the King's help." Roland's oldest spy said. "The Lombard nobles destroy the peasantry, your Majesty. In the name of the Holy Church, please help them. I've not seen so much want since I was a green soldier with Charles Martel, your grandfather. These Lombards take everything from the people. Heed this young boy's words." He beckoned to a small, fearful boy, mayhap ten years. The boy bent his knee. Michael nodded to him and his tale began.

"My ma, Sir, then my aunt…and, now, my sister — they all left us, disappeared. The men in the big cloaks, they took them. My brother and sister, my cousins… we searched and searched for them, but we cannot find them. We don't know what to do. My papa, he died trying to hold our cattle." The boy dropped his eyes to the floor as his tears spilled out. Others came before the king - spies, men, women and children- to describe the horror in Lombardy. It was a repetitious mantra: disappearances, killings, moving from ancestral homes, want and hunger.

The stories told of orphans, of entire families sold into slavery, of men selling lands held by their families for generations — all for a loaf of bread. The nobility, left in charge of Lombardy after Charlemagne's defeat of Desiderius, used every subterfuge, every dishonesty, every advantage to scourge the land. And they threatened, maimed, and killed anyone who objected to their methods.

"Help us, Sire. If you care nothing for Lombardy, at least help us save my friends." A young spy begged. "The whole realm is at risk. Hundreds starve to death." The hall rang with the voices of people begging for rescue. They offered their lives and those of their children if King Charlemagne would aid them.

"How can it be, Oliver? They enslave and starve their own people? Damnation! I am sick to death of these Lombard nobles. We wait no longer. Inform Janlur and the Abbot; the troops march tomorrow. I shall end this rape of Lombard as soon as I can." Charlemagne stomped out of the battle tent, overcome by the want and starvation the people reported.

Reversing his usual custom of wintering in a royal castle, the King marched to the Alps and established a camp. He wished himself in position to curb Lombardy betrayals as soon as spring arrived and allowed the army to move.

"We cannot dismiss our soldiers, Ganelon," King Charlemagne said to Ganelon's grumble. "Battle will begin as soon as the weather cooperates. We must defeat the Lombard nobles in order to save the Lombard people. What a travesty! We march now to stand ready to cross their borders." He shook his head at Ganelon's unhappy frown.

"Your criticism or your disapproval concerns me little, Sir. Soldiers fight whenever their commander needs them. For certain, the booty they take will soften their tempers." Charlemagne stared into Ganelon's face, his eyes never wavering.

"Such a pity, Ganelon." The commander looked at the King intently, angry because Charlemagne did not heed his advice. "You felt no such reluctance to massacre Saxon soldiers, did you?" The King asked. Ganelon's body startled; he looked around quickly, thinking to hurry away. "Nay, you led...even instigated...the Irismul carnage." Ganelon's face drained of color as his head snapped up.

"With no provocation, you murdered soldiers who surrendered. But, here, you're loathe to position our soldiers to overtake corrupt, self-serving traitors. I do not understand your values." Charlemagne frowned, then discharged Ganelon with a move of his head.

***

King Charlemagne knew he might well face a mass uprising of the Lombard nobility against him. Nevertheless, he marched into Lombardy early in March of 776. When the actual fighting began, only three dukes rebelled against Frankish rule – the dukes of Friuli, of Treviso, and of Vicenza.

In the king's eyes, the betrayal of these dukes sealed the fate of the Italian nobility. No longer did he show the Lombard nobles clemency. No longer did he allow them to rule themselves. Charlemagne's anger simmered and fed on itself.

He was unique, a king concerned for his people, dedicated to improving their lives. He could not understand the dukes. Rather than easing the suffering of the people or making an effort to strengthen the realm, the Lombard nobles seized the people's lands and possessions, even enslaving many of them.

On top of the nobles' greed, a disastrous famine swept through the land, extending the suffering and death. The unprotected populace was prey to any brigand or outlaw strong enough to work his will. Some, selling their small plots of land for food, became slaves in order to feed their children. Many, forced off their lands, left Lombardy, laboring in other countries. Others, stripped of their meager possessions, were destitute, sick and dying.

"I shall never trust these Italian nobles again." King Charlemagne fumed to Oliver. "From now on, those we name to oversee our laws in this dreadful land will be Frankish or Alamannian counts. They will do more for these people than their own nobility." He paced back and forth in the war tent.

"We make no allowance for Lombard laws, not anymore. We implement the laws I wrote for Lombardy during the winter. Put them in place. Abbot Fulrad will read them before the people. Tell the army to make camp; we stay until the laws are working, until our men are in place. Only then can we leave this God-forsaken place!" He began pulling parchment from the cases.

"Get Fulrad in here, Oliver, and, then, sit. I want copies made of all announcements. Messengers must go through Lombardy, take the new laws to the people." He pointed toward the tent door. "Go. Bring Fulrad. Let's begin." In very little time, Fulrad, Roland, Oliver, and Janlur made hundreds of copies of the King's words and his new laws.

"I call this first one my 'Italian capitulary.' Please evaluate it for fairness and clarity." Charlemagne told his 'copyists.' He read aloud. Overwhelmed by his words, not a single man wrote a word.

"This law is unheard of, Sire," Oliver said slowly. "It negates property transfers since the war and nullifies any sale which resulted in the enslavement of any man, woman, or child! And it applies only after our army passed through Lombard lands."

"Aye," Charlemagne replied. "The people accuse our army of devastating the land and their lives. They report the nobility – my overseers - gave them no choice, forced them to become slaves." He turned full eyes to Oliver. "Can you imagine…selling your child into slavery in the hope he will have enough to eat?" The King slapped his hand on his thigh.

"I will not have it; I will not! These are my people, by right of conquest. What kind of king would I be if, by my war, they're unable to survive? Nay, there must be an accounting. We will sort this out." He turned to look out over the now-green, verdant fields.

"This is the time to rescue them. I will prove to the Lombards I have their interests at heart."

"This is unheard of, Sire." Oliver almost whispered. "Your compassion for the Lombard peasants…it is a salve to my heart."

"Send a herald throughout the kingdom to inform the populace of our efforts." The King answered, nodding his thanks to Oliver. "The people will know I am concerned for them, much more so than their own nobility." *Aye, today I turn the common people against these nobles; they are the losers, of a certainty.* He smiled.

***

Although Charlemagne's daily burdens were great:

holding the Saxons at bay, establishing a working governmental structure for Italy, and attempting to establish an educational system for his realm, his personal life was bliss. After Hildegard's acceptance of Adelheid's death and the birth of Rotrud, he and his Queen became even closer. His laws to help the Lombard people brought tears to his wife's eyes and praise from her lips.

"Always you surprise me, Charley," Hildegard admitted. "Your concern for all our people is inspiring. This is not common in a ruler."

"Mayhap not. But if I am compassionate, my dear; it comes from your example. You worry and care for everyone, noble and peasant alike. Of a certainty, God sent you to me, sent you to help curb my martial spirit. I do look at power and rule differently from before, Hilde." He paused, holding a finger to his mouth. "Don't tell anyone my secret. I must retain my image of a hard, blood-thirsty warrior. It's the only way to keep the beasts at bay."

"And beasts there are a-plenty." She agreed as she rubbed his back.

***

As King Charlemagne and Queen Hildegard discussed the clothing they should wear for the upcoming evening meal, friend and foe alike arrived for a banquet. It was the first step in the arduous task of establishing a Frankish foothold in Lombardy.

King Charlemagne knew the Lombard nobles would act as if they were the conquerors. He hoped Abbot Fulrad's welcome would put the Lombard commanders at ease, avoid any unpleasantness. Abbot Fulrad would, firstly welcome them to the Frankish realm and, then, administer the oath of allegiance, one by one. As they made their vows, the King would state the support and behavior he expected. The purpose of the banquet was to assure them of their place in the conquered kingdom...and to show his strength. King Charlemagne hoped a generous banquet, focused on thoughts and commitments for the future. would underscore his forgiveness of their momentary lapse in allegiance.

Charlemagne pulled on his deep purple breeches and slid a pale purple tunic over his head. Embroidered down the arms and across the upper chest, the tunic boasted pearls interspersed with sapphires which lined the neckline and the hem. He pulled his long hair back, discreetly clasping it underneath the back of his tunic. The King's hair was so thick and 'fly-away' it was necessary to subdue it in some manner. Queen Hildedegard, whose dark hair and eyes lent mystery to her face, wore a dull-colored, lilac tunic and a full skirt of creamy-white wool. Around her neck lay a unique necklace of pale mother-of-pearl shards, glowing softly.

Hildegard moved to her wash basin to cleanse her eye; something was pricking it. She looked into the water and noted the paleness of her face. She looked worn and peaked.

"This will not do," she murmured to herself, frowning. Walking to a near-by bench, she picked up a periwinkle mantel and held it against her face. Immediately, color returned to her complexion. "My face is lost in this pale-colored tunic." She moved to her traveling chest, rummaged around, and brought out a bright navy blue-purple scarf. She wove the cloth in and around her headdress and set it properly on her head. Then, she returned to the wash basin. *Aye, that's better.* She turned to inspect the King's garments, just as he came to her side.

"You are beyond beautiful, my dear," he complimented her. "These colors suit you exactly, especially your headdress. You will become a model for the lords' wives." Hildegard shook her head. "Would you like to make a wager against me?"

"Charley!" Hilde exclaimed. "A wager, a wager on my husband's view of my beauty? I think not!" She laughed, tickling his neck. "Besides, Christian men do not make wagers."

"Ha!" The King responded. "Ohhh... but we do, my dear. We do, of a certainty! What is marriage but a game of chance?"

Chapter 10

FRIENDS AND CONFLICT

As Charlemagne and Hildegard dressed in celebratory clothes, Roland and Oliver entered the banquet tent. The two Peers complemented each other exactly. The rubies on Roland's blood-red mantle caught the light of the candles. His face glowed, making him appear slightly inebriated. His breeches were the same red as his mantle while his tunic was cobalt blue. Oliver, in blue breeches and a pale, blue tunic chose to wear his own red mantle, decorated with sapphires up the sleeves and along the edges. As they talked together, every maid-in-waiting, noble wife, and serving wench froze, captivated by the sight.

Roland, of a certainty, hardly noticed the attention. Originally from Brittany, he looked unlike most of the Germanic men in Charlemagne's court. His dark-brown hair was touched with gold. In a certain light, he almost had a halo around his head. His arched nose, thinner than his companions, and his high cheek-bones sent every feminine heart racing. He was the master of courtesies and never raised his voice to a woman, a child, or a servant. He invariably acted as fine as he looked. Even in mock sword practice, in jousting games, and in foot-competitions, he kept his temper under control, his clothing immaculate, and his manners polished. Always was he was kind to children and his beloved horses. Women fawned over him; men wanted to be him.

Oliver, on the other hand, was attractive to only the most discerning, man or woman. His hair was ash brown, his skin a lighter skin tone than Roland's. Roland was the picture of grace, with his lithe physique and long legs. Oliver, on the other hand, was heavy in the shoulders — muscled there and in his stocky legs. He was strong and immovable, rooted in the earth. Unfailingly courteous as well, he was unable to make small talk or lavish temporary praise on beautiful women. His value was in his character, in his integrity and in his honesty.

Few took the time to discover those characteristics. Alas, even though the court knew the King valued and loved both men, the average courtier or countess did not discern Oliver's gifts. The Peers, of a certainty, knew; but they did not discuss their colleague with others.

"Break your fast with me, please, Oliver," Roland urged his friend. "I have need of your counsel."

"Anything you wish to say, I will listen." Oliver replied, puzzled. "But I have little advice for you, Roland. You are more able in giving advice than I." He looked around worriedly.

"Nay, not this time." Roland replied, smiling. The two Peers took seats on benches to the right of the dais. A bit nervous about the disloyal nobles' attending the banquet, they both planned to be as close as possible to King Charlemagne…in order to ward off any unpleasantness.

"No one would dare attack the King here, Oliver." Roland whispered. "There would be no escape."

"Aye," Oliver replied softly. "But there are ever those who would martyr themselves for the glory of killing the King. It's from such as these he needs our protection."

Rinaldo, Ganleon, and Marc joined the table, just as the trenchers appeared, filled to overflowing. The smell of baking bread wafted over the camp as diners found seats in the banquet tent. Mouths watered with anticipation. Even the nobles, seated at the King's long table, turned their eyes to the serving maids.

For the first half of the meal, the maids had no worry about pinches, rubs, or uncouth grabs from the feasting men; all concentrated their attention on filling their stomachs. Oliver fed his favorite hound bits of fat and bones from his plate. The dog invariably sought him out, content to lie beside his feet and eat from Oliver's hand, rather than wander the tent, hoping for scraps.

"The Queen directed the cooks to create the best meal possible for this banquet." Oliver commented to Roland. "I saw Cook Burtson combing the forests for blackberries yesterday. Just this morning, he worried about the state of last year's store of acorns, so I hope the bread tastes as fine as it smells."

"If not, leave it," Roland suggested. "Look at all this food! We might eat for days on this plenty. Should we suggest the remains be given to the soldiers?"

"Nay, there's no need." Oliver responded. "Queen Hildegard already gave those very instructions. She allows no food to be wasted, even if the servers give it to the goats and hogs. But look at those lords eat! It appears they've fasted for days, not just since our morning meal." Roland looked up from his roasted chicken to survey the diners. He ate sparingly and simply, preferring roasted meat to those covered in sauces. His trencher held raw greens, carrots, parsnips, and cabbage. His one craving was for fruit tarts which he indulged more often than he should.

Here, though, was a smorgasbord of choices. There were meats enough for anyone's taste: boar turned on a splint for hours, a favorite of King Charlemagne; stuffed peacocks; roasted chicken; trout rolled in crushed pecans; pickled eels; and pork with potatoes. Though less popular with the diners, vegetable dishes crowded the table: turnips floating in butter; parsnips and parsley; a medley of beans seasoned with pepper; potatoes browned with bacon; and trenchers filled with greens, onions, and radishes.

When men began patting their stomachs and calling for more wine, the servers would bring desserts. Already this morning, Roland saw fruit-and-nut tarts cooling outside the cook tent. On the cooks' tables were cinnamon-sugared dough with peaches; blackberries and apple sauce; a salad of apples, walnuts, dried plums and heavy cream; and slabs of cake, sweetened with honey and preserves.

"This is the very time for an enemy to attack." Roland said to the men around him at the table. "Stuffed with food and dizzy with drink, everyone is an easy target." The men laughed good-naturedly, but Roland noticed that some of them pushed their plates away and sat straighter. Roland and Oliver smiled at each other, knowing the banquet chamber well-protected. King Charlemagne would never risk an attack with all the nobility sitting here beside him. Nonetheless, it is useful to keep men on their toes, Roland thought. He glanced at Oliver who slowly sipped his drink. Roland smiled, knowing there was only water in Oliver's flagon.

"My friend," he said, "let's talk before we are unable to think. Give me your thoughts on marriage, if you please." Oliver startled, his eyes boring into Roland's.

"Marriage?" His voice squeaked, then shrugged. "I have few thoughts on that noble institution." But seeing the seriousness in his friend's eyes, he continued. "I fear it, if you want the truth. I, myself, consider the idea from time to time. In the past, it made my stomach clinch. But, now…well, now when I think about it, I find a specific lady pops into my mind." He ducked his head slightly. "But, I must say, Roland, marriage is a huge step. Why do you ask?"

"…because I am considering it, too. Tell me the name of your interest, Oliver, would you?" Oliver blushed as Roland finished his question. *Mayhap, I should not ask so quickly, Roland thought. But if Oliver will name her, I may understand more about his views on marriage itself.*

"Nay." Oliver answered, tugging at his tunic. "I have yet to receive permission from her father, permission to ask her. That should be the first step, aye?" He looked at Roland for confirmation. Roland covered his surprise. *How has Oliver moved so far along…and I know nothing about this?*

"Aye, I suppose. Aye, that is the first step. You are firm in your decision, then?" Roland asked. "And you have a particular woman in mind? Oliver! You do surprise me!"

"I'm committed, but she knows nothing about my feelings and does not anticipate my interest." Oliver paused. "It does throw fear into my heart, Roland. I admit it freely to you."

"And in mine, as well." Roland agreed. He fingered his flagon, took a drink, and felt calmer as the wine went down. "But why now, Oliver; is this a sudden decision?"

"Nay," Oliver replied. "I have thought on it for some time, actually since Charlemagne's first little daughter, Adelheid, was lost. I always wanted children and," here he smiled at Roland, "for that, one needs a wife." He sobered quickly and continued. "Truthfully, my friend, I'm lonely. I would like someone to build a life around, someone who truly knows and values me." Oliver traced a streak of water on the table with his finger. He said no more.

"Seeing the heartbreak of losing Adelheid," Roland

said, "you must want this very much. A little child's death is enough to deter some men from ever having children...or from marrying, for that matter. The sadness almost destroyed the Queen."

"Aye, I know. But the comfort of her husband, the love he has for her, brought her back. I want that kind of marriage, Roland. I definitely do." Both men were lost in their own thoughts. And, then, Oliver again.

"Do you have someone in mind yourself? Many of the women in the court would jump at the chance to be your bride, Roland. If the court knew you were interested, women would proposition you twenty-four hours a day." He chuckled, imagining Roland surrounded by such eager females. "And it would not just be the maids, either," he teased. "Some lords would likely find themselves without wives." Roland smiled.

"I fear you exaggerate." He answered, humble as always. "It's not any woman I want for wife; only one interests me. But I've no idea if she would consider me." He laughed at Oliver's quick start.

"Aye, there are women who do not fall at my feet, my friend," he continued. "And one of them, of a certainty, is the one I would have." At that moment, King Charlemagne stood to propose a toast, a toast to peace in Lombard. Roland's and Oliver's conversation came to an end.

***

"I wonder who the woman is." Oliver muttered under his breath as he left the banquet for his sleeping chamber. He heard the drinking men, still imbibing, more completely losing their wits. Oliver shrugged; his thoughts returned to his own worry. *I'm surprised Roland asked my opinion of wives. Mayhap, such popularity as he enjoys gets tiresome.*

"It's true; Roland is the most sought-after of all the men at court—Peers or otherwise. He seems to draw women magically, all types and kinds. But just because you are sought doesn't mean you want the seekers." Oliver smiled to himself, then his breath caught. *What if he's interested in Jocelyn? She would never consider me then!* So unsettled did the thought make him that Oliver sat on one of the benches in the corridor.

"I must speak with Jocelyn," Oliver murmured. "I waited for her father to bring his sweet delights for the court celebrations; but Christmas and Easter are both behind us. He comes not." He thought back to King Charlemagne's words. "The Kind urged me to speak soon, and that was weeks ago. I must hasten." He directed his feet toward his chamber. "I must choose the best clothing I have to approach her. I shall ask her on the morrow."

***

Up at dawn the following morning, Oliver became more nervous as the minutes went slowly by. His stomach was so queasy he did not eat. He waited for the court to break its fast. Then, he set out to find Jocelyn. After almost an hour of diligent searching, the Queen told him Jocelyn was in the orchard, taking little Charles for a walk. Oliver hurried to the herb garden; the orchard was situated right behind it.

He walked rapidly toward the sound of a soft voice answering a child. Looking around, he noticed the air smelled of apple and pear blossoms. Entering the fruit trees, he passed into a wonderland of white and pink flowers. Under the sounds of a child's question, the lowing of near-by cattle, and pups' shrill barking was the buzzing of hundreds of bees—all busily at work among the blossoms.

"Gud morrow, Sir Oliver." Little Charles greeted him, as he popped from behind an old post which supported a side of the grape arbor. "Gud morrow."

"Good morrow to you, Charles. I trust you're having fun here in the orchard. Are there any apples ready to eat?" The lad laughed, his eyes wide and smiling.

"Nay!" He replied. "Apple's are babies; see?" And he opened his hand to show the small nub of an apple. "I didn't hurt it, Sir." Little Charles hurried to defend himself. "It was on the ground."

"I'm certain you didn't take it from the limb, Charles," Oliver assured him. "You could scarcely reach a limb now, could you?"

"Not yet, but soon, Sir Oliver. I grow fast." He declared. At that moment, Jocelyn came from the far corner of the orchard, waving to Oliver. He watched her approach and, then, fearing to be seen as discourteous, he walked towards her.

"Jocelyn, good…good morrow to you."

"And to you, Oliver. Look at these beautiful flowers! And the green leaves are a perfect setting. " She pointed to the fruit blossoms. "What brings you to the orchard?" As she spoke, they heard Charles calling Oliver's name.

"Charles, I can barely hear you," Oliver raised his voice. "One minute, we are coming your way."

"Whenever you can," was the answer which floated back. Oliver raised his eyebrow to Jocelyn as they both turned toward the King's son. He was manfully raising a fishing pole, trying to hold it erect. Oliver started to run toward him, but Jocelyn's voice stopped him.

"He's fine, Oliver. He loves holding the pole…because it's so tall, I think. Don't hurry. He doesn't want your help-- just your praise, mayhap." And she smiled. Oliver felt foolish.

"It's clear I don't understand little ones." He admitted to his embarrassment. This is not a positive thing to say to the woman I wish to marry, he thought. "I don't want him to hurt himself, drop the pole on his foot."

"He won't." Jocelyn assured him. "And, if he does, he will learn something from such a mishap."

"How do you know so much about small boys?" Oliver asked, smiling. Jocelyn laughed.

"I just watch them," she said, "and try to imagine why they do things. Watching and listening give me valuable insights."

"...kind of like I do with the Peers?" Oliver asked. Jocelyn looked at him in surprise and, then, smiled.

"I suspect you get the same result." She suggested.

"Nay," Oliver replied, "not nearly as clearly as you do, be certain of that." Don't panic, he said to himself. *Do what you came here to do; you must.* "As for my reason for being here," Oliver plunged ahead.

"I've come to...to talk with you, Jocelyn. I would make an important request of you." He looked away over her head to the forest on either side. *I'm lost. I have no idea how to do this.*

"...of a certainty, Oliver. I will do all I can to honor your request. What would you have of me?" She sat on an old log, apparently willing to give him all the time in the world. Oliver sat beside her and gathered his courage.

"I apologize to you ... for this process, I mean." He fumbled. "I apologize for not following an expected custom; but I'm quite anxious..." His words faded away as he lost himself in her eyes. Shaking his head, Oliver tried again.

"I wished to speak with your father, first, Jocelyn. But it seems Count Hautgard isn't coming to court, at least, not soon. And I fear that...." He stopped speaking because his throat was so dry. He feared to continue. Jocelyn frowned, clearly trying to decipher the connection between a request and her father's absence.

"I don't understand, Oliver. What does a request have to do with my father?" Suddenly, she blinked and look away, toward little Charles. Can he be seeking to determine my interest in him? She asked herself. But, not believing such a thing possible, she immediately dismissed the thought. Oliver saw the confusion in her face and determined he couldn't wait for pretty words or inspiration. He took her hand in his two and looked into her eyes.

"Will you be my wife, Jocelyn?" He asked. "I promise to love you, to treat you kindly, to protect you from this time forth?" Jocelyn's eyes bulged in her face. Her cheeks turned a rosy red which, for some reason, bolstered Oliver's courage. Mayhap, she will consent, he thought. And that gave him the eloquence he lacked.

"The first step is a betrothal, of course," he continued. "But I know I wish you for my wife, Jocelyn. In fact, you are the only women in this entire court, in this entire world, I want. I love your intelligence, your kindness, your quick wit and your deliberative behavior. You think through your words, as well as your actions; and in that, you won my heart." What have I left out? Oliver wondered. Jocelyn stared at him, seemingly speechless.

"Oh!" He exclaimed. "And I love you. Jocelyn, I love you. I do not wish to spend another moment of life without you. I know I will love you more each day we have together, each day that passes." Still, she had no reaction. Oliver squeezed her hand.

"Jocelyn, would it please you were I to kneel at your feet?" At those words, she laughed, withdrew her hand and stroked his cheek.

"Nay," she replied. "Kneeling is not necessary, Oliver." Her eyes opened even wider still. He could see the short breaths she was taking, her pale face.

"Are you ill, Jocelyn?" He asked. She shook her head quickly.

"Nay, I'm not ill…just surprised. I did not think…I did hope…" She stumbled over the words, looking at Oliver shyly. "I'm surprised. I was not sure you had any feelings for me at all, Oliver—friendship, mayhap, but not feelings this important." Oliver took her hand again, pressing it to his chest.

"I have very strong, strong and deep, feelings for you, Jocelyn. Soon, you will be able to feel them, radiating from my breast."

"In that case," Jocelyn beamed at him, "I accept your proposal. I shall inform Queen Hildegard; you should talk to the King, I suppose. And I will send a missive home to my family." Oliver could not think, so nervous was he. *Was it possible she agreed?*

"Did you say 'aye,' Jocelyn?" He asked.

"Aye, I did." Jocelyn confirmed, her face bursting with laughter. Oliver pulled her to his chest. The kiss, he thought, the kiss will have to come later.

"I'm so happy, Jocelyn." He admitted as a deep sigh escaped. "I just want to hold you for a while."

"Hold me, then," Jocelyn whispered back, "and I will do the same with you." Before either heard his footsteps, little Charles ran up to them. He wrapped his arms around both their pairs of legs and looked up.

"Hugs are good." He declared solemnly as he smiled up at them.

***

Oliver went to King Charlemagne that very day to deliver his news. He felt this was a propitious time to announce his betrothal. The effort to subdue the Lombards was a success; the Saxons, though still belligerent, were at peace for now; and spring, the time of hope and renewal, was upon them.

Oliver found the King near the river, soaking his feet as the water rushed by. The spring melting dumped even more water into the rushing river. Flotsam rushed by, caught in the flow. The sun beamed down on Charlemagne's fair hair, the wind flicked his tunic back and forth. The King lay in the grass, exulting in the sunshine on his face.

"Are you a sun worshipper, my Liege?" Oliver asked quietly, smiling at the King.

"Always," Charlemagne answered with a smile. "Since Fulrad told me of Egypt and the pyramids, when I was six or seven, I believed my former life must certainly have been there. The heat and warmth light my soul, Oliver. Surely, you feel the healing power of this day."

"Aye, I do. But I have heat and light from another, even more wondrous source. I just asked Jocelyn to be my wife. She agreed, Charlemagne! Can you believe my luck?" Oliver laughed happily, sitting beside the King. Charlemagne sat bolt upright, looking into Oliver's face for confirmation of his words. He smiled, a smile which grew and grew.

"I cannot begin to tell you my pleasure at this news! My very best wishes to you; I wish you the same joy I have in Hildegard!" The King beamed. "Of a certainty, you are truly a brave man, Oliver. You appear to be willing, eager even, to bind yourself to one woman. May your union be a constant blessing, my friend." He grabbed Oliver's shoulders, gave him a huge hug, smiling and pounding his back all the while. "When is the lucky day, my man;

is it decided?"

"Nay, nay, you move too quickly, Sire. I just asked the lady for a betrothal. She agreed. We must take time to know each other, to be certain we can abide each other. I, myself, am certain. Time will only strengthen my commitment."

"Aye, you seem determined to me," the King agreed seriously. "And when do you wish this announced? I assume you wish to shout it to the world. Am I right?"

"Aye, you have the truth of it. But Jocelyn prefers to write her family; then, the announcement can be made. And I must dower her, your majesty. I know her family's manor and position, the regard in which they are held, and would appreciate your suggestion as to what is needed. I have no sister and, therefore, no idea of appropriate choices." Oliver shook his head, already overcome by all the customs which a marriage entails. "This is the difficult, confusing part."

"I shall consult my wife," the King replied, after a few moments thought. "She will know exactly. And she will be reasonable, Oliver. We would not want you destitute if the young woman found you undesirable…after getting to know you better." Charlemagne immediately regretted his words, seeing Oliver's face pale, his hands tremble.

"I'm teasing you!" King Charlemagne exclaimed. "For the Lord's sake, Oliver, you finished the difficult part—asking the lady for her hand. The rest is…" he paused. "The rest is do-able, a pain in the ass, for certain, but do-able!" He laughed, again pounding Oliver on the back.

"My goal is to survive it," Oliver replied softly as he wandered off.

The King laughed uproariously at his friend and got to his feet. If only attending to this wedding were my biggest worry, he thought. He walked slowly to Hildegard's tent to tell her Oliver's news, all the while worrying about the governance of his realm.

***

I must make a visit to Arstat's manor soon. Charlemagne decided. *Let me evaluate this Count's success in interpreting the law. With that knowledge, I'll know the extent of oversight the counts require. The laws seems clear to me but I cannot assume my counts rule with wisdom and mercy.*

Although Charlemagne was certain his non-Lombard overseers were necessary to keep Lombardy and its nobles loyal, he knew the weakness of individual men could undermine his entire governmental structure. He used the same hierarchy as the church to underpin his government's organization but feared the framework alone would not guarantee loyal followers or competent administrators. For Charlemagne, the Pope, as the head of the Church, and he, as the head of his kingdom, was a reasonable hierarchy. Below the invincible leaders were those who served, both the realm and their individual peoples. To do their jobs well, they must also embrace the King's vision, his hopes for the people. *Often, I know they do not.* He reminded himself. *Since military decisions for this battle season are made, I have time to visit Arstat and determine for myself his abilities and successes.*

With the destination and route chosen, the mobile court began its journey, this time headed for Fulda. King Charlemagne wished to ascertain, in person, if the duke rightly fulfilled his duties-- holding court, making legal decisions, sentencing wrongdoers and, generally, keeping the peace.

Charlemagne himself wrote many laws and regulations and, then, proclaimed them throughout his realm. His *mis-*

si dominici, quasi-ambassadors of the court sent to assess the success of the realm's nobility, reported the dukes' and counts' successes and failures to him. He took a serious interest in the methods which the nobles used to implement his laws and legal directions and in their concern for the people under their jurisdiction. After the missi dominici reported their evaluations, the King visited the nobility as they judged and punished the people of Frankland. The King felt he owed the soldiers, the peasants, the small landowners, and the merchants such oversight.

Hoofbeats pounded the dry earth, louder and louder the closer they came. Duke Arstat looked up at the sound. He stood quickly, shading his eyes with his hand.

"Are those the King's banners moving toward our court? Oh, God! Aye! Those are the royal banners." His breath caught in his chest. There is nothing to do but welcome him, the Duke thought. He hurried from the stables, shouting to his captain to muster his gurads and follow him to the courtyard, there to welcome the King. Arstat waited for King Charlemagne to dismount, then went to his knees in the early autumn dusk.

"Your Majesty, welcome to my lands. What a surprise to see you! I did not expect a visit." He rose slowly. "Welcome! Do come, come inside and refresh yourself." The Duke's words gushed from his mouth. "Truly, Sire, this is an honor." Duke Arstat beckoned to one of his couriers and sent him racing to find the Duchess. King Charlemagne beamed at him.

"Duke Arstat, many thanks for a hospitable welcome! I'll disrupt your household, your daily duties, as little as possible. We're well-prepared to camp with our soldiers. Out here on your practice field will do very well. Please, please, don't disturb your good duchess. Our needs are few."

"My Liege, I cannot allow it," Duke Arstat protested. "You must have adequate chambers. Many of my men patrol my southern boundary, so your escort may use their quarters. Some of your soldiers may double up with my small garrison or pitch their tents, as they choose. Sire, is the Queen with you? I trust your court is nearby?" He peered down the road, watching for the court.

"Marilla, my Duchess, will kill me if I do not welcome Queen Hildegard profusely," he admitted. *I must be certain to give the Queen adequate attention. Marilla is so taken with court events, so jealous of those around the King and Queen. I must make special inquiries after the Queen and provide many comforts.* Charlemagne laughed, knowing Duke Arstat calculated the amount his hosting would require. He could feel the Duke's distress.

"Nay, nay, Arstat, the court is far behind us; their route does not come this way. I'm here to observe your court sessions. You scheduled court sessions every day for the next two weeks, is that not true? At least, so my *missi dominici* told me. I have your missive right here."

"Aye, that is correct, Sire," Arstat confirmed. "I'll be happy to preview the cases for you at the evening meal, if you wish." He changed the subject. "I regret we shall not have the pleasure of Queen Hildegard's company. My Marilla will feel much cheated. She so admires court life and all to do with it. She often wonders to me how Queen Hildegard and the Queen Mother Betrada can appear so beautiful, having the court move so constantly."

"Hildegard asked for a permanent court, Arstat. But the request is premature. I must be out among the people and, now, they ask for Hilde much more often than for me!" The King laughed. "She wins the hearts of my people."

***

King Charlemagne's mobile court created its own, unique society. As each court member provided news and speculation to the group, intrigue and gossip increased exponentially. Indiscretions and conspiracies thrived. King Charlemagne received much blame for events and people about which he knew little. Because he had no interest in the nobility's games for place and position, he left many decisions to the Queen Mother. As the lands within his empire expanded, his control of those same lands decreased. Additional land rewards expanded his class of nobles but, also, weakened his influence.

Charlemagne and his court survived on the lands he appropriated for the crown. His growing need for land, his increasing effort to Christianize the peoples within his empire, his efforts to educate and expand the clergy, his need for booty and wealth—all kept the court moving. The King and Queen found their responsibilities repeatedly outweighed their ability to respond.

"All ladies are fascinated with the court, Sire. I know they yearn to entertain your wife. Oh, but I must ask..." He dipped his head. "The expected babe, has Queen Hildegard delivered yet?"

"Within the next fortnight..." the King replied, smiling widely. "None can say which day."

"Well, Sir, I wish her an easy delivery." The Duke answered, then moved back to the events at hand. "Your escort may billet where they choose, Sire. But you shall surely come inside with me!"

Duke Arstad made a good accounting of his hospitality that evening. Being caught unaware, Duchess Arstat remained in the cook room to direct the cooks and hasten meal preparation. She served a meal exactly suited for the King.

"Everyone knows, of a certainty," she said to her

cooks. "The king loves roast meat. Prepare the haunch of venison saved for Sunday's repast immediately. Turn the bellows more quickly and heat those coals. We must not lessen the King's appetite with a lengthy wait. You may concentrate on bread baking and additional meats. Sweet treats hold little interest for him." The Duchess spent every minute before the meal with the cooks. And much to her relief, the meal of venison roast, ham with applesauce, spiced eels with asparagus, and stuffed quail met with Charlemagne's enthusiastic approval.

After the filling meal, Arstat and the King spent a quiet, but talkative evening, speaking of next year's summer battles and of commanders, both old and dead, who must be replaced before the spring assembly.

"Who should direct the bowmen in upcoming battles, do you think?" Charlemagne asked. "Merchun's lost the strength of his arm. Try as he might, there's no overcoming the damage. I must find his land reward now, not the fifteen years in the future I hoped to have." The two men talked of battles fought and battles planned and, finally, laid next spring's march to rest.

"I'm content, Arstat," Charlemagne commented. "You have a firm grasp of my wishes for the Frankish realm. There's much to be done, to bring this about; but this is my destiny. You and I both must persevere. Tomorrow we leave this topic behind and speak of your legal duties. I'm here to review your court, to see the problems that confront you, to become more aware of the nobles' challenges. It's difficult to know which noble to visit during court sessions. All of you seem to hold court during the same months!" The King declared. Arstat smiled at Charlemagne but laughed nervously.

"We must hold court during the best weather, Sir," he explained, "before the winter snows begin."

"I know, I know. I wish to observe your methods: holding court, responding to petitions, judging those in your prison, resolving the inevitable disputes. I noticed, on our journey, that your manor completed its harvest. I saw stacks of hay and women cutting barley and rye as we marched. The harvest looks to be excellent. Only the nuts remain to be gathered, humm?" the King questioned.

"Aye," Arstat replied. "We hope for a short winter, Sire, so the food stuffs will last." He nodded. "As for the court, there're many decisions, even pronouncements, to be made." He spoke in a firm, sure voice but his brow wrinkled. Seeing the King stifle a yawn, Duke Arstat finished: "But you shall be weary on the morrow, unless you get some rest, Sire. I will conduct you to your chamber."

"Nay, Arstat," the King demurred. "I can find my own way. See you in the court, then, on the morrow." He soon crawled into his linens.

Chapter 11

RESPONSIBILITIES

The next morning in his chamber, the King broke his fast with oatmeal, milk, and a dollop of honey. He, then, decided to wear an embroidered tunic instead of his daily, linen overshirt.

"I must look the authority," he smilingly said to himself. "If things are amiss here, I must look royal, as I make my pronouncements." He frowned, remembering his primary reason for this visit. After his last visit to Arstad's court, the *missi dominici* deemed Arstat's judgments entirely too harsh and suggested the older son, Jared, take over Arstat's duties. Charlemagne was here evaluate Arstat's court and legal decisions for himself.

***

King Charlemagne entered the Duke's ballroom and looked around at the turmoil in the chamber. Petitioners crowded the space; men glared at each other and shouted, scrambling for a place in line. Soldiers, seemingly with no clear duties, wandered about the room. Men and women, as well, called for the judgments to begin. Charlemagne rolled his head to reduce its tension; his jaw clenched; his hands balled into fists. Everywhere he looked, confusion reigned. And, worst of all, Duke Arstat was out of sorts.

"Where is my chair?" the Duke demanded of his squire. It appeared to be an oft-asked question. "I've told you time and again to have it brought for these proceedings. I *will not* make decisions from any other seat. Find it, find it now!" Arstat tramped up and down, threatening dire consequences on everyone.

Petitioners pushed one another, scrambling for a better place in line. Guards stood impassive as squires, servants, and nobles pushed, bullied, or struck the criminals bound to each other. With loud chattering and hawking, poorly-clothed women hurried through the doors, offering pies and ale at exorbitant prices. Charlemagne's temper flared. *What mockery is this! People appear to be going to market...or to a fair. The only serious faces I see are those on the prisoners, bound so tightly they can scarcely keep their feet.*

"Silence." the King's voice boomed over the milling throng. "Silence, I say to you." Charlemagne paused for his voice to penetrate the dull roar. Unwilling to wait another moment for the clamor to cease, he climbed onto a near-by bench, stomped his heavy boots, and yelled again.

"Who the hell...?" a voice asked.

"What does that fool think he's doing?" Another questioned.

"Have mercy, is ... Damn! Is that the King?" Yet a different voice wondered.

"Who do you think you are? Throw the villain out! Guards, guards."

"Silence," Charlemagne repeated. "This court is not a way station for you riff-raff to ply your trade. This is a legal court, set up to deal with crime, complaints, and petitions. If you've no business here, get out. Get out of here, you trades people! Leave this room!"

"Under whose command?" came a question from the

open door.

"Under mine, Charlemagne, King of the Frankish Empire...and your Lord!" Charlemagne stretched to his massive height and glared around the hall, challenging every eye he spotted.

"Oh, dear me," moaned Duke Arstat. "Dear me. Here, here's my chair. I declare these proceedings now in session. All of you...if you have no petition, clear the court!"

"Take them out guards; hurry them out! Excuse us, King Charlemagne. We are not as efficient as your own court." If Arstat hoped to placate the King, he misjudged. The King's head snapped up as Arstat spoke, displaying a visage red with suppressed anger.

"Duke Arstat," Charlemagne replied, his face stern. "Where is your older son? Isn't he in the court today?" Arstat's mouth opened in surprise, his face puzzled.

"Nay, he does not attend court, Sire. But, Sire, if you wish, I shall send for him."

"Aye, do so." The King got down from the bench. He motioned to a guardsman and directed him: "Sir, please clear this court of hangers-on. I assume you know who they are. We've business to conduct here and decisions to make. Bring in more guardsmen to control these people. Be quick!"

"Arstat." Charlemagne turned back to the duke. "No more delays! Summon your son, this Jared. Do it now!"

Duke Arstat sent a guardsman to bring Jared, and a moment later, called the court to session.

"We shall see the repeat criminals first." Three guardsmen brought the prisoners before the wooden table placed in front of Duke Arstat's chair. The Duke grimaced as the men appeared and, hurriedly, placed a scented scarf under his nose.

"I feared you three would be here," he pointed at each

one, clearly disgusted at the sight of the dirty, emaciated men before him. "What have you stolen this time?" None of the three responded, just stared above Atstat's head.

"Why do you not look at your lord?" King Charlemagne asked the tallest prisoner. The man looked into the king's face and smiled.

"I did that, Sire, 'til my last time in court...last year, it was. Duke Arstat ordered the gaoler to beat me 'cause I looked into his eyes. The lesson don't bear repeating... at least, not from my view, your majesty." Charlemagne walked behind the Duke's chair and whispered in his ear.

"Duke Arstat, I wish Jared here for today's proceedings. Bring these prisoners back after the mid-day meal when, I do hope, your son will be present. Proceed with solving property or land disputes, if you please."

"Of a certainty, Sire," Count Arstat responded. His voice trembled, his hand shook at the mention of Jared's name. What does the King want with my Jared? He wondered.

Charlemagne walked to the writing desk in the front of the hall, sifted through the account book, examined the wooden stamps and pens there, and finally sat down. The Duke's copyist scurried to the table.

"Please, Sire, is there anything you require? What might I do to assist you? Is there anything you need?" The little man queried.

"We shall take the first petition of the morning momentarily," the King announced. "Arrange the petitioners in order of most serious infractions first, so we may proceed quickly." To the chagrin of many near the front of the line, the guards pulled men from the rear and moved them forward. Arstat's copyist walked forward and nodded to the first man.

"You are Germoine, are you not? I am confirming your

identity."

"Aye, I am." The prisoner answered.

"According to the record here, one of your neighbors accuses you of grazing your sheep on his land." Charlemagne stood and began pacing. The quiet in the chamber was total. The King walked to the corridor, glanced into the courtyard, glared around the room. His foot tapped the floor. He walked again. The longer he walked, the more agitated his movements became. He slapped his hand against his thigh, stamped his boots upon the rock floor, checked the view from every window. The eyes in the chamber followed him.

"Where is Jared? I demand someone bring him immediately." His words fell into the silence. Duke Arstat hurried to the King's side.

"Here, King Charlemagne. May I present my older son, Jared?"

"It's time you were here." the King nodded at the young man. "Why are you not prepared for assisting in this court? Why weren't you here, an hour ago, to lend your skills to these procedures? It appears your help, any you might offer, would be most welcome." He frowned disapprovingly.

Jared bowed low to the king, looked at his father, and replied.

"My Father told me not to trouble myself with these activities," he responded. "He does not want me engaged with this."

"Nay?" Charlemagne lifted an eyebrow. "Interesting. How do you feel about that?" Holding his hand out, he continued. "Nay, nay, don't answer me now. We shall speak later. Sit down and watch the proceedings. I wish you to learn a few things." Duke Arstat walked toward the King. The wrinkles between his eyes deepened. He rubbed his hands together.

"Sire, excuse me, I would interrupt…" Jared shook his head slowly. The Duke stopped, the sentence dead in his throat.

"Sire, your wish is my command." Count Arstat bowed to the King.

"I would surely expect so." Charlemagne commented dryly, turning his head to hide his small smile. For the next three hours, Charlemagne solicited and questioned the petitioners.

"Of what are you accused? Are you guilty? Who bears witness against you? Do you know this person? For what reason would he bring these charges? Can you resolve this between yourselves, if I leave you two alone? Describe the borders of the property that is in dispute? Does it lie alongside your farm plot; is it nearer to your home or his? How long have you had this disagreement? Really, for that long? Do either of you know when this boundary was set…by whom?" In each instance, he gave them a ruling: one which was definite, clear, and final. "Once a legal decision is made, the case is closed." He said to the court. "No one is allowed to utter a single comment. Do you all understand me?" As the time for the mid-day meal approached, the King rapped on the floor.

"An announcement… The court for petitioners is closed for the day. Those left must return on the morrow. I urge you to make some effort to resolve your disputes. Starting today, this is a court of last resort. Only if you cannot solve your problems will you come here. And you'll bring payment for the resolution: one count requires a melon; two count charges require ten eggs or a chicken and so on. These payments shall, then, be given to the poor."

"Small problems are no longer the Duke's concern.

His time is valuable; he must use it only for difficult, seemingly unresolvable disputes. This morning will be devoted to criminal cases. Is this clearly understood? For today only, we shall hear criminal cases when we reconvene after we break our fast. Judgments must be made; punishments meted out. Only if you are accused of a crime should you remain today. The rest of you, go home." Charlemagne knew Jared's eyes watched him all morning and made judgment. The young man's face reflected surprised at the King's tactics.

***

"Come with me, Jared," the King directed. "We have things to discuss. Duke Arstat, please send food to the south end of the spring, there where the ground is level. Your son and I will break our fast there, conversing together. No interruptions, if you please." Jared fell in step beside the King and led the way to the stream.

"I'm surprised you even noticed the small garden, Sire, though it is a sanctuary from the heat on even the warmest day."

"Oh, it's not the garden or its promise of relief from the heat, Jared," Charlemagne admitted. "It's the water. I love to be near water. Swimming, I believe, should be the sport of kings. And this is a private place, isn't it? You and I must speak of important changes."

"Of a certainty, Sire," Jared replied. "It is a private place." While feasting on crispy catfish and sweet, flaky trout, the King talked in a low, purposeful voice. Jared listened intently, realizing Charlemagne honored him by describing his personal view of justice.

"What I want to know, Jared," the King paused to choose another fish, "is the kind of man you are. I would know your character and your thoughts—from yourself. Never fear, I'll consult others later. But tell me of your fears, your weaknesses and any strengths you have proved."

Jared began to speak and, then, paused. "Let me organize my thoughts, Sire." I know I have some skills, he thought, but will their value to me hold the same value to my sovereign? *He waits. I have little time but must be honest. Who knows what he means to do with this information, coming from my own lips.*

"Sire," Jared began, taking a chance with the King. "I am loathe to give you an answer. But I will speak from an honest evaluation of myself, an exercise I practiced much the last few months. First, let me explain so I do not look so bad in your eyes." He fidgeted uncomfortably. "My Father clearly wished me not to involve myself in his concerns. Mayhap he considers me untested or, even, unproved. I disagree, naturally; but his will determines… and limits…my opportunities."

Charlemagne looked the young man in the face and said nothing, just motioned for Jared to continue. The King removed his boots, moved closer to the stream, and stuck his big feet into the water.

"Nothing like cool, wet feet, Jared, to reduce a man's heat. Come, join me." What a strange man, Jared thought, but he is my King. Jared removed his own boots and sat on the ground beside the King. He began to describe himself.

"I want responsibility, Sire. I am an excellent horseman, understand the beasts better than anyone in this court. And I do love them! Where else would one find such majesty, loyalty, and beauty? I can think of no better friend, not in a demanding situation or on a pleasant occasion." Jared spoke firmly.

"My education in the soldiery arts is extensive. I'm a

good swordsman but my skill rests in the bow. The bow suits me. I don't relish the blood and guts which come with a sword. To my mind the bow is clean and quick — a good way to die. I would wish a death by bow for myself. But my father won't allow me in the fight. He keeps me in tactics and, if not there, in supplies and accounts." Jared stopped speaking, controlling his resentment until he could continue. The king ought not see my frustration with the limits father sets, he thought; but what can I say to him?

"I'm good with numbers. I maintain records of crop yield, expenses, declines in inventories — that sort of accounting. Mayhap this gift for numbers helps me with tactics; I create defense plans to be used against marauders. Very seldom does my father attend them. But, when he does, the confrontation is seldom lost. There is logic in what men do, Sire; I seem to be able to anticipate their actions."

"But your talents are underutilized?" The King asked. "I don't remember seeing you in the summer tents? Have you seen battle at all?"

"Aye, Sire. I took a wound in last year's battle with the Saxons. An enemy soldier stabbed me in the leg and I fell from my horse. My father sent me straight to the herbalist tent and kept me there for more than a fortnight!" Jared ducked his head; the ignominy of it still rankled his pride. "I could've ridden in a week, Sire; but my father would not allow it."

"And you truly wished to return to the battle?" Charlemagne watched Jared carefully.

"Aye, Sire. The battle frightened me; I admit it. But a commander must return to his duty, respond to the challenge. Isn't that true…else his men will not respect him or follow his lead?"

"It is exactly so, Jared, exactly so. Now, take a break, here in the sun. It feels so fine, don't you think so?" The King asked. "I'm off to speak with your father."

"Arstat," Charlemagne sought out the duke immediately after taking his leave of Jared. "Summon your scribe. I need to give him directions before the court session today. In addition, I want him in the court as we deal with these criminal cases."

"Surely, Sire, if you wish. But this is irregular…for my court. Criminals have no rights. Surely there can be no interest in writing anything about them or their histories." Arstat's face wrinkled in distaste, his contempt for all criminals coloring his speech.

"I'm not sure about interest in their histories," Charlemagne answered. "But we must have records of their crimes. You had these men in your court before today? Didn't you say that this morn?"

"Aye, much more than once, Sire. They seem to live as criminals all their lives. They never learn from the imprisonment or restrictions or even the beatings we give them. It's a most distressing job, Sire, dealing with this offal, the residue of society. They are nothing to me." Arstat replied, "nothing but trouble."

"I see," Charlemagne said. "But you also understand they are the residue of *your* society. Abbot Fulrad would say they are your problem; your society made them. Mayhap, the society made them criminals, hum? But we'll continue this discussion at a more propitious time. Please send the scribe directly to me. I wish a few minutes with him before we resume our duties." Charlemagne sat on a nearby bench, waiting. Promptly, the requested scribe came into the hall. Charlemagne seated the scribe to his right and admonished him to 'set everything down in the record.'

"Send for Jared," the King directed. "I want him here

to hear these prisoners." Presently Jared sat beside the scribe, busily noting the records he created and memorizing his coded notations.

The first prisoner stood in front of the king. Again, the smell of him preceded his actual body. He knelt to the ground, acknowledging the king's authority. He tried to rise quickly but was slow and swayed as he finally straightened up.

"Have a seat on the floor." King Charlemagne directed. "You appear weak and your hands are shaking. Are you ill?"

"Nay, Sire, I not be sick," was the reply. "Last night and today be not my time, Sire; I not be on the sch'dule." The man responded.

"Your time? What does that mean? And of what schedule do you speak?"

"Why, Sire, just as always here. We eat only when the sch'dule says so. Mostly, that be every three days. Yep, last time I ate, it was two days ago at mid-day. Do feel a goodly time past." Charlemagne looked into the prisoner's eyes.

"You've not eaten anything for two days? Do I understand you rightly?"

"Exactly, Sire. I don't get not'ing til tomorrow; it is, at mid-day. That be the way of it here, Sire, for long as I 'member." King Charlemagne swallowed, thinking of his meal last night, breaking his fast this morning and, another meal, just a little while ago. He raised his brow at Jared and continued his questions.

"Why are you here?" He asked the man. "What is your crime? And, then, why did you do this evil thing?" Charlemagne had to ask specific questions because there was no record on this prisoner. He had no information about his wrong-doing. He only knew Arstat imprisoned him more than a fortnight previous.

"I not see what I done as evil, Sire. My children be hungry. The smallest one, my son, be so weak he can't cry. Be it evil to feed yourn children? I was full of their cries; I feel lost, Sire, every time they cry." The prisoner looked teadily at the King and, then, at Jared. Charlemagne stared into the prisoner's face. He labored to make sense of the tale. The criminal neither looked away or down to the floor; he gazed back at the King.

"You stole to feed your children," the King stated. Seeing the man nod his head, the king continued: "What did you steal and from whom?"

"I did take from the Duke here, Sire. I clumbed his peach trees, 'dere in the orchard, and loaded peaches inside my tunic. And I stole bread from a cooling rack, there outside the cooking room. They no und'rstand I got that. My oldest boy, he ran home wid the loaf--for the children, you see."

"You're stealing to feed your children," the King repeated. "What work do you know? Do you have a skill; do you till the fields? Will you work or do you like stealing?" The King's heart was rent. Would I steal to feed my children? He asked himself. *If there were no food, would I steal it? ...of a certainty*, he admitted to himself. *I would steal to feed myself, much more so to feed my children.*

"Nay, Sire, can't say I like the stealing, but there be no work for the likes of me. I was a soldier, a good man with a bow. But my first lord, he got greedy; eager fo' more land so he left, left fo' Normandy. Told us here to do whate'r we could. Some years afore, he took my lit'le plot and learn't me to fight. Like I said, I be good with the bow. When there's no fighting, we left to do the best we can. Most people here be hungry, Sire."

"I not say all men be good; you know that not be the

truth of it. But manys a good man do fall on ill luck and can't turn it 'round; manys of us do." The prisoner's speech faltered near the end; he appeared exhausted.

"Bring this man bread," Charlemagne bellowed. "Feed everyone waiting in line." Charlemagne waited for the man to eat his loaf, accompanied by a little apple spread. Jared sat stiffly, his eyes far away. His face was white, his hand methodically rubbing his left arm. The prisoner's face would have made them believe he dined at a banquet.

"Here, guardsman, cut this man's bindings. I would talk with him," the King directed. To Jared, the King added: "You and the scribe, look at these notes; see the number of these men your father accuses of stealing. Talk to them and get their reasons. Write them down. I wish to talk with this prisoner at length."

"Are you able to walk, my good man?" Charlemagne asked.

"Aye, Sire, I be full of energy after my meal."

Charlemagne put his hand on the thief's shoulder and steered him to the garden where he talked with Jared, just this morning. The King questionedquietly as the two men sat alone, occasionally nodding affirmatively. In a short time, the king and the thief returned, talking even more avidly together.

"And now," Charlemagne summoned the scribe, "what did these men do—in general terms, scholar, just in general terms?"

"King Charlemagne," the scribe responded, "they are all thieves. They steal food. They take the basics—potatoes, corn, oats—sometimes from the fields, sometimes from the storage bins. Mayhap this one with you stole from the orchards. Some few notations suggest others took jams, jellies, haunches of meat from the cooks' storage rooms."

"Are these notations yours, Scribe? Are they accurate?"

"Not mine, Sire. Duke Arstat contacted me a fortnight ago. I arrived here only three days back, it was. But no matter - the notations themselves make no sense." The Scribe admitted. "I believe a man would steal meat… but steal jams and jellies! Not likely, he'd be a fool. Jams and jellies are extras, things hungry people don't think on. I thought, at first, I misread this record. The script is so primitive. But this kind of notation appears by many of these prisoners' names."

"Jared, what do you see in this?" The King asked, turning to Arstat's son. Jared shook his head in dismay, embarrassed for his king to witness such cruelty in his father's court.

"I'm unable to speak of it, Sire." Jared acknowledged. "I didn't know…I did not dream…such want shadowed our people." He dropped his eyes, afraid their unshed tears would fall before the King's stare. Charlemagne could see Duke Arstat hovering around the edge of the hall.

"Arstat, come here," Charlemagne directed. "What's the history of imprisoning men who steal food? How are they caught; under what circumstances are they judged? Why imprison them when they might work off such indebtedness? What happens to their families when the men are in prison?" Arstat's temper flared quickly. Snapping back at the King, he responded.

"I decide their punishment, who else? I will not have this offal walking about my land. I put them in prison where I can contain them. Aye, we feed them every two or three days. Let them understand real hunger! I imprison all I can, make them an example to others. They don't

166

deserve the food needed to keep them there." Charlemagne looked fixedly into Arstat's face, unable to fathom such contempt for life.

"I'm relieving you of this responsibility, Duke Arstat. Anything this onerous for you must no longer be your concern. You sit no longer in judgment of any of your people. Jared will supervise legal decisions. If judgment must be made, it will be his. You have no duty to my court. Do you understand?" Charlemagne asked.

Arstat stared at the King, stunned to silence. Yesterday night Jared warned his father to accept the King's directions, whatever they might be. Jared knew of Charlemagne's temper and suspected his father's precarious position with the King. Arstat nodded mutely, then turned and walked away.

"Free these men." Charlemagne directed the guardsmen. "Free them. They are going home to bid their families goodbye. They will join my army. As bonus payment they'll each get a measure of food, against their future booty, from me. The food they must take home to their families, to sustain them while the men are away. Find some clothes for them--first, a bath in the stream and, then, clean clothes. Use whatever you must from Duke Arstat's storehouse." He turned to the now unbound prisoners.

"Return to your families; take this food to them. Tell them you go to fight for your king." Charlemagne said to the disbelieving men. "I will feed you and give you work; you have no reason to steal from this day forward." Charlemagne spent the next day with Arstat's scribe, dictating laws and regulations to him.

"Now," the King specified, "copy these laws and post them throughout your lands. Make plans to read the posted laws to the people as you deliver them." He shook his head in disgust. "Eight months before this day, mymessengers read the very same capitularies throughout Frankland. But the dukes and counts seem not to have heard." Charlemagne always proclaimed new laws to the people and had the messengers read the laws, as well as post them. But, now, the King realized that some of the nobility embraced and displayed the laws and some did not. Some ignored or destroyed them entirely.

At first, Duke Arstat's scribe did not believe the basic rights granted to everyone. He dutifully recorded all Charlemagne dictated to him and sent couriers as the King required. The King commanded him to attend to any new capitularies which he received and to be certain the court and Jared knew of any changes in the law.

The Scribe's stature rose immediately to himself and to all in the court. He found himself responding to dozens of questions and, henceforth, became one of Charlemagne's foremost experts on the *capitularies.* He often traveled to other nobles' holdings to implement the King's revised directives. King Charlemagne gifted him with a fine horse some seasons later, for his service and, coincidentally, to ensure his unquestioned loyalty.

The King drilled Jared in his duties, explaining the interlocking legal system which sustained the realm. When he departed, he left Jared in charge and gave him a warning.

"I'll accept no more of your father's 'justice,' Jared." Charlemagnedeclared. "I'm stricken. I did not see his intent and his hate before this. Don't allow him to influence or to override your decisions. There will be visits from a *missi dominici* throughout the year to monitor your actions. These visits will never be announced; he'll come to review legal decisions and evaluate the laws of this holding. Don't disappoint me, Jared."

Jared served the court well. Years later he admitted

to Abbot Fulrad that he never liked the judging. It was a sore responsibility. But he did share the King's hope for improving the daily lives of his people and worked to that end. He was a fair and compassionate duke. The people's genuine appreciation for him filled his kitchen with baked bread and wild fruit for the rest of his life. Arstat, never quite understanding his deficiencies, brooded on the unfairness of his removal. He drowned crossing a flooded stream the next spring.

Chapter 12

FIGHTING AND GOVERNING

Charlemagne sent his Peers into areas which weren't on the year's annual circuit.

"I want our laws and *capitularies* implemented as soon as possible. There is no time to waste." But, as the King attempted to implement his laws, he found once again that life placed many burdens on his people.

A couple of weeks after returning from Arstat's manor, Charlemagne walked toward the cook tent, drawn by a crowd milling about. At the entrance to the banquet tent, Hildegard spoke with a group of agitated people. Noble women in fine cloth with gold chains clasped their hand together as tears slid down their cheeks. Maids-in-waiting, turning from onedistraught noble woman to another, urged the ladies to sit on near-by benches, soft with embroidered cushions, and brought flagons of water. The husbands, clearly touched by the talk they heard from an adjacent group, walked with hands clasped behind their backs, looked forlornly at their women's distress and mumbled to each other. A few children wandered from parent to parent, seeking comfort.

"There is an issue with the entire family." Charlemagne heard Queen Hildegard say as he walked up beside her. He noted her weariness and felt his stomach clench with worry. *Why didn't I stop sooner?* He chided himself.

After consulting with the herbalist, Charlemagne decided to stop a little earlier this year for the Yuletide. A longer rest in one location always lifted everyone's spirits. Besides, Hildegard needed rest. Carrying their fourth child, she suffered. Her legs were tight and painful, swollen from the summer heat and the lengthy march. Rotrud, who ran every waking minute, kept three women busy. There were nurses and maids to help, of a certainty; but Hilde was a dedicated mother, one who delighted in being with her children.

"Mayhap," Charlemagne mentioned to Fulrad, "if Hilde has more rest before the babe's birth, she will more easily recover her strength." Fulrad opined that a rest could not hurt, so the army camped as the weather became nippy, the air crisp. Not just Hildegard, everyone was grateful for the stop and suffused with excitement. Each member of the court dreamed of the days the court did not travel. A small number of court workers took such time to return home to families who lived close for a Yuletide visit.

King Charlemagne hurried to his Queen. He saw a group of agitated people milling around her.

"They must not return to work before both recover." He heard Hildegard's words. "I daresay one's recovery will aid the other. What a tragedy, especially at this time of year!" Charlemagne, catching the glitter of tears in her eyes, felt his heart thud. He was soon at Hildegard's elbow. She turned to speak with the court seneschal about provisions.

"They need everything. The hut burned completely to the ground." She put her hand on the seneschal's arm. "Talk with each child at court. I'm sure some of them will donate unwanted items, especially those woolen tunics which scratch so much!" She smiled, remembering the boys' reaction to a study, thick woolen overshirt, produced by a novice weaver.

"Something I should know about?" Charlemagne asked, dismayed by the sad faces. *Of course, this is her jurisdiction.* Charlemagne thought. *But her strain is so great, her exhaustion so unrelenting, I must spare her as much as possible. She is greatly troubled.* He looked into his wife's face. Hilde acknowledged his presence, her hand on his arm squeezed gently.

"I'm just hearing about an accident, Charlemagne." She said. "The court's primary cook, Jonas, and his wife, Clara — our baker — suffer from a horrible burning. They left us to visit friends who moved here after the Saxon uprising last year. You remember the Frankish families from Metz who were relocated, Charley?" She asked. "Their home was close by. Jonas' family went the day before last to greet them, intending to stay a few days. They found them doing poorly so Jonas' younger boys — Lucas and Nat — returned to our camp for food and clothing."

"As the families slept yesterday night, a spark from the cook pit flew into a pile of clothing and the house went up in flames. It was a quick, hot fire." She paused, wiping at her tears. "They are horribly burned, Charley, most horribly." She whispered to her husband.

"The healers, are they on their way to help them?" Charlemagne asked.

"Of a certainty. They offered little hope when they heard of the heat of the flames but try to decrease their pain." Hildegard shook her head sadly. Suddenly, an image of the family popped into the King's mind. He remembered both those boys — bright lads who impressed Abbot Fulrad with their quick, enthusiastic minds.

"Keep an herbalist with them," Charlemagne directed. "He's to try everything. When did this happen?"

"Just before we broke our mid-day fast, Sire," a stable-hand standing nearby answered. "We be breaking last spring's foals and saw the smoke. ...guess we saved 'um, getting them out of the hut, I mean. It burnt real fast, Sire!" The man had no eyebrows; the fire singed them off. He had bright red welts across his cheeks and forehead. Though he placed his hands behind his back, Charlemagne saw the angry, weeping burns on his fingers. The King dropped his head, struck again by the fragility of life in this harsh land. Leave off vigilance for one moment and disaster rushes in, he thought. A stable-hand stepped toward the King.

"Please, Sire; I have a suggestion. Don't think me a fool. I saw Lord Roland dunk a burnt mare in a mud bath! ... saved her life, he did! Do you think we can try it now with Jonas and his woman? Lord Roland said the mud drunk up the heat and kept the flesh from long-term harm—you know the angry, raw wound? It don't 'zactly lose blood. He called the burns "weeping" and thought the mud 'ud keep the thin, stretched look of the skin from hap'ng. Jonas' burn, it be bad, Sire. He and his woman gonna die... just herbalists' care won't be enuf to save them." Charlemagne caught his breath. The burns are this deep? He thought.

"Do it," he answered. "God knows Roland is creative. See to it now. Thank God, there's plenty of mud." The man ran toward the stable to get help, calling to people as he went.

Three weeks later, Jonas and his wife returned to the camp. Their healed scars were deep and monstrous, their skin puckered and rough. But each of their limbs moved easily, despite those scars. There was little strained, stretched skin; no heavy draining from the wounds and, now, very little swelling. Roland's method saved two lives and, as a result, the healers had another procedure to try in healing burns.

Hildegard engaged the weavers who busily made clothes for the family. Carpenters constructed tables and benches. The King sent soldiers to rebuild the family's hut and each court member contributed clothing. It was true. The noble ladies' hand linens and silk small clothes would do the women little good; but the spirit of the gifts was the value. With the tragedy behind them, the court looked forward to celebrating the Holy Days.

***

As always, the King waked well before first light and went to the chapel for early morning prayers. Coming back, he met Queen Hildegard in the corridor.

"My dear," the King began, as he grabbed her hands, "where are you off to and in such a hurry!" He kissed her forehead, as she stopped.

"Ah, Charley! I am to the chapel…to pray," Hildegard answered. "I see you preceded me again. What an early riser you are! Did you have your 'second' sleep?" She asked with concern. "You seem to sleep less and less, my dear."

"I practiced my letters, Hilde. You know how frustrated it makes me. I must." He added as he saw the shake of her head. "Be happy you learned to write early! I despair I'll ever be able to form the letters …so anyone can read them, I mean! But no worry! Our children will learn it effortlessly." The Queen kissed her husband's cheek and waddled off, supporting her large belly with her hand. Preparations for the Christmastide feast must begin and all wanted her direction.

***

174

Early the following morning, a messenger cantered into the camp, begging to be taken to Charlemagne's tent. Hildegard, dozing, wakened to the King's urgent voice, sending a guard for Oliver and Roland. She shook her head, knowing Charlemagne scarcely lay on his sleeping bench in the night. They'd had cups of tea and tarts after their prayers less than two hours ago. Hildegard struggled to wake completely, splashing water on her face. *Probably Charley heard the horse's hooves before the guards.* In less than fifteen minutes, Oliver and Roland came running.

"What's amiss?" Roland asked as Hilde opened the door of the chamber. "There's no threat to you or the King, is there?" His sword gleamed in his hands.

"Trouble here, my liege?" Oliver asked, looking around her for the King.

"Nay, he isn't here, but Charlemagne received a messenger. There must be some bad news from far away, else the messenger would not arrive this early, riding in the darkness." Hildegard said to Oliver. Just that moment, Charlemagne called from the corridor.

"Roland and Oliver, come. Hurry, please, here to the library." He blew a kiss to Hilde and stepped into the chamber as Oliver and Roland hurried to him.

"We march. The Saxons are on the move again. We must not delay." As he closed the door, he saw his wife grimace and look down at her swollen belly.

"The court will remain here." Charlemagne decided. "It will be too difficult for Hildegard to travel by cart again. Her due time is too close. Please, Roland, leave Rinaldo here with a large contingent."

"I will stay as well, Sire." Roland volunteered. "I want the Queen to have not a moment of fear or disquiet. Your route toward the Saxons is certain, is it not?" Charlemagne nodded his head affirmatively.

"Aye," he answered. "Our numbers will always over-whelm them. And our arrival will be a great surprise. I daresay the fight will be short."

"Then I guard the court, Sire," Roland emphasized, "and skip this one battle, this time." Charlemagne nodded in agreement and turned to Oliver.

"The army must move. Wake everyone. Tell them to prepare. We must leave as quickly as possible. Issue orders for no fires and no cooking this day; traveling sticks must suffice for the mid-day meal. Late yesterday, the Saxons took Eresburg and forced our Franks from the garrison. We must retake our fortress. A swift march will take them unaware. As news of our victory over the Lombard rebellion spreads, all believe we plan to linger here for months. Go. Prepare the army to march."

***

Although the movement of the army was not a secret for long, the King marched across the land and intimidated the frightened Saxons. They surrendered almost immediately.

Abbot Fulrad oversaw a mass baptism near the Lippe River. Thousands of Saxons converted to Christianity. Just as the mass baptism ended and Abbot Fulrad sang praises for the thousands of newly converted Christians, a messenger rode up, seeking the King. He asked only Charlemagne's direction and rode rapidly away once he had the information. Spotting Charlemagne astride Samson, watching Saxon prisoners bound and secured, the messenger jumped from his horse and ran to the King.

"Sire, sire!" He called. "Good news! Queen Hildegard delivered a son late last night!" Charlemagne winced as if a blow hit him in the stomach.

"And the Queen?" The King cried. "How does she fare?"

"She is well, my liege." the messenger assured the King. "She sent her own missive to you." He knelt and offered Charlemagne a small square of parchment.

All is well, dear. Hildegard's large, childish hand reassured him. *You have a beautiful baby boy, an heir and a spare!* She wrote with exclamationpoints. *He looks much like Rotrud when she was an infant.* Hildegard had added. *Come to us as soon as you can. I am tired but content.*

Well might you be joyful, my dear, Charlemagne thought as tears of relief rose in his eyes. Hildegard's weariness, her lack of energy during this pregnancy had him on edge, particularly during the last few weeks. His worry for her colored the days. But, now, at last, the babe was here! The King dismounted and knelt, thanking God for HIS blessing and for his wife's and child's good health.

"Please, dear Lord, protect them both." He prayed.

The King named Ganelon to plan the rebuilding of the fort at Eresburg. "If he builds, his talent will create, rather than destroy." The King mumbled to himself. He planned to return in the summer to evaluate Ganelon's progress.

"Plan the construction of yet another fortress on the Lippe, Ganelon. We shall name the new fortress Karlsburg. There seems no hope to conquer the Saxons for good, so we must bolster our battlements." He turned Samson toward the mobile court.

***

Charlemagne's commitment to spreading Christianity was not the result of study or of a true grasp of religious issues. He used the religion's structure, combining theocratic ideas with his search for power. Christianity's organization, its concentration of power and wealth at the top, and its pervasive influence gave the King a pattern for controlling his burgeoning empire. Along with control, Christianity also gave him a method for uniting disparate groups of people. Although Charlemagne was not a deep or abstract thinker, he understood the needs of his people for structure and strong oversight. He, genuinely, attempted to respond to those needs, as well as to draw the conquered into his realm.

Even as he used Christianity to unify the people of his realm, he valued the unique characteristics of the peoples he conquered and, generally, allowed them to continue to use their own historic laws and maintain their cultural values. Only after the Lombard nobles betrayed him did he insist on Frankish overseers there. He was, far more than conquerors before him, a beneficent ruler.

Yet, he required all those he conquered to convert to Christianity. He was relentless in subjecting them to missionaries, in relocating them into Frankish lands, in moving his own people into territories of former enemies, in demanding their oaths of allegiance--not only to him, but to his god as well. He used any method to unify his disparate realm into a whole. Of a certainty, there were men who worked against his efforts, those who yearned for complete dominion over conquered peoples. But, wisely or not, Charlemagne ignored their predictions of doom and vociferous criticism.

Of a certainty, the effort to create a cohesive realm, while respecting the different cultures and values of the peoples within it, was an ongoing exercise--one never complete during his reign nor after it elsewhere.

**

His experience at Arstat's court convinced King Charlemagne that his present legal structure and oversight were inadequate. He needed a more efficient organization for governing his people. He called in his advisers, including Paul, the deacon.

"Paul, who is the most effective organizer at court? As the realm expands, I need help in restructuring the realm's governance. I assumed my laws and proclamations went throughout the realm; but Arastat chose to tell the people only the laws he wished them to know. Many laws promulgated for the benefit of the Frankish people did not reach them. The nobility never implemented many of them. Or, if the people objected to a law, the nobles blamed me for it. Or, more often, they did as they wished, as in Lombardy." His forehead wrinkled; his hands rubbed together. He looked at Paul in dismay.

"This cannot continue! We must create an interwoven system, one in which no one man has too much power or can operate on his own. We must develop a method to evaluate the nobles' actions, to rate how well they fulfill their duties. First, we need a structure to oversee daily operations. We need specific laws and regulations to guide nobles and peasants alike. Then, we must have different people watching each other. And we need people to watch the nobles, to verify that they follow the spirit, as well as the letter, of the law."

"Aye," Paul answered. "I understand. You cannot trust men to implement your laws, not if they see some as punitive to themselves." Charlemagne nodded.

"Who can help us organize, create such a structure and determine the men we need?" The King asked.

"Seriously, Charlemagne, are you really asking this question? The answer is obvious."

"Obvious? Nay. I wouldn't ask if I knew the man."

Charlemagne responded. Both men turned slightly as Theodulf entered the chamber.

"You sent for me, Sire?" Theodulf inquired, setting aside his hat.

"Yes, Theo. Where's the scribe?" Charlemagne asked.

"As you requested, Sire, he waits outside, a competent fellow."

"I wish both of you to record the information the three of us discuss. We must ask questions of each other. Any law, directive, or procedure that's unclear - particularly one which seems to conflict with another - must be addressed and clarified. I ordered our mid-day meal with the cook, the evening repast as well. We can work uninterrupted. Fear not, I will feed you well!" Paul and Theodulf looked at each other, questions in their eyes, both unsure how to proceed.

"Are we the only ones dealing with these procedures and, humm, laws, Sire – the three of us?" Paul asked. "Forgive me, but I don't know what you want us to do." Charlemagne bowed his head, admitting he was unclear.

"Forgive me. I must explain. To be brief, then, I need to re-organize the realm's legal system and I need help. Identify our best organizer for me." Theodulf laughed aloud and looked at Paul.

"Is he serious, Paul?"

"I believe so." Paul nodded, a big smile across his face.

"What is so humorous?" King Charlemagne asked, his voice short and sharp. "This is a simple question."

"You, Charlemagne, you don't understand! Your question, excuse me, Sire, is laughable. You! You! You are our best organizer! Everyone comes to you for structure! You even designed the spice desk made for our mobile court...with suggestions on the amount of spice needed for a fortnight's sojourn! You are the GREAT organizer—

the most effective any of us know!" Theodulf guffawed loudly again. Charlemagne felt his face burn and quickly replied.

"Nay, Nay. I need help! I'm talking about reorganizing the entire realm!"

"So are we, my King." Theodulf replied. "So are we."

Paul summoned the scribe. Charlemagne began speaking, explaining his thoughts about court responsibilities, delineating his suggestions for the new governing structure. The three men analyzed and evaluated each point.

"Let's start at the top and work down, shall we?" Charlemagne asked. "Our current oversight is too loose. While in Arstat's court, I discovered the nobles do not always see fit to follow rewritten laws, nor do they revise procedures to implement them. They rule with a 'selective legal system,' one composed of laws they like. We must institute oversight, more control of their actions and interpretations. We need another layer of officials, I suppose." Hearing no objections from his advisers he continued.

"As for governing duties, I propose that our present Bishops be responsible for all affairs: those of the church and those few areas in which the church has no direct interests. It's critical for me to trust those who make and implement decisions. Since I recommend and appoint the Bishops, they will oversee and preside over the operations of the counties. That'll be the largest land division in the realm." He continued. "The bishops may name their underlings...with my approval, of course. As we organize and name these officials, our rules will give the original group guidance. Subsequently-named persons will be trained by the first group of trained officials."

"Before you move forward, Charlemagne..." Theodulf stood up. "I have a thought. Excuse me, Sire; but you need to reexamine your idea of bishops overseeing everything." Theodulf plunged ahead, knowing his words were directly opposite to those suggested by the king.

"Go on." Charlemagne replied with no hint of his thoughts on Theodulf'sdisagreement.

"I know your view and your hopes for the church, Sire; but its influence can be negative in certain situations. For example, the 'forgiveness concept' of the Christian church could, conceivably, wreck havoc in judging and sentencing criminals. The sanctity of marriage may cause a Bishop to look away from a man's brutality to his wife; I know women who have died from beatings. The 'head of the family,' as the church defines him, may not be held accountable by the clergy, by these same bishops. Your interest in supporting trade encourages money-lending. One who donates vestments to the church or who supplies meat to the church's larders may be allowed to charge more to borrowers. I say we must oversee the clergy just as stringently as we do secular officials." Theodulf concluded. He struggled to defend his remarks.

"Bishops in charge of all affairs gives them too much power and too much freedom...in my mind." He concluded. Charlemagne looked steadily at Theodulf.

"It appears you have given lengthy thought to church officials and power, Theo." He commented.

"I have," Theodulf replied. "I served as a gather of information for my father. I was, in fact, a spy... before I identified a vocation for myself. Following Father's direction, I wandered around his lands, identified emerging needs and made every effort to understand the interests, as well as the hearts, of my father's retainers. Of a certainty, it was an education. I became a cynic. I don't believe Christianity or the church will purify men's minds. Forgive me, Sire, for my disagreement!" He smiled tentatively and explained.

"You must institute checks for a system to work. I see nothing among churchmen to encourage me to trust them or to place my reliance on their judgment." Theodulf ceased talking. I have offended the king, he thought to himself; but the truth must be stated.

Charlemagne sat quietly, holding a pen which all three men knew he could not use. His organizational skills were as effective as Theodulf and Paul described. But he couldn't write his thoughts, commit lists to the page or even copy headings with sub-parts. He could not master the art of writing, try as he would. No matter, Theodulf thought. *He will think it through, organize units in his head, and develop a masterful plan for all to follow. I've seen his magic previous; he is a consummate planner.*

"Theo, you raise important questions." Charlemagne allowed. "Some I did not think of. I'll use this same method as I consider all areas which need organization. I must use people with experience in specific areas to help me restructure governing units. I will choose the Bishops, the clergymen who

work with them, and the nobility responsible for secular concerns. Each official will watch the others and all will report to me." He could not tell if his words pleased Theo or not.

"This way I'm in control of each person and every cog in this empire." He shook his head. "How can I keep it all balanced and functioning?" He shrugged. "I must; there is as yet no one to help."

"Beg your pardon, Sire." Theo replied. "You trust too easily. The oversight you describe may help. Just question men's motives more. Will you do that?" Charlemagne paused in his scribbling and nodded affirmatively.

"I will try." He answered, his face wrinkling in thought

at Theo's words.

Oliver entered the chamber just as Theodulf and Paul the Deacon left. They needed additional parchment and ink. After agreeing to join them, Oliver spoke to Charlemagne.

"Sire," he began, "nothing to worry you yet. But I thought you would want to know; the Saxons are on the move again."

"Now?" The King questioned. "…now, in the dead of winter, what are they thinking?"

"If I could answer your question, I would be a prophet, indeed." Oliver replied. "Mayhap, they're taking up positions; mayhap, there's a power struggle so some wish to remove themselves. The point is, all around the realm, Saxon tribes are moving. In the end, we know they won't wander too far; but you need to be aware of their present movements." Oliver waited patiently, allowing King Charlemagne time to digest this worrisome news.

"Aye. Well, no one—not even the Saxons—fights in winter, Oliver. Let's keep our eyes on them. Disturb no one else with this news. Tell Janlur, of a certainty; he can put the other commanders on semi-alert." Charlemagne looked intently at Oliver. "Or did Janlur tell you? I know he has spies on all the roads because….he always describes their skills." And the King smiled.

"No, Sire, these are our spies—Roland's and mine, that is. …news from a courier who just got to court in the early hours, before light." Oliver replied.

"We'll keep alert, Oliver. No other action needs to be taken now. We're here for Yuletide, for God's sake. Let's keep that holy time as blessed as we can."

Chapter 13

FRIENDSHIP

As Hildegard recovered from the birth of her second son, she took time to celebrate Jocelyn's and Oliver's betrothal. Oliver, with Queen Hildegard's assistance, identified Jocelyn's dowry. He and Jocelyn journeyed to Septimania, accompanied by Rinaldo and Theodoric, to receive Count Hautgard's blessing. As much as Oliver wanted Roland to accompany him on the journey, he had not the heart to ask him. *God knows, I don't wish him heartache,* Oliver thought, *not heartache I unwittingly cause.*

***

When Oliver told the King of his betrothal, Charlemagne sent for Roland. Charlemagne didn't know exactly how to tell Roland of Jocelyn's betrothal to another but felt the news should be relayed immediately. His Peers, their courage and understanding, always surprised Charlemagne; but, this time, Oliver outdid himself. Some three days after Jocelyn agreed to the betrothal, Oliver told Charlemagne he wished to inform Roland of his plans. From Jocelyn, Oliver now knew of Roland's possible interest in her.

"It will be easier for you both, Oliver, if I speak to Roland alone." Charlemagne replied carefully. "You two are like brothers. Neither of you knew of the interest of the other. News of your betrothal will be best coming from someone else. And, since I know and love you best—both of you--it is my duty." He looked sadly at Oliver's bowed head.

"Jocelyn felt his interest, Charlemagne," Oliver said, "but she thought it had to do with the colt they trained together. Myself, I was totally unaware of it." He shook his head, plunged one fist into the other hand, and shrugged. "I know not what to think."

"Why didn't he confide in me, Charlemagne?" Oliver asked, even as he realized he would not have known the words to answer such a declaration from Roland.

"It's good he did not." The King assured Oliver. "You both found the best of women and, having done that, you sought her out. I think it easier if he believes you know nothing of his own interest in her. You say Roland never gave you a name, did not identify the woman he favored?" The King asked again, longing to be certain. At the negative nod of Oliver's head, Charlemagne sighed. "It would be awkward…for this to be between you. And, since he said nothing to Jocelyn, he will imagine she suspected nothing as well." Charlemagne knew the role he must play.

"Let me speak with him. I'll think of something diplomatic." The Kingpromised. "If only Carloman were alive, my little brother was ever the diplomat; he would find exactly the right words to say to Roland. Let it be." Oliver nodded and left the battle tent. He was no more than thirty yards away before there was a scratch at Charlemagne's tent door.

"Come." King Charlemagne called, turning toward the tent flap.

"My Liege," Roland began, "you sent for me?"

"Aye," the King confirmed. "I have some news which

you should know. It concerns one of the Peers, one close to you. It's momentous news and, thereby, I hope you will share it with happiness and love."

"It sounds serious. What is the news and who does it touch?"

"It touches all of us, my dear Roland." Charlemagne answered quietly. He had loved this young man as a brother, ever since Roland left his own home at ten years to live with King Pepin and Queen Bertrada. Roland's mother, afraid of conquest and marauders, married her second husband, Ganelon, in unseemly haste after Roland's father died. That atmosphere soon became intolerable for Roland, so he came to live with his aunt and uncle, Charlemagne's parents. He is my younger brother, Charlemagne thought. *I must be gentle with this.*

"But it touches Oliver the most. He is betrothed! I, myself, am celebrating because his bride is one of Hildegard's most constant and beloved companions, Jocelyn Hautgard." The King talked on, giving Roland time to digest the information. "You remember, Roland? When you and I visited Hautgard in Septimania, after hunting down that outlaw band, Jocelyn was not at home? She was visiting her mother's sister. And, then, not much later, both Hautgard daughters—Jocelyn and Maria--and Hildegard joined the court."

Charlemagne stopped talking, watching Roland carefully. Upon hearing Jocelyn's name, he froze in place—so much so that he moved his upraised leg to the floor, in very slow motion. Roland's face blanched white; his eyes popped in his head and, then, clouded over.

Charlemagne turned to pour ale from the near-by flagon. In times of shock, everyone turns to spirits, he thought, so this might strengthen Roland. He did not like the drink and wished others would avoid it; but that wish influenced others little. In this particular case, the King considered the wine justified. He consciously struggled to make his voice light and carefree.

"We should celebrate this, even if Oliver is not here this minute!" He forced enthusiasm and excitement into his words. "Here, Roland, take a drink to his good luck and happiness!" He handed Roland the flagon and watched his Peer swallow the liquid quickly. Roland did not seem aware of the over-large serving the King poured him.

"Let's do this well," Roland answered. "How about another?"

"…of a certainly." Charlemagne replied, sipping his own flagon of water as he filled Roland's flagon. I would not make him drunk, he thought; but, mayhap, it would not be a bad thing today. Roland took another drink from the flagon and, then, yet another. Abruptly, he set the flagon on the table.

"I'm shocked. Although I do toast Oliver's good health and good luck, I cannot believe he is to marry… and his betrothed is Jocelyn Hautgard. Are you positive, Sire, of the woman's name, I mean?" He asked, turning a troubled face to the King.

"Aye, it's certain," Charlemagne confirmed. "The bride's father accepted the betrothal pledge and the bride agreed. Oliver offered a plentiful dowry: his land near the castle in Fulda; the filly you train; three chests of household plate and linens from his mother's manor; and a newly-born colt of his own. It is near-to-all he owns, I believe."

"Ever was he generous," Roland answered, "to those he loves."

"Indeed. His goods are noteworthy but do not compare to the worth of the man."

"I agree completely. He is the best of us all. I wish him

all happiness." Roland added, finally smiling at the King. "He deserves the best. I could not wish him a more suitable wife than Jocelyn. She is a gift...for any man wise enough to love her."

"I believe that true," the King replied, astonished at the direction of the conversation. "They both wished you told before anyone else...because you are a much-valued friend." Roland nodded slowly, his eyes filling up. He looked into the King's face.

"I do hope I'm worthy of such friendship." He answered, taking his leave of the King. Charlemagne watched Roland exit. He checked the mist in his own eyes, more than touched by both Oliver's and Roland's efforts not to hurt each other.

What produces this kind of gentleness? He wondered. *If such a situation developed between Rinaldo and Marc, they would be fighting as soon as a betrothal was announced. Ganelon would cleave a rival in two and ask questions later. What is it that makes men rise above themselves, above their own inclinations?* His face knitted, his eyes locked on the floor. He puzzled over the question.

He wanted to say it was religion, a sure and focused concern for the will of God. But, try as he might, he could not believe it. He knew too many good men - men who fought well, who were honest and forthright, men who would give their own lives for a fellow soldier. Many of them were not religious at all, not really. They might swear to be Christians; they might even obey the commandments and Church law; but many did not care about others.

So, is it possible to make men care for one another? Charlemagne asked himself. He thought of Oliver and Roland: two good friends, Peers almost always in competition. He thought of his own friendship with Abbot

Fulrad; they did disagree and fight each other, but their affection and concern remained. He analyzed Hildegard's friendship with Gisela.

"What do these relationships have in common?" The King asked himself.

"They are characterized by respect of the other person, by appreciation, and by understanding. How do we reach these conclusions?" He wondered. "How do we judge, evaluate, and respect our fellow companions?" Charlemagne walked around the battle tent; he went for a long ride on Samson; he watched soldiers fishing in the shoals of the river. Finally, turning Samson's head toward his court, he found his answer.

"Ah," he sighed. "The friendships grow because we think about each other. I mean, we analyze our own reasons for admiring someone, the advantages the person brings to our lives, the contributions the individual makes where ever he or she is. We think about their characteristics, their strengths and, aye, their weaknesses as well. Then we evaluate their influence on our own lives. Aye, much of this is subconscious; but it takes place. And, then, we understand the reason we chose them as our friends." King Charlemagne smiled calmly, though, in truth, he felt like shouting. Loyalty and respect are most profound, he thought, when we *learn about one another*, when we think of the other's values, commitments, and concerns.

"That's it! I must encourage my people to think. Doing so, they will, also, come to reject certain people. We understand certain people will not share our values or our interests; so we are not eager to be around them, do not wish to learn more about them. It is as I told Fulrad... years ago." The King remembered. "He asked me the reason I sought out men from other lands, why I wished to know them. He particularly mentioned Ibn Abn. I told him what?" He wrinkled his forehead, trying to recall his exact words.

"Ahh, I told him those men were like me…moving through strange lands to understand the world, seeking friendships to learn the secret of winning people's loyalty, identifying differences to better understand our similarities." The King, feeling as hopeful and frisky as a spring lamb, laughed aloud.

"I have it; I have it!" He cried. "The people must be taught to think. With that skill, we can know ourselves, learn about others, and create a paradise!" He began that very day to devise a more effective educational plan for the realm.

"My first effort must be with the clergy." Charlemagne decided.

During the amenable weather of autumn, he began traveling to the monasteries. He identified for himself the very small number of churchmen left who could read and write. He recruited these to teach their fellows, excusing them from other duties to extend instruction to their peers. At the same time, he expected the literate monks to offer education to those who worked for the monastery --be they kitchen hands, stable boys, or bishops. Most workers declined the offer; but the monastery schools, nevertheless, were filled with students. This progress, while slow, was encouraging. With various types of promotions and largesse, Charlemagne rewarded the clergy who encouraged their own monks to become literate. But he quickly understood much greater efforts must be made to reach even a small portion of his growing realm.

Contrary to the monks' deteriorating skills, it appeared the nuns maintained their commitment to mass education. They required novices to receive instruction in reading and writing, as well as in general healing. The nuns seemed to guard their knowledge less carefully, freely shared their instructional methods with each other, and educated all who entered as novitiates, as well as the children—boys and girls both—who studied in the abbeys' schools.

As he visited the monasteries and the abbeys, King Charlemagne urged those seeking God's will to respond to the Lord's directives and teach.

"Men do not learn through their own stunted abilities," he told them, "but through analysis and discussion, through comparing and contrasting, through disagreement and challenge. Be certain your students have equal parts of all." Consulting with Paul the Deacon, the King sent out calls for teachers. He advertised all over the realm. Men flocked to his court, braying about their skills and begging to prove their abilities. He looked and listened and hoped, but, still, was less than pleased with those who came to offer their services.

Weeks later, Abbot Fulrad made the mistake of asking about the King's educational project. Charlemagne--his brow furrowed, his heart heavy-- did not hesitate to tell him. In a few moments, his frustration boiled over.

"Even the copyists are unable to read the letters or the words they transfer from one parchment to another!" He shouted to Fulrad. "As the artists decorate and illuminate holy materials, a monk describes the drawings and enhancements they should make. One monk, do you hear me, only **one** monk is in charge of all the illuminations! This very same monk describes the embellishments which he envisions, even if he cannot read the passage the illumination illustrates! What a heinous situation!" The King glared at the Abbot; he was beside himself with anger. Seeing Fulrad's mild reaction, Charlemagne threw several containers on the floor in rage. All of a sudden, he jumped up and down on the broken baskets.

"How can the people know the scriptures?" the King raged. "How can they be accountable for their misdeeds, if they can't read about the misdeeds themselves? Imagine! The words are being lost! Literature and scholarly writings are disappearing. No one values them." He would have wept were he not so angry. "They'll be lost forever!" Pointing at Fulrad, he shook his head.

"I know the people are hungry; I know the barbarians are overtaking us all. But how can we sustain ourselves? Where is the history of the past; where are the volumes which point us to the Lord's path? Lost! Lost! Destroyed and lost through ignorance." He was livid. No one dared enter the room, so afraid were they of his temper.

"I've loved learning all my life! Words—poetry, treatises, chants--refine our spirits. Words, well spoken, paint pictures; provide understanding; influence minds; and produce power. This loss, this tragic loss of learning, is stupid! How is it possible--holy men unable to read? Just fifteen years ago, all the monks at York read! They were masters of disciplines. As boys, the monks tutored us--not by our sitting at their feet but in listening to them argue, explain, compare." Charlemagne was overcome, outraged at the lack of learning in his monasteries. He almost wept. The Abbott stood as far from the King as possible, trying to find words to interrupt the ranting.

Unthinkingly, Charlemagne caressed three books Paul the Deacon rescued from a burned monastery. Paul found them under the body of a dead monk, stabbed in the back by a barbarian spear. Charlemagne clasped the three, all written in Latin, to his chest. Hildegard, hurrying ahead of little Charles, rushed into the room.

"What is all this shouting, Charlemagne? Your roaring fills the court! What so distresses you?" She walked to her husband, motioned for little Charles to sit beside his father and poured herbal tea. "Drink this and calm yourself. Your shouting accomplishes nothing; you frighten everyone."

"Hilde! How did this happen…this ignorance?" She heard him moan.

"No one… there's no one who can read! These holy men are illiterate! They cannot read nor converse about important things. Who'll give the people moral direction? Such is not the province of a king. Who'll interpret the Scriptures? Who'll teach the children? People must read and write; they must do sums! We cannot build trade if no one can count! We are without men who can think! Who will help? How can I repair this catastrophe?" The King's face was pale, despite his anger-flushed cheeks. His very mass seemed to shrink.

"Charlemagne, I don't know the course you should take. But I assure you; shouting isn't the first step. Please sit down and explain this all to me quietly. You're the King; you can put this to rights. Look around your library and calm yourself." Hildegard knew the mention of 'library' would get the King's attention and she was right. He sat back, looking thoughtfully at the codices and parchments around him. He busied little Charles stacking pages of parchment. Then, just as he opened his mouth to speak, there was a rustling outside.

***

"Aye?" Hildegard answered. Before the word was from her mouth, Jocelyn rushed inside. "I must see you, Queen Hildegard." Words tumbled from her mouth. "I must call off this betrothal and I need your direction."

She slumped down beside Hilde's feet and burst into tears. Hildegard looked at Charlemagne, raising her hands in bafflement.

"I do not know." Hildegard mouthed to the King's unasked question. Then, she gathered Jocelyn up, put her arm around the young woman's shoulder, and led her toward her tent.

"What nonsense are you spouting, Jocelyn?" Hildegard asked quickly, steering the girl toward the tent door. "Do you wish the entire court to hear of this folly? Stop weeping and control yourself. You must desist! Or every woman in court will be descending on us." Jocelyn looked at Hilde in horror and, immediately, wiped the tears from her face with her hand. She stood up straight, walking slowly.

"We don't want that, Hilde." she acknowledged quietly as the two walked, ever so slowly. The Queen glanced at Jocelyn and enunciated her words slowly.

"Walk past my chamber, exit at the chapel, and move toward the river's edge," she whispered, "where we may have a smidgen of privacy. Let everyone think we are going for a stroll. Aye?"

"Of a certainty," Jocelyn replied, as she made consciously moved slowly and struggled not to cry. Her eyes filled with tears but she held her head high, trying to control her emotions. As they drew near to the river, Hildegard saw her groom waving a bridle at her. He walked between two docile horses, holding them steady.

"The King sent me, my Lady," the groom greeted them. "He said you two needed to ride a little." He placed the two bridle reins in Hilde's hand and backed away, looking for something to help the women mount their horses.

"Let's ride, Jocelyn," Hilde directed. "Charlemagne is right; we need to talk away from here. Can you mount?"

She asked, looking quickly at Jocelyn. Jocelyn nodded, took her reins, and stretched to pull herself on the horse. Hilde's groom hurried to her, a gourd under his arm.

"Stand on this, my Lady." He set the gourd beside Hilde's horse. She nodded, stepped on the gourd, and slid onto the horse, pulling herself up into the saddle.

"Thank you, Jess." Hildegard said as she nodded at Jocelyn and followed her. In no time, Hildegard cantered behind Jocelyn along the river's edge, steadily putting the court behind them. Some half a league on, Hilde reined her horse in and slid from her saddle. She tied the horse under a tree where she could crop grass and waited for Jocelyn to do the same. Then, the two women spread a linen under a huge oak and sat down.

"Now," Hildegard began, "what is the trouble?" At her question and sympathetic demeanor, Jocelyn once more burst into tears. Here, in this secluded spot, Hilde let her cry. If she gets this out of her system, mayhap she can speak to me coherently, she thought. Jocelyn sobbed as Hildegard held her hand and made soothing murmurs. After a barrage of tears, some cumulative sobs, and a little whimpering, Jocelyn seemed to have herself under control.

"Forgive me, Hilde. I guess life got to me today…in a way I could not deflect." Hildegard nodded.

"Tell me about it," she said softly, squeezing Jocelyn's hand in support.

"I came face-to-face with Roland," Jocelyn explained. "Up until now, I tried not to be where he was. I mean, I made an effort to avoid the places in the camp which he frequents. But, today, I decided to pick blackberries. There," she pointed near the edge of the forest. "And I paid no attention to the horses' hooves…until he called my name." She looked into Hildegard's face.

"Oh, Hilde, it was horrible," she admitted. "He was pale and sad. Obviously, he wanted to hurry by me, but knew it would be impolite to say nothing." She wiped a tear as it wandered down her cheek. "I greeted him. All I could say was 'Good Morrow, Roland.'"

"And...?" Hildegard asked. In her heart, she preferred to hear none of this. It can only hurt, she thought, this sharing of another's pain. But I must listen...and help her, if I can. Jocelyn wept again. Giant tears rolled unheeded down her face.

"He said 'Good morrow to you, Jocelyn. I trust you are well.' His eyes darted from spot to spot, as if hunting a place to hide." Jocelyn added. "Then, he looked directly into my face and said: 'I wish you great happiness.'" Jocelyn sighed and rubbed her eyes. "I began to wish him a good day when he spoke again."

"'I regret I did not speak my mind to you,'" he said, "'when it would have made a difference. But I do want you to know I wish you and Oliver all the best. He is as fine a man as any of us will ever know. I do hope we can all continue to be friends...after you two are married.'" Jocelyn hiccupped and laid her head on Hilde's shoulder.

"I feel such a heel, Hilde. I did feel his interest in me; but I gave him no sign of my suspicion. If I had, everything might be different. He looked so sad and hopeless there, sitting astride his horse. It broke my heart; it did! Roland is so good, so generous, so quick to help those in trouble. Women like his handsome looks; it's true. But they also value his gentle heart, his kindness to them, his courtesies. How dare I hurt him?" She looked into Hildegard's face. Oh, dear, Hildegard thought.

These are not thoughts she should be having. It was Roland who missed his chance, Roland who did not speak nor tell her his wishes. Jocelyn cannot blame herself. What shall I say to her?

"Why don't you cry this out, whatever it is, Jocelyn. We'll talk when you finish weeping?" Hildegard asked. Jocelyn meekly bowed her head and began sobbing once more. Minutes passed. Jocelyn seemed unable to dry her tears. As she patted her eyes, another flood of tears would rise in her eyes and spill onto her bodice. In fact, her tunic looked as if she were already caught in the rain. Hildegard sat quietly, arranging her thoughts. *I wonder if she wept like this before. I hope this is the last of it, for certain.* Finally, Jocelyn stood up, went to the river to pat water over her eyes and returned, sitting beside Hilde, again, on the linen.

"I think I can talk now," she said quietly, "without tearing up, I mean."

"Good," Hildegard responded. "You needed to cry and get this out, Jocelyn; but you are completely misdirected in your thoughts. Are you crying for Roland or for yourself? Do you regret the choice you made, to marry Oliver, I mean?" Hildegard dreaded asking the question; but it must be answered. Until today, she thought Jocelyn chose Oliver's betrothal freely and eagerly. Now, she did not know. Jocelyn appeared totally beaten. Jocelyn frowned at Hildegard's question, opened her mouth to respond and, then, closed it without uttering a word.

"I...I...I felt so sorry for him, Hilde," she finally said. "His entire body sagged; he is so sad and seems reluctant to speak to me. It's tragic; don't you think?" Hildegard shook her head. *Lord, give me wisdom as I speak.*

"Nay, Jocelyn," Hildegard replied. Jocelyn's head snapped up, her eyes glaring.

"How can you be so cruel?" She snapped. "How can you feel no pain or sadness for Roland? I broke his heart! I can feel it...even if you think not!" She spit out the words.

"I surely don't mean to be cruel," Hildegard clarified. "But I don't see Roland's circumstance as tragic. The only tragedy is he waited too long to tell you his feeling. That was his choice, Jocelyn. We will never know, nor do we need to, the reason for his hesitancy. But, if he wanted you for his wife, why didn't he speak? What held him back? He knew Oliver planned to ask a woman in the court to be his wife. Roland even told Oliver he, too, had a love interest!" She exclaimed. "But Oliver is the one who took a chance, who asked you to marry him. Do you regret that he asked you?" Hildegard paused. "Do you now yearn for Roland's declaration...before Oliver, I mean?" Jocelyn did not reply. She rolled her long hair around her hand, pulled it tightly, and released it. She smoothed out her tunic, fingering the embroidery around the neck, as if it were sewn in gold thread. She shook her head slowly but said nothing.

"You see," Hildegard tried again. "I'm confused. You were happy with Oliver's proposal, even enthusiastic, less than a fortnight ago. You went to your parents' manor to secure their permission. You accepted Oliver's dowry. These tears, your ragged feelings, make no sense... unless you want a betrothal from Roland instead." Jocelyn did not even indicate she listened.

"Is that the way of it, then?" Hilde asked.

"I did not say that," Jocelyn mumbled. "I did not say that at all." Her voice rose considerably.

"Then, why do you cry?" Hildegard inquired. "As I said, your behavior is very confusing to me. I don't understand your quandary." She made an effort to be comforting. "Why are you so sad, Jocelyn, unless you feel you made a mistake — a mistake in accepting Oliver. Aye, I acknowledge Roland has regrets. He wishes he could change his lack of action. He may wish to go back and relive previous days…and decisions. I'm sorry he will not have something he wants. But none of this is significant, if you are content in the decision you made."

"I don't know," Jocelyn moaned. "I don't know. I was completely happy with Oliver. I did not even think of Roland. But, then, seeing him; imagining the words he might have said; worrying he is disappointed…I feel very unhappy now." Hildegard did not respond. I have no way to advise you, she thought. *If you do not know the man you want, there is no one alive who can reassure you or challenge you.*

"I cannot help you, then, Jocelyn," Hildegard admitted. "But I will tell you this. If you are unable to choose between these two men, you should not be betrothed at all, not to either one of them. A betrothal encourages you to get to know the person, to determine if you are temperamentally suited, to ascertain if your values and goals as a couple are compatible. A betrothal must not be used to compare two men; it is about only one man. If you have no interest in the reality of marrying Oliver, you should end your betrothal. It's the only solution you have." *I have said enough.* Hildegard decided. *Jocelyn must reconsider her decision and be positive of it. I do not envy her.* She stood up, went to the horses and walked back toward Jocelyn.

"We should return to the court," she said. Jocelyn nodded and stood.

"Thank you, Hilde,for your words. I apologize if you think I misled you. I know you never had any doubts about your love for Charlemagne. I am a fool."

"On the contrary," Hildegard answered. "I knew I loved him; I did not know if he loved me…or if he loved me enough to accept it, to marry me. You have no such question with Oliver. There is no doubt of his affection.

Do you want him? That's the question, as I see it."

"Aye," Jocelyn agreed, "that is the question."

"Just remember, Jocelyn, Oliver was the one who made you laugh, who talked about the subjects you most love, who made an effort to entertain and engage you. He knows you well and loves you; he makes a huge commitment, asking you to wed." Hildegard turned her horse next to an old stump so she might mount, as did Jocelyn. They rode together back to the court.

Chapter 14

Declarations

"What is he doing?" Oliver muttered under his breath. In the distance, he saw Roland stop to talk to Jocelyn. "Mayhap, he is offering her his congratulations." Oliver reassured himself. "He's being polite; after all, we are all friends." But his words did not lessen his concern.

As Roland rode off, Jocelyn's posture looked different. Her shoulders drooped; her head hung down; she walked very slowly. Only moments before, moving toward the blackberry bushes, she was energetic, even seemed to be singing. I will leave her be, Oliver thought, not admitting to himself he was afraid to approach her. Promising himself, he would speak with Jocelyn after the mid-day meal, he walked along the river path, going to meet little Charles for fishing. The warm morning, the sun lighting every step toward the water, defied the emptiness he felt in his chest.

"I have one, Oliver," little Charles called. "Help me pull him out!"

"Nay," Oliver laughed. "This is your catch, little man. Just hold the pole until the fish tires. You have the strength to land him yourself. That's the pleasure of fishing."

Charles nodded grimly and grabbed his fishing pole more tightly. I must do as Oliver says, he thought; he always gives the best advice. Charles adored Oliver. This

Peer always talked to him as a person, not as a little boy, and Oliver never called him 'little' Charles. That 'little' always rankled the lad's heart. He knew, all too well, he was 'littler' than his father: not as brave, not nearly as big, not as jolly or determined. Charles tried ordering the stable boys around, as he saw his father direct others; but the boys responded to him inconsistently. Usually, if a Peer were close enough to hear Charles' directions, the stable boys would do as he asked. If it were only Charles and them, they sometimes ignored him.

How can I make Poppa proud of me, Charles asked himself, if no one obeys me? *Maybe, that's the reason everyone calls me 'little' Charles—not because I'm small and young; but because I cannot match Poppa...and never will.* A shout from Oliver diverted his thoughts. He looked toward his pole and saw the huge fish at the edge of the water. Charles jerked his pole toward the bank; the fish lay on the ground, flopping weakly. He dropped his pole and ran to his fish. Oliver came up, picked up the fish, and strung him on a thin willow branch.

"What a beauty, Charles," Oliver praised him. "You did a fine job of landing him. This will taste wonderful tonight; you should share him with your mother, father, and Rotrud."

"What about baby Carloman? Would he like fish?"

"He may," Oliver nodded, "but I suspect he's too little to eat it just yet. Maybe, next year you can fish for him. What do you say?"

"Aye," the boy replied, then added. "I'll be bigger so I can catch a bigger fish. Maybe the whole court can help me eat it!" He smiled so happily at Oliver that Oliver laughed and, then, nodded his head in agreement.

"We'll work on it. Let's take your fish to Cook. I think it's about time for your lessons." He suggested.

"Pro..bly so." Charles agreed with little enthusiasm. Oliver squeezed the boy's shoulder.

"We'll fish again next week." He promised as they put away their poles.

"Don't forget to sprinkle water on our worms, here in the gourd. We don't want them to die." As they walked toward Fulrad's tent, the King called to them from the horse line.

"Good morrow to you both." Charlemagne raised his voice, waving. "Did you have luck fishing, Charles?"

"Aye, Poppa. I have a big fish for breaking our fast," little Charles answered back. "Oliver and I are taking him to the cook tent."

"Excellent," the King answered. "If you are going to your tutor, please send Oliver here to me." Little Charles looked at Oliver and nodded his head toward the King.

"Guess we both have 'sponzbilities,' Sir Oliver," he said sadly. "See you at mid-day."

"Aye," Oliver agreed, glancing toward the King. "Good luck with your lessons. Work calls me as well." Charles grimaced and plodded slowly toward the Abbot's tent. Oliver walked quickly to the King and bade him 'Good Morrow.'

"...and to you, Oliver. I need to speak with you," he said, holding the tent flap open for Oliver who stepped inside. "What kind of fisherman is Charles?"

"He does well. He's still learning patience and quietness." Oliver smiled. "But he does well in landing the fish. He does love fishing, you know."

"Aye," Charlemagne acknowledged. "I see that in the number of times I see him with his pole. And you are a fine fishing companion: quiet, patient, observant. He could not have a better teacher." Oliver inclined his head to the King but said nothing. King Charlemagne turned to his work table.

"I've a question for you, Oliver." The King began. "I'm developing a curriculum for the academy which I hope to establish in the court. I want the children to learn academic subjects, as well as appropriate skills. It's easy to name the subjects: mathematics, languages, geography, literature, reading and writing, and some little philosophy — as they are able. But, the skills — I'm stumped."

"Do you mean life skills, Sire?" Oliver questioned, "... or some ability to earn a living?"

"I mean to include learning the worth of things, so our people can exchange goods or labor for goods and not be cheated. You know, basic mathematics." The King explained. "But, the help I need from you is a determination of the soldiery skills desirable for the boys. Hilde listed the skills all young women need: basic sewing; weaving on the loom; carding and dying of wool; the roasting and boiling of foods; baking; and managing a household budget. What say you the skills a young man will need?"

"Let me think on this," Oliver begged as he took a seat. "Give me a few minutes." King Charlemagne nodded and turned his attention to his list of 'lessons.'

Oliver muttered to himself, wrote down words, marked them out and, finally, sat to stare out of the tent's opening. In a quarter of an hour he turned to Charlemagne and spoke.

"I'm ready to give you my suggestions," he said. "Will you evaluate them closely? I find it difficult to make a concise list of skills; everything seems important."

"...my problem exactly, but I want the scholars to teach skills and processes---a way of thinking."

"Well," Oliver answered, "here are my suggestions... for all the good they are."

"They will not stand alone, Oliver." Charlemagne replied. "I polled several people to get their opinions, but your suggestions are the most important. Let me have them."

"I would require developing skill with the sword. If swordsmanship is taught correctly, a young man will learn to plan ahead; to identify his opponent's weaknesses; to co-ordinate his footwork, arms, and brain; and to be aggressive and to retreat in quick succession. Skill with the javelin is less necessary. It mainly polishes technique and develops elegance, if the man already handles a sword well."

"Interesting, go on."

"Use of the dagger is critical," Oliver continued. "A man's effectiveness with the dagger depends on quick responses; on the ability to evaluate another's strength; on body stability and co-ordination, as well as on knowledge of the body's vulnerabilities. A fighter must read another's personality in close, hand-to-hand fighting. Is your enemy a hot-head, a calculating fighter, a risk-taker-- strong and rooted to the ground or quick and mercurial?" Oliver stopped speaking and looked into the king's face. "I would, of a certainty, assume good horsemanship and riding skills."

"You see?" King Charlemagne's smile covered his face. "I knew you would give me exactly what I need. You identified the necessary skill and the reasons for it. Kudos to you, Oliver! Thank you, as always, for the excellent workings of your brain!" He slapped Oliver on the back and beamed at him.

"You just helped outline the curriculum for young men in our palace school, my friend. With any luck, we will extend this instruction to the entire kingdom." Oliver held up his finger.

"Something else?" Charlemagne asked.

"Aye. If we might teach the languages and tribal speech of all those within the Frankish kingdom, Sire, it would be a great advantage. We have such disparate peoples with differing languages and customs. If more of our people could communicate with others, the realm would be strengthened and so would your rule."

"It is as you say," the King agreed. "We shall incorporate as much as we can. But we cannot educate our children forever. Finally, they must take their places as adults, with corresponding duties."

"Aye, but the better prepared they are, the more prosperous Frankland, don't you think?"

"...Of a certainty." King Charlemagne answered, "... Of a certainty."

***

Oliver no sooner left the King's tent than his worry about Jocelyn and Roland returned. Why would a word or two from Roland so subdue Jocelyn? He asked himself again. Then, he smiled.

"I would have her always happy," he realized, "though that is not possible. Still, I would have it so." He went to the practice field to wield his sword.

As Oliver parried and feinted with Theodoric, he thought only of Jocelyn: her pale, pink-tinged lips; her full bosom; her muscular legs—strong from training her colt and riding often. He remembered the ease with which she talked of her father's 'sweet delights,' of transportation problems in delivering the sweets to far-off manors, of efforts to curb baking costs when nuts were not plentiful. *She is intelligent and well-informed, he told himself. We have many interests in common. And she love animals, as I do, though her favorite animal is, without doubt, the horse and mine is the dog. The more I know of her, the more perfect she*

207

seems. His heartbeat increased with the hope of such a wife. Oliver startled at his own thoughts.

"I should tell her these things. How else will she realize I adore her?" He shook his head in dismay. Speech was not his strong suit; he much preferred to listen. "But, sometimes, one must speak," he muttered, "so as to be taken seriously."

***

In the meantime, Jocelyn fled to the orchard. An old manor, long since destroyed, once stood no more than two hundred yards from the court's present camp. Yesterday, the court's older children finished gathering the last of the peaches and plums. Many of them dried now in the sun for later storage. Although the nobles contributed to the King's support, in exchange for military protection, their largesse was not unlimited. The court seneschal gathered food and fodder from any source he could tap. Consequently, unclaimed fruit in abandoned orchards; wild blackberries, blueberries, grapes and strawberries; walnuts, pecans, and acorns within the vast forest –the court harvested it all as they followed their seasonal journey. Jocelyn squeezed an apple on one tree, and, then, moved to another.

"They're not quite ripe," she spoke aloud to herself. "But it won't be long now. These apples are firm and hard, bursting with sweet juice. I hope we can pick before the court moves again." She sat at the foot of an apple tree, aware of the absence of bees' buzzing. Their constant hum was a commonplace sound in the orchard. All the blossoms became little apples, she thought; the bees are gone for this season. Thinking of bees, she naturally thought of honey and, from there, her thoughts went to love.

Who am I to turn down a true love? She asked herself.

It's clear Oliver values me and truly wants me for his wife. I remember my delight when he asked me! So, what's happened? She deliberately put the question to herself. Nothing happened, she answered, except I feel sorry for Roland. *And why should I?* Jocelyn stood up quickly.

"Aye," she re-iterated to herself. "Why should I? He never spoke of marriage to me. He never said he cared for me as Oliver did." *What if his attentions were mere flirtations, meant to pass the time? Mayhap, he's seeking to make another woman jealous?* "How short-sighted of me, to think Roland's unhappiness has anything to do with me. I do fool myself."

"Ha! He successfully escapes all the plans and dreams of half the women at court! He is courteous and pleasant, ever charming to all of us. How I misjudge…to think he is interested in me alone! He just likes women. I am one of many to woo, to flatter, and to entertain." Jocelyn allowed she might be over-reacting in this assessment of Roland; but she had no evidence he was truly unhappy because of her betrothal. She wandered back to the apple tree, plopping down near its trunk again. She leaned her head against the tree and thought of Oliver.

"I am a practical woman," she told herself, recalling her mother's favorite expression. "And practical women do not yearn for romantic interludes or flowery words." *But,* she reminded herself, *Oliver offered you a proposal from his knees; and he spoke of the reasons he loved you. Surely, those were romantic.*

"Aye," Jocelyn admitted, "they were; and they did warm my heart. But the thing I liked best was his nervous nature…nervous because he feared I would not accept him!" Jocelyn laughed aloud, delighted she recognized Oliver's hope and secure in her acceptance of his request for a betrothal. She sighed with relief.

"I worked that out," she assured herself, "but, just to be sure, I will think again about this in the next few days. I have plenty of time." Jocelyn left the orchard, cutting across its corner as she headed toward the noble women's gossip tent. Actually, it was the tent in which they gathered. But, to Jocelyn, gossip seemed the reason for its existence and, indeed, for their meeting with each other. Aye, she thought, they do embroider, sew, and card a bit of fine wool. *But most of their energy goes into talking... talking about others, usually in a critical fashion.* She ducked her head in the tent door, just as she heard a voice call for a drink. The day begins, she thought, serving these women and serving them once again.

***

As Jocelyn went to the women, King Charlemagne came from his battle tent to enjoy the sunshine on his face. We must soon begin our journey toward the Christmas location, he thought. *I would not get caught on the move, not with the threat of snow.* He looked at the sky. *It seems so benevolent, pale, blue skies and warming sun; but the sky and the weather change in a heartbeat.* He walked toward the edge of the forest, scarcely twenty feet from his tent door. *I must implement a reorganization of the realm. I must, even if the entire structure is not in place. Yet, I heard such frustration in Theodoric's words. Is the clergy as corrupt as he suggests? Is there a way for me to control their excesses until the worst perpetrators are gone?* He passed into the shade of the forest trees, looking around for a place to sit. Spying a felled log, he pushed it with his toe.

"I don't want wood beetles and grubs as companions this morning," he said aloud. "They may stay in their rotting wood for I will not disturb them." But his shoe did not dislodge crawly things, so he sat.

"What can I do about the clergy, with the corrupt ones?" He asked himself, not for the first time. Suddenly, he rose. "The Church must be reformed. I will root out the wickedness, identify those who no longer follow the Lord's teachings." He rubbed his forehead. "It will be a risk; many will ask how I am qualified to judge the Church's holy men. But, God requires certain actions from me. I know he made me King to undertake specific tasks for Him. Now, it's time for the Church to do its part."

"These priests, bishops, and monks must help me Christianize the heathen. It is the Father's will! HE leads us in reforming the Church! This mission allows me to demand much of the clergy. I'll use Fulrad as my mouthpiece and spread my ideas to the monasteries, to the abbeys, and through them, to all the people." The King hurried back to the court, pointing the guard at his door in the direction of Fulrad's tent.

"Summon the Abbot, Hans." The King demanded. "Tell him to report to me immediately." The King waited impatiently for the Abbot, anxious to begin his important cleansing of the Church.

"Abbot, we need more checks on the religious orders." He spoke as Fulrad pushed back the tent flap. "Some of your so-called 'priests' are corrupt beyond even my imagination. They're untrue to their vows: accumulating rich clothing, supping on exotic culinary dishes, buying manor houses and opulent furnishings. I won't even mention their sexual proclivities! How can those trained in sacred traditions be such lecherous, lustful men? Tell me, I demand an explanation!" Charlemagne stomped around the room, overcome with outrage and impatient indignation. "What do you have to say for them? What?" He glared at the Abbot.

"I don't know who you're talking about." the Abbott responded. "If you chide men for a little drinking, carousing... Unhappily there are always indiscreet, dishonest..."

"Indiscreet!" Charlemagne thundered. "I don't refer to small choices, Fulrad! Their behavior, their worldliness threatens the foundation of the Church! Indiscreet! Surely you jest; are you BLIND? Do you close your mind to flagrant violations which everyone sees? Do you uphold NO standards? Hear me! You're the problem — all of you in authority who don't care, you priests and bishops who do nothing to cleanse your followers!"

The King paced continuously, swinging his huge arms, taking great gulps of air, making shadow kicks at the furniture. Abbot Fulrad was silent. *I have no legitimate response. The king's descriptions are correct.* He admitted to himself. *If anything, Charlemagne underestimates the church's problems. I have no solution. The immorality and greed are beyond my power to influence. I don't have the strength to control the bishops and priests, to say nothing of the monks.*

"So, good Abbot, you cannot help me, hummm?" Charlemagne waited for some response. "Then, I must overhaul the church myself. Gather the bishops and other abbots... or, better yet, plan a journey. You'll visit each church and monastery in the Frankish realm to carry directives. As head of the Church, I'll dictate religious capitularies to impose order and righteous behavior. Monks, priests, all religious clergy must accept my standards of behavior or pursue another calling. You're the darling of the bishops. Take command of them."

"But, Sire," Abbot Fulrad interrupted. "You haven't the right. You're not the Pope!" Charlemagne ignored the Abbot's words.

"The bishops are to elevate the deserving. You judge if the bishops are honest or not. And if not, you **will** deal with them; they'll be released from service, excommunicated. Aye! That's exactly what I'll do—put them out of my church! After a suitable time, those who are still recalcitrant, any who refuse to rehabilitate themselves, will also be dismissed from the service of the Holy Church. Have any questions, Fulrad?" Charlemagne looked at the Abbot. His face was pale; his mouth moved like a fish struggling for air.

"You cannot, your Majesty, you MUST NOT do this." He deliberately controlled his voice. "The brothers will rise in rebellion; the Church will collapse."

"So be it," Charlemagne answered. "A collapse would be easier to repair than the needs of my proposal. With a collapse, I can dismiss everyone and start anew. My plan, though, requires forgiveness and rehabilitation, not to mention the time necessary to implement changes. We must act to save the institution—while still denying its low level today. Or do you have a plan? It occurs to me; you offer no solution to redeem this rotting institution."

"I? Nay, Sire," the Abbot gulped. "I acknowledge all you say. But I see no way to reverse the current situation. Mayhap, it ....." the Abbot stopped in mid-sentence.

"There's no 'mayhap,' Fulrad!" The King exclaimed. "There's only 'shall.' The changes I've described shall be put into place immediately! This filth ends—the fornication, the thievery, the deceit! I'll clean the Church of its corruption, or I'll destroy its very foundations! God pity and forgive all those who do nothing, who allow our beloved faith to come to this low ebb. I cannot. I shall never forgive this laxity or the inherent evil it breeds. I'm only able to speak with you because you are my father. I know your soul. For the present, be about my business."

213

The next morning Abbot Fulrad received a note from the King which bade him delay his trip for ten days. Rising in the early morning, King Charlemagne labored to re-write ecclesiastical expectations of churchmen. He needed more time, he told Fulrad, to complete his directives.

'Study these changes as you travel.' the note directed. 'I wish you to distribute them to the clergy, all over the realm. With the *capitularies,* you will find instructions for oversight of all religious undertakings, as well as the manner in which newly named servants of my Christian church are chosen. Our governing structure applies to the Church's business, as well as to the affairs of the realm. Eventually, this structure will embrace and control them both.' Fulrad shook his head in consternation and went to the King but he could do nothing to soften Charlemagne's changes.

"Isn't it time little Charles was out among the people, Sire?" The Abbot asked, just before he left the King. "He should be meeting the nobles, cementing their loyalty to him, making friends with their sons. He would enjoy traveling with me, of a certainty." Charlemagne considered the Abbot's request. He had a vague sensation of fear and responded quickly.

"Not this time, Fulrad. I must first be certain of the realm Charles will command. 'Tis too soon for such decisions. For the time being, he can meet families of the nobility as the court travels. He's a bit young to bear such a responsibility. Nay, Poppa kept me close until I was twelve or so. I'll do the same with Charles." He saw the Abbot's disappointment. "I do thank you for your concern. I know Charles' welfare is at the forefront of your mind."

Chapter 15

FRIENDS, OLD AND NEW

"The constant motion is making me sick." Queen Hildegard moaned into her linens. "Will we never stop? Surely, we travel far enough for one day!" She placed a wet linen on her brow. "If I must climb from this cart to cross another river today, I will run screaming into the water! With this big belly, I'll have no trouble floating." Thinking to provide some comfort, Charlemagne had consigned a bastarne for Hildegard's comfort; but the amphibious cart frightened her. Only a covering of leather at the cart's openings prevented the water's flowing in.

"Charley is afraid for me to ride so late in this pregnancy." She fretted aloud. "But this cart is much rougher than my horse. I asked him to allow us to remain at one of the castles. But he won't hear of being parted from the children."

"Oh, if only he loved us all a little less..." She sighed. Hildegard was surprised at herself. *How could she say such a thing?* "Nay!" she cried. "Shame, shame on me! Thanks be to God Charlemagne is kind and loving to us, each and every one. I see too much of a husband's control and callousness in other families, in this very court! Dear God, please forgive me." She begged. "I am so weary."

Hildegard turned to look out behind the cart. Both little Charles and Rotrud rode in and out between the wagons. As always, her son shouted, raised a miniature sword and called to the Peers as he rode by. Rotrud, just as predictably, sat atop her small horse, quietly concentrating on her riding. She talked quietly to her mount. My dear children, the Queen thought. *Thanks be to God they are alive and healthy. Losing Adelheid almost killed me; I worry for these two every moment and for little Carl.* She glanced down, unconsciously rubbing her distended belly.

"This babe I carry seems uncommonly heavy." The Queen murmured to herself. Hildegard was weepy, exhausted from the constant travel and nauseated by the carts' unremitting motion. *Are we never to stop for the night?* She wanted to shout.

Charlemagne changed their route the day before yesterday so she was in an unfamiliar wood. She prayed. She literally closed her eyes and begged God for a hostelry. There was a network of them throughout the empire, run primarily by monks--monks and clergymen who, by their religious vows and vocation, promised to receive and refresh travelers. How welcome such services would be, Hildegard thought. *I know there's not a single noble house for miles yet.*

Just as Himiltrude feared she could go no further, one of the King's governmental evaluators, a *missi dominici*, rode up beside her cart.

"Excuse me, Queen Hildegard. I secured food and lodging for you and the babes in Count Lenfur's hunting cabin. The Count refurbished an abandoned dwelling some years ago and, now, offers its use to you. I told him you could not grace his court; it is more than twelve furlongs away. But the hut is less than half a metre off this road, my lady."

"May God bless you, Missi Zorna," Hildegard responded. "I am more grateful than you can know for this kindness. Thank you for seeing my distress. I'm in your debt, Sir. May God bless you."

Carefully controlling his face, the *missi dominici* smiled in acknowledgement of her thanks. He didn't allow his pity for her traveling state to show. How much he asks of them! He thought. No allowance is made for pregnancy or illness or for too many cares. To the children, such trips can be joyful and exciting. The women, though, suffer over-much, and must never complain.

At last, we can stop! Hilde almost wept with thankfulness. *I feel stronger already. It must be the rough stones embedded in this road; the wagon seems to strike every one of them and dip into every hole. I'm unable to take the motion, probably because I'm well along in this pregnancy.* She patted her belly, just as a cramp hit her in the back.

"Ohhhhhh," Hilde breathed out. "Mistress Diltan, please send word to the King. The babe is coming. We must delay here for a day or two." Hilde did not worry. Her women were with her, including the midwife. At the last minute of setting out, the woman insisted she share the Queen's cart. Now, Hilde was very thankful such was the case. Three days later the Queen and her court joined Charlemagne's main contingent.

He rode to her in the night, of course, overjoyed to find her delivered of twins, Louis and Lothair. And he proudly escorted them all to the mobile court's new location. Once Hildegard and the babes arrived, the court left for the spring assembly, this year in Paderborn.

There, the talk was all of strategies to overcome any Saxon incursion. King Charlemagne was too realistic to think the Saxons would surrender to his power.

"They will rise again against us," he told Roland, "probably led by that new commander, who they think can save them. What is his name: Weeder...?"

"You mean Widukind, Sire?" Roland asked. "...the leader from Westphalia?"

"Aye," Charlemagne answered. "He will be their next leader; his name was on every lip when we overtook the Saxons last year. They do think him a god, it would seem."

"I cannot confirm that, Charlemagne. Mayhap, he's their best fighter and, thus, commands respect and loyalty. I am certain the Saxons would value a man who promises victory." He looked up, hearing a lone rider approaching. Just as Roland turned to leave the tent, the captain of the guards dismounted and scratched on the tent's door.

"Come, come," the King directed. Roland held the flap open.

"Sire, there is someone requesting an audience. He waits at the eastern edge of the Pader River." The captain announced.

"And who is it, Captain Podtrecht?" The King asked. The captain shrugged dismissively.

"He says his name is 'Sool er ah mahn eeb na all rabbee' (Sulyaman Ibn-al-Arabi)," Podtrecht answered. "But I think he's a mangy coward, fleeing from his country and down-on-his luck." Charlemagne's eyes flicked to those of Captain Podtrecht, to Roland, and back to the captain's face.

"And why do you dismiss him, Podtrecht? Is it your habit to dismiss those who give you their name...even if you mispronounce it like a barbarian? Or, mayhap, his looks – being different from yours – are distasteful to you?" He glared at the guard, slapping his hand on the desk.

"We are in assembly here, Captain! This is the very time for friends and enemies to approach this gathering.

Escort the man here... and treat him with respect." The King ordered. Captain Podtrecht, appropriately chastised, nodded and hurried from the battle tent. Roland left to bring the Peers to the tent.

Years ago, during a trip to the East, they met Sulayman Ibn-al-Arabi and learned his value to King Charlemagne. Indeed, the two kings were fast friends. Courtesy demanded the Peers greet him and welcome him to their land and the assembly. King Charlemagne called for tea to be prepared, placed additional cushions on his benches, removed two richly-embroidered tunics from his traveling chest and placed them on his sleeping bench. Then, he went outside his battle tent and waited for the Captain to escort Ibn to his tent.

"Ah, Ibn!" King Charlemagne exclaimed as the captain and Ibn-al-Arabi rode up. The King walked quickly to Ibn-al-Arabi, offering a hand as Ibn dismounted. The King kissed his visitor on both cheeks, clasping his shoulders as he did so.

"I am so happy to see you; welcome to my camp!" He said. The captain, with his mouth hanging open, turned, bowed to Ibn, and hurried away.

"You are the last man I expected to see but you are welcome, indeed!" Charlemagne assured him as they entered the battle tent. "How are you old friend and what brings you in search of me?" Charlemagne looked Ibn over carefully. He seemed in good health, even if his face appeared tired and pale. He and Ibn genuinely liked and respected each other. Their friendship formed years ago when their fathers conferred. Even more so than his father, Charlemagne delighted in Arab culture. He appreciated the beauty of its women, of a certainty, and enjoyed the methods of food preparation. From time to time, he waxed eloquent about shish-ka-bob and yogurt. Each time the King thought of a sheik, he wished Frankish people held him in as great esteem as the Arabs seemed to hold his friend. *What a joy to be a sheik! Ibn, as his father before him, commands great respect and obedience.*

"They are kings, for certain, Poppa," he said to King Pepin years ago. "The Arabic rulers do as they choose and expect obedience. No one seems to judge them, whatever they do."

Ibn al Arbai was the powerful Arabian governor of Barcelona. The borders he and Charlemagne shared near Septimania bonded the two men together. They respected each other and maintained a cordial relationship. Charlemagne, ever interested in different peoples, was eager to increase good will between Ibn-al-Arab and himself. Also, he remembered the value his father placed in his friendship with this line of Arabian sheiks. Both Ibn-al-Arabi and Charlemagne had visions of extending their realms, using each other in the process. Ibn got right to the point of his visit.

"You're the king of the West, by all the stories and songs I hear, great Charlemagne! I come to do you homage. Please accept these exotic creatures for your park in Aachen," he offered. Arabian men brought in Egyptian ducks, peacocks, and other brilliantly colored birds for the king's delight. "They will glorify your name and your exploits."

"If only I were as you name me, King in the West, sir," Charlemagne replied, smiling. "I fear there are several kings in the West." Ibn-al-Arabi shook his head in denial and replied.

"If there are several, Sir, you are the best of them. Of that, I stand convinced." Never immodest, Charlemagne delighted in hearing such greetings from the governor of Barcelona.

"Believe you are a King, Charlemagne, and it is so. As a king, tell the world you are my comrade and my supporter. With you at my back, Lion of the North, the threat which now rises from Umayyad Caliph of Cordoba will be as leaves in the wind!" Ibn enhanced his speech. "He is a snake, slippery and full of guile, hungry for power, and eager to subjugate us all." He knows Poppa aligned with his father against the Umayyads of Cordoba, King Charlemagne thought, pleased with Ibn's view of his value.

"Help us to defend ourselves, Charlemagne – I and Husayn of Zaragosa. We vow submission to your rule."

"Do you now?" King Charlemagne asked. "Such a vow lightens my heart, Ibn. Husayn previously swore his support of me, though I did not yet require it of him. I would know your need, Ibn Al Arabi; your realm and mine share similar interests. As my father always said, 'allegiances are the direct result of friendships. And our friendship is firm and strong.'" Hummm, Charlemagne thought, helping Al Arbai will go far toward my conquering part of Spain.

"Then, help me defeat the Umayyads," Ibn al Arabi repeated. "Many Arab leaders oppose this fool from Cordoba! With your lead, they will join our armies and certain defeat will be visited on the Umayyad Caliph." Charlemagne, imagining yet more lands and booty for his realm, eagerly offered his support.

"Dear friend," the King said, "let me know when you need my army. I shall march for Barcelona immediately. You know; you have only to ask. We shall meet in the days to come." He bowed deeply as Sulayman Ibn al-Arabi bowed, mounted his horse, and left the assembly.

The next morning three different commanders summarized Saxon activities, the tribes' movements, and the location of their camps. They identified the weakest Saxon tribes and their territories. Afterward, commanders and Peers met to plan battles for the upcoming summer fighting.

In short order, Charlemagne hurried his troops toward Aquitaine, calling his soldiers — spread far and wide throughout the realm — to meet him there for the battle season. Once his soldiers gathered, Charlemagne intended to march for Toulouse, all the closer to Sulayman Ibn al-Arabi should he send for Charlemagne's help. As the court settled into a semi-permanent camp in Aquitaine, Gisela, the King's sister, arrived from her abbey.

***

"Where is little Carloman?" She asked, eager to see her newest nephew. "I yearn to hold the sweet thing." She smiled at Hildegard as they shared plums and peaches.

"You should see the blossoms in the orchards, Gisela." Hildegard laughed. "The fruit trees, mayhap because of the milder winter, burst forth this spring, bringing us unusually flavorful fruit. These plums are filled with sweetness." Gisela nodded and took another plum, delighting in the crisp, juicy taste. "Here," Hildegard said, "let me send Rotrud to Mathilde. She can bring Carloman to visit us in the orchard. It's mild enough for him to be out." Rotrud scampered off, eager to bring her baby brother to their outing.

"Ahh, Gisela! It seems all I do is birth babies. Tell me everything happening in your abbey. And what about the new novices who joined you just after Christmastide? Can you say if all of them are meant to be nuns?" She listened to Gisela's stories of the abbey; but, soon, looked around in confusion. "Where is Rotrud? I sent her for Carloman and Mathilde some goodly time ago."

"Let me see what's keeping them." She told Gisela.

"Usually, Rotrud is quick in running errands...unless she stops to play." Hildegard didn't hurry. She knew Rotrud likely played with the babe herself, having quickly forgotten her aunt waited to greet him. Rotrud spent much time with Carloman, humming to him, patting his full belly, and generally providing oversight of the nurse's care of her brother. Hildegard was almost into their sleeping tent when Rotrud stumbled out. Her eyes were wide, her face white and chalky, and her expression miserable.

"Ma-Mam," she whispered.

"We're waiting for you and Mathilde to bring Carloman." Hildegarde looked at her daughter. "What's the matter? Your Aunt Gisela is anxious to see Carl. Is he still sleeping, Rotrud?"

"No sleep, Ma-Mam. Nay. Carly gone. He not here to play." Rotrud answered, her brow wrinkled. She turned to pick up a ball and stick.

"Mathilde and Carloman are gone? They must be close; let's look for them, shall we?" Rotrud shook her dark curls and sat in the dirt to dig a small hole. Hildegard stuck her head in the nursery tent, just to be sure no one was inside. The tent was cool, but empty of people. Carloman's linens lay mussed together in his basket. But the coverlet which they always tucked around his little feet lay on the floor, seemingly discarded. Hildegard's mother's heart knew immediately something was wrong. She dashed from the tent and called for a man-at-arms.

"My Queen?" He responded as he hurried to her.

"The babe," Hildegard tried to remain calm. "My babe and his nurse aren't in here; did you see them leave the tent?"

"Don't you remember, Queen Hildegard?" The man answered. "Not so long ago, you went into the tent and took the babe. I saw him in your arms. You didn't speak to me but left carrying him in the yellow linen sheet." He spoke very decisively, looking at the Queen with a questioning expression. "You did have on your blue cloak, Highness." Hildegard felt faint.

Oh, Dear Lord, Help me! Please don't let this be happening. My baby, my dear, beautiful boy, where is he? She stumbled, remembering the pain of losing Adelheid.

"Hurry to the training ground, Sir. The King's there, watching the horses' being broken. Bid him to hurry to me. Make haste, man; make haste!" The Queen summoned another soldier as he passed a few steps away. "Bring a guard unit to me quickly. Look for Captain Ross; he's the man I want. Tell him I need trackers, men who are swift and well-versed in trailing." The soldier started to question but, seeing the Queen's distress, hurried to do her bidding. Hildegard turned to find Rotrud staring at her.

"Come here, my dear one." Hildegard opened her arms and Rotrud raced into them. "Matilde seems to be taking Carloman for a walk. You know how he loves the outside. The day's yet warm so I'm sure he'll be fine. But I do worry, not knowing exactly where he is. Can you bring Queen Mother Bertrada to me?" She asked her little daughter. Hildegard knew Rotrud realized something bad was amiss; but, mayhap, the errand would lessen her fear. "Tell her to come to our tent. Can you do that, dear girl?"

"Aye, Ma-mam, I go to Queen Mam." Rotrud replied as she ran toward Queen Bertrada's tent. Hildegard, heading towards her own tent, heard hooves pounding, racing in her direction. As she turned, Charlemagne swung off his horse and came to her.

"Is anything wrong, Hilde?" he asked. "The man-at-arms seemed concerned, but only said you summoned me forthwith." Hildegard reached for her husband and cried.

"Charley, the babe, the babe and Mathilde are missing! I don't know where they are. The man-at-arms told me he saw me take Carl out of the tent." She spoke in brief, rapid sentences. "Charley, it wasn't me! I came to fetch him for Gisela to see. I sent Rotrud to get them; but she didn't come back. Charley, our boy's gone!" She broke into tears, sobbing on Charlemagne's shoulder.

In an instant, Charlemagne summoned five soldiers away from their duties, gave them instructions to reconnoiter the camp area, and took Hildegard into the tent.

A few minutes later, Gisela raced into the tent. Seeing the fear in her brother's face and his tender concern for Hildegard, Gisela knew something was wrong.

"What?" she asked, her voice breaking in fear.

"We can't find Carloman," Charlemagne responded gravely. "It may be overreaction; but neither he nor Mathilde is here, where Hildegard left them. How did you know to come here, Gisela?"

"I waited, first for Rotrud to fetch Carl and his nurse. Then, Hilde came to find Rotrud and bring them all back. Neither of them returned, so I ran here to see. Oh, Charley, what can I do? Is there some place I can look for them? Did the nurse take him for a walk or, mayhap, she visits with other court women?" Gisela's worry transferred to her steps; she paced back and forth. "He's barely two months old; what is the nurse thinking – disappearing with him like this?"

"Gisela, we must assume there is some evil afoot. Let me look around inside, see if anything looks out of place." That said, Charlemagne squeezed his sister's shoulder, pushed Hildegard into her arms, and began examining the baby's bedclothes. Close to the bathing trough, he saw a flash of light on the ground. Bending over, he picked up a small, miniature blade. It looked to be a part of a very delicately made sword—obviously an ornament of some kind. It appeared costly.

"Gisela," Charlemagne held the piece up. "Ever seen anything like this before?" Gisela steered Hildegard to a bench, gave her some ale, placed a heavy linen coverlet over her lap, and came to where Charlemagne stood.

"Nay," she answered as she handled the ornament. "It definitely belongs to a woman, though, too delicate for a man to attach his cloak." Just as she finished speaking, the guard whom Hildegard asked to fetch trackers came up.

"Sire," he said, bowing to the king. "Queen Hildegard asked for trackers. Our five best are just behind me. On the way here, we found one of the queen's ladies; she has a head wound and lay under a torn mantle. She is unhurt but for a large bruise on her forehead. But she's groggy and speaks hesitantly yet. I do fear something is amiss."

"Did you question her?" Charlemagne asked as he looked frantically at Gisela and, then, Hildegard.

"Aye, Sire, of a certainty." The guard replied. "She remembered little; she walked to the cook tent to bring tea for the Queen. She knew Gisela was in camp. Then, she says, someone grabbed her; but she remembers nothing else. I believe someone or something hit her on the head, Sire."

"Take her to the healer," Charlemagne answered, as Hildegard came to the man. "Then, spread your trackers out in a circle and work outwards. Look for signs of one person, mayhap of two people, leaving the camp. There can't be more than one or two. How many more would be able to enter the camp...and this tent unseen...and leave with my son?"

"Please, Jaythor, bring my babe back to me." Hildegard begged as she clutched the guardsman's hand. "I will come with you." She squared her shoulders and took a step forward.

"Nay, nay, Hilde!" Charlemagne answered. "Nay, you cannot. Stay here to comfort your other children. We will search until we find Carloman. No one can get far, not carrying an infant. Whoever has him must be on foot. Our men at arms would have heard and investigated a rider. Calm yourself, my dear. For a certainty, our boy will be back in your arms before nightfall. Rest here." Gisela came up to Hildegard and hugged her shoulders.

"Let's bring Charles and Rotrud here," she said. "It's time I saw my older nephew. We can have cider and tell stories while the guards and the trackers search. We must be brave for the children's sakes, Hilde." Hildegard shook her head in understanding and sent Gisela to the stables for little Charles. Her tears fell silently as Gisela left the tent.

Chapter 16

WATCHFULNESS

On the other side of the orchard, Little Charles fought to hide his disappointment. The apples were not quite ripe. Nevertheless, he would not disappoint the horses; so he picked the small, green fruit, hoping their crunch would make up for the tartness. Looking around, he saw the Abbot's gray horse between two of the tents. Where's A'bot Fulrad?Little Charles thought. *That's Nellie...but who rides her?* He turned again to look over his shoulder, watching the gray horse. She pawed the ground as someone tried to mount. *He's not the A'bot 'cause this man's tall and thin.*

"No one else rides A'bot Fulrad's horse." Charles muttered. "What's she doing off the horse line anyway?" He turned toward the tie-line through the low-growing bushes. He stopped. He heard voices, trying to whisper but with limited success. Not recognizing them, Charles stopped behind a copse, its leaves caught in the new thorns of the holly tree alongside. The holly tree's berries hung in great profusion.

"Guess it's gonna be a cold winter," Little Charles murmured to himself.

"Mount up; here let me hold him. Mount up. We must flee quickly." A deep, gravely voice pierced the air. A hand reached out to hold the gray horse's bridle.

"I can go only so quickly...with all these skirts. Let go of me. Here, hold the child; I must have two hands to mount! You hurt me and who'll nurse this babe?" The female voice was low, so quiet Charles could barely make out the words. But the voice was familiar.

What babe is she talking about? Charles wondered. *Many of the women in camp have babies; but who would try to mount with a baby? That's pretty hard.* For reasons he himself did not understand, Charles stood silently where he was, trying to get a glimpse of the man and woman. He saw the edge of a mantle but only for a moment.

"Could that be Ma-Mam's mantle?" he asked himself. "Nay, she's with Aunt Gisela. Then, who?" He stood, trying to understand someone's mounting a horse with a baby. *There are mantles like Ma-Mams at court but that one is the very same color as Ma-Mam's. She spread it for me yesterday to hold the blackberries we discovered along the forest edge.*

He saw two horses step away from the tie-line and walk into the trees. They seemed to move slowly, as if the horses were not healthy.

"Something's not right." Charles whispered as he hunched down, preparing to follow the horses. He turned to see one of his father's guards coming toward the horse tie-line. Charles ran to him.

"Roderick!" The boy shouted. "Roderick, someone is taking two horses. They didn't ask for them, just mounted and rode off! The horse master is at the cooking tent; no one talked to him. I'm sure of it." Charles ran up to the mounted soldier.

"Good boy, Charles!" The soldier answered. "Can you show me exactly the direction the horses went?"

"Aye," Charles answered. "I saw them ride into the wood."

Here, give me your hand." Charles raised his arm and

felt his body rise from the ground. He soon sat in front of the soldier. "There's no time to lose, Charles; sit tight. Hold onto the pommel. Can you do that for me?" the soldier asked. Charles was speechless.

"Now, which direction did you say?"

Little Charles pointed to the wood. Roderick's horse moved quickly in the direction of Charles' arm. The soldier made a high, chirping sound. If he hadn't felt the rumble in the chest against his back, Charles would have looked in a nearby tree for the bird which made the trill. But he knew the sound came from the soldier. Very soon, out of the corner of his eye, he saw two additional soldiers start toward them.

With hand signals, Roderick motioned the other two to each side of him and indicated they should move quietly forward. In a moment, other men filled in the semi-circle which the three, mounted soldiers anchored. The horses moved slowly as their riders walked side by side, searching around them. The normal sounds of birds, snorting horses, and the scurrying of small, woodland creatures ceased as the men spread out among the thick trees. All of a sudden, there was the cry of a hawk! Charles' mount bounded forward toward the cry as a soldier in the distance, shouted "Halt!"

A soldier, hidden in the trees, jumped from his horse to restrain a woman while another man held the reins of a second horse. In no time at all, Charles was looking into the face of Mathilde, Carloman's nurse.

"What are you doing out here, Mathilde?" Charles asked. He startled as he realized his little brother was in her arms, pressed against her chest. He slid off Roderick's mount and ran to Mathilde.

"Let me have Carl," he said. "Don't hold him so tight! He can't breathe! See? He's wiggling. Don't drop him!"

As he spoke, Mathilde turned; Carloman slipped from her arms. Charles grabbed for the baby and caught him quickly, just managing to keep him from hitting the horse. Roderick was beside him in a minute, steadying Charles' arms with one hand and grabbing Mathilde's arm with the other.

Before Charles could make sense of it all, his father rode up, yelling for the soldiers to protect his children. Charlemagne jumped from his horse and rushed to little Charles and Roderick.

"The babe is safe, Sire," Roderick reported. "Thanks to Charles, all ends well." Roderick winked at Charles and gave him a big smile. Charles frowned, confusion all over his face.

"Because of me...?" He mouthed. "Why, what's the trouble? Carl likes me to hold him; he isn't even crying." Little Charles reassured his father. "He's fine. Poppa, what's wrong?" His eyes zeroed in on his father's strained face. "...something bad happen?"

"All's well, my boy," King Charlemagne replied. "You're a hero. We must celebrate your quick eye! My boy, you just rescued your brother!" Charlemagne lifted his son into the air and planted a huge kiss on his forehead.

"You just saved your brother's life, lad. Three cheers for my brave son!" The King called to all who surrounded them. Many cheers rose from the soldiers returning from the field but none cheered so loudly as the King.

Charles still didn't understand clearly but could tell the cheers rising in the air were for him. He blushed, smiled, looked at the ground in confusion and ended by kissing Carl, just as Poppa had kissed him. He didn't know what else to do. Long was the celebrating that night. Everyone was up much later than usual. King Charlemagne described little Charles' keen eyesight and quick action and held him snugly on his lap. The lad smiled sleepily at everyone. Even Carloman seemed happy, sleeping off and on, then waking to nurse lustily.

***

The next morning Charlemagne summoned his Peers before breaking his fast.

"We will eat and plan together," he announced. "If you made appointments, please cancel them. You will be busy with me for the rest of the day. We reconvene within a very short period." As soon as the King spoke, the Peers looked at each other and sat down together.

"No need to waste the day, Sire." Oliver responded. "As dawn broke, each of us re-arranged today's plans. After we recovered little Carl, we all agreed to gather and to discover some explanation for yesterday's scare. More importantly, we need a plan to protect your children. All of us," he nodded at his friends, "are in readiness to begin." Oliver smiled, hoping Charlemage understood their great concern. Charlemagne, touched by the support of his friends and advisers, cleared his voice and acknowledged Oliver's words.

"I thank you all, dear friends. I know you love and value my children—sometimes more than I do," he laughed. "I am in your debt. Thank you. Let's begin our task, then. I was remiss in not taking previous attacks seriously." At their startled expressions, the King explained.

"All of you do not know... This is not the first danger aimed at my family." The Peers shifted nervously. "There were different incidents over the years which I dismissed – not believing anyone wished to harm us. But the attempt to kidnap Carloman yesterday convinced me. My family is in danger. I need advice from each of you." He fingered his signet ring. "I know there are those among you who feel my brother,Carloman, died under mysterious circumstances. This, very frankly, didn't occur to me at the time of his death. It may well be your suspicions are true."

"Some few months after Poppa died, there was an attack on my life, one in which the assassin mistook Roland here for Carloman. The assassin was clear in saying he had orders to kill us both. I dismissed his words; he seemed no more than a braggart to me. Though I killed him, it is clear I didn't end the threat against me and mine. You also remember I was hit during one of our autumn hunts."

"You speak of the attack with the strange arrows, don't you, King Charlemagne?" Seneschal Eggihard asked. "I thought you woefully unconcerned after the incident." The King nodded.

"Aye, the very same. But, again, I saw these events as coincidences; I thought myself just at the wrong place. But I can't believe this any longer, not with yesterday's daylight effort to spirit my son away. Even more worrisome, the attempt included the willing cooperation of a long-time nurse! Can anyone here explain this? I need to see some rhyme or reason in Mathilde's betrayal. Hilde and I talked, over and over in the night, about Mathilde's part in the babe's abduction. We understand it not."

"She is held now in a prison tent, guarded day and night by three men. Other men guard her accomplice in a separate location. So far, I've made no effort to question either of them." Charlemagne wanted to puzzle out their motives and secure evidence before he let anyone approach them. *The more I know, the more they'll tell me. I am certain of it.* The King thought to himself.

"Our first concern is the safety of your family, Sire."

The Abbot voiced everyone's worry. "Some extra guards and greater protections must precede talk of the thieves or of their punishment. For me, there is no reason strong enough to threaten the life of a child. We must put protections in place immediately; no further threat is acceptable. I must say, Charles is a credit to your house, Sire. A less observant child wouldn't have raised an alarm. Such a consequence frightens me a great deal."

"I now think it easier and more efficient, if I respond to my lady wife's appeal for a permanent court. Moving the court, my children, all those responsible for our daily comforts are formidable tasks, made all the more dangerous by constant change and constantly changing persons. If a long-retained person, one we all trusted, put my son in danger, what is the danger from those only recently in our retinue?"

"Exactly," Roland agreed. "Although you must still travel, visit nobles, interact with the people, a permanent physical court is easier to protect, Sire. And it seems reasonable that those settled in a permanent court will know your children, indeed all court members, better. In such an environment, any stranger or interloper would stand out, garner immediate attention. But we say nothing which sheds light on Mathilde's betrayal. Is there any explanation for the woman's actions?"

"We may find such an explanation and we may not. The real question remains: who is behind these attacks? You suffer from threats, your majesty, just as have your children – Charles in the burning tent and, now, Carl with this abduction. And we do know about the suspicion around King Carloman's death. Who gains from your death or the death of your child? What would a kidnapper demand of you, in exchange for your babe's life: ransom, advancement, land, the realm? Who benefits from harming or killing your children, for committing such a dastardly act? Who is behind these threats?" Paul the Deacon asked.

"Your enemy, cloaked in various clothing, has always been Desiderius, King Charlemagne." Abbot Fulrad replied, his voice firm, evidencing no doubt. "He surely set King Carloman's wife, Gebnega, against you as he plotted to obtain the throne for her boys. I daresay he never intended for either of your nephews to rule. Desiderius himself yearned to be King. Gebnega's boys were only shadows for him to lurk behind. The arrow which so wounded your leg and caused such loss of blood came from a mountain tribe in the Lombardy region. 'Tis likely befouled money changed hands for such an attack. You were surely the target; there's no denying it."

"Who was closest around King Carloman before he made his last visit to our court? Desiderius hosted him in Lombardy and hunted with him as well. Might all these attacks be his plots? Men in stealth undertook them all — the effort to kill you, the attempt to kill Little Charles in burning your tent, this recent kidnapping of Carl, the illness and death of King Carloman. These perpetrators are expendable, those who would hardly be missed... except for that young lord. He was proud and inexperienced, one any good, fighting man could surely defeat." Abbot Fulrad nodded his head.

"All these incidents have Desiderius' hand on them. He plots yet, even though he's cloistered in a monastery." The Abbot's eyes flashed; his face, ruddy and flushed, appeared blood-red. He took quick, angry breaths, overcome by the evidence he, himself, laid before the group.

"Your evaluation is well-reasoned, Abbot." Roland responded. No one saw him enter the room; but it was clear he had heard most of the conversation. His face was tight with restrained anger, his hands trembled. He spoke slowly, distinctly, keeping tight control over his voice.

"But since Desiderius is a prisoner in the Corbie monastery and his son, Adelchis, is in exile in Byzantium, neither of them implemented this abduction of the babe. Even if Desiderius voiced the idea of a kidnapping, he is able to offer little assistance and no money. I know Adelchis; he would have nothing to do with this." His eyes moved around the room, seeking answers. "More to the point, who does Desiderius still influence? Can anyone answer that question?" Theodoric raised his hand and nodded at Roland's words.

"Here is our first need. We must each obtain all the information we can about Mathilde, about the man being held by our soldiers, and about those who still follow Desiderius. For certain, information from each will form a pattern to enlighten us."

"Aye, let's each make an effort to explain this puzzle." Charlemagne agreed. "In a fortnight's time, we gather to put the pieces together. But, in the interim, all of you institute safety measures which better protect my family. Those who go to question people, be discreet and alert." Roland left immediately to gather information about Mathilde.

***

"Mathilde?" Cook Barston confirmed the name to Roland. "Aye, she was a good kitchen worker, one of the best. I b'leve she left here for the nursery. Yep, I'm sure. She went to help Queen Hildegard with the babes. But I'd have her back in a minute! She was a good worker, a good 'un."

Roland's raised brow, the frown between his eyes, reflected his surprise. Everyone he asked about Mathilde's character and personality spoke well of her. Each was kind and positive in his evaluation. How wise of the King not to let the court know of Mathilde's part in the kidnapping! Roland thought. *We seek honest evaluations of her. But she almost seems two people. We know she helped spirit Carloman out of the tent and was on a horse taking him away, yet everyone speaks of her loyalty and dependable nature.* Roland turned his attention back to Cook Barston.

"Tell me," he said to Barston, "did she have many friends in the court retinue? I know the king's children thought her great fun, but was she out among people her own age?" Roland had no idea if this information would tell him anything about Mathilde's purpose in kidnapping the babe; but he might obtain some insight from its answer. He needed to know all about her. *I must understand her motives. Then, maybe, I can link her with the instigator of this act. Mathilde ,herself, did not plan this abduction.*

"Aye, all the court workers like her; she was sought out; she was." Barston stated. "She so loved reporting on the ladies of the court: 'splaining their tunics; their hair — how it was dressed each morning; the trinkets diff'nt ones wore; who was dressing like another. You ken how women be, Lord Roland, talking and looking and comparing theirselves. O'course Mathilde could just watch and report. She's not a noble's daughter. But.." Barston laughed gleefully, "she did have her dreams, always hoping to catch the eye of a lord, or a Peer, or a soldier. She wanted the lord, o' course; but ranking soldiers, she especially liked them, you can be certain!"

"She's of marriageable age. Was she interested in a permanent bonding, do you know?"

"Nay, she looked far above herself. She wanted pretty trinkets, clothes, pillows — silk and the like. The foot soldiers, some asked her, but she not encourage them.

Nay. Mathilde wanted to rise, I be sure of that." Barston waited for another question from Lord Roland.

"Who were her friends, Cook Barston? Do you know who spent time with her?" Roland tried again.

"Aye," Barston nodded his head, laughing. "Lord Oliver's squire, he always hung 'round her, even when her duties took her all over the court. Guess he had hopes for his chances. He do be a good-looking lad."

Roland thanked the head cook for his help and summoned Oliver to his tent. The two wished to compare information about Mathilde. Hearing of Roland's interest in his squire, Oliver offered his friend beer, cheese and bread.

"Let's compare what we've found, Roland," Oliver responded. "Both of us examining the information might clarify some of our questions." At that moment Oliver's older squire, Jervey, came into the tent.

"Do you need anything, Lord Roland?" he asked. "I'll fetch you more beer...or barley soup to accompany your bread and cheese?"

"Thank you, Jervey, for checking; we have sufficient food. But I wonder if you'll give me some information. As you know we're trying to discover the reason for the kidnapping of the newly-born prince. We're asking questions about anyone who took care of the King's children. What is your opinion of Mathilde and the other nurse, Sophia? Would both of them fight to protect the children? Mathilde, particularly, appears to spend most of her time with them. Would she be afeared if any were in danger? Do you know her at all?" Oliver carefully couched his words to his squire. Jervey blushed to the roots of his wavy black hair.

"Tell you the truth, Lord Oliver; I did fancy her. She was always laughing, 'making eyes at us' — as my mother would call it. She was clean and neat, always looked dressed for a visitor, you might say. But I was nothing to her. Lots of us, squires and soldiers too, hoped she might favor us. But she wanted none of it. She has a mighty high opinion of what she might get: nice clothes and pretties—far more than the likes of me could ever do. I never got the idea she wanted a family, nor a husband, either. She wanted pretties, lots of them. I did, one time, see her wear a scarf belonged to little Rotrud; I don't hold with that. The scarf was a thing for a princess! She valued those things…any kind of pretty trinket. She's a good-looking girl; I tell you that." He paused and ran his hand through his hair. "Sophia, now, I know nothing about. She seems to stay pretty close to Lord Janus' wife. I think she's content with her place…not like Mathilde."

One of the kitchen girls breezed into Oliver's tent. She came to take the dishes and left-over food back to the cook area. She did not expect to find anyone in Oliver's tent and so paused, confused when she saw Jervey.

"Come right on in." Jervey smiled. "The trenchers are ready to go back to the cooking tent. Say, do you know Mathilde?" Jervey asked her. With a brief curtsey, the girl piled the leather cups - now empty of beer - the wooden plates, and the left-over heel of cheese in the largest trencher and nodded.

"She 'splained how to put my hair on top of my head." She laughed, blushing. "Keeping it there takes tight braiding and Mathilde showed me how to do that." She realized the Peers were in the room. Startled, she ducked her head, picked up the large trencher and hurried out.

Oliver and Roland nodded at each other, threw their mantles across their shoulders, and walked together to Queen Hildegard's tent. The nursery tent was next to hers. The Queen's serving wench told the two Peers the

Queen herself was at the river. Little Charles and Rotrud delighted in bathing, much to the Queen's pleasure. The servant described the spot where they would find the three of them. The two men headed toward the river, comparing the information they each gathered about Mathilde. Hildegard saw them approaching, waved at them, and hurried toward them.

"Good day to you both." She greeted them. "Your stroll would lead some to think you're relaxing; but I know you better. What's the worry?"

Roland smiled and winked at Oliver.

"No way to fool an astute woman," he replied, "and this is far more difficult when the woman's the queen!" Hildegard smiled in return and offered the men a seat on a near-by log.

"Excuse my poor, cushionless seats," she said, "but you won't find a lovelier place to rest. The tents seemed so confining to me, all of a sudden." Her head instinctively turned to her children, calling to each other in the water. She watched them intently, then turned back to the Peers.

"I'm afraid to take my eyes from them. I'm doing my best to cover it; but I trust no one to watch them now. If I were to lose my children by a moment's lapse in protection, I should never recover." She sat at the end of the log, rubbing her hands together unconsciously.

"Relax a little, your Majesty." Roland tried to comfort her. "Every eye in the camp is on your children. No one will infiltrate this court again. Oliver and I are trying to define Mathilde's motive in this. How long did she work in the nursery... almost a year? Do you have any insight about her? Do you think her capable of harming the children?" Hildegard shook her head from side to side.

"Nay," she answered. "I don't believe she would ever

hurt them...or allow them to be hurt. But she might agree to assist someone whose true plan she didn't know. After this horrible scare, my original impression of her haunts me." She shrugged. "Mathilde is a shallow girl, very immature. She looks for comfort and rewards. She delighted in dressing Rotrud, in choosing both children's clothes of a morning, in bathing and 'petting' them. She served serve their meals and kept them neat and clean. But she had no patience with their curiosity, with their pleas for stories, nor with the games they dreamed up."

"Aye," Gisela agreed as she walked up. "With a good heart, Mathilde responded to my requests for attending the children's physical needs. She always was more biddable if I promised a pretty trinket. It might be worth nothing; but if it pleased her eye, she would work very hard to please me and get it. But I did not judge her inexperienced. I believed her trustworthy and responsible."

"Aye," Hildegard replied, shaking her head. "Her youth has nothing to do with it. Mathilde works for the things she values; and those things are, often, near worthless trinkets. Though this was not exactly your question, Roland, my answer is this. She would forfeit the children or me or you for a pretty reward." Hildegard put her face in her hands, reliving again the horror of the empty tent.

"And so," Oliver began, "we must determine who offered her a trinket, who asked her to bring Carloman to them. I think all of us would just as lief not know her reward. I fear its cheapness would tear our souls." Oliver paused, overcome by this breach in the court's security.

"We continue to talk to people," Roland interjected. "Queen Hildegard, if you think of anything of import, anything at all, please send for us immediately." With that, he and Oliver bowed to the Queen and to Sister Gisela and left the queen's tent.

"Charlemagne promised he would talk with Mathilde," Roland said to Oliver. "May God ease his way and find us some answers."

"You two," Gisela called. "Wait a moment, please." Gisela quickened her steps and caught up with the two Peers.

"I've a question. Don't tell anyone I said this; but I'm discomforted. This is the third time there's been a direct, if unexplained move, against my brother's family, against his children. Do you believe the incidents can be linked?" Oliver's face paled; Roland looked at his friend and then, nodded, at Gisela.

"It looks suspicious to me." He replied. "But the King will not listen. He declares these people - unconnected to an enemy - are acting alone. I did beg him to be serious..."

"...as did I." Oliver interrupted.

"But he says I overreact." Roland spread his hands in exasperation. "Can you convince him of your concern, Gisela?"

"Nay, he says the same to me. We must all stay alert and keep as many eyes on the children as we can." Gisela answered.

Despite the mystery and wariness at his court, King Charlemagne's engagement in the affairs of his empire increased. Try as the Peers and the court nobles might, they could shed no light on the attemptedkidnapping of Carloman. Even after several months, neither Charlemagne nor the Peers had any insight into the theft of his son. The Peers could identify no conspiracy; neither could they find the whisper of a threat. The King safeguarded and over-saw his family's security as much as possible, but other duties demanded his attention as well.

***

Ibn al-Arabi finally sent a request to his friend, Charlemagne.

//

Charlemagne, my friend,

The governor of Sargossa agrees to submit to your rule. With his cooperation, your strength, and my army, we can overcome the fool in Cordoba. Meet me at the border of Toulouse and Septamania three weeks hence. We shall combine our armies and conquer.

Soon,

Ibn

//

"We march for riches and booty!" King Charlemagne told his soldiers as they headed south. Using his famous 'pincer' movement, the King directed one of his divisions to cross the Eastern Pyrenees into Spain; the second division crossed the Western Pyrenees.

Ibn Al-Arabi and Charlemagne's armies were to meet at Saragossa, a city controlled by the Arabs, in the Emirate of Cordoba. But when King Charlemagne appeared, the governor of the city reneged on his promise of support and refused to open the city gates. Enraged by the break of faith, Charlemagne laid siege to the city and waited. He camped for six weeks; but, hearing of another Saxon rebellion, he knew he must return home. Just as the King summoned his commanders, Roland hurried into the King's tent.

"Sire, we have a serious problem," he said without preamble. "The court seneschal, Eggihard, does not wish to burden you; but we have little recourse. Over the past weeks, the people here provided much of the food for our soldiers and the court, but they can do no more.

Their food is running low. They now face starvation, like their neighbors, and gaze into the questing eyes of their own children. They, understandably, refuse us any more provisions. They are even unwilling to sell foodstuffs to Eggihard. We must take Sargossa and end this siege."

"Call the Peers and commanders together," King Charlemagne responded.

"This siege profits us nothing." The King announced to his Peers. "It is true; I would delight in controlling northern Spain; but I dare not over-extend our resources any longer. The Saxons threaten our people once again. We're going home." He looked at each man in turn as they nodded their agreement. "Be on guard as we withdraw."

King Charlemagne ended the siege and left Saragossa behind. As the great army headed north, a messenger rode up to the king and handed him a rolled parchment. He thanked the man and thought of his likely hunger.

"Go to the cook-tent and eat before your return journey." Charlemagne said.

"Aye, Sire, as you say. Thank you." The messenger responded.

King Charlemagne unrolled the parchment. Long after he scanned the brief message, he sat staring at its words. The message almost stopped his heart. One of his newly-born sons, twins less than four months old, was lost, felled by a high fever.

'Please, I beg you, Charley.' Hilde wrote. 'Ride to the court as soon as possible. We all need you. Lothair is gone; I fear greatly for Louis. Come to us.'

"We turn north," the King decided. "We go to our own lands to engage the Saxons once more." King Charlemagne said not another word. His thoughts were with his wife and children, with the repeating sadness of losing yet another small babe. Hearing the noise of the army's movement, he suddenly realized Roland rode beside him. He nodded a greeting.

"Sire, may I suggest my contingent guard the rear of the army as we leave?" Roland volunteered. "You will, then, not have to maintain your own rear guard. And it will encourage our brave, fighting men...if they know there's a full regiment behind them. Some of those attacked the other night, outside the gates of Sargossa, are grievously wounded.Starting for home gives them strength. We shall take up the rear."

"A good suggestion, Roland." The King responded. "Let them see our backs." Roland turned his horse just as the court seneschal rode up beside him.

"Mayhap, when the people see the army leaving," Eggihard said, "they will be willing to sell us grain. Let me come with you, Roland. There still is much to do to feed the court."

"I welcome your company." Roland answered.

"I march with you also, Roland," Anselm announced. "Since we move toward home, I must schedule the judicial calendar for the King's return. Your slower pace will aid my thoughts. His Majesty's judgments will be sought by various Counts as we move back into Frankish lands."

"We'll travel together," Roland replied. "I could ask for no more appreciated companions."

Roland, always prepared, hung his traveling bag on his saddle. He bade his own personal regiment - men he specifically recruited, men dedicated to him - to while away an hour or so. All were free to relax while waiting for the Peers accompanying him to gather their belongings. Roland cobbled his great steed and sat with his back against a large tree. He waited only a short time. The men in the rear, soldiers and leaders all, were quick about their errands.

Roland got up to check his bags, patting one to be sure his gift to Jocelyn was safe. He had bought a ruby necklace from a jewel-maker outside Sargossa, knowing it would lie beautifully against her pale neck. It must be a wedding present, instead of a betrothal gift. This was the single time he allowed himself to admit he wished Jocelyn for himself. *But no one must ever know.* He told himself--not for the first time. *Oliver was both more certain and more swift than I and to him belongs the prize.* Roland smiled sadly, well-aware of the jewel he lost. I'd like to think she would have chosen me, if I only declared my interest before Oliver, he thought.

I put no value in the nickname the court gives me: the 'most handsome man in Christiandom.' "I surely don't think myself 'handsome,'"Roland muttered. "Looks wouldn't win Jocelyn anyway." *But I do know people always like me. It's been true since I was a small boy. But coming here, to King Pepin's court, made my reputation. I can't take credit for serving my king well; King Pepin and Charlemagne formed me.*

Roland's denial of his considerable looks was consistent with his personality. Everyone in the court loved him—for his daily conduct, for his chivalrous code and for his innate kindness. Even his soldiers commented on his gentle spirit, soft-spoken voice, and obvious concern for everyone. His position of older brother to the young boys at court described his orientation to everyone he met: helpful, caring, and protective.

Chapter 17

RONSCEVALLES

Waking up from a short nap, Roland heard someone approaching and got to his feet.

"Ready to ride, Roland?" Gelic asked. "Let's take up the rear and turn toward home, shall we?" The Peers mounted their horses and sat waiting for the last regiment of Charlemagne's troops to pass. The bulk of the army was now before them. Oliver raced up and stopped before Roland.

"I'll not be back here with you, old boy. I chose to come to the rear, but the King wishes me to ride ahead and scout for the most passable heights. We will ask much of our mounts on this march. He wishes to treat them gently and asks for the most level mountain paths we can find." He explained.

"Take good care and watch your back!"

"Aye, God speed, Oliver. I'll join you at the mid-day meal one day hence," Roland responded. "At the least, we are on our way home…whatever there is to face." Oliver nodded, raised his hand in farewell and rode forward.

The great army headed north, moving slowly because of the number of men, several thousand strong. As Roland suggested, the most dearly wounded were in a forward group, an effort to spare them the dust of so many thousands of feet. Roland held his forward troops back.

"Relax, men. We'll bite enough dust as we follow. Our mounts suffer more than we from it. Take the time to check your gear. We'll eat as we ride this night; but there'll be hot food as we camp. Has everyone got bread, cheese and traveling sticks?" he asked. Seeing the affirmative nods, he gave directions.

"Dismount for now. Walk about. We'll move forward, just as soon as this last contingent passes."

Roland waited as the dust from the soldiers' feet settled, then called for his men to move forward. They marched slowly as the troops ahead of them navigated the Pyrenees. Roland looked around at the mountains.

"Now's the time to halt for the day. These ravines will be treacherous as the sun goes down. Roncevaux Pass is right before us." He commented to Eggihard.

Suddenly, small stones pelted his head and his horse's rump. He looked up, just as he heard a cry rise from the rear. With only the small stone's warning, attacking Basques swarmed over Roland and his rear contingent. He and his troops were vastly overwhelmed, confused by the attack itself and by the ferocity of the Basque troops.

"Betrayed; we're betrayed!" Belic cried. At that moment, Eggihard turned to cut down a soldier advancing behind Belic. As his ax found the man's chest, Egginhard saw Ganelon, far away on a hilltop, urging Basque soldiers to the battle.

"Our own betrays us." Egginhard muttered as he fell to his death, an arrow through his back. Belic raced to Roland's side.

"We're o'ertaken, Roland. Sound the horn! Sound the horn!" Belic shouted.

"Nay, Belic! We can overcome them." Roland answered calmly. "Hold your sword high! These damn Basques will not overwhelm us! They're not Frankish men! Strike with your sword! Strike! Let your anger give it strength!" Roland smiled at Belic, even as he rode quickly to confront another soldier.

By the time Charlemagne became aware of the attack, everyone in the rear regiment was dead. Oliver, galloping to the rear as furiously as he could, saw the backs of the Basque soldiers as they rode away, scattering to conceal themselves in the mountains on each side of Ronscevaux Pass. He raced to a scene of total carnage. Nothing was left standing. Men and horses lay bleeding where they fell.

Oliver kneeled on the ground, shaking with grief and horror, listening to the crying shrieks of horses and the soft moans of dying men. Slowly gaining control of himself, he checked on the men who were still moving. He killed many of them – to be kind, to end their suffering. Eventually, he rode back to King Charlemagne to report. His head hung in shock and grief. Scarcely able to believe the massacre, the army paused to bury its comrades and turned once again toward home, weary beyond measure and overcome by sorrow.

***

The court mourned for all its lost men. Charlemagne, especially, seemed unable to move beyond the tragedy. He and Roland were close friends. Roland was almost his shadow, following Charlemagne everywhere, becoming the very personification of a Peer. And he was not the only loss to the King's well-being. Both his justice minister, the count palatine Anselm, and his seneschal, Eggihard, counted among the dead. The loss of the regiment, his friends and counselors was a catastrophe. It significantly undermined the King's confidence in himself. Even Oliver, now the closest friend to Charlemagne, worried over the King's muddled thoughts. But, finally, the King realized the deep sorrow must be put away; all had to reclaim their hopes and direction.

"You must speak to the court and to your soldiers, Charley." Hildegard urged him. "Everyone loved Roland and all feel his loss keenly. Others did not know Anselm and Eggihard as well. You and I, of a certainty, loved them but the court followers mourn them less."

"But Roland's sacrifice, his example of courage and loyalty, you must speak about him to us all. People are afraid of their own mortality. If such a soldier, such a shining light, can be snuffed out so quickly, what is the hope that an average person can survive? You must re-instill their hope. It is your duty."

"I know, Hilde, I know." the King replied. "But I'm at a loss; I can think of nothing adequate to say. Roland was larger than life and enriched all of us, just by being himself." Searching for a means to help his grieving people, King Charlemagne decided to offer a memorial service each fortnight until the Yuletide in honor of the brave men who died. Now, weeks later, the overwhelming sorrow was still with them.

***

On this, the third such memorial, Charlemagne laid a wreath of flowers in a small, now deserted, chapel along the court's route. As he bent to lay the flowers, he saw little Charles standing across from him. The boy looked beaten: his head cast down, his eyes red-rimmed, his clothing dirty, his hair plastered close to his head.

"Dear Lord," Charlemagne muttered, "my son is defeated, defeated by grief." He surreptitiously looked at others at the ceremony. All were slumped; many wept.

The King recognized his own sorrow in the faces of the court. Yet, as he glanced at his Peers, he saw resignation, strength and hope. "They have overcome their sorrow, and so must we all." Charlemagne turned to face the grieving soldiers, raised his right fist into the air and shouted.

"Long Live Roland of Brittany! Ever will he live in our memories, as will all those who succumbed with him. Long live, Roland!" And then, contrary to previous custom, the King began to speak.

"Take heart from your sorrow. Remember the ideals which these men lived: concern for each other, aiding the less fortunate, supporting their King, fighting for a better life for each of you. We do them no justice by wallowing in sorrow, by postponing our work, by dreading the next battle. They died working for us. We must live working in their memory. Cast off this sadness! We mourn them enough. They would wish us to move forward. Remember their lives! And rejoice we knew them, loved them, and have our memories of them to sustain us." The King finished speaking, his eyes scanned the mourners. He caught Theodoric's eye. Theodoric nodded imperceptibility. Charlemagne felt a core of sorrow leak from his heart. He knew he, himself, was now able to abandon his immediate sorrow and finally move toward the celebration of these remarkable men's lives.

"Go now," he said, "and be at peace, as our friends are at peace. They found their great reward." The whole company knelt to pray...for comfort, for courage, for the will to battle another day.

"Please join me by the river," Charlemagne invited. "We are having a sumptuous picnic. And I wish to parade our newly-trained colts and our newly-selected squires before you. This day marks our looking forward, no longer back."

***

Little Charles felt exhausted. He fled from the memorial to collapse on the forest floor. The weeks of mourning for Roland and his own personal loss of his uncle undermined the boy's spirit and, more importantly, clouded his usual sunny outlook. Charles knew he could never take Roland's place as a Peer. He couldn't; he was to be a king. But his uncle's death left him bereft. He couldn't imagine life without Uncle "Ro." He was gone; the world would never be the same again.

"Who'll practice sword play with me? Who'll help me with my numbers? I didn't learn near all Uncle "Ro" knew about horses, even about the baby ones!" Little Charles cried. He found it hard to believe he still had tears to shed. A slight scuffle of stone caught Charles' attention. He pushed himself to his feet, straightening just as his father's hand pushed a limb aside. The King came into the forest clearing.

"Are you here grieving alone, son?" Charlemagne asked. "You and I both need to help each other. We need to speak of your Uncle Roland and remember him."

"Nay, Poppa," little Charles replied, shaking his head. "I cannot speak! I cannot live without ever seeing him again." The lad sobbed, slumping back to the forest floor. He could hardly breathe past the huge fist in his throat.

"Oh, my son, you are not looking in the right places. You see him every day, my boy." Charlemagne answered softly, walking over to sit beside Charles on the ground. "You see him in so many things. When you hold your sword, Roland reminds you to lean to the left when you parry. He directs your hand 'just so' when you brush Samson, so as not to irritate the scar on his shoulder.

Adding and subtracting may never be easy for you; Roland will still be explaining sums to you when you're 40! I will just..." Charlemagne paused as Charles put out his hand to stop his father's words.

"But, Poppa, how did you know....?" Charles seemed bewildered.

"Oh, I know more than you imagine." Charlemagne assured him. "Your Uncle Roland reported your progress, as well as your blind spots, to me. He was extremely proud of you, Charles. You probably didn't realize Roland was eager to spend time with you. He said you really didn't need his direction with the horses - that you have a natural affinity, an understanding of them. He told me adding numbers is a challenge for you. You're better with the axe than the sword. I often envied Roland the time he had with you." Little Charles lay his head on his father's shoulder and squeezed his hand.

"I've decided to correct the loss. We'll ride together every day when I'm not on maneuvers, my boy, if you're willing. And we will speak often of your Uncle Roland. As long as we remember, he will never die."

"Dear Poppa, I want to." Charles murmured, crying quietly, his arms around Charlemagne's knees. The King sat with his son, waiting for his hiccups to subside. He did not realize the depth of little Charles' grief over Roland's death. I should take lashes, the King thought. *Mayhap a beating would make me more aware of others' struggles.* Little Charles stirred, loosening the grip around his father's legs.

"Poppa, I'm so worried. Do you think I could have saved Uncle Ro? I mean...like I helped with little Carl?" Charlemagne startled.

"You mean...when you heard the horse nicker and wondered about a babe the woman spoke of?"

"Aye." His son replied.

"Nay, no one could save Roland, Charles. He died in a battle, a fierce battle." He hugged his son close as Charles nodded his head. The boy gave a mighty sigh. Charlemagne felt a twinge of concern. *Can it be the lad saw or heard something worrisome?*

"What made you uneasy about Roland, Charles?" The King asked quietly.

"It wasn't people talking, Poppa." Little Charles answered. "It's more…a feeling, a worried idea." He shook his head, unable to explain to his father.

"Why don't you tell me about it?" Charlemagne asked.

"I heard Granpa Ganelon tell his captain something. I remember, when I heard him, it made no sense 'cause I couldn't think how he'd know such a thing."

"What did he say to his captain? If you can remember exactly his words, it would help me." Charlemagne made every effort to keep his voice neutral. He knew Charles explored all parts of the camp. And the soldiers, impressed by his eagerness to learn, welcomed them in their tents, at their tables, and among the horses. "Was it when you helped someone with a horse, mayhap?"

"Nay, Poppa. I was 'zamining (examining) Rotrude's pony's foot. He limped on our last ride. And so, I was kneeling under his neck. Grandpa Ganelon told that captain, the one with the long nose? …that we were resting soon, not making a long march, I mean. He said 'we don't march much today, not today.' He said. I didn't understand 'cause the wounded soldiers waited in front of the bowmen. You know, to start our march home…. before Uncle Ro fought, I mean."

Charlemagne held his breath, willing himself not to over-react and frighten his son.

"You did well to tell me, Charles. I'll ask around and

get to the bottom of it. But, don't you worry. None of us could have saved your Uncle Ro. War takes many of our fine men. You know that."

"I know." Charles acknowledged, though Charlemagne saw him wipe his eyes once again.

***

As the King comforted his son, the Queen was intent on giving some comfort of her own. She noticed Jocelyn rush away after King Charlemagne's words at the memorial. Hildegard went to find her.

After a brief search, the Queen came upon Jocelyn in the stables. Her pale, silk tunic was covered with hair and smudged along her belly where she had leaned over her horse, grooming her. Her eyes, swollen from weeping, looked bruised. Her headdress lay in the corner, under the trough. She looks an outlaw's wench, Hilde thought to herself. *Likely, Jocelyn's grieved more completely than any of us.* She watched the young woman's desultory brushing.

"Are you coming to the picnic, Jocelyn?" Hildegard asked, ignoring Jocelyn's sadness. "The turkeys and roasts on the splints are crackling with goodness. Come, your horse looks quite presentable. Do you plan to ride her before the court today?" Jocelyn barely acknowledged Hildegard's presence; she shook her head disconsolately.

"Nay," she answered softly. "I shall give the colt away. I find she has little interest for me now."

"What?" Hildegard asked, frowning in surprise. "What a poor idea! What an unreasonable thing to say." Her tone firmed. "Jocelyn, you must make peace with Roland's death, just as the rest of us. There is no more time to wallow in sorrow, to punish yourself."

"Punish myself?" Jocelyn asked. "Why would I do

that? Nay, nay. I have no interest in the colt any longer... not now. She just reminds me Roland is gone." The tears slipped from her eyes; but she ignored them.

"And you think this honors his memory, do you?" Hildegard asked sharply. "Look at yourself! You act as if death is foreign to our world, as if you should be immune from such sorrow! You did nothing to contribute to Roland's death; you are blameless. If you value the truth, think on this. Roland died the way he would have wished — serving Charlemagne, helping to keep the realm safe!" Hildegard stepped closer to Jocelyn. "Why do you belittle the man's sacrifice?" Jocelyn looked at her sharply, a retort on her lips.

"But I do not!" Jocelyn protested. "I love him even more for giving his life. I do!"

"Nay," Hilde objected. "You do not. Instead of speaking of him--of recounting his humor, his training skills, his ready smile, his spotless attire — you hide from all his friends and nurse your own sadness. This reduces his sacrifice to the mediocre, to the unnecessary, Jocelyn. Can you not see that?" Hildegard was disgusted. *Roland lived his life with vigor, with happiness and, aye, with being thankful for his opportunities. How dare these people negate the man...by feeling sorry for themselves, for thinking only of the man they lost, NOT the man they knew!*

"Everyone should be living enthusiastically in Roland's memory." Hilde said. "His sacrifice allowed others to continue to live safely, to come home. You all do dishonor him." Jocelyn said not a word, just stood staring into Hilde's face.

"I shall honor him," Jocelyn finally replied. "I shall honor him by giving up my own happiness." She shook her head. "I've decided not to marry. I will cancel my betrothal to Oliver." Hildegard's heart skipped a beat. How can she be so dense? She asked herself. *What good can come from such a choice?*

"Aye," she replied, "that choice will do a great deal of good, for a certainty." She tried to soften her voice but knew the sarcastic edge was there. Jocelyn startled at Hildegard's words. She stepped back.

"And what shall be your reason, I wonder?" Hildegard continued. "You and Roland were friends, nothing more, Jocelyn. No matter what fantasy you build in your mind, Roland never declared a love for you. On the contrary, he wished you happiness with Oliver. Again, you do dishonor him. If he wished to speak and did not, for love or you or of Oliver, he made his choice. He didn't choose to disrupt your relationship with the man who had already spoken for you, the man who loves you." Hildegard stopped speaking to let her words sink in. "How will you explain your disavowal of the betrothal to Oliver?" She asked. Jocelyn spread her hands in misery.

"I...I...will tell him I no longer care for him..." she said.

"Then, tell me to my face," a voice replied. Hildegard's breath caught. *It's Oliver! He's in the stable. Oh, my God, he heard Jocelyn!* She turned to look over her shoulder.

Oliver stood with a bridle in his hand, staring at Jocelyn. He face was pale, his eyes wide in shock. He grabbed his horse's bridle to steady himself.

"As a favor, Queen Hildegard," he nodded to her, "please give me a moment alone with Jocelyn." Hildegard nodded, passed Jocelyn, and walked quickly from the stable. She felt the young woman's horrified stillness as she left.

"I would like an explanation, Jocelyn." Oliver said. "I, of a certainty, will not hold you to a betrothal you no longer wish. But I would know the reason you do not care for me. I had no warning of this change in your affections." He ceased speaking, looking at Jocelyn intently. "It's impossible…" Jocelyn recovered herself. "I find I do not wish to marry, do not wish a home and family." Her voice strengthened as she fell on the idea. "I am quite content as a maid in the court and would take that as a vocation." At the last word, she turned to look at Oliver.

"You sound almost a nun," he responded, "though your ambition surely does not match the sisters'. Am I to believe you were fond of Roland, loved him; and, he, somehow, misled you? Since a relationship with him is not possible, you foreswear me as well?" Oliver dropped his eyes and scuffed the straw underfoot with his shoe.

"You cared nothing for me…all this time?" He asked quietly.

"Nay, nay," Jocelyn answered, even as she knew Oliver would disbelieve her response. "There was nothing between Roland and me. He was a friend who taught me much about the training of colts. …nothing more."

"Let's assume such was the case," Oliver replied. "Then, I need to know the reason you 'no longer care for me.' I believe those were your words to the Queen." He shrugged his shoulders, his eyes piercing into her face. "You did care for me once; but, now, you do not. Tell me, what caused this reversal? I must understand the reason for this change in your affection." Jocelyn did not respond. She had no answer for him. She shook her head slowly and turned toward the open door.

"Nay, Jocelyn," Oliver moved in front of the door. "I will have an explanation. Oh, do not trouble yourself. I consider our betrothal rescinded, as of this moment. But I will know your reason. What explanation am I to give the court and the King…when he asks me, as he will?"

"I cannot tell you," Jocelyn shouted. She saw the arch

of Oliver's eyebrows, the frown between his eyes deepen. She knew she made no sense.

"Have you dishonored me in some way, then?" Oliver asked. "Or did you embarrass yourself? I heard no indiscretion; but then, I would be the last to know, hummm?" At his implication, Jocelyn grew angry. She bit off her words in response.

"There was no indiscretion; I do assure you," she stated. "I do not wish to identify a reason. Reasons do not matter. If you accept the betrothal is ended, it is finished." She stepped around Oliver and hurried out of the stable. Oliver slowly closed the door, standing with his arm around his horse's neck. After long moments, he mounted and rode out, going toward the river and the court picnic.

Within a matter of days, winter was upon the Frankish realm. The court settled in the Aachen manor. Court members vowed to heal their spirits so they all might look forward to spring with renewed hope. Three days later, Jocelyn realized Oliver was no longer at court.

The winter was long; the ice and snow brutal. Even though spring brought battle planning, everyone welcomed the changed weather.

***

The annual assembly of Frankish chieftains ended. All agreed that the most insistent threat rose from the Saxon's previous, late autumn rebellion. Because of the Roncesvelles attack, Charlemagne's army did not get to Saxon lands before the winter set in. Now, defeat of the Saxons was his most important task. Already, several tribes were on the move. Gathering his fresh and rested troops, Charlemagne marched, once again, toward his most stubborn enemy. The older soldiers joked with each other, well-used to the King's urgency in battle.

"You don't need to tell me our route, Rufus," a grizzled old veteran said to his companion. "We left Sargossa to punish them last summer before the sadness hit us all. We knew Saxony would be first on our list this battle season."

"It would be refreshing to have a new foe, don't you think?" Rufus replied.

"Ha," the old veteran, Franks, laughed. "The only reason the seasons change is so King Charlemagne can attack the Saxons once more. You'd think he'd grow weary of the constant battle! Sometimes I wonder about the point of it all. We just massacre a group of them, force them to swear allegiance. They surrender, vow they will accept the Christian faith." He shook his head. "In another year, we're back...doing the same thing again."

"Right. Don't seem useful to hold a knife to a man's throat in the name of religion, does it?" Rufus asked. "We not showing much 'Christian spirit,' huh?"

"You know, Rufus," Franks replied. "I got little use for this religious stuff. I just want to earn my keep and go home to help my woman and lit'le ones at harvest time. I did drop seeds in the soil this last month...before the King sent out his call for troops. I wish I could think this battle coming up would be the last one. My woman needs help with the planting and the hoeing...aye, with the harvest, too. 'Dem crops keep us through the winter. It be hard work for her, without my hands 'dere to help. As for this new religion, seems to me the old gods did right good. I can't see much change with the Christian god. We still struggling, much like always." Franks added.

"The olde ways, they was good. I did hate when the commander cut down the Saxon's tree, though! You 'member the name the Saxons called it? Immisur, was that it?" Rufus asked, shaking his head.

"Like you, I try to follow the ole ways. Them I can understand. I know the tree meant something else. What did Garston call it—a simbul?" Rufus asked, his brow wrinkling.

"I asked my nephew about that. He got himself a job at court. All of 'em call the tree a 'symbol', means it stands in place of something else. ...kinda like the full moon means women think about love." Franks explained.

"The tree was called..aye, Irminsul - that's the name. The Saxons believed their tree held up the world. Now a thing like that, we ought to just let it be! I see no need to chop it up. Men do strange things, 'specially kings!" Franks cackled.

"You can laugh 'til your hair be white," Rufus added. "But I figure the felling of that tree gave us a fortnight more of battle. Maybe that's the reason the Saxons marched agin us last season. And here we be fighting them now! Chop down a sacred tree? I'd be mad myself and I'd fight more fierce, be I a Saxon! There are some beliefs cause no harm. One of them was that tree." Rufus declared. Remembering something else, he continued.

"Did you know? Some of those Saxon families we captured last year, Lord Theodoric moved them 'round close to my place. People roared mad at first, didn't want 'em there. But my Barston, he's a friend to one of the Saxon lads."

"'Popa,'" he said to me, "'this lad's a good one; he showed me about fishing.' They caught enough fish for our family and his, too. 'Course, the priests be there pushing all the God talk down their throats."

"Hell, man, be careful. Don't let the King hear you!" Franks warned. He knew his and Rufus' views of the battle were very different from those of the king. In fact, were he at the King's banquet table, Franks would never believe the King's description of their last battle.

***

Charlemagne finished discussing the battle against the Saxons with an envoy from the Arabian peninsula.

"It was a hard-fought battle." the King declared. "One can but admire the strength and courage of these Saxon soldiers."

"Were many of them close to you, Poppa?" little Charles asked his father. "Did you feel afraid to fight in the battle?" Queen Hildegard looked over at her son. How unusual for him to speak at table, the Queen thought.

The mid-day repast was often so long, with poetry readings and philosophical discussions, that weariness overcame her eldest son. He practiced with his little bow every day to strengthen his sword arm, just as the soldiers, squires, and Peers honed their own skills. Sitting at the banquet table was a silent effort for him, for the talk sometimescontinued for hours. A delegation of holy men and scholars shared in today's meal. Now, led by the King, they debated the use of Latin in church services.

The Queen smiled at them, excused herself, and herded her children from the table. Charlemagne did not often require them to join the court in the banquet hall; but, this day, he asked Charles and Rotrud to help him welcome the holy men. The Queen stepped aside and nodded at her children.

"Welcome to the Frankish realm." Little Charles said to those at the long table. "Come back to visit us."

"Happy to see you." Rotrude curtseyed, watching her father from the corner of her eye.

Queen Hildegard said her goodbyes and led her children from the room, thinking to take them to play with

262

this year's puppies. But, seeing Rotrude's heavy eyes, she decided on a mid-day sleep instead. Tucking, Rotrude in, she heard a shout from little Charles.

"Nay! Nay! I don't want to use a sword," the boy screamed. "Leave me alone! I'm tired of my friends; I don't want to see them. I'm sick! Leave me alone. Let me be!"

Queen Hildegard rose slowly; her body awkward with her sixth pregnancy. She went to her son's sleeping bench. Whatever upset little Charles did not waken him. He slept but not quietly. Tossing and turning on his sleeping pad, he grimaced with determination; and, it seemed, some frustration. Hildegard felt his forehead and discovered it was hot and damp. She dipped a cloth in cold water and gently wiped his face. Charles struggled from sleep, saw his mother sitting beside him, and burst into tears.

"Ma-Mam," he cried. "I'm sick. I feel hot and sticky." He threw the linens off and sobbed in great gulps, a much more serious reaction than his mother expected. He looked at her seriously.

"I don't want my sword anymore, Ma-Mam. Can I give it to Carl, do you think?"

Not want his sword? I seriously doubt that, Hildegard thought. *This is the boy who dragged his sword behind him.... when he was too small to raise it!* Hildegard gently rubbed his back while removing his breeches. They felt wet from the sweat which drenched his body.

"We'll talk about your sword later. For now, I'm going to sit here with you, Charles. You're hot and sweaty. Let me get you some dry clothing. I'll stay until you sleep. Relax now. You need extra sleep and shouldn't eat again, I think. See if you can sleep until dark." She urged. Hildegard rubbed her son's shoulders and stroked the back of his head.

"Ma-Mam, don't think I'm lazy," the lad mumbled. "I feel bad. Mayhap, tomorrow I can have a holiday...no practice." Charles' voice was low, muffled by the covers. Queen Hildegard's constant back rub, gentle and soothing, made his eyelids droop.

"Sometimes it's just too much. The boys all fight me hard; and, then, if I'm about to best one of them, the others warn: 'Be careful, don't hurt the prince. Don't make him your enemy.' When someone warns them, by saying that, my friend stops fighting! I can never just win; there always has to be the talking. What is all this fighting...." His voice trailed off as Hildegard's hands worked their magic.

The Queen continued to sit by her eldest son, massaging the tension from his young shoulders and comforting him with her presence. The King, coming in to bid her adieu before his next battle, found her crying silently, still rubbing little Charles' back. He motioned Hildegard to leave Charles' sleeping bench and walked her outside.

"What's the matter?" The King asked. Charlemagne couldn't bear to see Hildegard cry. He felt an utter failure when he saw her unhappy. Her tears, especially, he couldn't take. "Surely, Charles isn't seriously ill. He ate a large serving of stew, currants, peaches and cheese at table."Hildegard stared, surprised the King noticed his son's appetite.

"Nay, he's not sick in the usual sense, I think. He's much quieter lately, seemingly absorbed in his own thoughts. I need to sit down and talk with him. There's some problem which I haven't identified. After our midday meal, he was agitated, not at all himself. I'll ask your lady-mother to oversee the kitchen tomorrow. I must find some answers to little Charles' behavior." Charlemagne, knowing his wife wouldn't be denied in concern for her child, hugged her goodbye and reminded her to be safe.

"Me, safe?" Hildegard laughed. "You're the one off into battle again, Sire. You're the one who needs safe wishes."

"This will be an easy foray," the King replied. "The scouts have described the enemy's fighting style and weaknesses. We greatly outnumber them. Look for me in three days' time, mayhap two will do it. All will be well." Charlemagne took his leave.

"Goodbye, my dear lord." Hildegard smiled as he left the tent. With just the usual small twinge of worry, she returned to her sleeping son. She sat down, put her feet on a bench, and began to review the last few days, concentrating on Charles' behavior. The room was warm. Charles made little mumbling noises in his sleep; and soon, Hildegard herself quietly snoozed in her chair. Queen Mother Bertrada stuck her head in the door, saw the two quietly sleeping and withdrew. She gave strict instructions no one was to enter the tent; the weary two needed rest.

Chapter 18

Resolutions

Hildegard awoke some time later, glanced around to orient herself and glanced over at Charles. His legs were close to his chest; mayhap, he's cold. The Queen thought. She arranged a linen cover over him and gave him a small kiss on the temple. He smiled briefly but remained asleep. She remembered Jocelyn's entrance, her dressing Rotrude and their leaving. She relaxed on the sleeping bench.

"I can only kiss my boy when he sleeps," Hildegard murmured quietly. "He doesn't want to seem a baby, so my kisses must be given in secret. I hope he knows I love him dearly." She walked to the tent door and asked the man-at-arms to bring her bread and cheese. "Nay," she replied to his inquiry. "Little Charles won't be eating as yet."

After her meal of warm grain mix, barley bread, and goat cheese, Hildegard sat down again to puzzle out Charles' behavior. All of a sudden, he sat up in bed, slapped the covers, and frowned. She moved quickly to his side, just in time to hear him murmur.

"Please, don't kill him. He's a good king." The lad said. "What will we do? Please don't kill, Poppa." Charles whimpered once and, then, was silent. Hildegard watched his face, grimacing with strain and fear. Slowly, she patted his arm, trying to reassure him. Charles sighed, lay down and settled into the bed linen, quiet once more. The Queen left her sleeping boy and sought out Rotrude.

It was near dusk but Rotrude was picking pears from trees in a neglected orchard, one which once stood adjacent to a long-forgotten village. Jocelyn was making her a crown of blossoms.

"Is Charley sick, Ma-Mam?" Rotrude asked with concern, as her mother approached.

"Nay, I believe not, Rotrude," Hildegard replied. "He just seems exhausted...and troubled to me. He hasn't been himself lately. Do you know anything about it?" Rotrud was the observant one. She noticed all the happenings throughout the court. Hildegard felt no surprise when Rotrud shook her head affirmatively.

"He's changed, Ma-Mam." Rotrud responded. "Before, if he teased me, he was sweet, too. But now, he doesn't talk to me." She sniffled. "He doesn't talk to anyone." She rolled a pear on the ground. "He waits for Uncle Ro to come back." Rotrud was silent for a moment, then she spoke again. "He won't play games; he won't sing...or listen to stories! His rides with Poppa stopped, 'coz of the fighting."

"Does he talk about fighting or about being tired of battle training?" the Queen asked her daughter.

"He just wants to make Poppa happy. He told me he has to fight hard, like Poppa. He wants to fight when Poppa does, beside him." Then, she looked frightened. "Will Poppa let him fight? Will Poppa do that, Ma-Mam?" Before Hildegard could answer, Rotrude continued. "He wants to be a fighter. He fights with his knife and gets real tired." Rotrud obviously saw and heard much to arrive at this opinion. There was no doubt in her voice.

"No matter how excellent a soldier he becomes, he'll not go into battle any time soon; I can promise you that." Hildegard said before thinking. *What is my boy imagining?* "I had best go back and check on him, Rotrude. He doesn't rest easy." The Queen said as she turned toward the tent.

Queen Hildegard checked inside and found little Charles still asleep. She left the tent again to sit in the sun. She remembered little Charles' dedication in the practice yard, staying late to smooth his thrusts and begging Oliver to fence with him. Last week he asked Charlemagne for permission to watch the bowman; he wanted to try to make a bow by himself. Of late, he spent even more time than usual at the stables, currying his horse and rubbing oil into the bridle. When Hildegard told him not to neglect his studies, he told her soldiers had to learn to stay alive, that was the most important lesson of all. Hildegard was abruptly still.

"Oh, dear Lord, please help me. He's afraid Charlemagne's going to die. It all makes sense: learning to be the best soldier, practicing sword play over and over, trying to improve his aim with the bow, hoping to go to battle—to protect his father." Hildegard almost wept. *I know exactly the battle my son is waging with himself. God knows, I've the same concerns…every time there's a battle.* Hildegard laughed at herself, remembering the times she begged the King to choose a permanent home for the court. She so yearned for a single place to live. But, truth be told, she would no longer stay behind when Charlemagne fought than she would run away. *I must stay in close proximity to the battle; my being there protects him in some way. My worry would be unbearable, if I were not near. So, Charles is afraid, just like his mother. What can I do to help my boy? The Christ knows, I search and search but find nothing to help myself with the self-same worry.*

Once, Hildegard identified little Charles' problem, she went about her daily affairs, delving for some solution. Her mind and heart, both, worked to devise some answer for him. She knew it would take time. She had to digest this, analyze and think. She worked on the problem with all her heart. The Queen thought of all the mothers who worried over the fates of their sons. She found scarce comfort.

Thinking of all the men who fought and the constant nature of battle, she noticed dust rising from the on-going battle in the distance. Hildegard didn't, however, imagine the enemy's thoughts.

***

The young enemy soldier lay on his stomach and looked over the ridge as his uncle whispered beside him. As far as he could see, men atop horses ringed the valley. He thought the original Frankish deployment huge. It, however, was nothing compared to the thousands of additional soldiers marching now into the valley. Jurst didn't realize the battle still raged until his uncle pitched forward, an arrow protruding from his back. He looked around panic-stricken, having no idea where to run or, even, if he should run. He fell forward as his uncle's arm pulled him to the ground.

"Under me," his uncle mumbled, as blood trickled from his mouth. "Get under m' body and don't move." His uncle's fingers pulled his sleeve and, suddenly, became lax. Jurst lay on his back and pushed to raise his uncle's broad shoulders. As he slid from under them, he felt the slow, sticky trickle of blood seeping from his uncle's wound. He grabbed his uncle around the chest in fear but just as quickly realized this would catch someone's attention. Jurst wiggled back under his uncle's chest and flung his arm across his forehead. Unknown to the young man, blood from his sleeve smeared across his face. The dark blood marked him as grievously wounded.

At the very moment he laid his head back, the first of Charlemagne's soldiers reconnoitered among the dead. A soldier not far from Jurst moaned softly and got a sword in his gut for reply. Jurst heard the slow 'whush' as the air left the dead man's lungs.

If I wait, I'll be so fearful that I'll never escape. I'm not hurt. I can sneak away. Jurst was afraid his trembling would dislodge the body atop him. A burly, gnarled soldier walked among the dead and wounded, kicking bodies for any signs of life. Jurst held his breath as the soldier kicked his foot. Jurst let it flop as much as possible, hoping it appeared lifeless.

"Looks like battling with the Saxons is never going to end, don't it?"

A grey-haired soldier said. "Gods! How do we tell Franks from Saxons? What a bloodbath!" The older of the two soldiers shook his head.

"Mighty bloody!" His companion answered. "The dirt's wet with blood. How many wounded are there?" He looked over to his left. "The healers are coming down the ridge now."

"It's too late for most of these poor souls," his companion observed. "We'll start at the edge of this field. We need to line these bodies up. Here, I'll move the Saxon bodies; you get our men: living on the right, dead on the left." Franks directed, staring at the battlefield.

Jurst let his body go limp. It'll be dark before they get up here, he thought. *I wonder if anyone I know is still alive.* Jurst lay there, spending the last three hours of daylight listening for movement or moans around him. His uncle's men were all in this area. Despite his heightened awareness, Jurst could hear no sounds of life. *I have to move as soon as dark comes. I can sneak away in the forest.* Jurst began to wiggle from under his uncle's body. He heard voices.

"This was a massacre—on both sides, murder of all who stood." A deep, throaty voice spoke.

A large man, almost as tall as Jurst's older uncle Wundkind, clasped the man beside him around the shoulders.

"Who's the butcher here, Larson, us or them?" He asked.

"Don't make no mind, King Charlemagne. It all seems butchery to me." Larson replied.

"No other way to describe it, no other way, old man. Burn the bodies—as quickly as you can. I'll send more men to assist you." The large man said over his shoulder as he walked away into the night.

*So...*Jurst thought. *That's Charlemagne. A shame he wasn't cut down, just like my uncle here. May he rot in hell!* Jurst, unseen, glared at the man whose troops killed his uncle and massacred his friends. *Mayhap, I'll help him along the road to hell.*

***

"Rinaldo, I need to you to spy for me." Charlemagne said to his Peer.

"Of a certainty, your Majesty. Where would you have me go?" Rinaldo replied.

"You stay right here, son. I want you to be more alert than usual to the 'doings' of the court. I've information which may concern betrayal." The King rubbed his forehead. "We may have a traitor within the court. There's no proof, just my worrisome doubts. Keep your eyes and ears open. Oh, aye! And spend some time with the com-

271

pany captains, can you? I especially want to know who speaks of Ronsevalles, of the attack, of those we lost."

"Sire, can you give me any particulars…as far as individuals, I mean to say?"

"Nay, of that I'm not certain, Rinaldo. Look for anyone who seems to have had early knowledge of the Basques attack. We did not see its beginning and could tell nothing but that a massacre took place."

"You can't think one of ours commanded this, Sire?" Rinaldo's voice reflected his shock.

"Nay, I refuse to think that now…which is the reason I want you to listen and evaluate. Get some of the younger Peers to help you. Soldiers may talk easier in front of them."

"As you say, Sire. I will do my best." Rinaldo replied.

***

With each battle won, Charlemagne sent missionaries into Saxony to convert the people. Often he relocated the captured peoples out of Saxony to another part of his realm. The King was relentless in demanding all conquered people convert to Christianity, as well as swear allegiance to him. He wrote laws and regulations to rule each conquered tribe. In this year, 779, he also penned the 'Capitulary of Herstal' which established and described the ideal Christian kingdom.

When the battle season ended, Charlemagne once again delighted in the cultural offerings of his court. He surrounded himself with scholarly men — poets, orators, theologians, philosophers — and urged everyone to learn from them. For this mid-day meal, a group of intellectuals, scholars, and young monks joined the King's court.

They traveled the road to Parma, journeying to the holy Church there. In various missives, the Pope urged young monks to join the journey, both to be exposed to the want and poverty outside the cities and to strengthen their abilities to care for themselves. This group's delight in being in the midst of a large throng showed in their glistening eyes and wide smiles. Abbot Fulrad prevailed upon their leader, Paul the Deacon, to extend their journey and spend some days with the court.

Charlemagne, welcoming those he hoped would provide support and teachers for his educational plans, made an effort to remember each and every name, as well as their final destinations. He begged them to take seats, sup at his table, and enjoy the court's entertainment. 'Though we may be mobile,' he was fond of saying, 'we are not barbarians lost in the wilderness of ignorance.'

As a rule, Charlemagne ate well and was generous in welcoming travelers to his table. He did not countenance drunkenness and had high expectations of his companions' behavior. His young children were often at table with him and he demanded decorum and self-control for their sakes. Because his time was so dear, the King used the mid-day meal to pursue his interests and to encourage thought and informed discourse.

'Court entertainment,' as he called it, varied daily from poetic readings--often by the poets themselves--to astronomical discussions, to a rendition of old German fairy tales, to philosophical or theological discussions. In the company of religious pilgrims, priests or bishops, conversation might easily turn to church law or interpretations of existing religious tenets.

Charlemagne's thoughts often reflected a blend of Germanic traditions, Christian beliefs and pagan ideas. The Frankish king used his formal banquets as an opportunity to put forth ideas and gauge reactions. Such information was useful before he promulgated specific legal and ecclesiastical changes. In this group bound for Parma was Paul the Deacon. He often joined other illustrious thinkers in King Charlemagne's court and, like others, made his home there for months at the time.

This evening, there was double cause for celebration - the arrival of the pilgrims and the birth of the King and Queen's second daughter after Adelheid, Bertha.

***

"Now I have two beautiful buds." Charlemagne bragged as he stroked four-year-old Rotrude's hair. "You look like your mother, Trudsy; but your baby sister has my eyes and hair. Let us dare hope she will get some of your grace and quickness, not her Poppa's big... legs!" He laughed.

"Na-a-y, Poppa." Little Rotrude objected, shaking her head back and forth. "My little Bertha is boo-ti-ful! She is tiny; no big legs. She has her legs! She is MY baby; isn't she Poppa?" Rotrude looked at her father intently.

"Aye." Charlemagne reassured Rotrude. "You must share her, just sometimes." He interjected as he saw the worry line appear on Rotrude's face. "But she IS your baby, a sister at last!"

"She won't be mean to me. Louis is mean. He pushes and he pinches hard. But if he hurts Bertha, I throw him on the ground." She spoke fiercely, determined to protect her baby sister. The Queen, taking the hands of her two older children, bade the visitors a good afternoon and urged Charles and Rotrud to follow her. As much as the King loved talking with his precocious daughter, he must host the visiting party.

"Come," Hildegard said to her children. "We must rest before swimming in the river later." She bent down between them, seeming to straighten their little tunics.

274

"What do you say to the visitors?" She whispered.

"Happy to see you," Rotrude piped out, making a half-curtsy toward the monks and smiling broadly. "We hope to wel..kum you here again."

"A safe and pleasant journey," Charles added. The King nodded at them both, patting Charles on the shoulder as he passed. Then, Charlemagne gave all his attention to Alcuin, the Anglo-Saxon scholar leading the group.

Anxious to strengthen his plans for educating the people, King Charlemagne invited Alcuin, the famous scholar from Tours, to visit his court and to meet the other leading scholars who resided there. The King did so wish Alcuin to head his Palace School. Alcuin was one of the most renown intellectuals of his time--a prodigious scholar who, while not a holy man, commanded much knowledge in religion, philosophy, literature, language, and the fine arts.

This group of learned men, accompanied by the young monks, traveled to Rome to meet with the Pope and to discuss liturgical traditions. The court, while respectful and humble toward its spiritual guests, used this opportunity to celebrate. Visitors were, after all, sometimes months apart; and, during battle season, there was no time for parties and lightheartedness. This night there were poetry readings, a small dramatic presentation, songs and music, as well as speeches. Most of the welcomes and thanks were mercifully brief.

After the meal and entertainments, Charlemagne approached the scholar from Tours and asked for a private moment. They spoke at length. Near the end of their conversation, Alcuin gently refused King Charlemagne's offer of employment in the court's Palace School. The King, disappointed but still determined, spoke more directly to the scholar he so admired.

"Your influence will be far-reaching, Alcuin." Charlemagne continued his argument. "I mean to provide education to everyone in the realm. We start with the children and, then, expand learning to the adults. At first, the children or their parents may determine their educational goals. Many will prefer to be apprenticed. I know and accept the choice. But others will want more. As our plans unfold and various opportunities arise, all will be expected to have formal learning. We will develop trade, expand the goods we offer, teach our people dialects and languages other than our own. We must, in short, develop better choices for the Frankish people. For this, there must be education for everyone. I can't wait any longer to begin! I mean to implement basic, educational plans immediately." Alcuin still shook his head. His refusal moved the King to try another argument.

"As the director of my Palace School, you'll lay the educational foundation for this entire realm. Think on it!" Charlemagne urged. "You will have complete freedom. You'll define the content of a liberal education. You'll be free to choose the teachers, the methods to use for instruction, the length of a student's study. It'll all, every bit, be in your hands! If a thing is possible and you wish it done, so shall it be. I will, I promise, support your every request. We shall create a world of learning! How might a true intellectual, the most effective teacher in this world, refuse such an opportunity? Your influence will link with mine. You'll have complete autonomy to develop an academy, a center of learning and intellectual discussion, as well as to expand our scriptorium, to preserve the world's great writings. You'll personally direct the copyists and send writings to the abbeys, monasteries, to all centers of learning. You will be the creative force; all educational decisions are yours."

Alcuin listened solemnly, impressed by this king's generosity, aye, but by his love of learning as well. Alcuin smiled, enthused by - it was true - by Charlemagne's passion; but he turned down the offer.

"I thank you for such an honor, Sire," he responded; "but I cannot leave Tours. It's the center of my universe. As tempting as your Palace School sounds, I cannot imagine myself any place other than in Tours. I am sorry." King Charlemagne bowed his head in disappointment. He vowed that the rejection was momentary. Not today, mayhap, but in the future Alcuin would head his palace school. He would bring the dream to life.

Wishing the travelers a restful afternoon, Charlemagne returned to his battle tent to think on the Holy Father's needs. On the morrow, he was to speak to Abbot Fulrad about Pope Hadrian's latest demands.

Chapter 19

Demands and Refusals

"What's wrong with the Pope?" Charlemagne asked Abbot Fulrad, his voice under tight control. "He demands too much. Always does he pursue me, ever trying to increase the holdings of the Roman Church. He never fails to ask; his requests make me weary. Can't he understand: there are many needs in Frankland, many undertakings which deserve support?" Charlemagne ran his hand through his long hair, trying to curb his temper. I must not complain to Fulrad, he cautioned himself. *It is possible he will send word to the bishops and other church fathers suggesting I grow weary of the Pope. But, it **is** the truth. His constant demands for more land, for additional protection from his enemies, for more believers exhaust me. The man is a locust, eagerly gobbling up everything he sees. Ha! His missives speak constantly of conquests for the Church...which I'm to undertake.*

Abbot Fulrad remained silent; he despaired of the King's reaction to Pope Hadrian and of the Pope's demands of the King. Hadrian may ask Charlemagne but it will obtain him little, the Abbot thought to himself.

"He makes a pest of himself, Sire." The Abbot answered. "His requests never change; he repeats and repeats. Why does he think you the only source of land. Why not turn to his Italian nobles? Surely, they owe the

Church allegiance...and conquests as well?" He looked at Charlemagne's irritated face. "You and the Pope both identify the same needs of the Church; but he feels you move too slowly in filling those needs."

"It is not my responsibility to make the Pope a land-owner, Fulrad," Charlemagne disputed. "I promised him nothing! His eyes glisten brightly on every piece of land around Rome. He is fanatical in trying to increase Papal property. And, now, he has the gall to demand I name Spoleto a part of papal lands! I will not do it. The Pope does over-reach."

"Aye," Fulrad admitted reluctantly. "He has a huge thirst for extending Papal control, I admit; but he strives only to secure the business of the church."

"And to secure his own power," King Charlemagne added. "I will read no more of his missives. He is insatiable. No more, Fulrad. You read the parchments he sends and reply to him. I am finished with this."

"But, Sire," Fulrad replied, "he does not wish my opinions."

"Too bad," Charlemagne allowed. "They are the only ones he is likely to get. I will not write to him or respond to these outrageous demands. Keep his letters to yourself. You may tell him I wish no more communications at this time. Thank God our realm is far from Rome." Abbot Fulrad nodded, trying to keep himself from rushing out of the chamber. Thank God, I do not have to interact with these two men in the same room, he thought.

As Charlemagne watched the Abbot leave, he heard the trumpet of a herald's horn. Soon, a guard hurried into the library.

***

"What is the meaning of this fanfare?" The King asked

the guard resentfully. "I expect no visitors."

"Sire, a messenger has just come into the camp. He asks for an immediate audience with you. Your majesty, it is the Lord Hildebrand, governor of Spoleto."

"Hildebrand?" The King asked. "He's come across the Alps to greet me? He is here in Compiegne? Ahh... interesting." Charlemagne smiled. "Very well, I am overjoyed to welcome him to our court.

"What have we here?" the King muttered to himself. "First, I get a missive from Pope Hadrian demanding the duchy of Spoleto for the Mother Church. Now, on the heels of the missive, I'm to have a visit from Hildebrand himself. Can it be? Do Hildebrand and the Pope hire the same spies? They share the same timetable, it appears."

Charlemagne changed his everyday tunic for one richer in embroidery and of finer cloth. The exquisite embroidery in gold thread, the rubies and emeralds embedded in its ornamentation, transposed him from the king of a region to the king of a realm. His brow wrinkled as he fingered his attire, though he waited patiently for his visitor. The King chuckled to himself.

"My dear King Charlemagne." Lord Hildebrand enthused as he knelt to the King. "It refreshes my spirit to see your Majesty looking so well. Had I realized the delight this visit to your court brought me, I'd have journeyed here a fortnight ago." He surreptitiously waved his hand as retainers brought in richly decorated chests, filled with gold, jewelry, rich tapestries, and sheer silk from the East.

"Welcome to my court, Hildebrand," King Charlemagne replied. "I'm delighted to see you. Welcome to Frankland! You make a long journey, do you not?" *Truth be told, Hildebrand looks fresh as a springtime blossom.* "It's almost time for the mid-day meal. Please, rest, refresh yourself, and join us at table. We have much to discuss, I think." Lord Hildebrand's eyes sparkled; he smiled ruefully.

"I daresay we should re-visit old alliances, Sire; reforge them, my liege." Hildebrand suggested.

"I've no doubt renewed alliances will be as propitious for you as for me." King Charlemagne agreed, his smile duplicating his visitor's. "Come, let me point out the banquet tent for you. We'll welcome you there in an hour's time."

Charlemagne and Lord Hildebrand re-iterated their support for one another. Charlemagne assured Hildebrand he still considered him the natural ruler of Spoleto. Since the fall of the Lombard kingdom, Hildebrand ruled the city. *I see no need to tinker with this agreement. Pope Hadrian can dream forever. I will not cede Spoleto to him, no matter how badly he craves it. Hadrian needs such a message.* King Charlemagne told himself. He felt invigorated by his decision. His satisfaction was short-lived, however, as news of another Saxon incursion into Frankland reached him. Hurriedly the next morning, even before his prayers, Charlemagne met with Hildebrand and re-iterated his support.

"But I must march, Hildebrand." Charlemagne said. "Thank you for this visit. Give a thought and a prayer to my army as we move west."

"By all means, Sire. Success in your journey and in your battles, of a certainty."

"Thank you; a safe journey home to you." Charlemagne replied as he hurried to his waiting army.

***

Even though the Frankish soldiers marched hurriedly, without rest, they had little difficulty quelling the attacks which greeted them just inside the border lands. The overwhelming numbers of the Frankish army simply overran Widukind's forces. Saxony, once again, fell to defeat. King Charlemagne restored a semblance of peace and turned south, marching toward Italy.

***

"I must make this trip to Italy." The King confided to Oliver. His Peer, just last night, returned from his self-imposed scouting expedition. He was pale, had lost weight, and was weary; but, at least, he was back home. "How are you, my friend?" Charlemagne asked.

"None the worst for wear, Sire." Oliver replied. "My grief for my lost marriage remains but I did find, Charlemagne, that running does no good. So, here I am." He half-smiled and shrugged. "And you, Sire. How goes life for you?"

"Right now, it could be better, to tell you the truth." The King answered. "I can postpone the trip no longer, Oliver. To Rome, we must go. Hadrian chafes at my 'lack of concern,' as he puts it. We will make our appearance, visit for a short space, and leave Rome quickly. Mayhap my past distance from him will make the Pope more amenable to reason. Had I no need of him, this visit would take place two years hence."

The King stared toward the horizon, clearly reluctant to begin the journey. But he promised the Pope a visit; and, it was now seven years since he was in the Holy City.

"I must go." The King repeated. "But I can use this journey to evaluate the political situation in Lombardy. After the Saxon battles, I found our palantine in Worms overwhelmed with judicial duties. Now is the time to evaluate palantine success in Lombard lands. There is a chance that the responsibilities of the office may be too demanding for one man. I cannot risk a Lombard noble's stepping in to 'aid the King,' as he would describe it." He shook his head, his face reflecting disgust. "I will never again trust the Lombard nobility." He looked thoughtful but, soon, turned back to Oliver.

"Let's march against our eternal enemy, Oliver. Glad to have you back among us. Many people missed you, particularly little Charles." He put his hand on Oliver's shoulder.

"Just a moment. Please do me a favor. Talk with Rinaldo about the task I recently gave him. I have reason to think there may be someone in the court who...does not have my best interests at heart."

Oliver turned quickly to the king and opened his mouth to speak.

"Nay. Say nothing now, Oliver. Just confer with Rinaldo. He'll fill you in on my suspicions. I grow more and more concerned for the safety of my family. See what you can find out: you and Rinaldo."

"Of a certainty, Sire. I'll talk with him immediately."

***

After the battle against the Saxons, Charlemagne hastened to dismiss his soldiers and marched to Pavia. He wintered there and in the early spring steered his mobile court toward Parma. During this journey, he found much disarray in the governing jurisdictions and a lack of clarity, both in judicial interpretations and in criminal sentencing. He even went so far as to write a charter himself for the merchants of Comaccchio. It was there he, again, met the scholar he admired so greatly — Alcuin.

"You simply must head my Palace School." Charlemagne begged Alcuin. "No one else can match your accomplishments. No one else can do for the Frankish realm all we need. I beg you, reconsider your refusal." Alcuin bowed his head, embarrassed at the praise heaped on him by the King.

"Sire," he said, chancing to interrupt Charlemagne's praise. "I do not wish to disappoint you. My best chance of that is to NOT take the post you so enthusiastically offer." He held out his hand to stop Charlemagne's response. "No man can accomplish all you hope. It is the work of two lifetimes."

"Mayhap," the King allowed. "But you are the man for the challenge. Do not disappoint me. I beg you."

Alcuin listened solemnly to the King's plans for educating the children of the Frankish realm. Despite his best intentions, he admired the King's hope, his enthusiastic fervor, his indisputable commitment. Alcuin saw, again, a generous king who loved learning and was intent on sharing it with his people. The cost of such an undertaking seemed as nothing to him. The scholar's eyes gleamed whenever the king quoted a passage, be it an old fairy tale or a speech from a Roman senator.

To influence a king, to teach his sons, Alcuin thought! *How is it possible the Lord gives me such a chance? The King already argued theology with me, whetting my interest in his 'philosophers court.' What an exciting place Aachen must be. The minds of the age gather there to talk, think, argue, and challenge each other!* Alcuin felt his resolve waver. *I would be his children's teacher - sons and daughters both. He wishes all the children of the realm to read and write.* Alcuin reminded himself. *How extraordinary! As I labor to open his son's understanding of mathematics, I can debate astronomy and mathematics with the King. All my life, I dreamed of such a place. But I cannot count the resources necessary to develop a center of learning and, thus, I never dared to consider it.* He looked into Charlemagne's face, took a deep breath, and responded.

"I would have the opportunity of transforming the Palace School from a training school, chiefly emphasizing military skills, to one which teaches the liberal arts? My charges would, mayhap, become the thinkers of the next generation? Aye, I understand that military skills would continue to be honed, of a certainty. But, now, the young men..ummm, the young people... would work harder — using their minds to develop concepts and think, as well as to plan strategies and perfect their skills." King Charlemagne nodded. Alcuin paused for a second. "Then, I cannot refuse this opportunity." *Such will never come again.*

"Sire, I am your man." Alcuin replied, smiling. "I will be the director of your Palace School." Charlemagne's delight in Alcuin's affirmative response touched his heart. The King startled with surprise, a huge smile suffusing his face. He slapped Alcuin on the shoulder, almost knocking him from his feet. Charlemagne grinned and laughed. Later, Alcuin swore the King actually gave a little skip of delight as he grabbed him to his chest and crushed him in a bear hug.

"I am so delighted!" The King exclaimed. "You answer my most fervent prayer, Alcuin. This is better than winning a battle, for more significant than being the victor in a war. You, my dear Alcuin, will be my commander against illiteracy, my tactician against ignorance! Welcome, welcome!" He shouted. "Welcome to the Frankish realm!"

"It will take time for me to make arrangements, Sire." Alcuin hurried to add. "I must make my return journey to Tours. There I shall gather my books - my most precious possessions - and journey back to you. Do you object to my bringing an assistant?" He asked carefully. "I have one student who shows great promise. I don't push him to become a monk, Sire; but he is a thinker, a scholar. Aye, he has a fine mind." Alcuin had a disconcerting thought.

"Of course, he may not wish to come..." his words trailed off.

"Of a certainty," the King responded immediately, "bring anyone you wish, Alcuin. No one can serve us better than a scholar of your own choosing. Aye, turn for Tours and travel back to us as quickly as you can. I'll try not to burst with excitement before you return to us!"

***

With Alcuin's acceptance warming his heart, the King continued to march south and arrived in Rome by Easter. He felt no warmer now toward the Pope than he had in years past. But, he made his own folly years before in a promise to visit the Holy City. *A promise made is a promise kept.* He told himself.

With worrisome *missi dominici* reports coming to him from across Italy, Charlemagne knew he needed a greater cadre of law enforcers or a supreme overseer whom the people took to their hearts, a ruler they could love. He decided to name his four-year-old son, Carloman, king of Italy.

But, first, he believed it necessary to change the lad's name. Honoring his father, Charlemagne planned to re-name the boy 'Pepin' and make him king of the Lombard realm. He would be the only 'Pepin' the king recognized. Then, his first-born--his hunchbacked son, Pippin--could never claim inheritance rights from his father.

Having made the decision, King Charlemagne never wavered. He urged his troops toward Rome. Drawing up to Pope Hadrian's front door, Charlemagne sprang from Samson and bounded up the stairs. The Pope met him at the top, knelt at his feet, and stood to bless the King. Hadrian kissed a silver cross which he hung around the King's neck. He draped an arm around Charlemagne's shoulder and urged him inside.

Despite the bitter missives which previously passed between them, despite the Pope's demand for Papal Lands and Charlemagne's steadfast refusal to give them, the two men met together amicably. By the time the two rulers--the ecclesiastical one and the military one--greeted each other, discussed celebrations for the King's visit, and agreed on ceremonial issues, Queen Hildegard and the court arrived. Hadrian welcomed the Queen, cooed over the royal children, and made a great fuss over the Queen Mother. Taking Queen Bertrada's arm, he led them into luxurious rooms within his palatial chambers.

"Do we linger long in Rome, Charley?" Queen Hildegard asked. "I know you promised the Pope a visit long ago. But I would like our youngest child born on Frankish soil." She reminded him as she rubbed her stomach. "Would it be amiss to leave quickly after Carl's baptism? I mean...Pepin's baptism. I shall never get use to this name change, my dear!"

"We can't rush away, Hilde." Charlemagne answered. "Pope Hadrian must not think us eager to leave his company." He kissed her cheek and pulled her into his arms. "I know you wish to hurry home, my dear. Give me a few days. We must have a formal ceremony for the baptism. And I wish Hadrian to crown both Carl...I mean, Pepin...and Louis." Hilde stepped back to look into his face.

"What? Crown them both...kings?" She asked, startled. "What do you plan?"

"Both boys must be crowned, Hilde." The King answered. "Then, there will be no problem when they are old enough to rule in their own names. It's necessary. Hadrian probably already realized the necessity. He told me he has an elaborate ceremony scheduled for day after next. We must strengthen their place, Hilde. They are my sons and must succeed me, just as Carl and I followed Poppa."

"But who will rule, Charlemagne?" his queen asked. "I remember some frustration between you and Carloman. Besides, Charles is your son as well."

"Aye, Charles is my first-born," the King confirmed, thinking for a brief moment of Pippin, the hunch-back. "His place is secure; he will rule as well. But, I must guarantee Carl - that is, Pepin – and Louis their places." He took her hands in his and spoke earnestly. "I see no hope for it, Hilde. Louis must live in Aquitaine; Carloman--I mean Pepin—will become King of Italy and reside here." Charlemagne grimaced. "Hell, how I wish we had named the boy 'Pepin' in the first place, Hilde! I cannot get used to this change in names myself." He glanced at her pale face, the tears gathering in her eyes.

"I know...I know. Pepin is but a baby but it must be done...and he must live with his people. Anyway, our son Pepin, who used to have the name 'Carloman,' will be crowned and named King of our Italian provinces. The people will love him all the more for living among them. Think of his angelic face. The same advantage comes from sending Louis to his new home as speedily as possible." Charlemagne explained. "I will not risk losing the hearts of the people in Aquitaine, not from lack of a king. I simply must place Louis on the throne."

Hildegard wept copiously, but silently, into her shawl. She knew the king would respond to political necessity, as he saw it.

"You've no concern for a mother's need or a child's security," she answered him sorrowfully. "How can you take these babies away from their family? Neither will know each other; their other brother and sisters will be strangers to them. It does seem unnecessarily cruel, my King."

"Ruling Aquitaine wasn't as I expected, Hilde," the King admitted. "You see the reports. I administered it according to the Frankish pattern; the organization seems to have been effective. But I've no loyalty from the people. An administrator doesn't make a king. The people there are restless. Little Louis will give them a monarch they can see, one who will become a symbol of their region. They still follow many of their own laws and habits. Louis is young and pliable; he will learn their customs. Aquitaine will become his home. At his age, he'll remember nothing else and will truly become an Aquitainean. This will cement his influence. Pepin will do the same for us in Italy. Political needs demand this, Hilde!" He held his breath, trying to control his temper. Then, pointing at her belly, he continued.

"Surely, you can lavish attention on the babe you now carry. It will be birthed soon; you'll have much mothering then." Queen Hildegard knew further protest was useless. She bowed her head in defeat and returned to her children. In three days time, a double ceremony was held at the Basicilia.

***

Pope Hadrian chanted softly as he baptized little Pepin, nodding for him to sit as he poured water over the boy's head. Pepin flayed at the Pope's hand, wrinkling his face, preparing to voice his objection to the cold water. The Pope wiped his face with a white linen, then bent to whisper in his ear. Hildegard stepped forward to go to Pepin, to wipe his wet hair; but the King blocked her steps.

"Bless you, my child," the Pope intoned. "I baptize you, Pepin--son of Karolus Magnus--in the name of the Father, and of the Son, and of the Holy Ghost."

"World without end, world without end, world without end." The monks chanted in the background. As the chants died away, a single bell, light and melodious, rang in the inner sanctum of the church.

"As the bright purity of these notes echoes through the people, reminding us of God's love and salvation," the Pope said, "may your present innocence guard you from evil, draw you closer to the Heavenly Father, and direct your steps toward service to God above and mankind below."

He handed Pepin to Hildegard, whispering she should change his clothes and moved to the altar in the nave. Jocelyn hurried to the Queen, handing her a rich set of miniature breeches and tunic, all in red silk. Hildegard looked back and saw Louis already dressed in a matching set of blue silk. He waved happily at his mother and smiled. Quickly helping Pepin to step into his breeches and sliding the tunic over his head, Hilde tied his waist ribbon and wiped his wet hair with her hand linen. She set him on his feet.

Pepin went to stand beside the King, taking the hand Charlemagne offered to him. With a young son on each side, King Charlemagne moved slowly and stately down the central nave of the Church, smiling and nodding to those he recognized. The Church was filled to overflowing. Many congregants were weeping, but smiling widely at the two little boys. At the top of the nave, a temporary altar was in place. Here, Pope Hadrian stood, waiting for King Charlemagne and his sons.

"Come, my sons," the Pope beckoned to them. "I shall now name you your father's successors. As of today, you become kings in your own right. Kneel here, in front of me." Pepin took Louis' hand, looked back at his father, and moved to stand directly in front of the Pope. He bent over, whispering quietly to Louis. Louis shook his head negatively.

"Aye, you must kneel, Louis," Pepin repeated. "After the Pope says a few words, we are to eat lemon cakes and play with the puppies in the Pope's stable. Wouldn't you like that?" Pepin asked, smiling.

"...if I can have a puppy," Louis replied, his eyes intent. Pepin stepped back, unsure how to respond. He turned to his father. The King nodded imperceptively, then smiled.

"Poppa will let you choose a puppy for your very own," Pepin spoke softly to Louis, as every face in the first row smiled. "Now, though, you must be quiet." Louis nodded solemnly and turned a sunny face to the King.

"The two sons of our beloved King are duly baptized," the Pope continued. "Unto them, Pepin of Lombardy and Louis of Aquitaine, I do bestow the title of 'king' with all the duties and privileges such a rank provides. At this time, their father, Karolus Magnus—known to us as Charlemagne the Great--does rule over them; but, in time, they will succeed him. Pepin and Louis will share, along with their older, beloved brother Charles, the rule of our Carolingian realm.

"May God the Father guide and keep you," the Pope prayed, "directing your steps, purifying your thoughts, increasing your wisdom. In the name of God the Father, God the son, and God the Holy Ghost."

Charlemagne stepped in front of his sons. Slowly and

very deliberately, he kissed first one and then the other on the forehead. Next, he removed his own crown, placed it on Pepin's head, and kissed both his cheeks. He removed the crown from Pepin's head, returned it to his own, then removed it once again, placed the crown on Louis' head and kissed both his cheeks.

"To you do I entrust my kingdom." The King's voice boomed out. "Love it, protect it, and work your mightiest for the people." He took a small hand of each son in his own, big hands and led them from the church.

Outside the door, cheers and whistles greeted them from the huge throng. The boys bowed and waved and, then, hurried through a side entrance back into the Church. The people turned to partake of refreshments in the courtyard, the tables bending under the celebratory food provided by Pope Hadrian.

***

In a matter of days, King Pepin moved into the old castle at Pavia. The abbot of Reichenau, Waldo, and his brother Wala — two of the King's oldest friends and counselors-- ruled in Charlemagne's stead in Italy, as Pepin's regents.

Despite Hildegard's initial bafflement, followed by her entreaties and cries, the King escorted his youngest son, three-year-old Louis, to the border of Aquitaine. Sitting atop his horse and arrayed as a soldier, Louis crossed over into Aquitaine, claiming the land he stood to eventually rule. Louis, decked out in his finery, gloried in going 'for a ride.' In no more than three days, King Charlemagne and his court began their journey northward, leaving both small boys to their newly-given kingdoms.

***

Little Charles and Rotrude were thankful to remain in the mobile court. They understood, much better than either of the younger boys, that their brothers were away forever. The excitement of the Rome visit wore thin. Although the older children knew there was nothing to be done, they missed and worried for their young brothers.

"Life changes too fast." Rotrude told Charles as they talked once again about their brothers. "I know they will cry for us, Charlie. What can we do?"

"There is nothing," Charles replied wearily. "There is nothing, Rotrude...just pray they will be happy, I guess. We should find something to take our minds away... away from missing them, I mean." He turned at the sound of the trumpets.

"What's that?" Rotrude shrugged, little concerned with trumpets.

"They announce someone," Charles said to her. "Someone important is coming."

"They're coming for Poppa; you know that." Rotrude pointed out.

"Aye," Charles agreed. "I hope it doesn't stop our march. I miss everything about home."

"So do I." Rotrude agreed as the two watched a pair of magnificent gold and red striped banners approach their camp.

Later, Rotrude thought often of those trumpets. She had no reason to fear them or to imagine any sadness about them. But her memory of this day, colored by the trumpets, haunted her in later years. The 'someone' who entered King Charlemagne's camp was none other than a representative from Queen Irene--the Queen Regent for her son, Constantine VI, emperor of the Byzantine empire. Her chief priest begged to see King Charlemagne. The King received him immediately.

"It is a pleasure to welcome you to my court." The King began, wondering greatly at the reason for the man's appearance. "As you may have heard, we journey home, after installing our sons as kings of Lombardy and Aquitaine. To what do we owe your joyous appearance?" Charlemagne asked.

"I shall move directly to the reason for my mission, Sire," the priest replied. "Queen Irene, hearing you were expected in the Holy City, dispatched me to confer with you. I missed you in Rome by no more than five days."

"I regret you needed to extend your travels," King Charlemagne replied, still mystified at the need for such a journey. "I could not linger in Rome; my kingdom needs tending. You appreciate those duties, surely?"

"Of a certainty, King Charlemagne," the Priest replied, shuffling two rolls of parchment. "I have an offer for you from Queen Irene. May I speak frankly and with you alone?"

"Please, I beg you," the King replied, leading the priest toward his tent. The two men settled as Charlemagne sent his guard for mead, fruit and cheese.

"Sire. Queen Irene sent me to present an agreement to you, an agreement for the betrothal of her son, King Constantine VI to your oldest daughter, Rotrude." He explained. "Here is the contract." He offered the King a parchment. "…the betrothal agreement, Sire. It is profuse in its benefits to you, if you do not mind my evaluation."

"I shall determine its attractiveness." The King replied coldly. Surprised, Charlemagne never dreamed of this. Rather than being excited, he felt sick to his stomach and, then, he bristled. *Rotrude is only six! How dare anyone think of betrothing her. She's but a child.* He looked glumly at the priest.

"I need time to review the parchment. Please join us for the evening meal. I shall have a tent prepared for your party."

"Do not trouble yourself, Sire," the priest demurred. "My men are even now erecting my tent...there on the other side of your camping area. Nay, we have our own tents and provisions. I thank you, though I do anticipate joining you for the evening repast." He bowed once. "I leave you to peruse the offer, King Charlemagne. Any questions I shall be happy to answer after our meal." So saying, he left the tent, mounted his horse, and disappeared. The King rolled the parchment around in his hands, uninterested in opening it.

"Summon Queen Hildegard," he said to his guard. "Bring her here immediately." He ducked back into his battle tent and opened the missive. Waiting for the Queen, Charlemagne read every word on the parchment three times. It was brief and to the point. The priest was correct. The terms of the betrothal were generous, even allowing King Charlemagne and Queen Hildegard to determine the date of the proposed wedding. 'When you consider the princess ready' the missive said.

"Is anything amiss, Charley?" Queen Hildegard stuck her head inside the tent door, her body following immediately. "The guard seemed a little agitated."

"Nay, my dear," the King answered, "...not amiss, exactly, just unexpected. Take a seat." He walked around the tent. After circling twice, Charlemagne came to sit beside his wife and spoke softly to her.

"We have here a missive from Queen Irene in Byzantium," he said.

"Oh," Hildegard replied, "I do hope she's well. There are no attacks on Constaninople, I do hope." She started to stand, her concern obvious.

"Nay," King Charlemagne answered, pulling Hilde-gard back on the bench.

"Nay, there is no threat to that kingdom." He took Hilde's hands in his and kissed her forehead. "The Empress asks for Rotrude's hand, for her son. She offers a betroth-al between our Rotrude and her son, Emperor Constan-tine." He felt Hilde's whole body stiffen; her eyes opened wide with fright; her hands jerked from his grasp.

"But she's only six, Charley!" Hildegard cried, the an-guish clear in her eyes. "She's a baby!"

"Aye, of a certainty," Charlemagne agreed. "Do not think the worse, Hilde. There will be no wedding for many years. Nay, nay." He patted her shoulder. "No de-mands are being made. This is a proposal for a betroth-al. It is true; the empire's demands are spelled out here, in this missive; but there is no mention of a date for the marriage. In fact, you and I have complete freedom to de-termine the marriage date---six years from now, eight or ten? That decision is left to us and us alone." He handed the parchment to Hilde and rose to bring her a flagon of water. Hilde drank, almost unknowingly, as she read and re-read the terms of the betrothal proposal. She passed her hand over her eyes.

"These terms are generous, are they not?" She asked her husband.

"Aye…more generous than I can imagine. Almost ev-ery decision is at our discretion, Hilde. I cannot believe it!" He exclaimed in relief. "I would not, myself, dare to ask for some of the things Irene and Constantine offer. You saw?" The King asked. "Constantine is offering a sizable lot near the castle; a manor some three furlongs from the heart of Constaninople; chests of silk, teas, and woven cloths; jewelry to be made according to Rotrud's design—jewelry with rubies, jade, and amethysts - and a small cottage near the sea. I do not understand such generosity." He added to his wife.

"She is a pearl without price," Queen Hildegard responded seriously, "a precious gift, husband, one on which there can be no price."

"Aye. But this betrothal is generous in the extreme. I say we sign now. We shall include our wish for Rotrude to come to the marriage willingly. That is our protection of her. If, later, she does not like this marriage, we will deny her to the emperor. How like you that?"

"Can we demand such a thing?" Hildegard asked.

"Of a certainty," the King laughed. "Constantine and Irene may not accept it; but we can make the offer. What say you?"

"You're right. We will never see the like of this again. We must one day wed her, I know. This is a generous offer; let us hope it stands the test time will bring."

"Aye," the King agreed. "We hope for the best for our girl ...and make the best we can."

Chapter 20

REGRETS AND TRUTHS

Although her younger brothers left Charlemagne's court months before, Rotrude still often thought of the day they went to their own kingdoms. She was sad, not completely understanding the reasons which made the leave-takings necessary. But, thankfully for her spirit, she enjoyed the celebration of her sixth birthday. The excitement and party partly dulled the reality of Louis' and Pepin's absence. Rotrude began talking to her new doll, a present from her grandmother. In just the past few days, she found the doll a good confidant.

"The time I feel safest is when Poppa plays with me." She told her doll. "Sometimes I'm afraid for him to come home; he might have a bad hurt. I can tell--when his mouth looks small and tight-- he has a hurt place, even if he doesn't say it. Then, he looks right at me but doesn't see me at all. I can tell when Ma-mam is worried, too." Rotrud sighed.

"I hope Ma-mam's mouth is not flat tonight, and that her eyes aren't red," she continued. Talking to her doll lessened Rotrud's worry. "Ma-Mam does not have...we don't have parties together anymore either. I guess walking with a baby inside is hard." She whispered.

"Did you say something, Trudsy?" Charlemagne turned his head. He looked over at her from his bed on the floor. Only a moment before, Rotrude bandaged his hand and urged him to eat. "You see too much of your father's blood, don't you, my girl?" The king noticed his daughter's dark curls, the slight tilt of her forehead. "I didn't hear you clearly. Did you ask me something?" He rolled his body onto its side and propped on an elbow, looking at his elder daughter all the while.

"I'm thinking about Ma-Mam and the babe, Poppa." Rotrude replied. "A baby is lots of work...to grow one, I mean. I wonder why ma-mams have so many. I don't want any babes." Rotrude continued, seeing her father's attention. "Giseli, Mora, and Santiree say babies cry and fuss most of the time. When do ma-mams get to play?" Charlemagne kept himself from laughing outright and replied, a reply meant only for himself.

"I expect if they played less, there would be far fewer babes," he answered without thinking. "But you don't think about that." He saw Rotrude's face wrinkle with increased attention to his words. Trying to deflect her thoughts from his comment, he spoke. "There are so many babies because the Lord God wants more people for HIS work. And so, he gives us babes." The King resorted to previous explanations, knowing Rotrude much less interested in God than in babies.

"Aye... HE wants lots of them, I guess," she agreed, leaving the subject entirely. "What should we do next, Poppa?" She and her dear Poppa spent the morning together, riding into the hills to check on the wild apples. Eastertide was long over but blossoming flowers dotted the countryside. Apples were Rotrude's favorite fruit; she imagined it must be true for her Poppa too.

"When I'm bigger, I will learn to make the sticky food for you, the kind you like to put on your apples," she volunteered.

"...sticky food?" Charlemagne's face wrinkled. He had no idea where that came from but, suddenly, he remembered all the blossoms Rotrude admired.

"Ahh, aye. We talked about apples and the many ways to cook them. Oh, you mean the sweet sauce for the apples. Aye, you must learn all you can about food, my dear girl, though I imagine you won't have much time to spend in the cook tents."

"Poppa, what do you mean?" Rotrude's voice rose in astonishment. "Girls and Ma-mams must be cookers! Ma-mams cook!" Rotrude clearly valued kitchen skills and expected her Poppa to do the same.

"My dear, my dear," Charlemagne answered, laughing softly. "You're much too beautiful... to ruin your face in front of the hot ovens. You must tell the cook tent workers what to cook, how you want the food prepared and such. For those duties, you need to know as much as possible about food, its preparation, spices and such." Rotrude raised her eyebrows and looked at him with much skepticism.

"I will be a good cook." She insisted.

"Of a certainty." Her father replied, smiling at her determination. "You, also, will plan, choose gifts, and entertain visitors who come to court, I expect." The King smiled at his daughter. "You'll be the center of the garden; trust your Poppa's word. Bertha, too, in a few years..." Rotrude's voice caught; she looked at her father in amazement.

"Poppa!" She exclaimed. "You called me beautiful! That's for Ma-Mam and ladies. I'm a little girl."

"But such a dear one." Charlemagne observed. "You and Bertha are the Lord's precious gifts, as different from each other as day and night. Everyone in the court adores you." All of a sudden bashful, Rotrude hid her face in her hands and giggled.

"Poppa, I only want to be your girl..and Ma-mam's, too." She ran to give her Poppa a hug.

"If only I could keep you, my Rotrude; if only it were in my power..." Charlemagne murmured into his daughter's hair. Promising another orchard visit to Rotrude on the morrow, he begged his leave of her and went to the library to review his most recent revisions in church doctrine.

Charlemagne nodded with approval at the chants he introduced for the religious services. Just last week, he asked Abbot Fulrad to distribute the reforms and the musical additions to the church fathers. Hadrian has the chants by now, as well, Charlemagne thought. *They will be sent quickly throughout the realm. Under the Pope's seal, the priests, bishops, monks, and nuns will incorporate them into the Church liturgy.*

***

Charlemagne's summons to Queen Hildegard to discuss the Byzantine betrothal for Rotrude re-awakened the Queen's thoughts about Jocelyn. Hildegard knew the young woman broke her betrothal to Oliver and now drowned her confusion in work.

Six week before Jocelyn had asked the Queen for responsibilities in fetching and bringing for the court's noble women. Hildegard agreed with Jocelyn's request to serve the noble women in their dressing chambers and sent Jocelyn to them. But, less than a fortnight passed before Jocelyn begged the Queen to allow her to return to the nursery. Rotrude and Bertha both cried at Jocelyn's absence, of a certainty, and continued to ask for her. So, Hildegard was happy to have her back.

Jocelyn worked willingly and with competence, but

she was a shadow of her former self. She seldom smiled, though she joined in the children's games, kept them reasonably clean, and drilled them in their lessons. Even though her duties lightened because Pepin and Louis were no longer at court, the lessened responsibilities did not seem to help her spirit.

Hildegard watched from afar, much disturbed by Jocelyn's obvious unhappiness. She sighed deeply. She had no criticism of Jocelyn's industry, just of her personality. She seemed to have lost the light of her soul.

"She's so unhappy. I must set things right." Hildegard, surprised at her own daring, went in search of Oliver. If he seems unhappy as well, she told herself, I must find some way to help them both. She summoned him to the garden she was creating.

"My liege," Oliver greeted her happily. "It's good to see you here, working in the herbs." He smiled. "I can only imagine how hard it is for you to leave them behind as we journey throughout the realm. I admire your persistence in continuing to gather and nourish the plantings." Hildegard nodded at him and smiled, surprised he noticed her diligence.

"I so love to see things grow, Oliver," she admitted, "though some would say I do go overboard with growing babies." She shook her head vehemently. "Every living thing must be nourished, loved and protected, if it is to survive. I simply attempt to do that…for the plantings and for my children."

"Aye," Oliver replied. "I know and I admire it. But, still, it must be heart-wrenching to get them started and then have to leave the plantings behind. You never see the fruits of your labor."

"Aye, not only the plantings," Hildegard reminded him. "My dear little boys are behind us now, much to my regret." Oliver squeezed her shoulder. He would have cut out his tongue; his last wish was to remind her of the sons in Italy and Acquitaine. Hildegard saw his regret and spoke quickly.

"Forgive my boldness, Oliver. I beg your pardon before I speak. Know my next words reflect only my concern for you." She looked into his eyes. "Are you content?" Oliver looked at her sharply, refusing to take her meaning.

"...content? As content as a peace-loving man can be, in the midst of constant war, I suppose." He smiled sadly. "I long for peace, Hilde. I know Charlemagne must protect his realm; but the bloodshed, the constant battles... There must be some better way."

"I continue to hope." Hildegard replied. "My prayer is that today's battles will make it unnecessary for my sons to fight tomorrow. It may be a vain hope but I, like you, yearn for peace." Oliver nodded his head, seeming ready to bid her goodbye. Hilde hurried to continue the conversation.

"I worry for you, Oliver," she plunged in. "It's difficult to seek peace among those who love fighting. The heat of the battle seems to warm some men's blood...so they live for the excitement. I know this is not so with you and, as a result, I know you are often alone--not only alone, mayhap, but isolated from your fellows, Peers and all."

"You describe my place exactly, my liege. But I don't find being alone a punishment. It is only when the 'alone' becomes 'loneliness' that I suffer." He caught himself, surprised he admitted so much to the Queen.

"And this 'loneliness,'" Hildegard continued, "is it with you often?"

"Aye," Oliver confirmed, "much more often than I like and much more often than before." He looked directly into Hildegard's face. "My hope was to be married by now. But it was not to be." Hildegard opened her mouth to reply; but Oliver's words rushed from his lips.

"It's sad and difficult, Hildegard. Jocelyn is perfect for me. She exemplifies all those traits I value in a woman... and she is beautiful besides. I miss the hope I had for our union." He spoke softly.

"Then, you love her still?"

"Aye, I do." Oliver admitted. Hildegard nodded slowly and made her decision. "I shall love her all my life."

"Then, I shall see if this relationship can be renewed, Oliver." Seeing his surprise, she smiled. "Nay, do not ask my plans or my methods. I wish to prevent her from making a life-time mistake. I first needed to assure myself of your continued interest in Jocelyn... before I approach her."

"It's no use. She made her decision. Had I known she fancied Roland, I would never have spoken of my love for her." He hesitated. "I know I have little to offer, compared to him. She hid her true feelings from me."

"She did not love Roland, Oliver." Hildegard contradicted him. "I believe her confused and unsure of her own inclinations." As she spoke, Oliver's eyes bored into hers.

"Is it possible; do you truly think?" He whispered, more to himself than to the Queen. "Might I still have a chance with her, my liege?" Hope blossomed in his eyes. "I cannot compete with a dead man, you know. Gone from us, Roland is even more perfect in death than he was in life." He rolled his shoulders and shrugged. "To be sure, I don't wish to pressure Jocelyn to get her." He wiped quickly at his eyes, but not before Hildegard spotted the moisture there.

"I confess to you. I have little hope left."

"I'll do my best to see if you should hope, Oliver. My heart tells me happiness is possible for the two of you. But I will be certain...for your sake. It breaks my heart to see two people so well-suited for each other apart. Jocelyn was, at one time, not clear in her own desires. Mayhap, she begins to understand herself better these past months. I'll do my best to determine her interest and her feelings for you. I promise," she made the sign of the cross across her breast, "not to lead you astray or give any undue hope. If you trust my good intentions, I may be able to change your 'lonely' state." Oliver nodded imperceptibly.

"If only you could, my Queen," he replied. "For this particular woman, I would be grateful, even until my death."

"Don't die on me yet, Oliver," Hildegard warned. "Dead you have no need of me. I would not work a miracle for a man who cannot appreciate it!" She laughed with relief. Now, if only she could encourage Jocelyn to admit her unheeded feelings. Hildegard was positive Jocelyn loved Oliver still. *She just needs to have some understanding of his worth.* As she turned to leave, Oliver knelt and kissed her hand.

"God speed, Hildegard." He said softly.

If I can work a miracle here, help Jocelyn know her own heart, please God, work a similar miracle for my Rotrude with Constantine...when the time comes." Hildegard prayed silently. "Do you, Father in heaven, also, believe in a heart for a heart?" She lifted her eyes upward.

Infused with excitement for her mission, Hildegard decided to confront Jocelyn sooner, rather than later. She stopped one of the King's guards and asked him to summon Jocelyn to the herb tent.

"Tell her I'm hanging herbs and would like her assistance," she directed the guard. "We may have our evening meal together here, instead of the banquet tent. Please let the King know of my plan."

"Aye, my lady, right away," the guard replied as he hurried off.

Hildegard walked slowly to the herb tent. As soon as the court's annual trek began in the spring, she collected early-growing herbs, planted seeds, and trimmed cuttings. She offered herbs and cutting to noble manors, to peasants for their little plots, and among the farmers.

The herb tent was her domain alone, except for the herbalist who accompanied the court in its travels. Today he roamed the woods and hills, collecting watercress and young, tender, peppermint. He seldom worked in the tent. As she entered, the Queen picked up a small gourd, filled with seeds. *If I soak those seeds, they might grow more quickly. I'll wait for their rough husks to soften before I plant them.* She scooped soil as Jocelyn stepped into the tent.

"Good morrow, Queen Hildegard," she said, just the hint of a smile in her pale face. "I trust you are in good health."

"I am good in body, my dear," Hildegard replied, "if not in such good spirit." Seeing the young woman whose voice, often, soothed her children, Hildegard vowed to make Jocelyn re-consider her rejection of Oliver. She did so want her to find a good husband.

"I appreciate your prompt appearance, Jocelyn. Please, call me just "Hilde" today, if you will. I long for a friendly voice which addresses me as a friend, not as a queen."

"As you will," Jocelyn replied as she came close to Hilde, hugged her, and rested her head on the Queen's shoulder. "I miss our laughing conversations and wild speculations--back when we were young and carefree, back in our 'life before the court' world."

"My dear Jocelyn," Hildegard answered carefully. "You should be just as carefree, if not more so, now than then. You have an assured place in the court, are beloved and admired by all those who matter, and won the hearts of two fine young men—even if you did not jump at their attentions." Hilde forced a smile into her voice, one filled with more delight than she felt. "My dear, you are young and carefree still. If not, I must know the reason why not." Hildegard held Jocelyn tenderly, hoping to elicit some secret yearning or, at least, a denial of her words. Jocelyn stirred, gave the Queen another squeeze, and backed away.

"All you say may be true. But I feel old, broken, and used up, Hildegard. The joy of life seems to have slipped out of me completely." She shook her head and stood straighter. "But I came to help with the plantings or is it drying of herbs? Isn't it too early for hanging and drying?"

"Aye, it's too early for preserving the herbs." Hildegard acknowledged. "But I have discovered a secret. Seeds, like the dill here, dried early give a delicious taste to cucumber pickles. Since discovering this secret, I dry a few handfuls of dill seeds as they form--if I can find them as we move through the realm. It is a particular fancy of mine."

"Anything which eases your heart, you should have, my dear." Jocelyn said earnestly. She thought, often, of the two small boys far away in Aquitaine and Lombardy, living without their mother. "Though we must be brave, small delights and unexpected kindnesses keep us afloat." Seeing Hildegard understand her meaning, Jocelyn hugged the Queen once more.

"You and I both need tender care this day." Queen Hildegard affirmed.

"You know my sorrow; but, tell me Jocelyn, why are you unhappy?"

Jocelyn did not answer but tucked a work-linen over her tunic and began spooning dirt into Hilde's planting gourds. "Do you wish not to talk as we work?"

"Nay, I delight in speaking with you Hilde, as always. It's just...I'm not good company. I feel miserable, but I don't know the reason for it. My life is much as it's always been." She hesitated, as if remembering.

"I want to thank you again for giving me leave to return to the nursery. Maria said Countess Hertzog was livid when told I was no longer available to oversee her wardrobe." She laughed in great delight. "You can't imagine the sewing, the alterations, the decorations she wanted for her clothing! What an old ninny she is! How can a woman of such weight—5 stones, at the least—imagine she will set styles for the court?" She sobered quickly. "I didn't realize how much I prefer children to grown women." Jocelyn's voice was so serious Hildegard laughed in spite of herself.

"You are a gift to the children, Jocelyn." The Queen said. "They do their lessons, particularly practicing their letters, with more enthusiasm for you than they do for me. We're delighted you are back where you belong." She glanced sideways at Jocelyn's face. Her lips reflected a hint of a smile. But the sad, lost expression of the last months remained embedded there.

Hildegard took the tender stems of the dill plants and gave them to Jocelyn.

"If you will bind three or four of these together, I will hang them in my traveling basterne on the morrow."

"I'll use this grape vine to bind them," Jocelyn replied, nodding.

"It occurs to me," Hildegard spoke again. "Your life is

not the same as before, after all. In fact, the court changes enough that one season never duplicates the same season from years past. There has been constant change since we came to court, don't you think?" Queen Hildegard asked. Jocelyn paused in her binding, thinking deeply.

"Aye, I think you're right, Hilde. But my life, well... my life, except for a brief time, demands the same from me — the duties of a maid-in-waiting. And I have the same rewards one year to the next."

"Then, mayhap, it is this: the rewards of the court are less exciting now." The Queen commented softly. "Let's examine your life. Before and after this 'brief time' you mentioned, were you happy?"

"Before, of a certainty, I was." Jocelyn volunteered nothing more.

"But not after?" Hildegard persevered, hoping Jocelyn would not cut her off and refuse to talk.

"Nay, never 'after.'" Her eyes looked into Hildegard's face and, then, darted quickly away.

"The answer is clear," the Queen declared. "We need to examine the events occurring during this 'brief time.' That seems to be the turning point - the time when you went from being happy and content to being miserable. Isn't that what you said?" She waited, determined to make Jocelyn examine her unhappiness.

"It's fair to say; aye. All of a sudden, I am quite miserable--not just unhappy. Hilde, I am bone weary; I have no energy and little interest in anything. Only your children can lift my spirits. And, not to remind you of your own sadness, but the lads' absence is a trial for me as well." Tears sprang to her eyes, tears she tried to prevent the Queen from seeing. She stooped quickly to retrieve the gourd she dropped and wiped the tears from her eyes.

"But this unhappiness arose before we left for Rome."

Hildegard declared, refusing to move from the subject at hand. "I first saw your sad face months ago, Jocelyn, just about the time Oliver left for his journey to Aachen." At mention of Oliver's name, Jocelyn seemed to shrink. Her pale face turned lighter still; her lips trembled; and she knocked gourds and seeds off the planting table onto the ground.

"I felt badly before that, Hilde." She objected. "Of a certainty, the butchery at Ronscevalles deadened us all. I remember sadness and confusion; the massacre - of Roland, of Egginhard, all the rest - deepened my spirit even more. Don't you remember the state of the court in those tragic days?" She breathed deeply, wondering at the ache which rose in her heart. "Roland, you remember, Roland spent time with me, helping me train Miranee. She is such a good mount; he deserves all the credit."

"We all miss him," Hildegard replied. "I expect we who knew and loved him will miss him all our lives. Even before the attack, it was a particularly difficult time for you — Roland on one side and Oliver on the other. I can't imagine your strength in seeing them both, knowing they both delighted in your company."

"Nay, I didn't believe their interest, Hilde. It didn't seem possible to me." Hildegard put a hand on each of Jocelyn's shoulders.

"Aye, you did know it, Jocelyn," she emphasized. "Both of them were seeking your attentions; you cannot deny it. What is the good in objecting to my words?" Jocelyn shook her head, no longer trying to hide her tears. Hildegard pulled Jocelyn to her chest and spoke.

"Why are you crying, Jocelyn? Search your heart; give me the true reason." She urged.

"...because I hurt Oliver so much, Hilde. He asked me to be his wife. He was so nervous and dear, Hilde. His words made my heart sing!" Jocelyn paused, sobbing. "And, then, I turned against him. He did nothing to earn such treatment! I'm so ashamed. Thinking I might get a declaration from Roland, I dismissed Oliver—both his feelings for me and mine for him. How could I be such a fool?" Hildegard didn't answer the question. But she wanted Jocelyn to continue to examine her feelings, so she pulled her friend on the bench beside her.

"Why did you do it? If you were happy with Oliver's betrothal offer, why even think about someone else? You and Oliver were a perfect match." Hildegard chanced to add her opinion.

"I was so flattered; I guess." Jocelyn bowed her head, her shoulders trembling. "Just think, Hilde: the 'most beautiful man in Christiandom' was spending time with me! Roland kept seeking me out, even helped me train my colt. The attention muddled my head."

"I was, also, shocked at the noble women's attitude. They envied me, Hilde - me! ...the quiet, accommodating girl who everyone admires for her 'goodness,' for her refusal to flirt, for her distaste in seeing the soldiers teased. I often reprimanded my silly sister, Maria, and her friends—always giggling and seeking attention from any man they chanced upon! And, then, I acted just as they when the man they all dreamed about—young maids and noble wives alike—spent time with me and seemed to enjoy it." Jocelyn clung to Hildegard's neck, her tears wetting the Queen's scarf and the bottom of her headdress. Hilde held Jocelyn, made 'shushing' sounds, and rubbed her back as she cried.

"And you let Oliver walk away without a word?" She asked. "Surely, you didn't mean to be so foolish."

"I was so ashamed; I let other women's values cloud my mind." Jocelyn admitted. "I didn't know what to say to Oliver. If I admitted I felt flattered by Roland's attentions, I suggested I preferred Roland to Oliver. If I seemed unreceptive to Roland's attentions, I would alienate Roland... and the noble women would deem me foolish, even ungrateful." Jocelyn pulled away from Hildegard, wiped her eyes and face, and stood.

"In the end, I accomplished one thing. I drove away the man who truly loved me," she said morosely. "Forgive me, Hilde. I didn't mean to break down to you. You, of a certainty, don't need to share my sorrow; you have more than enough of your own."

"But I do share it, Jocelyn. You are my friend; I would not see you unhappy and I, of a certainty, cannot allow such unhappiness to last."

"What do you mean?" Jocelyn scarcely paid attention to Hilde's words. She poured water from a near-by flagon over her hand-linen and wiped her face. She removed her headdress, fluffed her hair, and replaced the headdress. She felt Hildegard looking at her.

"What do you feel for Oliver now?" Hildegard asked, holding her breath, though she didn't realize it.

"...now?" Jocelyn repeated, staring into Hilde's eyes. "I'm not sure." Hildegard glared at her, dismissing her words with a disdainful look.

"Not sure? Come now, Jocelyn. Only you and I are together in this room. Be truthful with me." She saw Jocelyn's confusion and changed tactics.

"Never mind. We don't need to talk about it now. But I do want to know if you feel anything for Oliver...anything at all." Jocelyn stared at Hildegard, frowning as she tried to decipher meaning in her words.

"Feel for him? ...now, you mean? What are you asking, Hilde?" Jocelyn inquired. Queen Hildegard shook her head.

"I've told no one, Jocelyn. You alone are privy to my next words. Just the day before this one, Charlemagne and I agreed to a betrothal for Rotrude." She held her hands up in a defensive position. "I know! I know! She's too young. But the problem with royal children is betrothals are more political agreements than anything else."

"I ask you these questions for my daughter's sake! I need to know about other women's hearts, their motives, their feelings for a man...as they arise. And I trust no woman's heart more than yours."

"I don't understand." Jocelyn admitted.

"I'm being convoluted, I know," Hildegard replied. "You see, Jocelyn, I loved Charley from the moment I saw him. I didn't admit it to myself, naturally; but he had my heart. All through his denials of his feelings, through the times he drew near and backed away, I never stopped loving him. I am asking you if you knew you loved Oliver...even before he came to you, before he asked for your hand. Of a certainty, you interacted with him at court. He was no stranger to you; neither was Roland. Who garnered your interest first?" The Queen asked intently.

Jocelyn walked around the planting table. She dipped her hands in pots of soil, sniffed small sprigs of herbs which were barely above the ground, and pressed basil leaves before holding them to her nose.

"Let me think on it." Jocelyn replied, looking over at Hildegard. The Queen stood silently, waiting. Finally, she picked up her spoon and began to fill several gourds with soil. She took a flagon and poured water over the soil. Jocelyn said nothing. Queen Hildegard dug up several small plants and transplanted them to larger gourd containers. She did not look, again, at Jocelyn, not wanting to influence or to pressure a response. Hildegard had almost lost herself in the planting when she felt Jocelyn's hand on her arm. The young woman took Hilde's hand and squeezed. She shook her head as the tears rolled down her face, yet again.

"It was Oliver, Hilde," she whispered. "It was always Oliver I loved." She sat, again, on the planting bench and wept.

Chapter 21

BEGINNINGS

Alcuin did not linger in his old home. The enormity of the challenges awaiting him in the Frankish realm fevered his brain. He packed, took his leave of his colleagues and his students at the monastery in Tours, and now reconnoitered his workroom. He tried, in these last few minutes before departure, to finish a translation which the copy master needed in the scriptorium. *But, this foolish monk gives me no peace!* Alcuin bent over his book, signaling his need to get back to work. The monk stood in front of him, saying nothing. His reading interrupted, Alcuin look up.

"And so, Brother Mithris, what exactly is your dilemma?" He hoped 'dilemma' was the correct term for he listened to little the man said. *I must get this translation finished!*

"I don't see how I can help you."

"Oh, but you can, Master." The monk's honeyed voice reverberated through the room. "Why must you go to Aachen? It's a mistake, in my opinion." He grumbled, dropping his eyes and his voice in imitation of regret. "We know you've requested many copies of manuscripts. The scriptorium's awash in new parchment, nibs, inks — all manner of materials since the King's request arrived. As I told the bishop, we need all the copyists we can get to respond to the increased work." The abbot glanced nervously about the room, wet his lips and, with hands behind his back, continued.

"I need to transfer Angilbert to the scriptorium. He's an excellent copyist and has some training in the illuminating art."

Alcuin startled; he didn't anticipate this request. For several previous years, he nourished and guided Angilbert, ever since he accepted the boy from his destitute parents. He did not consider leaving Angilbert in Tours; he planned to take him to Charlemagne's court. Alcuin wasn't sure the boy wished to be a monk but he could not imagine leaving him here. Mayhap, Angilbert deserves his own choice, Alcuin thought. Brother Mithris shifted back and forth, clearly eager for Alcuin's decision.

"Why do you ask for Angilbert...when there are many more experienced artists among the young men?" Alcuin frowned. "I announced my travel more than ten days ago. Why do you ask for help now?" Mithris shuffled his feet, looked out of the casement but said nothing. Alcuin was immediately alert.

"Oh, it's not possible, Brother. Angilbert comes with me to King Charlemagne's court." Alcuin explained. "The lad needs polishing. He appears to have some true poetic talents; and, being surrounded by beauty, laughter, and all ages of people—not our staid, quiet brothers—might give him opportunity to prove his talents. Do you think him an accomplished poet, Mithris?"

"Oh, to be sure." Brother Mithris responded. "His sensitivity, kindness, and beauty would be appreciated, surely, in Charlemagne's court. But I fear he might be overcome by the richness there; misled by pomp and ease, so to speak; toyed with by those comely, palace girls." Abbot Mithris' upper lip curled with distaste, as his eyes widened in appeal. Alcuin noted his uncharacteristic fidgeting. It filled him with foreboding. *Something evil is afoot here.*

"It's a request I will consider, of a certainty," Alcuin politely replied. "Thank you for being concerned about the boy's future. I'll make a decision before we leave." With a dismissive turn of his head, Alcuin returned to his translation. Some minutes after Brother Mithris left the room, Alcuin summoned his page.

"Holson, summon Angilbert, please. I need to see him; it's fairly important."

"At once, sir." Holson replied, knowing any degree of 'important' from Alcuin meant immediately. "I shall deliver your summons at once." Holson scampered out the door.

Mithris' request seems ill-considered, Alcuin thought as Hobson left. *Young Gil has yet to show a sliver of interest in the scriptorium.* Alcuin translated a few more lines of text. He heard running feet, a quick knock, and Gil stood before his work table. The lad's sandy shock of yellow hair stuck out in all directions as he impatiently smoothed it away from his eyes. His face, flushed from his sprint, was alive with eagerness and pleasure at being summoned. Ahhh, Alcuin thought, what a delightful picture; how beautiful he is. Alcuin's thought stayed his hand on his pen.

"Hummm," he murmured, "can his looks explain Brother Mithris' interest in the boy?"

"You sent for me, master?" the young man asked. "I came as quickly as I could from gathering leeches."

"You're certainly prompt, my son," Alcuin answered, acknowledging Angilbert's speedy response to the summons. "I have a question for you. As you know I was to leave today for the court of Charlemagne. Now, my departure must be tomorrow, but my concern is for you, for your future. My absence affects you greatly, for I'll be unable to continue your lessons. Brother Mithris asks for your skill in the scriptorium. What do you think of his request?" Alcuin watched the boy closely, noting the immediate tautness of his jaw, the furtive eye movement, and the tensing of his shoulders. There was a minute or two of silence. The lad obviously tried to phrase his words.

"I'd choose another vocation, master, if I may," he replied. "I don't wish to be a copyist. It may be premature to say but I hoped to continue studying with you and, perhaps, become a.....poet?" His response was hopeful, though his head hung in doubt. Alcuin looked steadily at the boy, the closest to a son he would ever have. Angilbert had always been bright, inquisitive, and eager to please. He did have some literary talent; but a poet, Alcuin wasn't sure.

"I must confess; I thought to have you accompany me to Aachen." Alcuin said in response. "As you know, King Charlemagne finally cajoled me into acceptance of a post there, to head his palace school. I journey to his court to begin this task. The King's dream is to encourage all interested men, and women, boys and girls to learn — especially reading and writing. Although I haven't said it to the brothers, I doubt I'll ever return to Tours. Aye, quick forays back and forth;" he explained at the lad's frown. "But by my acceptance, my life moves in a different direction. I pray I'm not immodest, but I believe I can provide some service to the King and his court."

"What say you to going to Aachen, Gil? I am loathe both to dismiss you from my service and to remove you from my life. This gives you little time to decide. Forgive me. I assumed you would come; but you must make your own choice. I must not do it for you."

"Oh, master!" Angilbert's eyes snapped with pleasure. His smile ran across his face. "Nothing, nothing would please me more than to serve you in Aachen. I wish you to direct me in my choice of vocation. I tend my love for God daily, but I don't feel drawn to taking vows. Can you accept me if I don't continue in the Church?"

"Aye, my boy; I have my own doubts about you as a monk. ...not that you are untried or unworthy," Alcuin hastened to add. "But you've had so little choice in your life; it would delight me to offer you more than one road. You are well-educated and might become a scribe, work in a counting house or even become a teacher of languages. Shall we agree you are to accompany me to Charlemagne's court then? After some interval, we'll speak of your long-term vocation." Alcuin queried. "And should I speak to the Abbot for you or do you wish to take your leave of him?"

"Oh, my thanks, master! I do so wish to accompany you. It's been my hope since you sent word from the King's court two fortnights ago." Angilbert's eyes danced with excitement. "Nay, I don't wish to speak to the Abbot. If you would tell him of your plan, I'll spend the time gathering my linens and clothing."

To Alcuin's discerning eyes, the boy looked decidedly uncomfortable, just speaking of the abbot. He noticed Gil never spoke the abbot's name.

"Aye, make haste then, my boy. We should leave at sunrise and you need some rest. Please meet me at the stables; we'll break our fast some distance from the cloister; we have long days ahead of us." Alcuin turned back to deposit certain books in their traveling cases as Angilbert left to gather his own belongings.

Before retiring, Alcuin sent for Abbot Mithris. With no

preamble, Alcuin went directly to the subject.

"Brother Mithis, Angilbert's accompanying me to the court of Charlemagne. There he will choose a vocation and make his home. Please select a scribe from Brother Marcus' class to assist you in the scriptorium. And, Brother Mithis, bear in mind the strictures which the Church sets against sexual appetites. Our priests and brothers must be pure and maintain decorum in all their actions." Alcuin noted Brother Mithris' discomfort, his attempt to cover his response to the implication in Alcuin's words.

"Bishop Tonlos's in charge of Tours. His elevation has already been announced; Abbots Hornio and Stropis will be assisting him. Be aware, Brother Mithis, many are watching." Alcuin spoke as he quietly closed the door on Brother Mithis' back.

***

Alcuin and Angilbert left the Tours monastery an hour before sunrise, the first step of their long journey toward the Frankish court. Angilbert was so grateful to be accompanying his master he overworked himself. At the evening campsite, he was a dutiful lad.

He prepared an evening meal and concocted several tasty dishes to encourage Alcuin to eat. As Gil's skill improved over the years, he often tempted Alcuin's palate. It was not uncommon for the scholar to forget meal times, being consumed by his reading and research. Now, though, Gil reminded him to eat.

After the meal, Angilbert cleaned the bowls and spoons, whistling quietly as he worked. After packing food for their mid-day meal, hejoined Alcuin at the fire.

"I detect a more enthusiastic interest in this trip's food preparation, Gil." Alcuin teased. "You'll make a fine cook, given another ten years to practice on your long-suffering master."

"I daresay you'll survive, Master," Angilbert looked up, beaming at Alcuin's light tone. "I must thank you once again for allowing me on this journey." Angilbert's smiled stretched over the whole of his face, his eyes glowed. "It's the answer to a dream...to continue learning from you and to join the biggest court in Christiandom."

"I wouldn't say much about the bigger court, my boy." Alcuin replied. "I'm certain the Byzantine court in Rome believes their court, if it may be called such, outshines all others. But, you may be correct. For a king, Charlemagne's realm far exceeds others, perhaps even the influence of the Pope himself. I'm delighted to bring you, Gil. I can't imagine life without your scintillating presence." Alcuin often complimented Angilbert on his cheerful countenance and sunny approach to life. He was a joy to have around, so Alcuin was reluctant to question him.

"I don't wish to may you uncomfortable, lad." Alcuin continued. "But I sense a strong effort, on your part, to avoid Brother Mithris. If this is your individual reaction to the man, I can accept it and will say no more. But do the other lads, also, try to avoid him?" Angilbert's jaw tightened, his hands clasped each other behind his back. He stared at the fire, keeping his eyes averted from Alcuin's face.

"I don't wish to spread tales, Master," the lad replied. "I myself have made all effort to avoid him."

"Aye, I did notice." Alcuin responded. "You understand, then, the reason I repeat my inquiry. Do the other lads, brothers or workers alike, attempt to avoid Brother Mithris?"

"Only the comely ones, Master." With reluctance, he finally looked into Alcuin's face. "I did all I could, Master, in finding tasks which sent the boys out of his presence.

Seeing the way things were, many of them volunteered to scrub the pots, muck out the stables, and spread manureon the fields. But, as you know, the Brothers' needs must be met. And Brother Mithris did ask for much." Angilbert answered.

"Were all the lads troubled by the man?" Alcuin probed.

"Nay, Master, only the most pleasing looking—the ones with light hair and eyes; the ones fit from work in the garden and fields; the ones who would delight the eyes of young women, Sir." Angilbert bent his head, his neck muscles taunt in the firelight.

"There is much amiss here, Gil." Alcuin understated his reaction. "You are saying Brother Mithris has an unhealthy interest in some of the initiates. This interest is so befouled some lads need protection? Would you define the man as a predator?" Alcuin's heart squeezed; his mind balked at this reality. He scuffed his shoes in the dirt and rubbed his hands.

"Aye, Master," Gil replied. "My answer must be aye. He does control the lads. But he's not interested in *just* the initiates, Sire; all who work in the monastery are easy prey to him." Angilbert stood up, put a shrub on the fire, and brought Alcuin a tankard of water. Alcuin took the water gratefully. He felt a great need to ease the dryness of his throat, beyond the huge lump of bile which threatened to spew forth. He took a drink and coughed. Angilbert smiled.

"My words make doing simple things difficult, don't they, Master?" He asked. "I didn't know what to do! I knew you would believe my report of Mithis but feared he would blame another lad....and dole out punishment. Truly, Master, he's a hard man, hard and very selfish." Angilbert's eyes dared Alcuin to deny his statement.

"Aye, I see you were caught in a quandary, lad." Alcuin agreed. He squeezed the boy's shoulder. "Call Pross, please. He needs to return to the monastery. We two will be safe without an escort; this threat needs my immediate attention." Angilbert nudged Pross in his bedroll where he was almost asleep.

"Forgive me, Master," the servant apologized. "The meal was overgenerous and so tasty. I drifted off to sleep as you two were talking."

"Pross, I regret I must waken you," Alcuin apologized. "But, you are to return to Tours quickly. You may wait 'til daybreak but, then, hasten back and deliver this missive to Bishop Tonlos."

"As you wish, Master," Pross replied. "Take care and stay safe on your journey. I hope to be on my way before you wake."

"God speed, Pross," Alcuin and Angilbert said together. "Thanks for your company and your good humor." Alcuin added. "This is not an easy journey for you but you do the monastery a great service. Manuscripts will need to be brought to Aachen, somewhere near summer's end. You're to bring them for me... to the King's court. I'll reward you well then."

"May I ask the contents of your letter, Master?" Angilbert questioned later. "I know this isn't my right; but I do fear reprisals from Mithis toward some of the lads."

"Rest easy, my boy," Alcuin answered. "I directed Bishop Tonlos to transfer Mithis to the old monks' conclave. Its closest village is Stuttgart...by about ten hours. He'll have no one to prey upon there. There are just good--some very religious--old men who pray, argue good and evil deeds, and know all about each other. His days will be full of boredom and frustration."

"That should do, Master. Now, maybe the lads can

concentrate on their duties and their studies." Gil answered simply.

***

Alcuin's and Angilbert's journey moved forward. They pamperedthemselves, riding leisurely through the warm spring days, sheltering or getting wet from the brief morning showers, and generally enjoying their duty-free journey. Many days after setting out, they arrived at King Charlemagne's court. The King summoned them immediately and welcomed them with joyful exuberance, with tasty fruits and fresh-baked tarts. He conducted them to a new tent, furnished for their exclusive needs and assured Alcuin he could settle in Aachen. His Palace School needed a permanent location.

"I cannot ask the master teacher of my realm to move with the court. As much as I would like you with me, it's not practical. Angilbert may wish to accompany the court from time to time; but I'll not require your constant presence, Scholar. You must be settled. All who need your advice and counsel will be able to find you."

"Alcuin, I'm so thankful you're here at last! You are the architect I need for my educational plans. What a glorious world we shall create, Alcuin, what a world! But," the King continued, "I would seek your advice about an immediate question."

"Please refresh yourselves from your journey and join the court for the evening meal. Might we talk before the meal begins? Or....maybe I'm asking too much? I know this was a long and difficult journey. Do you prefer we talk on the morrow?"

"We shall be at the banquet tent, Sire, as soon as possible. Angilbert and I both anticipate becoming members of your esteemed court. I must bathe off the dust from this journey and change my linen. Then, I'll meet you in the banquet tent." Alcuin assured the King.

***

"What do you think, Scholar Alcuin?" Charlemagne asked as he and Alcuin talked late into the night of Alcuin's arrival. "I don't want my daughter used for alliances. But the request I described came directly from the Queen Regent in Byzantium. She proposes the betrothal of our children, her son to my daughter. Who knows where such an alliance might lead? And I hesitate to offend."

"My son," Alcuin replied. "I've just arrived; I have no experience or learning in marital alliances. Being ill-equipped to offer advice, my only thought is this. Kings often agree to marriages for their children which, in the fullness of time, are not honored. Rotrude is six years, didn't you say? Much can happen during such a lengthy betrothal." Alcuin looked directly at the King, knowing he needed a definitive answer. But he was unable to give it. "To unite both branches of Christianity, wouldn't that be a great accomplishment for a king?" he asked. "And, I think, you have time to determine the true benefits of such a joining, should you wish to re-examine the agreement later."

"Aye. True. I made it clear long before this. My children may agree or refuse any betrothal at an appropriate age. I can't fathom requiring them to marry, as I say, without any concern for their preferences. I guess I got this from Poppa. Aye, my Queen and I agreed to the Byzantine offer in principle. But we did insert our wishes into the betrothal. This is a pre-betrothal agreement, in effect until both children are older and able to form an opinion of the other. Thanks for your thoughts, Master Alcuin. You've unburdened my mind," the King replied.

Within a fortnight the pre-betrothal messenger arrived for Queen Irene in Constantinople. An invitation for Rotrude to visit the Byzantine court followed on the heels of the pre-betrothal acceptance. It was a trip which Queen Irene asked Rotrude to begin immediately. But, at Queen Hildegard's urging, King Charlemagne postponed Rotrude's departure until new clothing could be sewn and the Queen could further drill their daughter in courtesies of the court.

***

Although preparations for Rotrude's journey consumed Hildegard, she did not forget Jocelyn and Oliver. Since her separate talks with them, she knew the rift between them must be repaired. She considered several ways to bring that to pass. Their relationship and her need to devise a plan for helping little Charles deal with his fears of his father's death taxed her energy.

"Both these situations need resolution," she said, "before Rotrude begins her journey. When this babe I carry joins the world, I can spare thoughts only for her. Hilde readily admitted she wanted another daughter. She glanced down at her growing belly.

"Spring is here; we begin our travels through northern Italy tomorrow. And the battle season will soon be upon us. I need no additional concerns weighing down my spirit."

The Queen decided to implement her plan to help Charles and use a similar location to re-unite Jocelyn and Oliver. She feared Jocelyn might reject Oliver a second time if things did not move forward quickly.

With his hope rekindled, Oliver mooned over Jocelyn at all the court functions and caused increasing speculation. He loved her well; it was clear to everyone. But the court ladies began to question his reluctance in announcing his interest. Their insatiable gossip and growing speculations were enough to disgust a woman in much less fragile condition than Jocelyn. It is time I do something, the Queen told herself.

***

Queen Hildegard sent a guard to summon little Charles to the stables. Their outing was planned days ago but postponed because of bad weather. This clear, warm day was perfect to begin their search. Abbot Fulrad met the Queen standing by the door, waiting for a stable-boy to bring her horse.

"Good morrow, my lady...off for a morn's ride?" He asked.

"That I am, Abbot," the Queen replied. "Charles and I go in search of crabapples."

"Not yet." Abbot Fulrad answered. "It's too early for them, Hildegard. The apples are yet nubs; the fruit yearns for sunshine and long days of warmth."

"Of a certainty, Abbot. But I'm looking for the very little nubs. They are a potent addition to sweet jams. We won't be here when the fruit is ready to be picked and cooked. I wish to dry the new nubs for later use," she explained. The Abbot looked unconvinced but nodded as he hurried by.

"Good hunting," he replied.

Hildegard promised Charles access to every sweet in the cooking tent, cajoling and begging him to be her scout...for early crab apples. If she were to speak freely with her eldest son, Queen Hildegard knew she must have him alone, away from the ready ears at court. Charles, though little interested in the crab apple search, finally resigned himself to accompanying his mother.

"Ma-Mam," Charles called. "I'm saddling your horse; be there in a minute." As soon as Charles toddled, he'd followed Roland everywhere, absorbing Roland's knowledge of horses. Talking about horses was like a tonic for both of them. Charles spent days in the stables and drank in the stories and legends of famous horses' great deeds. He learned much, some from observing, some through trial and error. Now, the nobles and even his father's horsemen, sought Charles' opinion when anything was amiss with the destriers or the plow beasts. Instinctively, the horses trusted him. Asked about his affinity for the horses he always replied: 'I never ask more from them than they can give.'

"Ma-mam, ready to go?" He called, leading the horse toward his mother.

"Do you need help mounting her?" He offered his mother his hand to steady her step up.

"Step the boulder, Ma-mam," he directed. "You can mount more easily from that height." When they arrived at this castle, Charles placed the large stone beside the stable wall and urged the ladies of the court to use it to get atop their mounts.

"Thank you, my dear," Hildegard replied. "Your hand does make me feel more secure. Now, I'm settled. Is your horse ready?" Hildegard asked, looking around.

"Yes, Ma-Mam," Charles responded. "He and I went for a gallop before you broke your morning fast. We had two morning meals already, if you can believe it!" Hildegard smiled and took up her reins.

"Lead the way, my dear," she directed. "We need to search for those crab apples. Everyone seems amused by my need for them. But just let them taste the fruit spread; they will be singing my praises. We must be careful in not taking too many, though. The fruit should move through its normal cycle as always. Someone who usually journeys this way may look forward to gathering crab apples. Who can say?" Charles shook his head in mock despair.

"Oh, Ma-mam," he replied. "You concern yourself needlessly for these little crab apples. God put them here to be eaten. I'm sure HE cares not if they are eaten now or two months from now. And, besides, your need for the apples is a good one. What can be more important than good-tasting fruit spread?" Queen Hildegard started to respond, but looked up at Charles' face. He held his smile in place, trying not to laugh aloud.

"Charles!" His mother exclaimed. "I know this is not a very important task; but it gives me time to talk to you alone. Court ears and whispers do limit our conversations together." Charles sobered and rode back to give his mother a kiss on her cheek.

"Say what you will, Ma-mam," he told her. "No one is listening to us out here." And he waved his arm over the empty fields. At his words, Hildegard rode forward, enjoying the sun and the warming day. In a few moments, she began probing her son.

"I know your Poppa wouldn't approve of this question, Charles; but I feel it should be asked. You're the firstborn of our children and, as such, will rule most of these lands when your Poppa is no longer able. This is a sore duty. And a choice you did not make. People would not like it, at first," she continued honestly, "if you choose to refuse this duty. But I, myself, want to know if you would prefer a vocation in the Church. I can defend such a choice, if you wish to make it. The realm will be divided among you, Louis, and Pepin, of course. But you, being the eldest, will bear the greatest responsibilities. Mayhap, you don't like the look of this future." Hildegard stopped talking, looked closely at Charles and attempted to gauge the honesty with which he would respond. She ought not have worried. He looked directly into her face, his eyes steady and forthright.

"Nay, Ma-man; I wouldn't like the Church. If any of us would make the choice, Louis should choose a church vocation. Nay, I'm content to rule, though I weary of the need to practice sword play so much! I like the planning of battles and deciding who should do what. I learn a lot as I watch the commanders plan strad...gy. Is that the right word?"

"I believe the word is 'strat-e-gy.'" Hildegard told him. "You never tell me your thoughts on battles and soldiery, so I'm interested in them." She tried to speak lightly, both to disarm her son and to indicate interest without pressuring him.

"I did wonder last battle season if Poppa would allow me to make a different choice. I thought long about it," Charles admitted. "But, truly, Ma-mam, I like my tired body when I fight. I yearn to be a good swordsman. I practice every day to be as good as Uncle Ro was. Yet, I know practice must continue, skills must always be improved."

"I like for the stableboys to do as I ask, not because I'm a prince, but because I know the most. Did you guess? Even Abbot Fulrad asked me for training tips on one of the younger colts? I gave him my best advice. I hope I don't over-praise his horse. He IS my favorite!" Charles admitted, blushing a little, concerned he said more than his mother wanted to hear.

"Then, it sounds you are content with the path expected of you." Hildegard answered. "Do you fear the fight, my dear? I'm so afraid for everyone I know in a battle. It is so very fierce!"

"Nay, Ma-mam, I'm not afraid, not of the fight." Her eldest son assured her. "Sometimes, from the battles I've watched, there's not much fighting or the fight starts and stops and, then, begins again. I learned from the mock-battles. A soldier must pay attention to his fight, concentrate on what he must do. Bravery is in the do-ing." Charles frowned and looked down at his reins. Hildegard remained concentrated on his face.

"But I do worry, Ma-Mam, about all the soldiers fight-ing. Like you, I fear for the ones I know. A man can be strong, true, and brave; but that won't save his life. Uncle Roland was a great soldier; but he still died."

Hildegard never softened life's realities for her chil-dren. She knew only the strong would survive in their demanding, dangerous world. She knew strength came in physical body, of course, but even more so in spirit, and in daring and effective thinking.

"What should I tell Louis or Pepin or even Bertha when they admit their fears for the soldiers or of the fighting?"

"Tell them a true soldier is always afraid." Charles an-swered without hesitation. "He does what he must. And if death comes, he prays it's quick. I think many soldiers don't fear their own deaths. They fear the deaths of their companions." He shivered a little and continued. "I have yet to conquer that; I fear so for Poppa!" Charles fell si-lent, certain he'd admitted far too much to his mother. Hildegard's heart lurched. There it is, she thought, just as I feared.

"Charles," she said, "your knowledge of death be-gan at Roland's death and has, of a certainty, multiplied many times since. It's impossible to forget death in such a world as we have. It surrounds you at every turn. You are likely to conquer its fear for yourself, but not for the death of your father or for others close to you. How well

I know this." Queen Hildegard admitted. "I struggle with it every single day. And the more men I know in the fighting, the more difficult the struggle becomes."

"Roland left more than a legacy of honor and pride. He left us a sure knowledge of early death. We must each deal with the fear, Charles, every single day." She saw him sigh, thinking deeply. *I've tried to compose a talk for Charles, a way to help him leave this fear behind,* she thought. *But I failed utterly. I can't find the words because I'm still afraid myself. But I must comfort him somehow, to give him strength.* Carefully, Hildegard reiterated her previous thought.

"I guess, Charles, Roland taught us more in death than he ever did in life. He was a unique man, especially for this time and place. But he always made choices which were clear to him. He took pride in his battle prowess. He fought and killed because he believed good would result. He was not bloodthirsty or interested only in battle. But he fought because people were in danger, because the enemy attacked, because a success now might help bring a chance for success in later battles. And he trusted that all who battled with him made those same calculations."

"You can't choose for another. Your values may not explain another's motivations; but it doesn't matter. You respect those who fight, pray they fight for noble reasons, and do your best to protect them. Your choices and your reasons for the fight are yours alone. Just be certain they are true for you! Other people must make choices, just as you must. And, as they should not question your choices or your reasons, you must believe their choices are just as critical to them as yours are for you." Hildegard hesitated. Charles seemed to listen to her words. His taut forehead relaxed a little; his eyes were less forlorn.

"Do know this, Charles. Your Poppa doesn't fight to

leave you a kingdom. There may well be a kingdom to leave you; he surely hopes and plans for it. But he fights because he wants to unite these many peoples. He fights because he likes the success of conquering; he fights because power feeds his great energy. Understand my words, Charles," she cautioned him. "These battles may help bring Christianity to this realm; the spoils of war may help support the work of the churches. But your Poppa fights because he likes the fight. And it's to his credit he fights in the thick of the battle himself. To do less would make him a wretched coward. In your life, my dear boy, fight for good; the battle, then, will be worthwhile."

"Thank you, Ma-mam." Charles smiled at Hildegard. "I must think more about your words - to see if they are true for me. Oh, and I thank you...for offering me a choice, too." Charles pointed over his mother's shoulder.

"There are your crab apples, Ma-Mam," he laughed. "And this tree, the one on the left, seems to be filled with little apples. Great! We shall have fruit paste to last through the winter!" Hildegard nodded and moved her horse to the large tree. Eagerly, she picked two tiny apples, gingerly biting into their tart skin. At the first taste, she moaned. Then, she reached in her bag and brought out a soft apple from last year's harvest. She spread a bit of the crab apple juice over the soft apple and smiled. Soon, she munched happily. With a stern gaze, Charles wagged his finger at her.

"Ma-mam, be careful or you're going to have a sick belly," he warned. "I must take you home, away from all this temptation." Giggling together, they filled two small baskets with tiny apples and headed for the stables.

Chapter 22

MATCHMAKING

On the morrow, Charles rose with a good heart. His mind was at peace. His choice of soldiering, and his Poppa's choices as well, were necessary and needed. His mother, returning from her daily prayers, noticed his relief and felt her heart lift. She knew Charles already thought about his life and the realm's expectations of him. She was content with his choices.

"But, now," she reminded herself, quietly, "I must play match-maker with these two lost lovers." The Queen hurried to the stable, seeking out her favorite groom.

"Newton, I'm playing a game with the Lady Jocelyn. I wish you to take the great hound, the one with the black and white patches, to the orchard. Take something delicious for him to eat, touch the ground all around the orchard with the food so he can have a happy time smelling. Then, bury the piece of food and leave him there to find it." The young man smiled quizzically at the Queen. "He won't run away, will he?" She asked, a frown crossing her face.

"Nay, my Lady," Newton answered. "If he finds the food and eats it, he'll still search in the same places again, hoping more has appeared...by magic!" He laughed.

"Good, then," Hildegard replied. "I want no harm to come to him. I just want him to be in the orchard. You think the dog will cooperate?" She asked, in doubt herself.

"Aye, Jogalong will go, sniff, eat, and hope for more." The groom assured the Queen.

"Take him as soon after the mid-day meal as you can." She told him and hurried toward the women's gathering chamber. Serving girls laid out today's mid-day meal as Hildegard steeled her nerves and opened the door to the gossip arena…or so she called it. All eyes centered on the door and most smiled, seeing it was the Queen. She smiled at everyone and no one and picked up a flagon of tea from the table. As she looked over the tarts, her eyes scanned the room. Finally, as she was about to give up her search, she saw Jocelyn in the far corner, sewing.

Queen Hildegard slowly made her way toward the young woman, speaking to women who caught her eye, greeting those she had not seen for a day or so. Dawdling to speak to a newly-arrived maid-in-waiting, she saw Jocelyn look up and nod. Hilde smiled pleasantly to a group of noble women and moved to sit beside Jocelyn.

"Good morrow," she greeted the young woman. "I have a strange request, Jocelyn. Are you free to help me after breaking your fast?"

"Of a certainty, Queen Hildegard," Jocelyn replied. "Anything you need, you have only to ask."

"Then, I shall be back soon to voice my request," Hildegard said as she hurried out of the chamber's side door. My goodness, she thought, I almost initiated my plan without guaranteeing the other side's participation. She left the manor and crossed the herb garden to enter the courtyard where the men practiced their swordsmanship. Sure enough, there was Oliver instructing his squire and Rinaldo's newly-arrived squire as well. Hildegard smiled and nodded as she entered the courtyard, responding to the many greetings. Oliver saw her heading his way, so he turned to meet her.

"My liege," he greeted her, "may I be of some service to you?"

"Aye, thank you, Oliver," Hildegard replied. "I'm afraid one of the dogs may get hurt. Do you know the big black and white hound Charlemagne so prefers for hunting bear?" At Oliver's nod, the Queen shook her head. "The houndsman just told me he's missing. That would be nothing, but he may be tracking something he cannot manage. One of the stable boys spotted him in the orchard; but he could not catch him. Staige said he saw the Lady Jocelyn going toward the orchard after the dog. I know Jocelyn often takes the dog when she rides. If anything should happen to either of them..." Hildegard let her voice trail away.

"I doubt there's any danger, my Queen," Oliver reassured her. He appeared to have no worry about her tale. "But, mayhap, I should check on Jocelyn?" He looked questioningly at Hildegard.

"To lessen my worry, please do." Queen Hildegard tried to reflect deep concern in her voice.

"I'm leaving right now." He looked at her and whispered. "I'll take care of this myself, your Grace." He raised his hand to her and left. Hildegard rushed back to the women's chamber. Waving to Jocelyn, she hurried over to her.

"That beast of a dog you so favor, Jocelyn," she said, "disappeared from the kennel. Please check in the orchard for him. One of the squires discovered bear tracks down near the river and the houndsman wants all the dogs back here." Jocelyn startled, stood immediately, and hurried out of the chamber, almost running in her haste. The Queen nodded to the women on either side of her and slowly left the chamber. I have done my best, she said to herself. *Let love find a way.* And she smiled.

***

Jocelyn hurried toward the orchard, trying to decide if she needed to go to the kennel to get additional information. Nay, she thought. *Jogalong is my favorite. I cannot waste the time. If he catches bear scent or, even, the smell of a deer, he will bolt from the manor and not return for days. I must find him.* She almost broke into a run; but, imagining the stories likely to circulate around the court about her 'mannish' ways, she remembered to walk quickly. As Jocelyn left the manor by the front steps, Oliver passed the herb garden behind the manor, hurrying as well, intent on spotting Jocelyn. He did wonder at the Queen's disquiet.

"Only if there is a wild animal in the orchard would any danger present itself. And, with all the people around the manor, an animal close is unlikely." Oliver mused. Still, his thoughts ran, the Queen worries. He felt it is duty to relieve her mind. Oliver rushed into the orchard, the front entrance almost blocked by the newly-opened blossoms of the apple trees. Thinking he heard a noise behind him, near the forest's edge, Oliver turned his head to look over his shoulder. Trying to pick out a distinctive sound, he grunted in surprise when someone walked right into his chest.

"Ufft!" His breath caught as he steadied his feet. Looking down, he realized a young woman sat on the ground.

"Oh, please excuse me!" Oliver cried. "Let me help you up." He reached down to grab an arm. "I do apologize to you. I looked over my shoulder for ..." The words froze in his throat.

"Jocelyn?" He asked stupidly as he pulled her to her

337

feet. "Jocelyn, have I harmed you?" His eyes drank in her loveliness. Jocelyn was speechless. The color rushed to her face. She blinked rapidly to keep her tears in her eyes. Seeing Oliver's dear face was almost more than she could bear.

"Oh," she uttered softly. Then, she controlled her expression and withdrew her hand from his. "Nay, nay. It was not your fault, Oliver. I'm afraid I ran into you. I'm looking for Jogalong. He ran away, maybe from smelling a bear's scent. I worry that he might speed off and get into more than he can handle." She smiled at Oliver, seeing his rapt attention to her rather lame words.

"I, I...uh, I see." Oliver answered. "Aye, this is the spring of the year. Mother bears and cubs might be out; and if Jogalong ran into a mother, trouble would stare him in the face." He grabbed Jocelyn's hand and pulled her after him. "We best hunt the crazy dog, Jocelyn. You know the mischief he can get into."

Jocelyn walked beside Oliver, making no move to withdraw her hand from his. He is just as kind as before, she thought, watching his intent face scan the orchard. She felt Oliver startle.

"There he is!" Oliver shouted. "He's digging beneath the apple tree, there in the middle of the orchard. Follow me, Jocelyn. I'm going to run to see if I can catch him." And Oliver raced across the orchard, calling Jogalong. The dog looked up, recognized Oliver, and bounded toward him.

"Come here, boy!" Oliver shouted as Jogalong almost knocked him down. He quickly put his hand on the dog's neck and pulled him closer. Jogalong licked Oliver's hand and plopped down on the dirt. He wiggled all over when he saw Jocelyn coming toward them. Oliver untied his linen belt and looped it around Jogalong's neck. By then, Jocelyn was on her knees beside the dog

"How's my sweet boy?" She crooned as she stroked his head, holding the linen belt a little tighter. "Come." Jocelyn walked toward the kennels, holding the linen belt tightly.

"Would you like me to walk him, Jocelyn?" Oliver asked, hoping she would not turn Jogalong over to him and leave. "I would hate for him to tear or soil your tunic." Jocelyn handed the linen belt to Oliver, making certain her hand stroked his as he took hold of the belt.

"Aye," she replied. "You are more likely to be able to keep him close than I." She laughed the lilting sound Oliver loved so much. "He does just as he pleases around me."

"He's a good dog," Oliver replied as he tied a knot in the linen belt, "most of the time." Jocelyn laughed as he bent to rub Jogalong's stomach. The attention turned the animal into a lamb. Jogalong lay on the ground and turned his belly up. Jocelyn gave a delighted snicker.

"What a love hound, he is. Did he wait out here just to get our attention?" Oliver spoke before he thought.

"If I thought that, I'd have begged him to pull this trick long before now." Jocelyn's smile ended abruptly as she looked into Oliver's face. Before she could respond, Oliver reached out and cupped her chin in his palm.

"Oh, my dear," he whispered softly, "how I have missed you."

"...and I you." Jocelyn admitted as she put her arms around his waist. She gathered all her courage and looked into his face. "Oliver, forgive me. I was a fool...walking away from the finest man in the world." She held her breath as she saw Oliver's jaw clench and release. He turned his face away. *Oh, what have I done?* Jocelyn reprimanded herself. *I wanted only for him to know I care for him.*

"Excuse me. I must return to the manor." She reached down to pat Jogalong goodbye and to compose her face. Oliver's sober look brought tears to her eyes.

"Nay. You are not needed at the manor. I need you here. I need you so very much, Jocelyn, my love." He added as he drew her close to his chest. And, then, he kissed her—a dear, sweet, loving kiss filled with reassurance. Jocelyn's arms stole back around his waist as she hugged him tightly.

"And I need to be here…in your arms," she told him. "This is where I belong, now and always."

***

Queen Hildegard stood on the lookout for Jocelyn and Oliver when they walked by the herb garden, headed for the kennels. As she saw Jocelyn whisper in Oliver's ear, Hildegard's face broke into a gigantic smile. *Looks like my little ruse worked*, she gloated, *though both Jocelyn and Oliver will soon see my hand in their 'rescue of Jogalong.* But no matter, she thought, the problem between them appears to be a thing of the past. She began humming as she turned from the window, just before the first labor pain struck.

King Charlemagne hurried toward the birthing chamber. The court was on edge. The Queen was still in labor with no end in sight. Her birthing pains came closer and closer but the babe did not move. Charlemagne, more afraid of the birth process than of any enemy he ever faced, burst into the room, scattering noble women and servants alike. He walked directly to his wife's sleeping bench and took her hand.

"Hilde? How do you feel?" He asked, trying to cover the fear her pale, drawn face produced. "Is there anything you need? …anything I can do for you?" He stroked her jaw line and bent to kiss her atop the head.

"Would you stay here beside me for a little while, Charley?" Hildegard asked. "It seems this babe is reluctant to come into the world. It must be a girl." She smiled. "Rotrude and Bertha both took their time; do you remember?"

"Of a certainty," the King's voice boomed with false cheeriness. "They linger inside, gathering strength, so they may rule the court with their first breath." He laughed. "They know instinctively their father values persistence and dramatic entrances." The ladies in the chamber smiled at the King's light-heartedness, knowing he attempted to reassure and enliven his wife. Patting her shoulder, the King spoke softly.

"You rest, Hilde, rest as much as you can. I will sit here and hold your hand. Know I'm here and try to sleep a little." The midwife came to place another cold cloth on the Queen's forehead and nodded encouragingly at King Charlemagne. Many hours later, the Queen delivered a baby girl whom she named 'Gisila,' in honor of the King's sister.

"Take a message forthwith to Gisela at her abbey. Fulrad will pen it for you." Charlemagne directed his guard. "Tell her little Gisila, her name sake, arrived only moments ago and asks for her. Wait there for her to arrange her affairs and escort her quickly to the court. Four days hence, we march first to Mount Soracte. I would see my uncle's monastery and thank God for my newest daughter. Three days after, we move through northern Italy, from the holy mountain toward Florence. Bring Gisela along the same route."

***

As soon as Hildegard felt like moving, the King began his annual circuit. Gisela joined the court just as it was leaving Florence. Her presence among them and her tender solicitude for little Gisila and Hildegard both invigorated the Queen. Within hours of Gisela's arrival, Charlemagne heard laughter, accompanied by happy gurgles from the babe, streaming from the Queen's tent. From Florence, they journeyed to Pavia and, then, to Brescia. When the court arrived in Milan weeks later, the bishop baptized little Gisila. Charlemagne prayed, as he did for all his children, that Gisila would continue to be healthy and strong. Each birth of a child opened, again, the wound of losing his first little daughter, Adelheid. He and Hildegard prayed daily for their children's continued well-being.

"Since our new daughter is here, Hilde," King Charlemagne said, "it's time for us to honor Queen Irene's request. Rotrude must visit the Byzantine court. We must not delay this journey any longer." He shook his head slowly. "I know full well, dear, she is only six years old. But we did agree to the betrothal. And the Byzantine Court's king and Queen Mother deserve to see the pearl they will get. Don't you think so?" Queen Hildegard gazed at him blankly, unwilling to agree for Rotrude to make the trip to Constantinople.

"If we send her now, while we are still in Italy," the King patiently explained, "she will have less distance to travel both ways and, thus, be away from us a shorter time. She need not linger there, Hilde; but the trip must be made." Then, he had a brilliant idea.

"I shall ask her aunt to accompany her," he suggested. "Such journeys are the expected duty of holy women anyway. Gisela will be happy to go. And she is astute; she will analyze and evaluate every single person in King Constantine's court. None of them will suspect the mind beneath her nun's wimple." He laughed and looked at his wife. "What say you?"

"Aye, if Gisela can go, I shall rest easier." Hildegard replied, believing her sister-in-law the best one to chaperone her little daughter to the foreign court.

"I shall go to her at once and present our proposal." Charlemagne declared.

Chapter 23

KIDNAPPING AGAIN

The mounted escort halted to allow Rotrude and her ladies to walk about. The horses drank from the river; the men checked cinches, wagon hitches, and stored trunks. Rotrude sat at the river's edge, bathing her feet while her attendants wiped their faces with water-soaked hand linens. Their journey to Constaninople, begun just two hours previous, had them less than six miles from King Charlemagne's court.

Rotrude peered toward the thick reeds where her Aunt Gisela repaired her damaged clothing. As their cart bounced along the rutted road, a flagon of honey, brought for their oat cakes, overturned. No one noticed it until Gisela exclaimed at the sticky feel on one side of her tunic. The sweet honey soaked through her clothing. Although Rotrude assured her she smelled sweeter than any of them, Gisela took this chance to bathe in the river and wash her clothes.

Rotrude's attendants and the soldiers were already removing tunics and shawls for the sun shined hotly. With the excitement of the court's send-off in the past, the travelers' enthusiasm at the start of the journey faded away. As the travelers cooled off and waited for Gisela to reappear, two of the horses startled and jumped nervously.

"What's wrong with your gray, Monston?" the captain of the guard questioned his second-in-command. He did not finish speaking before two of his men wheeled and shouted.

"Men are approaching from the west, Sir!" Sergeant Moulston called.

Several men rounded the curve and galloped quickly among them-- burly-looking men with no identifiable house crest on their garments. Five of the escort soldiers rose to mount their horses. A bevy of arrows mowed them down. Three of the burly men rushed the three soldiers left on horses, stabbing the soldiers and their sergeant.

A man with a box slung across his back hurried Rotrude's maids into a single cart. One of the younger maids screamed. A bowman answered with a blow to her face. As she sobbed, Rotrude climbed into the cart, following her women. She prayed her Aunt Gisela would hear the noise and stay well away. As Rotrude stood upright in the cart, another man on horseback grabbed her at the waist and hoisted her across his horse. A bowman caught the leads of the cart's horses and led them away. Rotrude struggled with her captor; but he bound her arms to her side, just like a sheaf of wheat.

"Not you, little one; you come with me." He ordered.

Instinctively, Rotrude knew he was going to hurt her. The man's eyes were intent, staring into hers. His eyes are cold, Rotrude thought, cold and mad at something. She tried to 'squish up', to make herself small; but he held her across his lap. The pommel of his saddle bored into her back. Just as she thought they began a long ride, the huge man reined his horse, rode into the near-by forest and carried her into a tent, one screened from the road by small shrubs and bushes. Her captor shouted at two people shaking pillows and linens.

"Get out, you fools! I told you! I have no more use for you here. Find your way back to that rotten dwelling you call home!" An old woman and a maid scurried out. She could see the few furnishings inside the tent. The lounging pillows, scattered around the carpeted floor, were luxurious. A brazier burned brightly, even in the day's heat. The room smelled faintly of roses. Two more serving women unrolled rugs and linens.

"Get out, you two!" the man shouted at them. "Get out of here, now!"

Rotrude looked at the man's red face. Oh, no! She thought. *His face is just like Poppa's when he's mad.* Rotrude looked around. There was nowhere to hide. The man turned toward her bench, seemingly ready to knock her to the floor. Rotrude watched him come. She felt her heart thudding in her chest. All of a sudden, she remembered the serving boys at Cook Baston's hearth.

When the boys made Cook Baston very angry, carelessly spilling food from the trenchers or putting their fingers in the stew, he yelled at them: 'Mother of God, SEIZE me!' Rotrude overheard Cook tell the baker the call reminded him not to strike the boys. His duty, Baston said, was to make them into reliable kitchen help, not to beat them.

This man is mad, Rotrude thought. *Cook's words might stop him from hitting me.* Instinctively, she knew the big man would strike her, not just talk mean to her. As he reached to grab her shoulder, Rotrude shouted with all her might.

"Mother of God seize thee!" She exclaimed.

Her vehemence and unexpected yell stopped the man dead still. He looked at Rotrude in stunned disbelief.

"What you yelling at?" He asked, frowning at her. "Your pa, the king... he be known for his great faith.

What are you saying? You putting some kind of Christian curse on me? Do you use the 'evil eye' on people?" He spit on the ground at her feet. "Bahhh! No one said you had religious powers."

"Shit." The thief muttered. "I ain't risking a life-time curse for this deed." He turned from Rotrude and hurried toward the door of the tent. Just as he pulled the tent flap back, he stopped, turned and came back to her. He drew his knife.

"This'll let your Pap know he almost lost you," he said. He nicked her left leg far above the knee. Then, he ran from the tent.

Rotrude slid carefully to the floor, watching her blood bead atop her leg. Even when she heard a horse gallop up outside, she feared to move. *One of those other men might come inside.* She moved closer to the tent wall, thinking to squirm under it.

***

Riding up, Theo saw five of the King's guard lying in their own blood. Rinaldo and Lord Janlur parted from him. Rinaldo spotted a cart in the distance. Nodding in that direction, he and, then, Lord Janlur pursued it. Frantic that Rotrude and her women were hurt, Theo yelled at two men he saw disappear behind some shrubs. Seeing him, they urged their mounts and rode quickly into the edge of the forest. Moving slowly, Theo rode behind the shrubs and saw the tent, alone and unguarded. Hoping Rotrude and her women were inside, he didn't follow the men. He dismounted and hurried into the tent. There he found Rotrude, seemingly unhurt. With a cry of relief, Theodoric gathered her in his arms.

"Thank God, my precious girl," Theo stammered. "You're safe; you're safe!" Then, he spotted the blood running down her leg and grabbed her hands.

"Did they hurt you, my princess? Did they harm you?" Rotrude heard the fear in his voice. She looked at her leg, still bleeding. She did not understand this was her own blood until she looked into Theodoric's panic-stricken face.

"I'm so glad you've come, Uncle Theo," she sobbed. She clasped her arms around his neck and grabbed his tunic tightly. "Nay, he only nicked my leg. But it stings." Just a few minutes later, Gisela rushed into the tent and gathered Rotrude in her arms. Rotrude thought her Aunt Gisela looked even more frightened than she was. She quickly assured her aunt she suffered no harm.

"The cut is small, Aunt Gisela. It was the man's face that was so scary. He was mad, Aunt Gisela." Rotrude said. "I didn't know what to say or do." She turned to Theo and smiled.

"We must both thank Uncle Theo," Rotrude said. "He saved my life. I know it."

***

Charlemagne was livid!

"Who threatens my daughter? She's just a child! What does it merit someone to kidnap her? Is this for ransom, for revenge against me, or could this be an enemy of King Constantine?" He shook his head wearily. Being alert and protective of himself was one thing, but securing the safety of his family was a far more important endeavor. Even Charlemagne's restive nobles, ever on the look-out for any weakness in the court, were incensed at the impudence of this plan.

"What to do? Who do we punish? Someone must pay."

Queen Hildegard watched the King stomp around the room. She was still so afraid she was unable to think! Rotrude is just six years old, she said to herself again. *What can I do to protect my children? When the attempts were made to steal Charles and, then, Pepin, everyone thought Desiderius might be behind the plots. But Desiderius is locked in Corbie monastery! Kidnapping Rotrude would gain him nothing.* Queen Bertrada assured herself. *Who would kidnap my daughter? How could anyone hurt a child?* She wailed with terror and burst into tears, hugging her body as though to keep all of it together. *That nick on Rotrud's leg, so high on the leg, could only be a threat of ravishing! My dear, dear girl! How must we live to protect you, to protect all our children?*

"How can this happen a few hours from our court, Charley?" Hildegard asked the king. "Who's wandering our realm with such a purpose; who would initiate such an attack? Pepin's attempted kidnapping never produced a villain—only a servant girl greedy for ribbons and pretties. Were we wrong about that?"

"Can evil this gross be afoot... threaten children with the king's escort? Charley, we must have a permanent court. No more moving around the realm. No more! I will not chance my daughter's safety again. Even guarded with men we trust, the brigands almost took her!" Queen Hildegard gave a low moan of helplessness. "I'm not likely to disregard this warning, the warning cut on her thigh! What kind of animal would suggest such a thing? Mayhap, there would be no interest in ransom--just an assault on her, ruinous for her life and for the kingdom." Queen Hildegard shuddered as the King rushed to her. Sharing her fears of rape, Charlemagne took Hildegard into his arms, patting and soothing her.

I MUST reassure Hilde, he thought. *Gisila's birth took so much of her strength.* Each day the King paused to access his wife's health, noting signs of fatigue or pain.

"I swear to you, Hilde, we WILL find out. We must.

First, there was the effort to burn you and little Charles in our tent. The next attempt was to spirit little Pepin away. Now comes this near loss with Rotrude. Thank God Theo felt nervous about this trip and followed them! We must find who's plotting against our children." Hildegard stirred.

"Is it possible, Charley? I mean, maybe an enemy cannot kill you so he turns his effort on our children?"

"Oh, my God!" Charlemagne staggered, "you mean someone purposefully targeting them? Why them...why not me or you?" The King raged, full of fear for the safety of his family. Hildegard moaned low in her throat.

"Remember my wedding dress, the one that disappeared just before the ceremony? Remember? Might that be included in this attack on us?"

***

The Peers gathered around the King after the evening meal. Charlemagne looked at his friends and shook his head.

"We need fresh eyes." He stated simply. "I believe this effort to kidnap Rotrude is from the same hand which attempted Pepin's kidnapping. A servant girl's greed is too simple an explanation for that. All our investigations and questioning, what did they yield? Nothing." He shook his head, his face pale and drawn. "The madness of taking the boy in our camp, now the overpowering of Rotrude's guard--both these efforts require information from inside our court. We have a traitor. I'm convinced of it."

The men shifted uneasily. Their lack of success in identifying the mind behind little Pepin's abduction worried them all. And, now, there was this new threat, against a different child. Someone seemed almost to be playing with them.

"Send for your squires," Charlemagne directed. "Send also for the serving wenches. We must speak with them, determine if they noticed anything suspicious."

"Sire, I don't see the point." Theodoric objected. "We have questioned and interrogated, even threatened, all in the court already. We uncovered nothing."

"And that's the problem, Theo. There must be an answer; and it MUST come soon." The King declared. "I'm afraid I'm going to lose a child. Without God's help, both my sons and, now, my daughter might well be dead or injured. The price is too high! This is unacceptable. Do you hear me?" He began pacing the room. "I will not lose Hildegard to fear and worry, either. Already, I worry for the health of her mind. We must do *something!*"

"Ogier just returned from the Lombard court. Mayhap he discovered some trail there, something which will explain these plots. We thought Desiderius might have instigated the burning of little Charles' tent and... remember Lord Morston?" Count Janlur asked. "Could all this be interconnected?" He looked around at the worried faces.

"Let's ask Ogier if he saw or heard anything in Pavia."

All those assembled nodded in agreement, anxious to find any information to aid them in protecting the king's children. They remembered the circumstances of King Pepin's acquiring the throne, and all remembered the resentment King Pepin; and, then, King Charlemagne received. They themselves were loyal; but this wasn't true of all nobles, landowners, or even soldiers. But would any they knew harm a child--the king's child or another? Before this, none of them would have believed so.

"Call your squires and send for all the serving wenches." Charlemagne repeated. "The court's nobles can take care of themselves this day. We need to speak to these people, examine things they heard or saw. They listen with unjaded ears, see with new eyes things which you or I might not even notice." The King kicked the library table as he passed it. "The court is infiltrated, I tell you! We must identify the spies!"

Regardless of doubts about the value of the squires' opinions, the Peers summoned the squires and wenches. Paul the Deacon, newly returned from a religious journey, visited each cooking tent and the noble women who oversaw the maids-in-waiting. He relayed the king's command and returned, followed by chattering, excited young women.

Oliver immediately understood Charlemagne's point: the more eyes watching, the more would be seen. But how were they to discover relevant information; how to weed unusual events, idiosyncrasies or foolishness from significant reports? As the young people swarmed in, he sat in the back corner, thinking deeply.

***

The next morning, all the Peers gathered to develop plans for protecting the royal family. As they settled in the battle tent, a messenger introduced himself and asked for the King. The Captain of the Guard led him to the King's library tent and, then, went to the horse line, looking for Charlemagne.

"Search the messenger in the library." The King directed his second-in-command. "From this day forth, everything possible will be done to protect this court and my family." He rubbed Samson's neck and headed for the library tent. "I have little interest in messengers this day." He commented as he hurried forward.

"Sire," the messenger stood. "I have a missive here,

352

for your hands only. I am to wait for a reply, if it please you, your Majesty."

"Go to the cook tent to break your fast, soldier," the King replied. "Rest, relax. I shall summon you after I peruse the message." He sat at his library desk and unrolled the parchment.

"It's from Himiltrude!" Charlemagne's breath caught in his throat. What problem was there that his first wife would write him? He smiled as he remembered she always formed her letters better than he. Charlemagne scanned the first paragraph, more surprised at receiving the letter than at anything it would contain.

///

Charlemagne, greetings!

My pardons to you but I must make a request. It is for our
son and for his future. You must take him. He is uninspired
here. I

have done my best, Charlemagne; but Pippin needs your
influence

and your attention. He suffers from a lack of friends and a
lack of

place. Being the flawed son of a lady is not enough. Many
treat

him as a prince, despite my efforts not to remind him of that
station. He's more and more lost as the day turns to night.

Please help our son.
Himiltrude

///

Charlemagne winced at Himli's use of his given name; her formality hurt. I was always 'Charley' to her, he remembered, flooded afresh with thememory of his mother's banishment of his young wife those many years ago.

In the midst of all this worry for Hildegard's children, another of my children is threatened - Pippin, my hunchbacked son, King Charlemagne thought. Charlemagne spotted Abbot Fulrad coming from the baker's tent and beckoned to him.

"Please bring your writing materials, Abbot," he said. "We have a missive to construct." The King described his requirements to the Abbot.

"Be kind, Fulrad. This is the single request Himiltrude makes of me since she left the court. Our son deserves some of my attention; send for him immediately. Be firm in relaying we expect his presence within a fortnight. There's no time to lose."

"Of a certainty, Sire," Abbot Fulrad replied. "It's time he were here with us."

***

The attempted kidnapping of Rotrud set the court on edge. All the Peers sought to name the guilty party. Alcuin, so recently arrived at the court, could offer little insight. But he suggested Angilbert provide assistance to Abbot Fulrad. The Abbot set Gil to work on a set of questions to be put to each serving wench. The men sought to identify unusual behavior, a too-sure attitude, anyone within the court with overmuch ready coin.

Rinaldo and Theodoric questioned any court worker who supervised people. They were astonished at the number of people needed to keep the court functioning. Having his rye loaf in the morn, Theodoric often thanked God for the baker. But he found there was not one baker, but three of them! Food preparation took the numbers of a small army...or so it seemed.

"Rinaldo, how will we ever identify a culprit among all these people?" Theodoric asked. "There are, at least, a hundred suspects...and more coming every day. With the start of fighting just a few weeks away, this will be an impossible situation. We're getting nowhere!"

"I agree," Rinaldo nodded. "We need more help, so I suggest we enlist the help of Lord Janlur. He is an intimate of the court, long known and, thus, well-trusted. He is able to solicit rumors or opinions from nobles who will not talk easily to you or me. He is discrete, a man eager to serve the King, and with an astute mind beneath his attractive face. I will tell him my idea and get his evaluation. What do you think?" Theodoric was immediately alert. He dragged with weariness and worry, knowing their efforts weren't adequate to the task at hand.

"Aye, Rinaldo, what do you propose?" He asked with great hope.

"I suggest we fake a dis-enchantment with his majesty. Have someone begin talking against him, and see if anyone approaches the mal-content. A member of the court who seems at odds with the King will, invariably, gather interest and, possibly, expose a traitor. The person who criticizes Charlemagne should be someone innocent and trusting...all the more believable."

"If he'll do it," Rinaldo continued, "I suggest we ask Angilbert." "

"Let's describe our scheme to him and see what happens. If there's a traitor in the court, surely the person will befriend someone known to be upset with the King." Oliver explained. "Since this effort to kidnap Rotrude failed, we must believe the villain will make another attempt, or, perhaps, target one of the younger girls — Bertha or Gisila."

"That's a good possibility." Theodoric nodded. "But let's make this realistic; we'll describe our plan to the king. Mayhap he'll start a fight or demand a face-to-face battle. Do you think he can play the part?" Rinaldo shook his head. He wasn't sure about this suggestion.

"Wait, Theo! Suppose we set the altercation without the King's knowledge. Then, his response will be more believable and may bring jealous or disloyal nobles into the open. Dispirited troublemakers often elicit help from the naïve, the innocent, or the newcomer. They also speak more freely. We'll need to sift through all Angilbert reports to us—if anyone approaches him, I mean. It may be the evil doer will, carefully, try to feel Angilbert out, if only to learn what we know."

"Charlemagne does love a little drama, doesn't he?" Theo laughed. "I delight in watching him when the traveling actors perform; he's so very taken with the action, the plot, and the subterfuge. He's often led astray by the actions of one person or another!" He smiled widely. "...and his utter surprise at the end is amazing."

"Aye, he never has to worry about convincing anyone of much. He's the King and he hands out his pronouncements as easily as breathing," Theodoric answered. "He brooks little dissension, of course; but everyone obeys him, regardless. Such allegiance makes for obedience but, also, produces resentment. I wonder if this plotter is a resentful court member."

"I doubt it." Rinaldo responded, waving as Oliver came in. "These attacks against the children are too deliberate and too well-planned, too drastic, to be the result of discontent. Or so it appears to me. Nay, this is an on-going plot to gain power and to spread fear." Rinaldo paused, lost in thought. "I can't fathom the reasoning, though, for someone in the court to take this chance. These attacks only make the King angry, more wary, more resentful, when they occur. Whoever thinks this will intimidate the King knows him little or not at all."

"Aye, well-said, Rinaldo." Oliver agreed. "And this may well be the traitor's undoing. Although these forays had the possibility of deadly accuracy, each one failed. Thank God, they were poorly executed. Their multiplying only gives the King legitimate reason to crush the instigator. He'll do it with no mercy," Oliver predicted, "if we ever find the culprit."

"I hope to be traveling when the day arrives," Theo agreed.

"Then, let's implement our plan." Rinaldo said. He and Theo found Angilbert in the orchard and explained what they wished him to do. Angilbert beamed at them, flattered they requested his services.

"I shall do my best, Sirs," he assured them. "Shall we choose the date of this charade?"

"Oh, nay," Rinaldo and Theodoric responded in unison. "The time is now! Prepare yourself, Gil. We go to see the King." Theo smiled at Angilbert's initial panic but assured him he would carry out his part well.

In no time, Oliver located Lord Janlur and sent him to Theo and Rinaldo. Janlur led Angilbert to seek the king. They found him enjoying his favorite occupation--swimming in the river. The two men slipped into the water, floating toward the King.

In than less than fifteen minutes, the King's bellow rang out. Twenty heads jerked toward the sound. In the calmer curve of the river, the King and Lord Janlur swam rapidly toward shore. Angilbert lingered behind, treading water, allowing distance to grow between himself and Charlemagne.

Janlur talked furiously, slapped the water with his hands and strainedtoward the king. Charlemagne reached the bank, planted his hands on the grass and swung his body. He rose as his feet gained the ground. He turned, shook his fist across the water at Angilbert and shouted.

"You do overstate yourself, scholar!" King Charlem-agne screamed, a dark vein standing out on his neck. "How dare you speak to me so! God knows the devil's in your heart. You, bastard! I will have NO orphan ad-vise me on my translation! You have nought of learning which I respect. Where did you study--in the wilds of Britannia? You know nothing of classical writing! You're a fool! Stay out of my sight." The King shouted at Angil-bert as he hurried away from the river. Rinaldo turned toward him.

"Be gone, Rinaldo! Keep this poppin-jay away from me. I've nothing more to say to him." Charlemagne gained ground rapidly, his long stride moving him away from the swimming hole. Contrary to previous swims, this one neither relaxed nor calmed him. He was so an-gry he stumbled in his hurry to leave Janlur behind. Ri-naldo beckoned toward his chagrined friend and urged Angilbert to swim to shore.

"It's very cold there, Gil. Get out of the water. Don't delay. Ahh, I shall talk to the King at the evening meal. Don't fret! His temper has the best of him again. I know you meant no harm. Come! Come in and clothe yourself." I fear he will stay there in the water, Rinaldo thought. *He's not seen the King's anger, never received the brunt of Charlemagne's temper. I'll bet he never heard Alcuin even raise his voice.*

Rinaldo slid down the river bank and beckoned to An-gilbert, urging him to come from the river. Very slowly Angilbert shook his head, as if to clear it. He swam to-ward Rinaldo. In a few minutes, Rinaldo extended his hand to help the young man climb onto the bank from the river. Others in the water swam to the bank, came out and crowded around Angilbert. Some advised him not to worry; others watched and measured him. Angilbert shook his head, gestured negatively with his hand and hurried away. Rinaldo assumed a worried expression, looked after Angilbert sadly, and walked quickly toward his own tent. *This was well played.*

Over the next ten days, more than one court malcontent approached Angilbert. He talked with each of them but could find no evidence they had any real knowledge of Rotrude's abduction. The abduction, coming just before news of Charlemagne's first-born son's return to court, fueled rampant speculation.

***

Pippin, the Hunchback, arrived three weeks and four days later. Astonished that Charlemagne summoned him, Pippin said as much to his father.

"I don't know why I'm here." Pippin confessed after their initial greetings. "Oh, I'm excited." Even in his confusion, he knew not to offend the King. "It's been three years since our last autumn hunt; but I didn't expect this ...invitation, of a certainty."

King Charlemagne smiled. In his son's response was surprise, as well as judgment and implied neglect. And it's true, Charlemagne admitted. *I have neglected him: out of my sight, out of my thoughts.* He sincerely regretted his lack of care. He now resolved to correct his absence in his first-born's life.

"Your mother and I agreed you should join the court." Charlemagne said as Pippin's eyes grew large. "You need manly influence as you prepare for your future. My Peers, each of them, are brave, admirable men. It matters not which of them you emulate. You will become a finer soul and a better man. Each one is exemplary in performance, loyalty, and character. I do love them well."

"I consider being in your court a true boon, Poppa."

Pippin exactly matched his father's formal tone. "I yearn to distance myself from my mother's house. Not," he added hurriedly, "from lack of concern or care, but from limited exposure to the world and small opportunity to test my value."

Charlemagne, surprised at the maturity of his son's speech, approved of his words, his bearing and his acceptance of his new surroundings.

"So, we are all three content with this change," Charlemagne concluded. "Your education in the ways of the court begins as soon as you change your clothing. Remove your travel mantle, refresh yourself from the journey. Rinaldo, you do remember Lord Rinaldo from our hunt together?" At Pippin's nod, the King continued. "Rinaldo will accompany you to the hall for the evening meal. We have guests from Baghdad; you'll have an interesting exposure to another world at our evening repast."

"As you say, Sire, I go to change my garb in preparation for the evening activities." Pippin responded as he turned toward the door.

"Dear Lord, thank you for Himli! What a fine prince our son makes; she taught him well." Charlemagne's heart felt lighter than it had in many days. He turned to change his own dress. The caliph must be matched in clothing this evening. Charlemagne had just the tunic to outshine him. He hummed a liturgical chant as he disrobed, humming in a meter far faster than the church fathers would ever approve.

Pippin integrated quickly into the daily routine of the court. Oliver, ever kind and concerned about those who didn't have their own place, took a special interest in the boy.

"Pippin, how are you doing?" Oliver asked the young man a fortnight or so later. "Are you adjusting to the court and its routine? Do you have any continuing problems, challenges, or worries? This is a demanding court. Joining it from outside is a challenge, I know."

"Master Oliver, my biggest problem is always my appearance." The lad answered. "That will never change. I've adjusted to it all my life. My misshapen back, my crooked walk, the compensation I make for my balance....most people avoid me. They don't see past my freakish looks." He shrugged, as if dismissing his words.

"My mother adores me... and everyone in her house is kind. Here, life is very difficult. But, I must learn; I must make a place for myself. My father gives me this chance. So, I do not complain."

"Aye, I can testify to that. You always have a smile and offer a willing hand to everyone. Do you mind, though, if I share a life observation with you?" Oliver looked directly into Pippin's face and, at his nod, continued gently.

"I've found people in a group always react against anyone who's different. It seems the group's values become the only values worth embracing. And they attack anyone who does not support those values." Pippin's brow furrowed; his eyes narrowed. He didn't acknowledge Oliver's words.

"I've always been an outsider, Pippin." Oliver continued. "I left my own home at an early age, was an orphan before I was eight. I always felt myself less than other men in the lack of a family and in having no certain place of my own."

"Even here, valued by the King, I'm seen and judged as difficult, because I don't like fighting. If I can solve a problem through talking or compromise, I choose one of those methods every time. This makes me a coward, at worst, and a weakling, at best, in the Peers' eyes. I do wish you could have known your grandfather. He and I were alike in thinking."

"I understand you," Pepin interrupted. "It's common sense — what you just said--or so it seems to me."

"To you and me, aye," Oliver nodded, "but the Peers fight first. Action is their watchword. They don't talk or compromise. This is also true of your father. They like fighting and winning, of a certainty. But battle is in their blood; it's both a challenge and a reward for them." He paused, thinking deeply.

"I believe they value my meager talents; but, even so, there are moans of impatience when I ask a question. Questioning is anathema to a non-thinker." Oliver sighed deeply. "Even the King sees me as a rudder, if not an anchor. I'm the one who makes the effort to delay the rapid, usually aggressive, response of the others. I interfere with their warrior status, their enthusiasm for fighting at any provocation." Pippin startled.

"I cannot believe this!" he exclaimed. "I thought all Peers were equal and supported each other!"

"Nay, it's not so." Oliver responded answered sadly. "Nay, fighting is natural to them; soldiers fight. It's the only choice they imagine. They call any other course a weakness. Abbot Fulrad often supports my view; but even he advocates fighting is a necessary evil." Pippin knew his dismay showed on his face. I have had my fill of fighting, he thought.

"I learned early the art of losing a fight, losing so as not to be badly hurt." Pippin confided to Oliver. "My humpback interferes with my balance. And I can always be bested by one who moves quickly. Not because I can't fight," he added quickly, "but because I lose my balance and can, at that moment, be taken. Boys figure this out quickly. I never have a hope of saving myself." He stopped. "Is the world always unfair, Oliver?"

Oliver noted Pippin's use of his first name, instead of a title, and felt a thrill of. So, he trusts me, Oliver thought. *He trusts me enough to feel easy calling me Oliver. At last, I'm his friend!*

"Aye, Pippin." Oliver answered. "I can only believe the world or, its people--at least--are unfair. That is one reason men embrace a religious belief. They hope for some fairness and justice beyond the realm of men."

Pippin and Oliver turned back to the practice field. As Pippin parried with some of the squires, Oliver sat watching, wondering at the chasm between war and peace. On this warm, spring day, the swordfights were close and energetic. The fighters soon turned to the river for a bath.

"Come fishing with me, Pippin," Oliver invited. "The cook, Lawford, is waiting to fry fish for our evening meal, if he be invited to join us. How about it?" Pippin's delight showed on his face.

"Aye, Oliver! I'd like that. I've missed the taste of trout. Are we likely to hook any of those in these rivers?" Pippin asked.

"...if you can land one, of a certainty." Oliver laughed. "Great! I lost my fishing partner when Ogier journeyed to Lombardy, two or three fortnights ago. Since his return, the maids-in-waiting are more interesting to him than fish. It'll be great to have you! Don't worry about bait. I'll bring all the worms you need."

After their swimming-baths, the two met upstream of the court's site. There was a small, deep pool which provided a respite from the rushing, tumbling river waters. Oliver and Pippin baited their hooks and dropped their lines in the water. They stood about forty feet apart.

Oliver yearned to chat with Pippin. I'll let the lad be, he thought. *I'll bet he loves fishing because it's solitary; he doesn't have to pretend to interact. People don't expect men to fish together. I fish so I can avoid spending time with the courtiers and the drinkers of the court. Hah! King Charlemagne's dislike of drinking and carousing surely doesn't seem to influence his friends! Fishing helps me renew myself. Mayhap, it's the same for Pippin.* Pippin smiled as he worked his line opposite an old log in the pond.

"A likely hiding place for a fat trout!" He glanced over at Oliver who was removing his hook from a large mouth. "…a good one, Oliver?" Pippin called.

"Aye!" Oliver answered, showing his fish. "… not your trout, though! This is a b-i-g perch! It will make Lawford's pan, for certain! Had any luck around that log?"

"Not yet, but I have real hope; I want you to admit the difference between trout and perch…in their sweetness, I mean!" Pippin laughed. As he talked, he moved his line slowly through the water, walking at a snail's pace toward Oliver. Pippin felt a twang on his line as a fish pulled against it. He stopped, raised his pole to pull the line taut, and waited. He felt a jerk, snapped his line to sink the hook, and began raising his pole even higher. Oliver's mouth dropped open as Pippin's catch broke the water's surface. Not a trout, but a huge turtle dangled from the line.

"I'll never get him to land," Pippin muttered. "He's heavy." He swung his arm, rapidly depositing the turtle just beyond Oliver's feet. Gently, Pippin raised the neck, removed the hook from the beak mouth, rubbed the turtle's head, flipped it to its feet and pushed it toward the water. Oliver didn't understand.

"You catch it to let it go?" he asked, almost taking a step toward the retreating turtle.

"I never eat them." Pippin replied in a quiet but determined voice. "…guess I understand their panic. You see, I know exactly how that turtle feels, lying helpless on its back. It's just as difficult for me to right myself as it is for this turtle. A hump back, though uglier, is just like a turtle's shell." He sank on one knee to re-bait his hook.

Oliver pulled in his second perch, put another worm on his own hook and dropped his line in the pool beside Pippin's. *Who would think that fishing could be healing?*

Later, the two men presented Cook Lawford with enough fish to feed them, five soldiers and three hungry squires. It was a wonderful meal — all the more so for the interplay between the two fishermen.

Chapter 24

No Suspects

In the practice yard, the Abbot spoke to the squires. They'd had a long morning. reconditioning bridles and leads. Their mid-day meal consisted of a filling venison stew, brown bread and apples stewed in honey. Now, the Peers and their squires relaxed in the sun.

"Abbot Fulrad's not speaking to himself, lads," Oliver shouted. "Sit up and listen. His thoughts are important." All the squires from an eight-year- old beginner through the sixteen-year-olds, sat up quickly, turning their eyes and ears toward the Abbot. Oliver was never unreasonable in his requests of them; and, though he was far more serious than the other Peers, the squires all respected his words.

"I want you to realize your actions may influence others." The Abbot repeated. "Lads, look around. You're models for those who labor to become squires. They're watching and learning from you. Remember this as you make choices. We often adopt values from those we admire. Be sure your values and your actions are admirable ones which help build character. Keep testing your bodies and your minds," he added. "Some of you may be Peers before you're through."

The squires smiled at each other, hoping for just such a reward and trying to catch the eyes of their masters to indicate their hopes. Pippin sat quietly by himself, off to the side of the gathered company. *Why's the Abbot the one speaking to the squires? He wondered. I wonder why Rinaldo or Theo doesn't give his opinion and advise the squires. Is the Abbot the spokesman or are the Peers reluctant to speak?* Pippin stood as a guard walked up to him.

"The King requests your presence immediately," he said to Pippin. "He wishes you to ride with him; he'll meet you at the stables." Pippin nodded to the man and turned toward the stables. As he finished cinching his saddle, his father rode up beside him. Pippin mounted his horse.

"Son, how are you this morning? Thank you for joining me." Charlemagne handed him a fruit tart and rode alongside the river. He cantered, then galloped his massive horse as Pippin rode beside him, his horse at a canter to match the King's mount.

The King and his firstborn rode for several miles. Seeing the lather on his mount's flank, Pippin slowed to a canter, then to a walk. Charlemagne followed Pippin's pace. Soon, the riders dismounted to stretch their legs and allow their horses to graze. Charlemagne removed a leather bag from his horse— more tarts and sweet dough for the two of them. He and Pippin sat on the ground and leaned against an old oak.

"Looks like lightning got this tree." Pippin observed to his father.

"Aye, there's no protection from that." Finishing a piece of sweet dough, the King offered Pippin a tart and took one himself. "Tell me of your experiences in the court." The King directed, taking a bite of blueberry tart. "Are you busy enough; is there any time for fun?"

"My days are filled with practice, Poppa. With fighting practice, military maneuvers, battle tactics and my problems with grammar, I'm spent at day's end." He grimaced, then smiled. "How can grammar be harder than any of the others? Who would think writing could be so straining? Mother had a strict, demanding tutor for me at home; but we never wrote much." He shook his head slowly.

"I'm embarrassed." He admitted to the King. "The truth is: I feel stupid. Compared to Charles and Rotrude, I pen my letters like a five-year-old." Charlemagne made as if to speak, but Pippin hurried on. "Even Bertha and Lord Theodoric's grandchildren seem to get it better than I. The fighting is hard; the writing's harder. Mayhap, reading is enough, Poppa. Must I write as well?" Pippin ate a bit of tart, washing it down with river water. "Thinking of it, I don't feel hungry after all." He put the tart aside.

"You're at a disadvantage." Charlemagne hurried to explain to Pippin. "The younger you start to learn the writing art, the easier it seems to be. I'll never master it myself; started too late, I'm sure. But you are much younger than I. You'll grow into the skill." He insisted earnestly. "And, aye, it is necessary for you to learn."

"That relieves me, Poppa...that it's not easy for everyone." Pippin replied slowly. "I asked the master for something more to copy, to practice the letters. But the religious tract he gave me was hard to read and understand. It's more trouble than the copying's worth."

"A religious piece? Stupid monk!" King Charlemagne exclaimed. "He gave you an illuminated copy, I'm sure--one meant for beauty, not for reading. I'll speak to him, and tell Alcuin to make recommendations to your teachers. This monk has a copyist's mind, I would guess." Charlemagne chuckled to himself, though he sympathized with Pippin's frustration.

"Does Lord Oliver ever write his thoughts or, even, his philosophy down, Poppa? I should like to read a copy of his words." Pippin wondered aloud.

"Oliver?" The King asked, puzzled. "...not that I know of, though he has some hunting tales, I believe. I didn't think philosophy was your interest, though I'd be pleased if you developed an analytical mind. Would you wish to debate and share thoughts, my boy, as some of us do in the 'Philosophers Discussion?'" Not pausing for Pippin's reply, the King smiled. "How unusual – that want to read Oliver's thoughts." Charlemagne frowned: "...why Oliver?"

"Oh, because, Poppa! Master Alcuin told me he and Oliver discussed things. He said Oliver was a good thinker, mayhap the best in your court. The Master explained the reason for some of your campaigns to me. If he hadn't told me differently, I would think all you and your soldiers do is terrorize...to get people to obey you. Their fear of you gives you control over them." He shrugged but spoke earnestly.

"I believe many people just follow the strong men, do whatever is asked of them. Don't you think so?" He asked the King. "That's the reason I want to read something Oliver wrote—to see a thinking man's ideas." Pippin explained.

"Go on," Charlemagne responded, barely keeping his irritation under control. 'What is this about terrorizing people? Let me hear more of your thoughts."

"It's simple, Poppa," Pippin responded eagerly. But, then, seeing his father's jaw clench, he knew he angered the King; he overstepped some boundary. Pippin plunged ahead but paused to find the best words.

"It seems to me people are full of fear from your conquests. They see killing and more killing. People don't want to die. So, they do as you order: go to church, supply food for your soldiers, bring grain and fruit to your cook tents. They see your power, even your bravery." Pippin added. "But they don't feel they're your people. They serve you and flatter you, if they can, to stay alive. I talked to many travelers on my way here. They bring tales from the entire realm. And all I heard showed people full of fear, Poppa." Pippin wanted to be clear so he gave his father an example.

"Queen Hildegard said she and Uncle Theo approached the shepherds beyond the mountain and made friends with them. On her direction, the grain farmers take wheat and barley to the shepherds for the winter. The shepherds, then, use the grain to feel their sheep and supply mutton to your cooks. Through supplying the grain, the farmers survive to plant again the next year. And the farmers buy wool or even a sheep from the shepherds!" Pippin smiled, pleased with the circle of economic activity. "Isn't this smart?" Pippin, his words tumbling out, did not wait for his father's reply.

"But that's not all! Queen Hildegard takes the wool from those sheep, brings it to the weavers, and replaces the court tunics for cooks, serving wenches, bakers, and gardeners in the winter. Her coins to the shepherds buy needles, knives, carts and such for them. There is good feeling among them all; I have seen it." The lad looked very thoughtful as he continued.

Charlemagne sat still in amazement. The boy quickly grasped this 'circle of work,' of interdependence, he thought.

"In these weeks here, I watched and listened," Pepin forged on. "I knowsome people like you, even love their king." He explained, glancing into the King's face. "But those aren't the ones who fear you. Master Rinaldo and

Master Angilbert, too, talk to cloth merchants, to spice merchants, to those who supply parchment. They come when summoned, but not from fear of you nor to obey you. Instead, they're here to exchange goods, or, if not that, to make coins, to feed their families. This seems to me a good thing, this working with each other. War is bad; it brings death, and loss, and extra hate." Pippin was silent. This is a long way round to get Master Oliver's words to copy, he thought. *But Poppa should know the people's fear of him isn't a positive thing.*

"I must think on this, Pippin," Charlemagne answered. "...had enough of these sweet 'delights'?" At Pippin's nod, they mounted their horses and returned to the stables.

The next day, after his mid-day fast, one of the King's squires brought Pippin a treatise on 'Rationales for Keeping the Peace,' penned by Lord Oliver.

***

Returning from a walk alone the next morning, Pippin spied little Charles washing his horse.

"Little Charles, indeed." Pippin muttered, amused as he looked at the stocky ten-year-old. "He's almost as big as Oliver's squire." Charles groomed his pony with a stiff brush. When the little horse turned his head back to look at him, Charles immediately dipped a large flagon into the river and poured water over the animal's back.

"It's a hot day, Ter." Charles said as he poured an extra bucket over the little horse. The horse whinnied in reply and moved his back feet. He stood in puddles of water, the rivulets coursing down his sides and gathering around his hooves. But Charles knew he was happy; the horse delighted in being wet. Charles smiled to himself. How crazy I was, he thought, just two years ago. *How* could I have thought 'Terror' would be a good name for my horse! He's anything but scary! And he giggled.

"What's so funny?" asked a voice behind him.

Charles turned to see Pippin, the hunchback, skirting the edge of the river. He smiled at Charles, clearly amused by Charles' giggle. Charles didn't know how to act with Pippin. He liked the older boy; he was straight-forward, friendly - a hard worker who never expected special treatment. Charles knew he had a place Pippin could never claim, even though Pippin was his father's son as well. Charles didn't see this situation as fair, but he didn't how to change it.

"Good morn to you, Pippin." Charles answered. "I was wondering if I ever did anything stupider than naming my horse." He laughed aloud. "Sometimes, it seems, my mind stops working."

"I can't answer that, Charles," Pippin replied. "But I wondered about the name, 'Ter.' I supposed it had something to do with crying." At Charles' stupefied look, Pippin explained. "You see, Ter' sounds like 'tear' so I guessed they had some connection."

"Oh!" Charles cried. "What a good guess! Do you mind if I say that, Pippin? It explains 'Ter' better than my true reason. I could say his full name is 'Teardrop' since he is light-colored...clear like a teardrop. Or I could say I cried til Poppa got him for me."

"I wouldn't use the crying part, Charles," Pippin laughed. "It would be repeated, just as you were trying to be your bravest...and most grown up."

"Aye, saying that would make a problem, wouldn't it?" Little Charles answered, praying the older boy wouldn't embarrass him with the tale later. Sometimes, Pippin seems so lonely, Charles thought. *I wish he could feel included in something.*

"I wanted my horse—pony—to be bold. I thought a brave name would help him." Charles laughed again. "The 'Ter' really came from 'Terror.' It seemed the best name...at the time. In a few days, though, I worried the name was a mistake. Look at him! How can anything this pea size be a terror?"

Pippin admitted such a name was a huge stretch and laughed with delight at Charles' explanation. "He seems a good and decent mount, Charles." Pippin answered. "So I think 'Ter' is the best compromise. Just say Rotrude, as a little girl, called him 'Ter,' mixing the sound up with 'deer.' People will believe your explanation; they'll understand you wanted him to be swift...like the deer. You can be certain."

"Good idea, Pippin, I will. Only you and I will know the real name?" Charles replied, a question in his voice.

"Only you and I." Pippin agreed.

"What are you lads about?" Theodoric asked as he walked up. "Here are some tender shoots for my mount; look at her head straight for them!"

"I'm checking to see if Charles needs any help, finishing up his horse bathing." Pippin replied. "I think he's done, though. Anything I can do for you, Master Theo?"

Everyone in the court knew how much Pippin missed Oliver during his journey to find more soldiers. Oliver befriended Pippin when he first came to Charlemagne's court. He never expected less of Pippin than he did the other boys and never spoke about Pippin's hunch-back. They spent lots of time together, fishing and such. So, now, Theo or Angilbert tried to share time with Pippin. It was their way of honoring Oliver and his friendship. It also made the lad less lonely.

"Aye, lad," Theo replied. "Come with me to the cook tent. I need help carrying food to the men working the leather. Through some carelessness, rats got into the war steeds' bridles and ruined many of them. Now it's a race to get new bridles made before the summer battles. Come, Pippin, help me take the meal." Little Charles bade them both goodbye and turned 'Ter' toward the King's tent.

Pippin and Theo talked together as they packed leather pouches with food, remembering their last fishing efforts and the tasty meal they enjoyed.

"Where're the men working, Lord Theo?" Pippin asked. "I didn't see anyone near the supply tent."

"Nay, they're working through the night, near the cook tent. Sleep as they can, get up to eat and work again. I built up fires for them, should help them see a little better. They insisted on moving their tent and supplies away from the main camp; said they didn't want to keep everyone awake as they worked. So, we have about four miles to get to them, my boy." Theo replied.

Pippin and Theo spent some time gathering food, begging from every cook tent. The leatherworkers had no time to cook or leave their work. Pippin, seeing apple tarts cooling on a bench, asked the baker for the 'poor men working through the night' and netted tarts for all of them, including Theo and himself.

Feeling very proud of their success and looking forward to their own feast, Pippin and Theo mounted their horses to deliver the meal. They rode in companionable silence for a bit. Then Pippin turned a little toward Theo and spoke.

"I need your advice, Lord Theo. I hear different stories from different people. Some of it I can't make sense of." Pippin shrugged as if ignoring the problem. But the tense set of his shoulders told Theo otherwise.

"It's hard to know what people mean sometimes, Pippin." Theo assured him. "Even when they explain, you're only get part of a story. There's the reason Oliver and I say you must think for yourself."

"Oh, I understand, Master Theo," Pippin replied. "But when people say things which you understand later aren't true, what do you do? Do you, then, disbelieve everything they say, or just the things you can see you're being misled about? I feel uncertain of everything I hear now."

"Do you mind telling me what's troubling you?" Theo asked. "I don't want you to break a confidence. If your questions don't give away secrets, how about describing a situation—even if you don't want to repeat what someone told you?" He tried not to push the boy. Experience showed that, oftentimes, the less you knew about something, the better off you were!

Pippin frowned, sighed, and looked at Theo's concerned face in the deepening twilight.

"It's not someone telling me things, Master Theo," he replied. "Men don't confide in me. It's just...I feel wary when people seek me out and ask questions. I don't know if it's the subject itself or the tone of those speaking... Let me be direct. In several situations, someone misled me, deliberately, I mean. Someone told me his version of the truth and did not encourage me to seek the truth itself."

Theo was uncomfortable. *Where was this conversation going? Who knew what might have been said, wisely or not?* He saw Pippin's confusion and worry and immediately offered his understanding.

"Well, lad," Theo answered, "tell me what's confusing you."

"Could we feed the men and talk about this as we eat?" Pippin asked. "This roast smells so good I have to get something in my belly before I have the strength to talk!" He laughed as they tied the horses' reins and began to unpack the leather pouches.

It was some time later before the two got their own food and took leather mugs filled with water to sit cross-legged beside the fire. The men were at their benches, eating and working at the same time. Oliver and Pippin sat together.

"Did you know I was in Lombardy, Lord Theo?" Pippin began. Theo shook his head negatively. "I thought you didn't. Queen Gerbegna invited me there...to get to know her sons, she said. But that was a joke." He smiled wryly. "Her sons had no interest in me, especially after they saw my back. They didn't come anywhere near me, probably afraid my hump would attack them. Anyway, I knew in three days Mother made a mistake in agreeing for me to go there. It was bad, a very difficult time." Pippin stopped talking for a few moments. Just as Theo opened his mouth, the young man spoke again.

"I had to stay for a fortnight. Though there were escorts and contingents leaving every day, none traveled in the direction of Ma-mam's home. But it didn't matter. It was clear within a day of my arrival, I had to find my own way about and amuse myself until I could return home."

"Did anyone offer you activities or jaunts or training sessions?" Theo asked. He visited the Lombard court when Desiderius was king; the court had been a lively, busy place. True, Desiderius was now in a monastery, Charlemagne's punishment for his attempted coup. But the nobles were wealthy still so the court must reflect some of its former splendor. Pippin spoke.

"The seneschal told me the daily activities of Queen Gerbegna's sons but they never asked me to join them. Both boys are older than I, it's true. But they had no interest in me, were never friendly. Nay, I trained with the squires, often ate with them, too, and stayed out of the way. But here's the strange situation I don't understand."

Theo offered Pippin an extra apple tart and watched with delight as the boy demolished it in appreciative bites. Growing lads' appetites, he thought, are not affected by confusion, nor even by a father's neglect, it seems. Pippin thanked him for the tart and continued his story.

"The man who tutored the boys, Queen Gebegna's boys, often sought me in the library. I found him ill-prepared to teach, Lord Theo. Anyway, that's not the point. I want to describe this exactly, not color the tale with just my side of it. Let me think a minute to get it right." As Pippin sat quietly, ticking off his fingers, Theo took down the packs in preparation for a night by the fire. He and Pippin agreed they both preferred to sleep beside by the fire, under the stars.

The night was warm as creatures' stirrings formed a backdrop to the soft peeps from tree frogs. A cacophony of sound surrounded them. Theo sat back down just as Pippin continued.

"That master, the boys' tutor, asked me repeatedly if I knew King Charlemagne's children, if I visited the court as it moved through the realm and wintered at Aachen or Ingelhein. I told him the court never settled for more than a few weeks at the time. I emphasized I knew no one in the court well, most especially my father. He seemed surprised but, even more, very disappointed. The next day, he came out of the music room and walked me to the stables...to point out the best horses, he said. Ha! ...as if I could choose one to ride!" Pippin shook his head. "This day, he wanted me to describe Poppa's children — color of hair, height, color of eyes, and their dispositions."

"Aren't those questions strange, Lord Theo, coming from a teaching master, I mean? I told him I was at the court three years previous. He seemed shocked to hear it. But, then, he said anything I knew about my step-brothers and step-sisters would help." Theo, opening his mouth to answer, stopped at Pippin's outstretched hand. "Nay," he cautioned. "Don't say anything yet; hear all my tale."

"I repeated again I didn't know these children. I knew only their names and ages, which I gave him. Next he asked how much the boys practiced soldiery arts and if the girls were 'homebodies'. It's the very word he used. In my loneliness I told him I believed everyone was a 'homebody,' if they have a decent home. He seemed very interested in my statement, even told me it was of great importance. His interest, so intense it was, made me wary; so I told him little. Of course, I knew little to tell." Theo motioned for Pippin to stop talking.

"And when were you there, Pippin, at the Lombardy Court?" He asked.

"...just before being summoned here, Master Theo. I did not even go home to bid goodbye to my mother. I came directly from Lombardy to this court. I went there just after Yuletide for about six weeks. Is the time I was there important?"

"I see," Theo answered, shaking his head 'nay' to Pippin's question. Why does that time seem important? He wondered to himself.

"When the teaching master understood I had no real information about my father's court, others in Lombardy became friendly. At least, they sought me out to walk with me to sword practice and to evening meals. They were pleasant, sharing specially-brewed ale (as they said) and treats from the cook tent. It was a surprise to me, to realize how much they seemed to know about Queen Hildegard's children. I wondered why the teaching master didn't consult them with all his questions."

"Who were these people, Pippin? And what exactly did they say? Was the information true, now that you see the King's children and their lives?" Theo asked.

"I don't believe any of it was true, Master." Pippin stated. "These holy men and one maid, they talked like they were members of Poppa's court, like they lived in his court for years. One of the monks was hostile when I knew nothing to tell him. He asked if Abbot Fulrad hadn't taught me to respond to an elder's questions." Seeing Theo's confused face, Pippin explained.

"For example, one particularly friendly fellow said he knew Rotrude often made fun of me. He said she told stories describing stupid things I did: like falling off a rooftop, spilling the milk bucket bringing it to the kitchen, or teasing a puppy until it threw up its food. Lord Theo, the stories made me sound like a monster."

"Another monk declared Charles jealous of me...because I was the oldest son. He warned me Charles hungered to fight me on the practice field, to cut off my hump so I'd be normal. He sneered and said Rotrude and Louis told all the soldiers I was 'funny looking.' How could it be true, Lord Theo? Louis is just a child. We don't even know each other! Then another suggested I was no longer Poppa's son because little Carloman's name change to Pepin took my name and my place away." Pippin put his face in his hands, overcome by the derision implied in the words he recounted.

Theo felt sick. What's the point of inflicting all this pain? He asked himself. *Why would anyone hurt Pepin this way, especially about his appearance? Why draw attention to his difference...to hurt him or to get something from him?* Theo answered his own question. *But why must men be so cruel?*

"What do you think was the reason for these tales,

Pippin?" Theo didn't know if this were a cruel question. But he knew Pippin must learn to discount such dribble. He mustn't think anyone, certainly not his own siblings, would believe or say such things. "You must know these recountings are untrue." Theo declared, realizing Pippin needed to hear them denied.

"Master, it's not possible for me to know the truth. I know some people, seeing me, want to hurt me. They are usually cruel, hate-filled people. Mayhap, they wish to hurt anyone. I don't know where such hate comes from. I do know Rotrude would never, ever say such things. And Charles is incapable of such cruelty. Now that I'm here in this court, I am more convinced than ever. But why tell me such things? Do I exist just for others to hurt? Is that my fate?" Pippin spread his hands, begging Theo for an explanation.

"Pippin, Pippin." Theo grabbed the boy around the shoulders. "You must not believe such talk. These are only stories someone created to make mischief. It is, I believe, someone's effort to sever you from your father, from your brothers and sisters, from any positive feelings about this court. Such talk is the creation of a sick mind, one which hopes to create hatred, to encourage you to hate your father and your family. Woe to the ass who dreamt this! I would cut out his heart and be gleeful!" Theo spoke as firmly and as angrily as he could, his good heart wounded over the suffering Pippin endured.

"You must believe no one here wishes you harm. Think on the concern good Queen Hildegard has for you and know people here love and value you. Didn't your father welcome you immediately? Didn't you feel everyone was happy to greet you? Your treatment in Lombardy was a poison which is meant to spread all through your heart."

"Aye, this does seem likely. Aye, Lord Theo, you do have the right of it. But how can the court be harmed, if I'm hurt? I never saw these people, these Lombards, before." Pippin replied. "I wish them no harm. Truly."

"That is to your credit, my boy," Theo answered. "Tell me once more the questions you were asked, if you can remember. If not, we will waste no time on speculation. But I will tell your father someone in Lombardy continues to wish him ill...not a new reality, of a certainty!"

"Let me see." Pippin's brow wrinkled. "The tutor asked me Charles', Rotrude's, and Louis' favorite activities. One of the masters wanted to know if the Queen rode out often with her maids in attendance, or did she most-often ride alone. Another asked the sleeping hours of the King and Queen. A monk wondered if my father continues to swim at any opportunity, even in winter. The first master particularly asked about the children's lives: the foods they liked, their horses' names, their favorite activities, if they had many picnics or visits away from the court. I told them nothing of these things for I knew nothing. Mother told me of Rotrude's betrothal and of the likelihood she would spend time at the Byzantium Court. I told them of the an engagement but knew no details." Keeping his reactions in check, Theo asked a question.

"Anything else you remember saying to them? You had very little to tell, more than likely the reason they kept asking you questions. I would guess these are no 'masters,' Pippin. These men were spies for Desiderius or Adelchis."

"Mayhap." Pippin answered. "The only responses I made were general ones that everyone knew. But being here, I see the activities are no longer true. The teaching master said Oliver and Roland drank and caroused away the night hours with young wenches. He described musical contests at the evening meal where the contestants drank many flagons of ale. And someone said the Peers raced horses in order to choose the fastest ones for Oliver and Roland." Theo startled at the comment, at which Pippin laughed good-naturedly. Pippin pointed at Theo. "It's true; I did hear it. Oliver and Roland have huge reputations."

"Racing horses? That tale is true." Theo confirmed. "They really did choose their mounts by racing them! I know other stories, different interpretations which I will not repeat to you." Theo looked rueful as they both laughed, thankful to move beyond the painful memories Pippin recounted.

"Lad, we both need sleep. Here, I've spread our blankets near the fire. Rest easy; try to dream—only pleasant things, though!"

Breathing a sigh, Pippin took off his hat, patted Theo's arm and lay down. In a few moments, his face relaxed, he curled to his side and smiled. He was asleep the next breath. Theo watched the sleeping boy.

"...Such treachery!" Theo mumbled to himself. "Here is the answer to Rotrude's kidnapping--the Lombard Court. It's just as I heard in the court's whispers. All of Desiderius' antipathy still remains. Ever are there men ready to use old arguments and jealousies to obtain their own desires. Now, what to do? Mayhap, Alcuin can suggest a next step for us. I wonder when he'll get back." The scholar was on a trip to Tours to seek parchments for the court school. Already, he was late returning.

***

Luck was with them. The next afternoon, Master Alcuin arrived at King Charlemagne's court.

"A huge rainstorm delayed me." Alcuin explained to Angilbert. "There was no hope of passing through it. At least, our wait was in a dry cave, a great place for sleeping!" Alcuin looked pleased with his adventure but his delight in seeing Angilbert was obvious.

"Master, welcome back; I hoped you would be here before the sun rose again. We must speak. I have worrisome news but need, firstly, to tell you of events here since you left. You heard about the attempted kidnapping of Rotrude?" Angilbert described the still-fresh event, as well as reported on the birth of little Gesila."

"Theodoric formed a possible explanation of Rotrude's kidnapping. The plot likely originated in the Lombard court. We have hints of what may have happened there. You and I are both fond of Pippin. This concerns him. I fear his story has grave implications for the court. We must expect constant threats." Angilbert recounted Theo's explanation to his teacher and requested Alcuin's reaction to the events Pippin described.

"Theo waits your reaction, Sir, and requests your suggestions for what we should do next." Alcuin sighed, his heart aching at Pippin's experience in the Lombard Court.

"We must see the king." Alcuin answered. In short order, the three men requested an audience with King Charlemagne. He sent for them immediately.

"You must speak, Theo." Alcuin said. "Be as direct as you can but make no judgments yourself. Just relay the facts as Pippin gave them to you. There might easily be traitors in the King's court, as we speak. Do you understand?" They went directly to the King. Theo recounted all he heard from Pippin.

"And so," Alcuin concluded, "it appears an enemy of this court planned Rotrude's kidnapping. He or his accomplices had information about her betrothal and her upcoming journey to Constaninople."

Charlemagne looked from Theo's face, to Alcuin's. Then, he looked at Angilbert. All of a sudden, in a sharp movement, he slapped his left fist into his right hand.

"How dare he betray his sister thus?" he bellowed. "I will wring his neck!" The King stomped around the room, his steps increasing in rapidity, his fists hitting and hitting into his hands.

Theo watched the king, completely shocked. After all the information he told the King about plots and likely counter-plots, Charlemagne was angry with his son!

"Did you hear my words, Charlemagne?" Alcuin raised his voice, deliberately putting disbelief in his words. "You hear nothing!"

"Wait, let me speak!" Angilbert exclaimed. Charlemagne, for such a huge man, turned quickly and glared into Angilbert's face.

"Wait for what?" he demanded. "You want to wait? My own son betrays his family and you all just sit there! What treachery! He must be punished. He must be controlled, for his and my own good!" Alcuin strode to the King, grabbed his shoulder and turned him.

"Sire! Sire! Control yourself .You don't think clearly. Stop, this moment. LISTEN to us!" Like a past-ripe pear with no core, the King withered and looked at Alcuin, beseeching his help.

"You're acting a fool!" Alcuin shrieked. "No wonder men are hesitant to bring you a truth! Have you lost your senses? The lad is innocent of wrong doing. Innocent! Do you hear me?"

"Pippin doesn't even realize the Lombards used him! Where is your reason, that mind you're so proud of? Sit down! Pay attention! And listen, again, to Theo's tale."

Alcuin pressed the King down on the library bench and nodded to the two men. "Theo, repeat your information."

Theo held his breath for a brief spate, then recounted young Pippin's description of his visit at the Lombard court again. He admired Alcuin's many gifts--not the least was this one, helping to control the King's temper. He heard the Abbot could make Charlemagne see reason as well. The King, he knew, lost control very infrequently; he functioned well...most of the time. But when he did not, everyone paid - culpable or not.

Charlemagne sat in chastised silence, a tear running down his cheek as Theo, once again, recounted the contempt his children supposedly had for Pippin. When Theo described Pippin's experience at the Lombard court, everyone was silent.

Alcuin sat directly in front of King Charlemagne. His face was grim, his brow furrowed. He held his fingers before the King's face and began to tick off facts.

"You understand, Charlemagne, we defend Pippin. You hear he meant no harm to your children? He had no real knowledge of your plans for Rotrude. He repeated his mother's speculations to questions whose intent he could not imagine. Are you listening to me; do you hear me, Sire?" Alcuin questioned the King.

"I must be satisfied your anger does not affect your reason. Are you in control of your temper? ANSWER ME, damn it!" Alcuin, dumfounded by the King's show of rabid anger and now incomprehension, completely lost his own temper. Charlemagne gazed steadily at him.

"Aye." He responded in a muted voice. "Aye, I hear you, Alcuin." He smiled slightly. "You don't need to shout. I'm quiet because I see just how poorly I judge my son! I, who lead hundreds of men, see him in the worst possible light. What a fool I've become. What a fool..."

Angilbert let his breath out.

"Thank God for my Master." He whispered quietly to himself. He realized the weakness in his knees and quickly sat down. Theodoric muttered to himself as well.

"Thank God the King listens to Master Alcuin! I could never control him so; and who knows what he would do to poor Pippin?" Alcuin's voice broke into his thoughts.

"The single reason we came to you, Sire, was to alert you, again, to the threat against your house. Theo recounted Pippin's experience only to suggest the insidious nature of these plans. In truth, it matters not who attacks you, who kidnaps your children, who threatens your rule! If any one of you is dead, the damage far outweighs the identity of the assailant. But, knowing the source of these plots, you must act! You must, firstly, protect your family and, then, root out these traitors." Alcuin shook his fist.

"Be thankful your eldest son is innocent…and good in heart. Be thankful for his mother. You know she taught no treachery at her breast. Be thankful, you old bear! Praise God!" Alcuin challenged the King, content to give him time to think and to regain his control.

"Why am I king?" Charlemagne asked. "My advisers are so much more able than I?"

"Right father, right time, right moment!" Alcuin quipped. "Don't go into the doldrums, Sire. We must counteract the poison infiltrating your court. We've had too much delay and denial of reality already."

"Those of us here agree, Sire." Theo reflected Alcuin's urgency. "The threat is from Lombardy. From there came the attack on you at the hunt, Sire; the arrow which poisoned your leg at the river camp; the attack on Rotrude's escort; the effort to take Pepin and, possibly, the threat to Charles in the burning of your tent years ago."

"Everything points to a traitor within this court. There must be someone within, aiding these Lombards. Let us fervently hope a court noble is not the mind behind these attacks."

"Additional steps to protect your children will be taken today. I shall ask Renfrey to be responsible for expanded protection." Alcuin proposed. "The children are more vulnerable than you or the Queen. I daresay no harm came to Pippin in Lombard because there was no awareness you valued the lad." Alcuin could not resist the mild rebuke.

Charlemagne nodded in agreement, thanked the three men, and left for the stables — once more hoping for calm in riding his stallion across the land.

***

Alcuin and Fulrad spent many hours together, talking well into the early hours of the morn. King Charlemagne already directed them to identify the individuals who threatened his family. Contrary to his habit of imposing justice with his procedures and laws, in this threat the King left any corrective actions to the judgment of his trusted Peers.

Truth be told, Angilbert said to himself, I made tens of inquiries, inter-viewed soldiers, even followed people and watched them since the attack on Rotrud's escort. *There were no viable findings, nothing we can use to move against anyone. Neither did we identify anyone to watch or confine.*

"You know, Master," Angilbert voiced his thought. "Since it seems these attacks are Lombardy-based, we must review the behavior of every individual in the court and identify anyone who came to us from Lombardy during the past several months. Reviewing any more time would, I think, be useless. No one spoke of Rotrude's betrothal before her visit to Constaninople, no one other than the King and Queen to each other. And Pippin was in Lombardy after that time. So, let's look at those who entered court service, or even came to visit if they still remain, after our departure from Aachen at Yuletide."

"That's a reasonable plan, Gil," Alcuin concurred. "I know nothing more to suggest at this point. That's a place to start. I daresay this will be a long hunt."

Chapter 25

CHANGES IN THE REALM

Charlemagne vowed to leave the hunt for Rotrude's kidnappers to his Peers. He knew his temper would, eventually, hamper any of their efforts, so he determined to turn his energy to something else. He knew he must resurrect his people's hope in the future, somehow render them enthusiastic about learning, instill a hunger for learning and knowledge. *But how?* He asked himself daily. *What can I do to give them a new vision of themselves?*

He stared at the top of a red-haired lad's head. Startled out of his musings, he looked around, not quite remembering just where he was or what he did. *Oh, now I remember. My guardsmen are identifying likely-looking men for the wrestling bouts on the morrow.* The King shouted to two muscle-bound lads on the field.

"Hold him upright. If he upsets you, you are the loser!" The young men, Curt and Danis, grappled to hold on to each other, both acknowledging the King's warning. They were almost mirror images of each other: bulky shoulders, legs outlined by muscle, bulging cords along the arms, able to hold and endure.

Along with Curt and Danis, many of the men were exhausted. They started wrestling more than two hours ago; many of them now hung onto each other in order to stand. Control passed from one of the pair to another. If attention wavered or a limb weakened, the fighter fell to the strength of his opponent.

"Just look at them, Hilde." Charlemagne caught the Queen's attention. "They're desperate for a chance, for any hope." Queen Hildegard examined her husband's face. His forehead furrowed, his mouth drooping, his eyes outlined in unshed tears, he watched the men struggle. "They're so eager. Watch them, just for a space." Queen Hildegard hated these military spectacles.

"This staged combat is man's excuse for yet more fighting. I don't understand." She said. "Fighting dominates your lives. Can there be no end to it?"

With her husband's words still echoing in her head, Hildegard separated the contestants into two groups. One group, composed of well-fed and well-dressed nobles and an occasional high-ranking soldier, clearly derived great fun from the games, competing in good-natured spirit with their comrades. The other group-- mostly lean, unkempt men--fought with great dexterity and energy. Remembering Charlemagne's use of 'desperate,' Hildegard looked with new eyes.

"My dear," she said quietly to her husband, "aye, I see the desperation. They compete as if they have nothing to lose, don't they?"

"Assuredly so," the King replied. "They fight to be selected to participate in a hunt. In the past, I've invited some local man in the hunt to join a regiment or to compete for a training slot among our newest soldiers. At the last joust, I asked if anyone would like to apprentice as a cook. Their response, their interest, is shocking! The men don't really care what the job choice might be; they just want to get the offer of a place. That hope keeps them sweating, grappling, and trying to best each other! I can feel their hunger, the constant gnawing which urges them to push a little harder, to take a bigger risk—anything to make a chance for themselves. They'll grab any chance which comes."

"But, it's the young boys who captured my thoughts, Hilde. They look beaten at the age of twelve or fifteen. There is no hope in their faces."

"Our own boys often complain of having nothing to do. They declare they are bored with sword play, with riding the hills atop their own horses, with tending the colts and kennel dogs. Yet, the lads swirling around here turn eager faces to anyone who offers a crumb for an errand. They have no time to be bored. They strive to survive." Overwhelmed with concern and regret, Charlemagne almost wept. Of a certainty, he forgot the games and their attractions.

What can I do? How do we produce more food, get it to the people? How do I maintain the men's and boys' support, their loyalty? There must be an answer!

***

Charlemagne's realm had no coinage system. For the most part, his people traded and bartered for goods. His grasp of economic measures, small as it was, limited his ability to bring more plenty to the land. He understood, though, that his empire - whether composed only of Franks or including Lombards, Spanish, and Saxons - must develop trade. He knew the strength of Byzantium, including its spread of Christianity, lay in its ability to send both products and people throughout the world. And since he obtained food, yarn, tools, armor—well, almost everything—from those who dwelt within his lands, Charlemagne realized the power of one group supplying necessary goods to another group.

He constantly sent messengers to various small villages in order to encourage metal-smiths, stone-cutters, tailors, even cooks, and other trades people to migrate to his court. He kept them busy and well-fed; but the size of his court, like the size of his empire, kept expanding. There were never enough craftsmen, never enough skilled workers - no matter which particular skill the court or the army needed.

"Let's set a price on specific goods and, even, on services." Charlemagne said to Oliver.

"A price, Sire. How will we determine a fair amount? Pears in Ingleheim are worth next to nothing, so many grow there. But in Aachen, the price would double or triple. How do we allow for that?"

"Send for Alcuin," Charlemagne suggested. "He may have some idea."

Alcuin, Anglibert, and Oliver talked into the night, trying to create a fair distribution of prices for specific goods. Finally, Anglilbert held up his hands.

"Who are we to figure this out? We need to go to those who have this knowledge. We can sit and speculate all day but we cannot know if our ideas are realistic. Let's go to the experts on this."

"And who would that be?" Alcuin asked, his eyes red with fatigue.

"The seneschals, of a certainty!" Anglibert exclaimed. "They negotiate, procur, evaluate and use all the goods which pass through noble manors. Surely, there is a system already in place. True, they may barter; they may exchange one type of good for another; they pay more for cloth from Septimania than they do for that woven in Pavia, mayhap. But there must be some reason to their decisions and their costs."

"Aye." Oliver agreed. "Of a certainty, the seneschals know more than we about goods and services, for certain."

The seneschal, Marius, welcomed the men into his counting room. Reams of shelves held codices and parchments, all filled with transactions to support Charlemagne's court. Oliver, Alcuin and Angilbert felt immediately more hopeful as they took the seats offered them. Marius nodded as Alcuin explained their problem.

"We do have a system, of sorts, in place." He told them after Alcuin explained the King's demand that a coinage system be created to replace the practice of bartering. "Our prices...for good or services...are competitive so individual prices change often. One day pears from Ingelheim, that you mention, cost 2 coppers each; another day, they will be 3.5 coppers."

"But how do you know the cost on a particular day?" Anglibert asked.

"The simple answer is this. The cost of an item depends on how many people want it. If there is a large demand, the item is more expensive; if the demand is low, the item's price goes lower."

"And how do you keep up with that...changing prices all over the realm? It makes no sense to me." Alcuin replied.

"The realm does not matter." Marius answered. "Price is set by the man who has the goods or provides the service. Your only concern is if you can pay his price. He sets the price and takes the chance his goods may bring more or less money. If he travels to deliver his goods, his price may differ from place to place. The price is too high, you say? He must lower it or keep his goods for himself." Marius' face broke in a wide smile. "The demand for the item determines the price; that is all."

"So, all we need do is convince people that this 'coinage system' will work, will provide them with the items they need? Is that it?" Angilbert asked Marius.

"Aye. It is as you say. But you must pay men in coins for their labor. There must be enough coinage for them to buy the things they need. Local food – vegetables, eggs, milk - will require lower prices than tarts, tea, or spices. Many people will grow their own food, hunt for meat as they've always done, gather nuts in the autumn. They may use the foods themselves or sell it to others; but the prices will be similar in each region. Food unavailable in one place will cost more in another but that fact encourages trade. It will be 'bartering' with a monetary amount of value, rather than an exchange of products." Marius explained the coinage system of the Romans to the three men, emphasizing its simplicity and applicability to any realm.

King Charlemagne himself introduced the idea to his court, first to the nobility and, then, to the workers. From there, he sent couriers among the small villages and noble estates through which his court moved. The use of coins placed resources in the hands of people at every level of society. If he and his sons continued to increase the size of the realm, continued to draw more souls into their lands, opportunities to expand trade would rise.

Charlemagne encouraged tradesmen by establishing legal protections for them. He guaranteed a wage for their labor and encouraged them to move throughout the realm, hiring themselves out. He sought workers of iron, gold, and silver. His realm needed more shoemakers, carpenters, fishermen, soap makers, bird catchers and net makers.

Artisans did not overly concern him. They could be borrowed from the churches and monasteries, though enticing them away from the monks was often difficult. Only the monasteries had the wealth or the inclination to support aesthetic concerns; and, of course, all beauty in religion was but a reflection or praise to the glory of the Lord. The common people had little time or coin for the pursuit and support of beautiful ornamentation.

The people must have work. Charlemagne repeated to himself. *I must find some way to increase people's need for products, as well as their ability to buy such things. It's the only way the realm can support itself. But how can I do it? What methods should I use?*

Though Charlemagne yearned for the wisdom of his father, he understood King Pepin never had the answers his son so desperately sought. His father lived his entire life surrounded by the court, from managing the king's resources to surviving on them.

Poppa never thought of changing the structure of his society. But I, I intend to restructure it. I want a prosperous realm, one with educated, Christian people who have enough to eat, who learn and live without such wide-spread want and ignorance. He knew converting his people to Christianity would help him manage, even control them. If he could also offer a more stable, more fruitful life, his realm would prosper. And his sons need fight less often.

King Charlemagne looked again at the dozens of young lads milling about.

"Aye!" He cried in sudden understanding. "Aye! I must help them develop skills. All of them will not want to read and write. They want work; reading and writing aren't often required. Many, even now, would follow a trade, if the training existed."

"I'll ask the monks to initiate skills training, the skills needed in the manors—cooking, farming, animal husbandry, orchard maintenance. I'll bribe the tailors, the smiths, and the builders to offer more apprentice positions--not just the usual one--but three or four. The crown will pay them for their trouble. In time, we'll have workmen to send out into the realm; we'll have men with skills. Apprentice them, train them well and quickly, make them subjects supportive of Christ's teachings and loyal to their king! Here's the foundation for a more benevolent society and a prosperous kingdom." He sent for Alcuin.

***

Charlemagne continued his mission to conquer the Saxons. While he planned, described battle tactics, and mapped marches, his Peers centered their attention on the vulnerability of the royal children. The Abbot called Angilbert yet again to the library tent in order to evaluate their ruse on the King. Did Anglibert's perceived argument with Charlemagne root out any malcontents?

"After the scene at the river with the King," Fulrad said, "have any traitors come forward, Angilbert?" Condescendingly, he considered the young scholar. "Are you a good enough actor to attract a traitor?" Angilbert ignored the jibe and answered humbly.

"Nay, Abbot, no certain enemy of the King. Oh, several individuals approached me, of a certainty; but I take none of them seriously. One or two nobles tried to suggest they knew more...or guessed more...than they tell. ...But, hard, substantial evidence? Nay. There is no one to investigate further. What about you?"

"No one, absolutely no one approached me," the Abbot responded ponderously. "Of a certainty, my closeness to the king would probably prevent any such contact." He straightened his mantle around his shoulders and paced about. "Angilbert, this effort to steal Rotrude was the act of a disgruntled fool. There is no complicated plot. I am certain of it."

"No plot...because no one comes to you? Why didn't you warn us no one would approach you, Abbot? Alcuin and I both wasted our efforts, trying to encourage those who work against Charlemagne to align with me. Do you believe the King has no enemies? Is that your meaning?" He shrugged. "If so, our drama fails but we cannot undo the choice now. My unhappiness with the King's reaction, his anger at me...we play this to some conclusion." Angilbert inclined his head slightly and left the library.

"An ass, boy! You are an ass!" Fulrad Abbot exclaimed, as soon as Angilbert was out of hearing. "There's no traitor in the court. There are many disaffected lords, many jealous courtiers but no traitor to my King. I'm certain of it." He left the library tent.

***

As the Peers continued to struggle to identify Rotrude's abductor, the King decided to spend some time with Pippin. He began taking his hunchback son with him everywhere. He never wanted anyone to suggest he didn't love his first born son nor accuse him of being ashamed or embarrassed about him. Queen Bertrada's banishment of Pippin's mother, Himiltrude, still haunted his heart, even after all these years. Even if he didn't understand it, he knew Pippin's life was difficult and, often lonely. He hoped to ease those conditions by his presence.

Charlemagne, himself, was not unhappy. Hildegard, their children and his work filled his life. He readily acknowledged Hildegard's value to him and to his court. But his heart ached for poor Pippin.

Charlemagne, always secure in his place in the world, never tasted mistreated or marginalization. Central to the lives of many people, especially his sister, Gisila, he reveled in the security of his place. But he remembered his brother Carloman's anguish when he felt overlooked. Carloman grew up always defensive, forever worried about the opinions of others. King Charlemagne did not want such uncertainty for Pippin.

This world, Charlemagne mused, is for the strong, for the aggressive. *The quiet man, no matter the depth of his thought nor the polish of his appearance, is never noticed, nor much valued. For a craftsman or a clerk, a lack of attention from others may be an acceptable situation. But for one who soldiers, for one who makes decisions for people, for one who must rule — for a king's son — quiet strength is a tremendous weakness.*

King Charlemagne struggled with the necessities of fighting invaders, of demanding their immediate conversion to Christianity, of promoting laws to force their loyalty. Often, his actions clearly violated the church's teachings — teachings he swore to uphold.

"I cannot justify the constant killing; but I, also, can see no end to it." He often muttered under his breath.

***

Charlemagne's army moved forward to attack the Saxons early in the 782 battle season. Prince Widukind, whom all the Saxon tribes followed, led them in another rebellion against Charlemagne. The King wasn't particularly worried about the coming encounter. He held reassuring information from his forward scouts. His fighting men on war-trained destriers, his most disciplined force, far outnumbered the Saxons' horse soldiers. The King was well pleased with the caliber of these men. True, many of the infantry were free men who joined him of their own will. Those men and the soldiers supplied and maintained by the nobility comprised the bulk of his force. But he had a core group of soldiers who bore the brunt of many a battle, the professional men. They helped him maintain a large army, all the better to overwhelm his enemies and to keep his troops' morale high. He honored his fighters, fed and clothed them well. And experienced, battle-hardened commanders, often his Peers, led the Frankish forces.

Charlemagne made certain that stories of successful battles flew throughout his lands. He singled out deserving soldiers, praised and rewarded them. He never undervalued his fighting force. And he kept a watchful eye on soldiers who were lost and those who replaced them. He was a soldier's soldier and delighted in his relationships with them.

***

In this campaign, he sent a large army forward. The first contingent was under the command of Worad.

"For this engagement,Worad," Charlemagne explained, "you will lead the attack, just as you manage the court as Count of the Palace. As you move forward, sound your horn. Theo will, then, move toward you from the west. I shall pace my march from the South." He raised his eyebrows at Worad. "You understand the plan, do you not?" Worad nodded.

King Charlemagne moved his hand over the map, tracing the movement each regiment would follow. Oliver, Rinaldo, and Theo nodded in agreement.

"Remember; we all move within a minute or two of each other and will, then, arrive from three different directions and overwhelm the enemy. We must approach in a three-sided block; I will not have Saxons' breaking through our lines or create exits for their retreat."

"What about the northern approach?" Rinaldo asked.

"It's not a worry," the King answered. "Our closing vise will entrap the Saxons. This time we shall defeat them completely. They grow more bold and destructive with every rebellion. This constant battle will stop on the morrow."

The next morning, waiting behind a small hill, King Charlemagne kept his troops hidden. The soldiers were in place by sunrise and, still, they waited. The King hoped to march as dawn appeared but had, as yet, given no signal to the forward troops. *What is Worad waiting for? Is it possible he expects me to lead the attack, even though I explained the maneuver to him?* Charlemagne summoned a messenger and sent him to Rinaldo.

"Any word from Worad?" He asked. "We must move soon so all sides of the three-pronged attack are coordinated." Pacing up and down before his bowmen, the King listened impatiently for the sound of a horn. Oliver rode up.

"We are ready to move forward, Sire." Roland said, speaking softly in order to hear the battle horn. "Theo does wait overlong to move, does he not?"

"Aye. He must march soon," Charlemagne replied; "or the three prong attack will not work." Charlemagne heard quick busts of sound and saw ash-laden smoke in the distance; but hit and run strikes — typical of Saxon battle — were preliminary to full-scale attacks.

"It will take a short time for our separate contingents to get into place." He said to Count Janlur. "Who can be in a sword fight already?" He frowned with worry, looking to the Count for an explanation. "We saw the Saxons slap their own arms together last year, attempting to sound like a much larger army. Mayhap, they play at war again."

Suddenly, a horse raced down the crest of the hill.

A messenger, urging the horse toward the King, rode recklessly. The man acted strangely: shouted, waved his hands, and beckoned the troops forward.

"Help, Sire, need help!" He shouted as he fell from his horse directly in front of Samson. Charlemagne's big horse shied but quickly regained his balance.

Kerold, a commander to Charlemagne's left, blew his battle horn and raced away, an entire column of men following him. In only a moment his regiment poured down the hill into a battle where clouds of dust and, now, men's screams filled the air.

"It looks like a rout," Bernard shouted to the King as he raised his hand, leading his own men into the valley. "Forward!" Bernard yelled. Following Kerold's standard through the dust and chaos, Bernard's troops streamed toward their fellow soldiers.

"Oh, dear God!" Charlemagne held his breath. "Theo and Worad attack! They do not wait for us to get into place."

The King led his soldiers into the fray. His face grew red with anger as he saw dozens of men fall from their mounts, arrows sticking from their shoulders. Raising his own sword, King Charlemagne led his soldiers in a soul-wrenching battle cry.

At the sound, thousands of Saxons looked up to see a horde of Frankish soldiers pouring into the valley, their weapons catching the glint of the sun's rays as they attacked. At such an onslaught, many of the enemy threw their swords, bows, and daggers to the ground, standing in mute surrender. Charlemagne's regiment slashed and fought.

Rinaldo arrived with his soldiers, cursing and fighting as he led them forward. Oliver, coming from a different direction, saw hundreds of Saxon and Frankish soldiers lying on the ground. The soil was red with blood. Only the wounded moved. The only sound was that of the birds. They already gathered to feast on the dead bodies.

Combining the soldiers in Oliver's, Rinaldo's and his own contingent, Charlemagne's commanders gained control of the battlefield. The King, wielding his sword, cursed as he recognized first one and, then, another of his fighting men.

Rinaldo and Oliver herded Saxon soldiers into a near-by canyon. Their soldiers gathered weapons and commanders directed their troops. All waited for the battle's end to be declared through the battle horns. Seeing the large number of enemy surrenders, Charlemagne rode toward his commanders.

"What in the name of God happened here? Where is Theodoric?" He quickly scanned the battlefield. The dust was so thick all he could see were moving shadows. "Report! Report! Explain this carnage!" Oliver appeared out of the dusty chaos, a sword in each hand.

"I cannot say, Sire, what happened. The battle began long before our arrival. Worad's contingent is destroyed. There are many dead and many more wounded...our Franks, as well as hundreds of Saxons. I found Worad's standard, trodden near a small stream a half furlong away. No sign of him or of Theo. Chamberlain Adalgis-ile and Constable Geilo, though,... we found both their bodies. Pray we have not lost Theo along with the rest."

A few moments later, two soldiers hurried forward, carrying Theo between them on a bloody blanket.

"His wound is grievous, Sire," one of them reported. "He needs a healer quickly."

"Take him to that small hillock." Charlemagne direct-ed, pointing. "My healer comes forthwith." The King hand signaled a nearby messenger. Charlemagne turned to Oliver.

"What did Worad think—himself invincible? This is not the battle we planned! What did he do? What in the hell did he do? If we lose Theodoric, I'll have Worad's balls and those of his sons between my swords!"

Rinaldo turned around bodily. He shook his head in sorrow as tears streamed from his eyes. It was impossible to comprehend the number of bodies lying motionless. Charlemagne watched silently as grim and bloodied Franks herded Saxon captives, still more of them, toward the canyon. Rinaldo galloped to the King.

"Sire," Rinaldo shouted. "Praise God, Theo lives! He may ever limp and favor his left side, but his head is still upon his shoulders." Rinaldo pointed toward soldiers emerging from the battle dust over the canyon. "We found Worad's body; so, too, those of Constable Galio and Chamberlain Adalgis. Every man under their banners died." Rinaldo paused to catch his breath and coughed.

"Theo said the battle began before he arrived. Worad did not wait for Theo or us but attacked as soon as he sighted Saxons. There're many, many lost, Sire." Rinaldo's voice choked over his last sentence.

"How many enemy captives do we have?" Charlemagne asked, attempting to take his mind off the slaughter, to slay his anger. He slammed his hand against his thigh. "This is stupid! Damn it! How could Worad be so stupid?" He raised his eyes to the line of conquered soldiers.

"Look at them! I'm unable to feed this number of enemy soldiers! Damn it, how dare they live! Adalgis is gone! Constable Gailo, a good and decent friend, dead as well! What was Worad thinking? What manner of madness could lead to this?" Charlemagne's head sank, his shoulders slumped. Clouds of ravens and crows gathered. The

King watched them wait patiently in the near-by trees.

"Kill the prisoners," King Charlemagne ordered softly. "Kill them every one."

"Sire?" Count Janlur asked, not sure the King spoke the words he heard.

"Kill the Saxon prisoners. Do you hear me? We Franks leave a message, here at Verdun, to all remaining Saxons. Kill every one; do it now!" He thundered. By this command King Charlemagne condemned 4500 Saxon soldiers to their deaths. As the beheading began, Oliver rushed up, begging the King not to execute this great horde of men.

"You cannot do this, Charlemagne!" He cried. "These men do not deserve to die. They surrendered to you! Their deaths will not resurrect those we lost!" He looked into Charlemagne's blank face. "You must not kill these captives. This is murder!"

"I can and I shall," Charlemagne answered. "Leave me, if you have no other advice." Moments later, the King looked toward the River Aller. For the second time in a day, it ran red with blood.

Unable to prevent the slaughter and unwilling to accept the King's orders, Oliver mounted his horse, bade Abbot Fulrad and Rinaldo goodbye, and rode away. He and Jocelyn were never seen again.

***

"So, it's true?" Charlemagne asked the Queen several days later. "Oliver is gone?" It was an unnecessary question, of a certainty. He knew Queen Hildegard wept still. She and Pippin were the last to see either Oliver or Jocelyn. Hildegard quietly recalled the leave-taking.

"Riding away from the Verdun battlefield, Oliver sought Jocelyn out at the mobile court and asked if she still wished to marry him. He offered to release her from their betrothal. Jocelyn, unwilling to give up the best man of the court, asked only to bid me goodbye. She and Oliver gathered extra clothing and took their leave of me. Oliver, then, searched for Pippin and found him fletching arrows. He bid his young friend farewell." Hildegard brushed at her eyes. "I saw them both wave goodbye to Pippin and disappear into the darkness." Hearing Hildegard's litany, Charlemagne went to find Pippin.

"Aye, Poppa. He left for good. I searched for him everywhere. I begged him to delay, when he bade me goodbye. He just looked at me, tears streaming from his eyes. Poppa, I fear for his life! A thief can take him unaware. He has no heart for defending himself." Pippin cried.

"The scouts turned back from the search." Charlemagne confirmed to his first-born. "There's no sign of his route nor of his direction. We've searched everywhere we can. Be certain, Pippin: if Oliver wishes not to be found, he surely will not. I cannot believe the battle overwhelmed him so. He fights always with strength and honor. I can make no sense of it." The King shook his head, puzzled and grieving.

"Nay, Poppa," Pippin objected. "We both know it was not the battle."

Charlemagne looked at his son but said nothing. He wanted no explanation from Pippin, afraid of his words. The King, with a slight wound in his hip, returned to his tent. The Queen wiped the tears from her eyes as he spoke of Oliver again.

"I can't explain it, Hilde." Charlemagne said. "We can find no trace of Oliver's route. He fought brilliantly, as always. Why? Why did he disappear this way! Do you think his mind fell apart?"

"My dear, Sir." Hildegard replied coolly. "Oliver's

leaving has nothing to do with his mind. He honors his heart! He is sick to death of the killing, Charley. Surely you see that—the slaughter, the murder, the rape, the violence. Oliver was ever the seeker of peace. This, I believe, is his final acknowledgement. He knows peace will never come to Frankish lands. The battle and the killing will go on and on. He has no heart for it, not anymore." And Hilde began sobbing, clearly aware of this serious judgment of her husband's choices. The King left her, led the next fight against an outlaw band and was, once again, injured.

***

"Send 'nother man to fight, Poppa?" Bertha's eyes were wide with fright. "...it hurt?" She asked as she pointed at Charlemagne's wound, a red-streaked linen covered his bloodied leg. "You cry. I hold your hand." Her little two year-old heart ached for her father. She looked steadily into a face very much like her own.

The healer told the King to rest his leg because it was weak from the knife wound. Charlemagne swung his huge arm over the table, knocked everything to the floor, and lay down. Dark shadows spread over the hard-packed earth as the wound bled. Bertha admired her father's table-bed; but she could see her mother's tears as Queen Hildegard noticed the dark stain under the sleeping bench. *Ma-mam cries and cries*, Bertha thought. *She sick. What I do?* Ma-Mam and Poppa sick, she thought.

"Your leg sleep, Poppa?" Her mouth trembled. Charlemagne, hearing the fear and weariness in his daughter's voice, looked quickly at her. Her pinched face, the line between her eyes, the tense set of her shoulders all showed her worry and discomfort.

"Bertha," the King spoke kindly, "please fetch me

some roast from yesterday's meal; I'm so hungry. Oh, and ask the cook for an apple. I know the only ones left are old and dry, but bring one for me. You hurry back with the apple and tell cook to have Roderick bring the food." Charlemagne requested.

"I run, Poppa." Bertha called as she left the tent, hurrying toward the cooking fires. Charlemagne lay heavily on the table, trying to deal with his throbbing leg. The healer's probing was necessary; he searched for any bit of metal. But when the healer pulled the knife from his leg, its tip was gone. All feared it was caught in Charlemagne's flesh. But, despite dedicated probing, the healer found nothing. After all, the knife thrust went deep into his thigh, up to the handle. *Forget about it.* The King scolded himself.

"What's the matter with Bertha?" He muttered.

Of all his children, Bertha looked the most like the King. Charlemagne swore he understood her better than any of his other children. Watching her was almost the same as looking at his own face in the water.

"Why is she so drawn? She's pale and looks ill. She's seen me wounded before; but, aye, she didn't see the healer do his work before this." The King muttered. "Still, she was not close to the surgery, and Hildegard quickly cleaned the blood which poured from the wound. Ah, if only Hildegard could reassure her...but Hilde is exhausted herself." All of a sudden, the King understood.

"Bertha worries for me and for her mother. These pregnancies seem to be more and more difficult for Hildegard; her strength disappears so quickly. And any illness is frightening to a child."

At that moment, Bertha came into the tent, followed by a cook's apprentice carrying a basket. Bertha poured ale for her father as the cook's helper took food from his basket: roast from a wild boar, thick slabs of bread, a spread made from grapes, and two old, wizened apples — probably from the bottom of the barrel.

"Bertha, this is a meal for a king!" Charlemagne exclaimed, motioning for Bertha to stand close beside him near the table. "Thank you for getting it. Now, come-- my dear daughter--and share your ale with me." Bertha laughed aloud for the first time in days.

"Poppa!" She exclaimed. "Drink for you! I not like it, tastes like dirt!"

"Dirt? I suppose you may be right." Charlemagne smiled. "But come and put this spread on the bread for me; we can share the bread and this almost-dead apple." The King held the wizened fruit out to Bertha.

"Poppa, apple not dead!" Bertha screeched, laughing. She added. "It old." Her dear face reflected her delight in her Poppa's teasing and the sense he was not as badly hurt as she feared. She climbed onto the bench, taking a huge bite from the bread which Charlemagne offered her.

"Looks dirty…dirty brown, Poppa," she informed him, "but tastes good."

Charlemagne beamed at his daughter. Surely she is a pearl of great price, he thought to himself. *Such a dear, beautiful face.* Suddenly distracted, he stared in the distance. He had some appointment, later in the day. *Who was it with and for what?*

"I can't think what it is, not at this moment." He murmured to himself.

Nearby, Abbot Fulrad paced, his steps faltering as he stopped to stare out of the door of the tent. Catching himself, he resumed his circuit, straightening items on the bookshelves, fiddling with the lay of the rug, scraping candle drippings off the wooden tray. He knew the Queen Mother would rant at his carelessness. Wondering at this inane thought, Fulrad sat abruptly. A moment later he stood and hurried to the door.

"Find the King for me, Ailstar," he directed the guardsman standing outside the library tent. "Please, say I continue to wait for him in the library." He guessed the King did not remember this appointment. The Abbot suggested the King meet with him more than two weeks ago.

In the days between, he hoped to find some way to broach this topic. But he had failed. He could find no easy way to open the conversation. *What can I do? What can I say...without the immediate suggestion of guilt? If I had only anticipated this and could have moved early to nip...* Frustrated, he pounded the table, bruising his fingers as his church ring bit into his flesh. The pain was of no moment; his heart broke days ago. In that lay the deepest pain.

King Charlemagne scratched at the tent door open and rushed in.

"Forgive me; forgive me, Abbot. I forgot our meeting. I broke my fast with my little Bertha. She's frightened by this flesh wound," he talked quickly. "You should see her eyes, wide worry. I told the children I will let them pick apples from my shoulders at the end of the day. It gives them comfort." He smiled, remembering the sweet weight of the girls' bodies across his back. "They are so dear and ask so little of me." He sighed.

"But what's our agenda?" He asked, remembering Fulrad requested this meeting. "Is there some problem with the church doctrine we discussed? Have you heard from Missi Rodericks who just returned from Aquitaine? Nay," the King shook his head, "you scheduled this some time ago. Well, Abbot Fulrad, what is your pleasure?" Fulrad looked at the King. He stared so long Charlemagne moved toward him.

"Fulrad, are you ill? Your brow is wet, on this cool day.

Your face is flushed and your eyes, your eyes are blank. Do you have a pain in your head?" The King asked, concerned. "Dear man, what is it? Tell me. Surely, there can be no catastrophe this dire."

The King led Abbot Fulrad to a nearby bench and gently pushed him to sit. He hurried to the door to summon a healer.

"Nay, nay, Sire, please." Fulrad wiped his forehead with his already damp neck linen. "Nay, no healer, please; this MUST be a private audience." He stuttered out. Charlemagne, not understanding, was angry about his own confusion.

"You're not well, Fulrad. That's plain. There can be no talk when you can scarcely stand. Nay! We must call the healer."

"Sire, please; there is great evil afoot. We must speak, you and I." Fulrad's words poured from his mouth. "No one else, I beg you! Your kingdom is at great risk, Sire. You MUST listen." He stood and walked toward his king. Although the abbot seemed even more agitated, his stricken voice stopped the King who looked quickly at his old teacher.

"Then, speak, Fulrad." Charlemagne commanded.

"I'm at a loss, Sire, as where to begin." Fulrad responded, fumbling behind his back to draw a bench close.

"Please forgive me, I must sit. Excuse me, Sire. I must just say the words – straight out. I request your forgiveness before I begin. You and I must make plans...plans made today for immediate execution!" Charlemagne sat beside the Abbot. The Abbot immediately stood up, walked to the tent door, turned and spoke to his king.

"There are horrific rumors, Sire, evil and horrible whisperings which you must answer. I first heard the lies months ago. I know neither their origin nor their source;

but all is in readiness for foul, unchristian action."

King Charlemagne stood, walked to the tent door, and motioned the guard to stand farther away. He poured ale into two leather mugs and handed one to the Abbot.

"Please go on," he said, heavy at heart at Fulrad's agonized words. *The Abbot seldom overreacts to trouble.*

"There is talk...and there is belief, Sire. Rumors accuse you of unnatural acts, sexual depravations, and..." Charlemagne's mouth formed a rueful smile.

"Ah, Fulrad, there is ALWAYS this talk, to be expected of a monarch—and if not of a monarch, then of a commander. It's nothing." He sighed in relief. "Only the dispirited or the replaced believe such nonsense."

"Nay, Sire. This is more serious. Many believe the rumors. I caution you, Sire. I speak not of the usual soldier's tale, nor the bravado which creates outlandish exploits." Fulrad insisted. "Nay, Sire, this is an indictment of your behavior...with your young daughter ...with Rotrude, Sire. People accuse you of ravishing a princess - your own daughter. She's but seven years old, your Majesty! Still, the air is thick with rumor."

Fulrad bowed his head, locked his hands together behind his back and wept. Tears streamed down his cheeks. His shuddering back showed the effort he made to conquer his heaving sobs. His breathing and occasional moan dominated the room. In a moment the remains of his breakfast were at his feet. Fulrad crumpled to the floor.

Charlemagne could not speak. He, too, lost his footing--his legs giving way as the horror of Fulrad's words echoed in the room. He felt weak in the stomach, as if his heart's rapid beating squeezed his stomach into a wad of bile. He could feel his heart tearing, blood rushing from its torn flesh, drowning his breath in sorrow.

The silence stretched, neither man able to speak. What

more is there to say? Abbot Fulrad wondered. *Charlemagne's sexual prowess, his many conquests as a prince, his seeming lack of interest in holding a wife. Such behavior fuels this vile gossip. Though he is a good man who fights for a better life for his people, this weakness destroys him--his delight in sins of the flesh. People will talk and, unfortunately, his actions make him culpable. What CAN we do now?* Many minutes passed. Fulrad's words hovered in the air. The King was unable to move beyond them. But, even in his pain, Charlemagne knew the accusations must be answered.

"I must speak, Fulrad," the King finally said. "These accusations must be refuted...not only answered by me, but by Hildegard, by Queen Betrada, and—aye—by you, Fulrad. They must also be answered by the behavior— the love and trust shown me—by my dear Rotrude." King Charlemagne rubbed his forehead. "Aye, we must mount a counterattack. We must act now."

"Speak, Sire? You?" Fulrad asked. "Forgive me; I didn't hear your words." Fulrad pushed himself up from the floor, dazed and spent. His blanched face, his trembling hands, his weak knees all testified to the physical courage needed for rising.

"Fulrad, my friend," Charlemagne began. "Thank you for your courage. I know my temper didn't allow you to believe I would not kill you...after such words." He shook his head.

"I assure you; I'm in your debt. I also know, despite our previous relationship, you would never confront me with these allegations if you believed a word of them. Thank you, also, for that, my friend." The King hugged the Abbot, drawing strength from his old teacher. Together, Fulrad and the King walked to the Queen's tent. As the children's nurse went to summon the queen, Fulrad slapped his own face.

"Abbot," Charlemagned exclaimed. "What are you doing? There's no need for self-punishment. Cease!"

"Nay, my boy." Fulrad replied. "I'm myself again. Nay, I'm putting color in my face. Queen Hildegard must not see me upset. I must seem in control, as must you." He rubbed Charlemagne's cheeks roughly as he heard the Queen's footsteps.

"Abbot Fulrad, Charlemagne. I did not expect a visit." Queen Hildegard, looking into their faces, stopped speaking. "Is something amiss?" Her eyes widened as she saw the King. "What are you doing here, my Lord? I bade you farewell, believing this year's battles begun. Why are you here and not with the army?" The Queen was confused.

The process for beginning summer battles was precise and thorough. Every effort was made to follow time-honored methods on the first day's march. Both the Abbot and the King exhorted the men to fight their best; praying with them and for their success; recognizing the ranks, the insignias, the previous battle successes of each unit; building comradeship and mutual respect. The first march of a new battle season was the foundation for the season's successful conquests. The Queen, ever nervous about her husband's safety, was close to hysterics.

"Never fear, my dear. All is well." Charlemagne hastened to her side. "We postponed the march late last night. We still wait for the delivery of the destriers from Lombardy! I didn't relish creating new battle movements, necessary if we don't have the horses. I delayed our marching day 'til tomorrow. Forgive me! I neglected to tell you. I decided this in the hours, just before dawn. Please, please, my dear. I didn't think to cause you such a shock!" The Queen stared at Charlemagne, then moved her eyes to Fulrad. They looked sheepishly at the floor.

"Men!" she exclaimed, sitting on a nearby bench, fanning her face with her hands and tapping her shoe.

"This is not a propitious start, Fulrad," Charlemagne said. "We must tell Hildegard; it should be done now."

"Let me begin, Sire," Fulrad answered. He walked to the Queen, took both her hands in his and began. "My dear, we have a worrisome situation which requires immediate response. Please remain calm. The King and I have it controlled, so you're not to worry." "

"You must be aware: there is evil afoot. Nay, don't say a word!" He cautioned as Hildegard moved to rise. "Pray, let me finish. Then, I will answer every single question. Will you do that for me?" The Abbott did not feel nearly as assured as he appeared, nor did he know if he could answer "every single question." But he knew strength and re-assurance were his greatest assets with the Queen and would be, later, when he refuted the rumors.

"There are evil, vicious rumors around the court, having to do with the King's sexual proclivities. Nay, nay, I won't be graphic, my Lady. Suffice it for me to say this; much being said is impossible. But talk persists, doing its constant damage. In any case, the talk centers on the King's love for his children, especially Rotrude. As you can imagine, the suggestions are crude and barbaric. The rumors do not, as yet, touch little Bertha, mayhap because she is barely three years." Seeing the Queen's horror, Fulrad squeezed her hands. "We shall refute them all, of a certainty. You must be strong and loyal and, above all, loving and constant in your attentions to the King. There can be no hint you've even heard these dreadful accusations. Are you able to do that...for me, for the king, and for the realm?"

***

The whisperers of the court were always at work, jockeying for information, re-interpreting conversations, speculating when there was no cause. Such was the price of a kingdom, the dues of reigning, the cost of a monarchy. But never had the cost been this high.

Looking back, King Charlemagne remembered his disgust at court reaction to the dissolution of his second marriage with Desiderata, princess of Lombardy. Everyone, from the kennel master to the court candle-maker, offered an explanation for that failure. But, nothing prepared the King for this, this speculation Fulrad described!

"How can my love for my children — much deeper and purer than my love for anything else — be so besmirched, be so undermined? And what will such rumors do to them?" He asked his wife. "These children are dearer than life to us. How can we anticipate the whisperings the children might hear? How can we counteract them?" *And, poor Hilde!* All this coming, just as she enters the worst part of this new pregnancy, he thought. *She is already so big, much more so than with the previous pregnancies. I pray to God she does not lose this child. This new threat and worry will drive her mad!*

"The best way to counterattack this vicious talk is to place my relationship with my children directly in the people's faces. We shall publicize our every action. Everywhere we go; everything we do will be announced at court." Beside him, Queen Hildegard nodded. "The children's activities, even our gatherings as a family, will become public events, opened to as many individuals as can be included. There will be no hidden corners, no secret visits, no activities closed to the eyes of the realm." He sighed. "It will be exhausting."

Queen Hildegard, her ladies, the Peers, all hurried to implement Charlemagne's suggestions. The King and his family, especially the King with his children, were always on display. They were never alone, certainly not with each other. Little Charles, Rotrude, and Bertha began taking all their meals in the big hall. Ten-year-old Charles and Rotrude, who was now seven, found much excitement in this change. But the evening meal, often begun well after the children's usual bedtimes, exhausted them all, including Hildegard and little Bertha.

"Thanks be to God," Charlemagne intoned to Queen Hildegard late one evening. "Pepin and Louis are safe in their kingdoms. The Lombard and Aquitaine castles are sound. It's not necessary for them to play at this game."

"Good Lord, Charley, I did not think of our sons, so far from us." The Queen's strained voice murmured. "You're certain they are in no danger?" Her eyes were giant orbs in her face.

"I hold men's heads there in my hands, Hilde." The King replied. "They will give their lives for our sons. I strengthened the boys' guards; those castles are doubly armed. Fear not; they're protected. Be certain, my dear."

King Charlemagne increased the number of nurses and caretakers for his children and expanded the guard four-fold. Outings the children enjoyed with Queen Bertrada and her ladies increased. Singing periods, riding of ponies, orchard pickings, swims in the river, fishing expeditions, tea and jam parties, gathering of wildflowers, and playing with puppies now outweighed all other matters. Charlemagne ordered any activity which promoted the children's visibility emphasized. Two or three Peers and a bevy of court women accompanied them on all their outings.

Queen Hildegard sought various methods to keep everyone happy: delicious and filling 'sweet delights,' vast quantities and vintages of wine for the nobles, additional maids and servants to pamper participants, and games and competitions galore. She encouraged laughter; energetic, physical activities; and increasing consumption of favorite foods.

Months later, nobles complained of weariness and tunics which hugged their bodies. The children begged for longer naps and less running games. And the ladies looked bleary-eyed at everyone, their faces wan and pale.

"Please, Poppa, may we break our fast in our rooms?" Little Charles begged. "I want only to sit in my sleeping clothes and eat my porridge on my sleeping bench. In the early morning, the kitchen is so crowded! All the boys want to be my sparring partner, to go on errands together, to sit beside me, or to bring me another cup of milk. They even want to share my sticky bun! And, if I speak to someone a little longer, even to share a riddle or a joke, everyone else is jealous."

"Aye, Charlemagne; do make us another plan," Hildegard begged. "I fear one of us will make some small misstep and undo all the positive of the previous months. We're very tired, living in the view of so many eyes—so judging of us. Have you any other ideas?" The Queen did not hide the hope in her voice.

King Charlemagne looked at his wife. Beneath her eyes, she appeared to have bruises; her face was extremely white and pasty. Even her thick, luscious hair lay dull and flat on her head. Her belly was larger yet, though she said she was 'used' to the increased weight of her body.

"Aye, I have another idea and need your evaluation of it, Hilde,"Charlemagne answered. He held up his hand to forestall an immediate response. "It's an odious idea, I admit; but it might bring us some relief from this distress and intrigue. I believe the light we shed on our family life repaired some of the damage of the rumors. But I also know we cannot live like this forever. I cannot predict the efficacy of this new idea."

"And so," Hildegard asked, "what is it? Tell me your idea, dear husband."

"I propose we again send Rotrud to her betrothed in Constantinople. She must, after all, make the trip. The attack on her is behind us. Queen Irene and Prince Constantine are still waiting. We will add a codicil to the betrothal agreement. Abbot Fulrad will swear Rotrud is a virgin." Charlemagne saw Hildegard wince, holding her trembling hands tightly together.

"Nay, fear not. An examination is not necessary. Don't concern yourself with horrific imaginings. The Abbot will declare her pure and ally all fears. We will specify, again, that Rotrude has the final choice in this marriage. I won't sacrifice my children to alliances...tried that once myself with disastrous results." Hildegard smiled in sympathy and patted the King's shoulder.

"It might work. And it doesn't even have to be subterfuge. We can say openly we seek the best possible marriage for our oldest daughter. But, we will, also, respect her wishes. Ask Abbot Fulrad if such a codicil is seemly. I realize we cannot postpone this visit forever. This time, however, I'll accompany Rotrud and, possibly, take Charles with us as well. It's not too early for him to become acquainted with Constantine. Surely his mother will name him king soon. Rotrud will be frightened, otherwise, to undertake this journey a second time."

She gave Charlemagne a playful nip on his ear. The stress of the past several months took its toll on the King as well. He needed to be free to concentrate on the upcoming battles. Hildegard hoped the plans for this journey to Constantinople lay to rest all the vicious innuendoes. As if the threat of death is not enough, she thought, we have to deal with these obscene rumors as well.

The King and Queen planned Rotrude's visit to Constaninople for the end of summer, as the battle season ended. Once they made the decision, the mobile court journeyed to Aachen where they spent Eastertide. Before the next battles, Charlemagne wished to speak with Alcuin, to hear his plans for the palace academy and for the manuscript copying centers.

***

Alcuin established his academy in Aachen, the city which Charlemagne most loved. He brought parchments from Tours for the Aachen library and borrowed manuscripts from monasteries all over the realm. The monks and illuminators in his scriptorium copied Greek and Roman literature and distributed it to any monastery or abbey which promised care of the parchments.

Alcuin also experimented with writing styles and created the Carolingian miniscule script. The clear script proved invaluable for daily accounting, for messages and letters. The copyists found the script easier for people to read and used it in their illuminated manuscripts. The mathematicians delighted in its simplicity, finding it clearer for equations than their previously-used, unspaced capital script.

Combining his love of books and his highly-developed aesthetic sense, Alcuin directed the creation of the Golden Gospels, a series of masterpieces illuminated in gold and, then, written in gold on vellum or on purple parchment.

Despite many people's wishes, Charlemagne's court was still a mobile one, moving throughout the realm. Alcuin remained in the residence in Aachen and began building his Academy. He sought instructors from all known lands, attempting to acquire the best minds in Europe to provide a foundation for his educational efforts and Charlemagne's dream of a re-envisoned academy.

Chapter 26

CLARITY, MAYHAP?

Angilbert approached Alcuin as he unpacked parchments in the library.

"Welcome home, Master. I beg you not to abandon me when you make another journey. I waited here impatiently during the weeks you traveled so far away from us. I still feel I should have been with you." At Alcuin's indulgent smile, Angilbert broached his most immediate concern. "But there is no time to belabor this. I need your help in analyzing who sought and who planned Rotrud's abduction. The Saxon slaughter and, then, those horrific rumors seem to distract everyone from that still, unsolved crime: the attempt to kidnap the child."

"With fresh eyes, you may provide insight others are incapable of giving. Do you understand my meaning?" Angilbert inquired.

"I might notice something others missed or refused to consider?" Alcuin clarified for himself.

"Exactly so, Master." Angilbert confirmed. "At least, that's my hope. I plan to recount events to you. Then, you summarize all you hear from me and any conclusions you draw from my recital. Others volunteered for an interview with you, if that is necessary."

"Does no one wish to place blame for this kidnapping of Rotrud? Wasn't there a like threat to one of the children years ago?" Alcuin's frown deepened. "The child was a babe... I recall a tale very vaguely." His voice faltered, his eyes looked vague as he tried to remember. Even though he knew none of the King's children well yet, Rotrude was, so far, his favorite.

"I so wish we I were here at court when this kidnapping occurred."

"So far we can identify no one involved in the plan, Sir. In the attempted theft of Pepin, you remember, the child's nurse aided the kidnapper. But the man himself died before he could be questioned – good luck for those who planned the abduction. There're those in the court who believe someone murdered him. But no one has given any reason for the kidnapping in the first place. I find the casual outlook of the King and the Peers – of the entire court – unbelievable! Everyone appears to feel safe... despite these obvious breaches."

"In the case of Pepin, this nurse, Mathilde, is a very simple girl. She told the Queen the man wished to show little Pepin to a high-born lady. She suspected no threat. I sought any knowledge about Rotrude's kidnapping from her. I was sorely disappointed. She's easy to fool, Master. She believes anything a person tells her. I spoke with her several times. And, it's almost the same with Little Pepin's attempted theft. No one investigated that incident either. Even when I asked nobles in the court who might wish toharm the King...or the child...no one suggested a single villain!"

In their ignorance, they believe everyone satisfied with his life. They take no threat seriously. Open warfare, enemies marching on them, is the only fight this court understands. The same mindset applies to Rotrude's kidnapping. Ha! Some of these men should work in the church for a space. Their knowledge of power and struggle would increase exponentially!" Angilbert laughed at Alcuin's knowing nod.

"Is it possible for men to become so secure in their own beliefs or so comfortable that they do not see threats or danger?" Angilbert shook his head in confusion. "Now, despite King Charlemagne's curses, the will and interest in investigating Rotrude's kidnapping has evaporated. No one understands this serious, very real threat. The children and the Queen need protection immediately, especially the younger ones." Alcuin rubbed his eyes, rolling his shoulders to ease them.

"Aye," he replied. "Protecting them all is the most pressing need, Gil. My brief observations of the court since my return are limited, of a certainty. But awareness is no better than when I left for Tours. People don't understand the serious nature of these attacks. Proceed with your recitation of events and let us see if I can discern any connecting chords."

Angilbert quickly summarized both the previous attacks on the King himself and, then, the suspected threats to the King's children. The incidents with King Charlemagne were clearly an attempt to murder him. The attempts directed toward each of the king's three children were clearly to spirit them away. Someone designed the attacks on Pepin and Rotrude to steal them; the tent burning when little Charles was an infant was open to interpretation. Did someone really want to burn the boy alive?

"Each of the three children were directly targeted." Angilbert concluded. "In the court, they are always vulnerable. No one takes appropriate care. Don't you agree, Master?"

"...with no doubt, my son. It feels the King, in his ignorance mayhap, is unreasonably careless with his own.

But let me ask you. You are certain of Pippin the Hunchback's true innocence in all you relate? With his lack of place, he is not too young to understand he has little future as the King's heir or as a displaced mother's son." Alcuin bowed his head, saddened by the limited choices for Pippin, the son of a powerful king made useless by his misshapen back.

"Ah, he surely is innocent, Master. I daresay his present unawareness won't last forever. He's buffeted by jealous companions, by courtiers who flatter and fawn over him, even by missives urging his return to Lombardy. He is now, with the King's changing Carloman's name to Pepin, in a vulnerable place, one which he heretofore did not have. He must be changed by this. But until now, he knew nothing of plots against the King and avoided intrigue. I do assure you, he is blameless." Angilbert replied with no hesitation.

"Sit with me, my boy," Alcuin beamed at the son of his heart. "Your presence aids my thoughts and calms my agitation. You give me much to think on, the evidence and your suspicions as well." He sat on the cushioned bench, surrounded by the parchments he brought back from Tours.

Angilbert refreshed Alcuin's cup, opened his newest parchment, and settled into his corner, delighted for the reading time the waiting afforded him. After a lengthy time, Alcuin stood and stretched.

"The last part of the journey strained my legs, or I am, indeed, older than my days show." Turning to see if Angilbert listened, Alcuin smiled and continued. "Let me summarize my conclusions and see your reaction, Gil."

"Aye, Master, I listen eagerly. I feel we must act quickly, to safeguard both King Charlemagne and his babes." Angilbert responded.

"These are the salient points, at least as I see them," Alcuin began. "I will write them on this parchment. Sometimes writing highlights a point we might otherwise overlook." As he picked up his pen, the Abbot and Theodoric entered the library tent.

"Please, good friends, listen and correct my conclusions as to Rotrude's attackers...and the other frightening incidents." Alcuin invited as he motioned Theo and Fulrad to a near-by bench.

"Firstly," Alcuin began as the men sat down, "the perpetrators remain unknown to the King and his court. I know Mathilde helped to carry little Pepin (or Carloman) out of the camp. But it's clear to me from Gil's summary that someone used Mathilde's trusting nature. We apparently have no idea who that person was." He looked into each man's face and saw agreement. "The mind which planned this was, clearly, not the man who led Mathilde and the babe. This suggests a non-Frankish villain."

"On the other hand, the two direct attacks against the King came from enemy lands: a disgruntled Saxon alone on his vendetta and an unknown bow master. The firing of little Charles's tent came from a young Lombard noble who did not even know the King's face. Unknown men almost stole Rotrude; but they were men who certainly came specifically for her and knew of her journey. The knowledge in these efforts against the children suggests long-term watchers at this court and a single-minded effort to part these children from the court and from the King." Abbot Fulrad and Theo nodded in agreement. Theo added he believed all the incidents connected.

"At first glance," Alcuin continued, "I would think the threats unrelated. Look at the very different persons used to attempt these acts: a single soldier, a bowman, a young and untried lordling, a nurse, thieves or bandits with Rotrude. Nay, there is too much variance in these attacks for them to be unconnected." He looked into the eyes of each man in turn.

"I don't believe in coincidence, Sirs. The mind behind these efforts went to great lengths to dull our suspicions. I conclude there has been a continuous threat to the King, an effort to harm/kill him, even before he became king. Now, though, the threat is toward his offspring." He rubbed his neck and shook his head.

"Charlemagne viewed these threats carelessly, as did the entire court. We must guard the court and give over-due attention to the Queen as well. I cannot suggest with certainty the origin of this ongoing threat. The Abbot, be-ing the longest resident, must carefully evaluate my next words." He nodded at the Abbot.

"Please, Abbot Fulrad, don't hesitate to question my statements or my conclusions. I'm responding to infor-mation given to me. You, on the other hand, lived these events." Angilbert delayed Alcuin's next words with a question.

"Would you like the conclusions of Rinaldo and Theo-doric, Master? They sifted through actions, tales, others' thoughts..."

"Not yet, Gil." Alcuin answered. "Keep them in your mind 'til I present my thoughts. We'll be interested in the commonalities of all conclusions. My remarks are based on this assumption. There has long been an effort—a consistent, renewed effort—to destroy our King, by elim-inating him or by taking a child. Any of these acts against the children might destroy him, weaken his mind, if not his will and body."

"Therefore, I suggest the following points be discussed among major court figures, including those investigating this latest threat—Rinaldo and Theo. Court figures would include the King himself, Abbot Fulrad, Rodrick, Queen Mother Bertrada, Queen Hildegard, Gisela, and Lord Janus. You may add anyone else you wish. But, don't be fooled. There is much dishonesty in this court. Clear your minds of previous conceptions and examine everyone!"

"Here's my summary, as Angilbert requested." Alcuin expressed his conclusions. "These attacks define a well-calculated but fluid plan which sought different results as time passed. There was firstly the effort to assassinate the King. When this failed, his children became potential victims. Their vulnerability made them easier targets. Killing was not necessary, only kidnapping. One would usually expect a demand for money...or, perhaps, even a demand for the throne."

"King Charlemagne would never give up the throne!" Theodoric rose to his feet, his face red. "A mere kidnapping would never weaken his will!"

"Not so, Theo." Alcuin immediately answered. "Think on my words. Would you put a price on the head of your son? If asked for your property, your manor house, and your wealth for the life of your Geoff, would you hesitate to part with them?" Theodoric grabbed his head and nodded negatively, in misery.

"The King would make the same choice, Theo. Your Geoff would even understand the intrigue and power such a choice offered. Because Charlemagne's children are younger, they would not understand the choice; they would believe their Poppa would save them." Alcuin smiled at each man, understanding none would willingly sacrifice his child for a kingdom." "I, myself, would give up anything, if Angilbert were in danger."

"The lengthy nature of these efforts suggests the mind behind all these attacks is a single mind. These efforts come from one person or from a small group who share a devil's bargain--eliminate the present ruler of the Frankish empire. I suggest there is long-term enmity here, an escalating hatred of the King, a spirit willing to sacrifice much--children and babes--for its quarry. The men carrying out these attacks are probably away from this court, less the efforts would be more frequent and less bold."

"The man who plans has a devious mind; the attacks against the King were meant to kill him. The kidnapping of a child seems much worse. We cannot know the individual child's eventual fate. The fire set to little Charles' tent...or to his mother's tent...implies death by fire.

"Rotrude's journey, known in general terms by a handful of people, was not long-scheduled, talked about, nor described to even the court population. Hence, there must be a traitor within the King's immediate circle. Someone is providing information to the planner I mentioned. And the planner has influence and wealth to buy assistance and cooperation." He looked at the troubled faces of the men. "Little Pepin's fate, I cannot guess." Alcuin added. "I suspect he would have lived a few days at most but never returned to the King and Queen...regardless of Charlemagne's capitulation." Alcuin ceased his litany and looked at the three men in the room — very different, very gifted men. Now, they must evaluate his words and provide something of their own.

"Let's meet here after we break our fast at tomorrow's first light." The scholar suggested. "You need time to ponder my thoughts. We adjourn 'til the morrow."

Abbot Fulrad, Theo and Angilbert with slow steps, bent heads, and worried faces left the tent, intent on Alcuin's words. They vowed to evaluate his reasoning and accept it or refute it with critical analysis.

***

Later, in the small hours of the morning, Angilbert sat bolt upright on his sleeping bench. After leaving the meeting with Alcuin, he sifted facts, examined theories, considered villains. He gained little insight from the process. But, now, half-awake, he remembered one of Pippin's sentences. *The lad made reference to Abbot Fulrad, both when he first spoke to Oliver and when Angilbert and Theo questioned him later.* ...not strange in itself but I cannot remember what he said, Angilbert thought. *Why would Pippin mention Fulrad when he was speaking of Lombardy? I must have the time confused in my mind. Abbot Fulrad hasn't been to Lombardy in more than ten years; it had to be in 673 when King Charlemagne fought Desiderius in one of their earliest confrontations.* Angilbert lay back down, straightening his sleeping linens as he did so. But, immediately, he sat up again.

Aye, aye." He reminded himself. "Pippin said the Lombard teacher, the master retained for Queen Gerbegna's boys, asked him something about Abbot Fulrad. I must talk to Pippin at once."

Angilbert pulled on his tunic and boots. Flinging a mantle over his shoulders, he left to find Pippin. The lad was not in his sleeping chamber. Angilbert imagined a growing boy would be in the kitchens to quieten a hungry stomach or in the stables. His vote was, firstly, the stables.

I know that, despite his strength and ability to survive, Pippin is very lonely. And what is more loving than a litter of puppies? Angilbert explained his hunch to himself. *The King's favorite hound birthed six pups some weeks ago. Yesterday, they seemed at their most energetic stage.* There in the stables, near the oats and barley, Angilbert found Pippin.

"Lad," Angilbert greeted him. "Somehow I just knew you would be here. Isn't it a little early for visiting?" Pippin, his eyes shining with delight, shook his head.

"I can't resist them, Gil," he replied. "I've decided to ask Poppa for this one, the one with the circle of brown and black on her head. Do you think he would give her to me?" Pippin asked, longing in his eyes.

"Mayhap, we can influence him," Angilbert laughed. "But we need to plan the best approach. Before that, remind me in what manner Queen Gerbegna's boys' teacher asked you about Abbot Fulrad. I can't remember what the teacher said to you."

"Nay, Angil. It wasn't the teaching Master. It was a monk. Because I gave no answers to his questions, he asked me if Abbot Fulrad didn't teach me to reply to my elders. He appeared to think the Abbot schooled me in Poppa's court. I didn't understand the reason he thought I knew the Abbot. But, then, a noble asked me something and I turned away. Later I realized the questioner believed I lived in Poppa's court."

"So, this monk appeared to be acquainted with Abbot Fulrad, hum?" Angilbert clarified.

"Of a certainty. I got the impression they were friends...or, if not friends, surely knew each other well. Abbot Fulrad has been at Poppa's court for years, hasn't he? The way the monk talked, it seemed he and the Abbot once worked together. Is this important, Gil?" Pippin asked. "You're up very early to ask questions...almost like those answers are as important as these puppies?" Pippin laughed as Angilbert looked startled.

"...just trying to arrange things in my mind, Lad; that's all." Angilbert replied. He waved goodbye to Pippin and headed for Alcuin's chambers. As Angilbert feared, Alcuin was already awake.

"This mountain air must be good for you, Gil," Alcuin teased. "I don't remember your being a dawn riser back in the monastery." He laughed with delight at Angilbert's embarrassed expression. "And so, what is so momentous you are up before the cocks, my boy?"

"Master, I thought I clearly described events to you yesterday. But earlier this morning, I remembered a puzzling statement, one from Pippin. I'm sorely troubled by it."

"Explain it to me immediately." Alcuin directed, seeing the confusion and fear reflected on Angilbert's face.

"It has to do with Pippin's visit in Lombardy. You remember all we went through when telling the king about it- his anger, his blame of Pippin?" Alcuin grimaced and nodded. "When Pippin was in Lombardy, one of the monks at the Lombard court made particular mention of Abbot Fulrad. This is a jarring note to me, Master. Do I overreact? Is there an innocent reason for an acquaintance of the Abbot's to be spending time in a court which has, historically, been set against Charlemagne? Why would a monk friend of Fulrad even stop at Lombardy...if evil were not afoot?" Angilbert's face betrayed his concern.

"This may be an innocent event, my boy," Alcuin responded. "But the mention of Abbot Fulrad does imply some connection. Fulrad was the King's teacher years ago when he was a mere lad. Fulrad began at King Pepin's court long before Charlemagne became king; so his allegiance is long-standing...to father and son. But you're correct to be wary; let me think about it."

***

Later that morning, Alcuin sought out Abbot Fulrad. He found the Abbot in the cooks' tent, having a honey tart.

"Don't you fear ruining your appetite for our midday meal, Abbot Fulrad?" Alcuin asked with a smile. "I myself find the more tarts I eat, the more I wish to eat.

They're a great temptation."

"As for that, Scholar Alcuin, I must agree with you. I yearn for the sweet taste and am unable to resist its summons." The Abbot responded, completely unrepentant. From my observations, you're unable to resist ale and sweetened wine as well, Alcuin thought to himself.

"I do have a request, Abbot." Alcuin went straight to the point. "I have received a missive from my brothers in Britannia begging me for a copy of St. Augustine's last teaching. They do not wish illumination or ornamentation on the pages. So, I wonder if you could identify the parchment copy which is the easiest to read. Your knowledge of the library, from your years here, is much more extensive than mine."

"Aye, I know one." The Abbot smiled. "Aye, I know a parchment which will suffice. It's written in a plain hand, almost childlike. I will tell the monk in charge of the scriptorium to make a copy for you."

"Thanks for your help, Abbot." Alcuin inclined his head in appreciation. "You mentioned your long service at this court. Have you been here since the King was crowned, in 672 was it not?"

"Aye, here since then, of a certainty, but I was at King Pepin's court for many years before Charlemagne received the crown. I watched our King grow up...taught him all he knows, as they say!" Abbot Fulrad laughed.

"Oh, then, mayhap you can honor me with one more request, Abbot. I have need of a monk familiar with court traditions, an effective copyist, and, hopefully, a monk who served under you. The King wishes someone to begin an academy in Lombardy's Pavia and suggested I approach you for a recommendation. I would imagine time spent in Lombardy would be advantageous, but it's not required. Changes which people normally don't wish to embrace are often more easily implemented if initiated by one who is familiar to them, don't you think?" Alcuin asked. The Abbot immediately shook his head.

"Aye, people do trust someone they know. But, try as I might, I can think of no monk with the characteristics you mention. There was once a monk in our court who was distraught by Charlemagne's love of secular literature. But when he also saw St. Augustine's writings being read at evening meals, he became one of the King's greatest supporters. He didn't work for me, except for being here during part of my tenure. He was under Brother Bernard's oversight for he was a wonderful illuminator. The scriptorium brothers wailed for days when he asked to leave us."

"Why did he leave, Abbot; and where's he now? He sounds an ideal candidate." Alcuin controlled the interest in his voice and face.

"He's in Lombardy still. He transferred to a small monastery there. As I remember, it's near the Lombard court, though I daresay his influence is minimal in the chaotic environment of Pavia. There's been far too much change and intrigue there--always a trial for King Charlemagne." The Abbot finished, nodding his head sadly.

"Do you think this monk would consider a different duty?" Alcuin asked, innocently. "I dislike asking a monk to leave a beloved monastery, no matter the needs of the crown."

"Oh, I should think Brother Jedediah would be honored by your interest, Master Alcuin." Abbot Fulrad responded. "Shall I request his presence at court?"

"If you would frame the request, Abbot Fulrad, I would be grateful. First, let me be confirm with Charlemagne the number of clergy he anticipates assigning to Pavia. One of the duties of this position would be oversight of the *missi dominici* who travel there." Alcuin concluded. The Abbot's eyes lit up with interest.

"Ahhhh," he murmured. "Brother Jedediah would be delighted to garner such a position. But I will wait upon your command to initiate contact with him."

"Thank you for your generous help, Abbot." Alcuin replied as he left the cook tent. Alcuin summoned Ogier the Dane and spoke with him late into the night.

"When you went into Lombardy, you didn't find any evidence of plots to harm Rotrude, did you, Ogier?" Alcuin asked.

"Nay, Master Alcuin." Ogier answered. "There was much talk about King Charlemagne's court, though. It surprised me to see the Lombards so interested in our court. Much of the talk I heard centered around the King's unwillingness to choose a permanent court location. The Lombards appear to think it particularly "barbaric" that the Frankish court moves so often. They believe a royal court must have stone floors, tapestries adorning the walls, and candle-holders permanently secured."

"The nobility, men as well as women, speculated often about Queen Hildegard, about her lifestyle. And they made many self-righteous pronouncements about her concern for the common people. They even spoke of her agricultural plots and exclaimed when told the noble women mimic her efforts." Ogier laughed. "I do admire her so much, Master; she's not deterred from her chosen route by anyone or anything. And her heart is ever warm and good!"

"To be sure, Ogier. She's the jewel of this court...and of this King." Alcuin agreed. "Did you hear anything of a Brother Jedediah in the Lombard Court?"

"...for certain, Sir." Ogier exclaimed. "A more unholy monk I never saw! He gorged himself with meat and sweets, drank ale with the largest of the army's gluttons, and was most unkempt. Rumors reported he wouldn't turn down a 'roll in the hayloft,' Sir; but I didn't observe him in a compromising position. I thought I heard his loud voice one night, quite late from the stable. But I didn't linger to verify the speaker's identity. He's the worse example of a monk I've seen, Master Alcuin--a true stain on the Church." Ogier's mouth curled with disgust, his eyes flashed with his memories.

"What's his supposed function?" Alcuin asked.

"I never could determine it." Ogier admitted. "He met every courier and every rider who entered the gate. Often he took those entering to a nearby inn, feeding many of them. The unknowledgeable often complimented him on his Christian kindness. But I would swear he knew each and every rider, Sire, and questioned them. I felt he offered little real Christian support. He was one of those who questioned Pippin. Finally, the lad avoided him. Many times I saw Pippin spot him ahead and, then, turn in the street or, even, in the corridor and retrace his steps to avoid Jedediah and the men with him."

"Ogier, I wish you to take a missive to this very man. It will not be signed; but, if he cooperates with someone here, he will heed its summons. Please tell no one of your destination." Alcuin urged. "Can you leave before the sky lightens into the morrow."

"...as you say, Sire. I'll gather a spare tunic and retrieve my mantle. Let me stop by the cook's tent, as well as request a fresh mount. I'll return for your letter quickly." And Ogier left Alcuin.

Alcuin's missive was brief. He made a point of not signing the letter but sealed it in two places with plain wax. Its contents were simple.

Another failure.
All kits still alive and growing.
Disappear quietly,
come for new directions.
Speed is of utmost importance,
as is secrecy.

"Follow Jedediah very discretely, Ogier." Alcuin directed. "He's not to suspect a thing. I want to know what he does, exactly, in Pavia. If he leaves there, follow him. Give this ten days. If he still travels away from us, you turn and come home. When you arrive back here, report to me on his journey. Pay heed to your own safety; and know we all, everyone at court, is in your debt." Ogier nodded briskly and took leave of the scholar.

***

Ogier rode hard to Pavia and, from there, to the old Lombard court. Five days in the saddle utterly exhausted him. If he delivered the missive and Brother Jedediah left immediately, Ogier had not the strength to follow. He must rest. He rode out of town and found a small inn. After eating, he wiped down his horse, fed it an adequate--but not generous-- allotment of oats, and bedded down in the hay loft. All was quiet as he drifted off to sleep. Just as the sky lightened, Ogier mounted his horse once again and rode quietly out of town for a mile or so. Once beyond the sleeping sentries, he turned his horse back toward Pavia and soon clattered into the sleeping courtyard. He demanded to see Brother Jedediah immediately. A gnarled inn-keeper led him to a chamber near-by. Jedediah came to the chamber door, identified himself, and took the letter. He spoke gruffly.

"Wait for a reply." He did not invite Ogier in out of the cold nor offer him a meal.

Spattered with mud from his ride and wrapped in a worn, voluminous mantle, Ogier sat on the stones of the stairs and waited. Fairly quickly, the chamber door opened and the monk came out. Seeing Ogier, he spat.

"I've no reply. Refresh yourself." Jedediah added, throwing Ogier a coin for his trouble.

Ogier climbed on his great horse, rolled his mantle and secured it to the pommel. He moved quietly behind a near-by stable and waited for the monk to appear. Ogier turned his horse homeward as Brother Jedediah cantered out of the stable, alone and apparently in a great hurry. He rode quietly behind the big man, pacing his horse and himself for the day.

The big monk stayed on the main road, stopping often to confer with passing pilgrims and verify the route of King Charlemagne's circuit. After a brief inquiry to a traveler, he would remount his horse and continue his steady pace. He slept five to six hours of the night in a makeshift camp, apparently dead asleep. He ate no hot meals, apparently having brought provisions which he could eat as he rode.

Even though he got less sleep, Ogier prepared a hot drink at each night's stop and warmed beans and bread. He realized Jedediah rode toward Charlemagne's court and, so, he didn't need to keep the big monk always in sight. Still, he followed. Long before light hit the morning sky, the monk started out again. Now, he avoided travelers on the road and moved steadily north.

In due time, Ogier saw smoke rising from King Charlemagne's campfires. He slowed his horse and let it amble forward, keeping Brother Jedediah in sight.

The monk rode into the east side of the soldiers' camp, hailed a young boy and spoke to him. Ogier watched carefully. The lad ran directly to Abbot Fulrad's tent and went inside. He reappeared immediately, holding a loaf of bread. Seeing the lad's broad smile, Ogier surmised the Abbot rewarded the lad for his message. Ogier nodded, knowing the young boy and his family would eat much better this day. When Jedediah handed his horse to a stable boy, Ogier unsaddled his own horse and left him to graze. Jedediah headed immediately toward the river.

Ogier followed slowly and spied Abbot Fulrad walking rapidly toward the east. He didn't enter the camp but skirted the bank of the river. It seemed the Abbot and the monk walked in the same direction. Fearing discovery, Ogier slipped behind massive boulders at the rivers' edge. He knew a crevice between two large stones which looked out on the river and in the direction of the two men. He settled on a boulder as Abbot Fulrad raised his hand and looked toward the trees. Brother Jedediah came forward. The two men walked toward Ogier's hiding place, stopping just in front of the crevice between the stones. Ogier slipped quietly to the ground. Hidden behind the two seven foot slabs of rock, he easily overheard the men's conversation.

"I'm surprised to see you, my friend," Abbot Fulrad said to Jedediah. "I told you to wait for my message. You shouldn't be here."

"What are you saying?" the monk questioned. "You sent me a missive. You told me to come quickly. Here I am. What's your next pleasure — something more effective than a kidnapping or a rape, I would bet!"

"Shut your mouth, you dirty swine," the Abbot hissed. "I've not summoned you, letter or not. My plan did not succeed; it's true. But I don't need you. Why are you here?" The Abbot glared at the monk, fingering a leather whip which he held in plain view.

"Don't make a mistake you'll regret, Abbot." The monk growled, nodding at the whip. "You don't frighten me. I make more than two of you. Regret not following my lead? If I gave the orders, 'stead of the other way 'round, the King's wings would be clipped already, along with some badly used children. But, nay, you have to control everyone--preen your ego, I'd say. And, look, you've an-other botched kidnapping." Contempt dripped from his voice. His body slouched as he leaned against a boulder.

"Another opportunity is at hand." With exaggerated calm, Fulrad ignored the man's criticism. "The King's children plan to be in the orchard picking peaches when the court camps overnight at Rouens. Hide nearby and pick them off with arrows. One of them or all, it makes no difference to me. Let no one see or take you. Do you hear me? I will reward you as promised.Don't fail me in this, Jed," he warned. The Abbot glared at the monk.

Ahh, so here's the Abbot's henchman! Ogier's breath caught. *Dear God, what will Charlemagne think of this? He's not likely to believe me, not if the Abbot denies his plot.* He frowned, then he remembered Alcuin's part in this. *The scholar has some plan; I'll leave the surprises to him.* He looked at the two men, once again. *Fulrad is no match for this monk. He must know it. Only Fulrad's religious authority has power and it works very poorly to keep evil men under control.*

"Leave me be, Abbot." Jedediah answered. "This time you get the result you crave. I will not fail. When I hurt one of Charlemagne's children...or kill one...I'll contact you. Until then, stay out of the way and *act* innocent. In-nocence, of a certainty, does not apply to you holy men--leastwise not one like you!" He laughed uproariously and walked away.

Ogier skirted the huge boulders, keeping well out of sight as he slipped behind the trees and bushes at the forest edge. Although he was an expert in the ways of the forest's hidden perils, his life would be forfeit if Fulrad saw him. Small rodents bustled through the underbrush as birds called shrilly to each other. The impenetrable trees stood silently, sentinels guarding the forests' secrets. Ogier hurried to the guardsmen's tent.

"Lawrance, restrain the monk who's leaving the camp; he's there behind those huge boulders east of the river." He ordered. "You can spot him easily. In fact, you'll smell him afore you see him. His stained, torn cloak is dull brown, his head covered by a hood. Guard him in the prison tent. Say nothing to him, ask him nothing. But guard him well. You may provide food and water, no ale—no matter how often he requests it."

"Aye, Lord Ogier. I go myself for this duty." The guardsman answered.

***

Ogier went directly to Alcuin. He described his trip to Pavia, Jedediah's return and the conversation between the monk and Abbot Fulrad. Alcuin summoned Angilbert. The three men stood in front of the scholar's fire pit. Although spring warmth was in the air, all three men felt chilled. They looked miserably at each other.

"And so, here's the answer," Alcuin broke the quiet. "How do we present this to the King? He is ever loyal. His heart will break when he understands this friend, this teacher from his childhood, does so betray him. I confess; I find Fulrad's behavior difficult to comprehend. What does the Abbot hope to gain by harming Charlemagne's children? What can be more important than the love and high regard he enjoys here?" Alcuin stumbled over his words, overcome by Fulrad's betrayal. *What drove the Abbot to betray the King, a man who was a son to him?*

"Master, we must not describe this to King Charlemagne. I fear his temper will destroy us all, before he makes sense of the plot. We must, somehow, get the Abbot to confess. Can we use Jedediah to show the Abbot's betrayal? Might the King confront them?" *Only then will the truth stand uncovered to Charlemagne.*

"Aye, such a revelation would be the most effective course; but, how, my son, how to bring it about?" Alcuin asked. Angilbert hung his head. He did not know. But his humor rose quickly.

"I've described the result, Master; you must devise the method."

"Ha!" Ogier laughed. "I understand your regard for each other! This repartee makes each encounter a delight! When all this is settled, I simply must spend more of my time in your company." Then, he sobered.

"I have a suggestion. It'll be by the grace of God if my idea produces clarity. But, let's summon this monk before the King and have the Abbot in the room with them? If we're lucky, Fulrad or Jedediah will make a mistake, will interact poorly with each other, and arouse Charlemagne's suspicions. Guilt often produces unsought confessions. If this produces any reaction, we may, then, pursue it to its conclusion, without accusing anyone." Angilbert suggested, even as Rinaldo shook his head.

"I fear the King's temper. When angry, he often over-reacts and rushes to a completely incorrect conclusion. Master Alcuin, do you think this will work? I know it's risky. Mayhap, you have a better plan?" Ogier implored.

"Nay, I do not. This idea is brilliant, Ogier—to have them confront each other. But if neither of the men says anything, bringing them together will cause us three serious repercussions. As Angilbert said, the King's temper may mow us down. We shall bear its brunt when Charlemagne realizes we imprisoned Jedediah. There's no good if we're forgiven after we lose our heads. Secondly, Fulrad will have reason to criticize and attack us all. In the worst scenario, we may be banished. And, lastly, in a fit, the King may give Jedediah full run of the court. He may complete his dark deed. I fear for the children." Alcuin paused.

"Sobering, isn't it?" He looked around at his compatriots. "Despite these worries, I believe this idea is worth the risk. ...a priest, who would murder a child? I would gladly give my life to end this barbarism."

"If you two agree, I will approach the King." Ogier suggested. "I know, as you and Angilbert do not, his passion for theatre. He loves the dramatic and participates in plays in the banquet hall himself. He always delights in playing the villain's part. I suspect this will start as a lark to him...if I can set the scene appropriately."

"Do as you must, then," Alcuin agreed. "But as the drama unfolds, remove yourself from his sight." Alcuin worried about Ogier's safety-- about all of them, if the truth be told. He and Angilbert already agreed to expose Fulrad to the King but Ogier did no such thing. His safety was a grave concern.

***

Ogier requested an immediate audience with the King. Because it was early morning, Charlemagne summoned him into his sleeping tent. The King had just returned from his daily prayers.

"A splendid morn to you, Ogier! You are up and about early. It must be the promise of spring in the air. Do you have an entreaty for me on this beautiful morn?" The king asked. He was in fine humor, hopeful the sadness and dreariness of winter would soon be behind them all.

"Sire, good morrow to you. An exciting possibility just arose. I want your help. We have the promise of a splendid homecoming for one of our court members." Ogier smiled broadly, hoping to convince Charlemagne of his delight.

"During the night, an old friend of Abbot Fulrad arrived in camp. He, Jedediah by name, has no notion Abbot Fulrad is a member of your court. He told us they were once brothers in the same monastery but lost track of each other and have not seen one another in many years. It's possible this Jedediah was in King Pepin's court for a brief time."

"Some of us thought we should bring them together, not telling either his friend is here! Such a reunion will gladden every heart, remind us all of long friendship!" Ogier raised his eyebrow at the King. "It's likely to provide a bit of spice in our long litany of criminal cases this morn. What do you think?" Ogier attempted to fill his voice with suppressed laughter, suggesting this unexpected reunion would provide entertainment.

"Over the years, both of them have changed, I do not doubt. Easy recognition and remembrance may prove difficult. As the 're-uniter,' you may need to call their names, one to the other," he suggested slyly. "Wouldn't it be gratifying to reunite old friends and, then, to honor them at the evening meal? We celebrate Louis's birth date tonight, don't we?"

"Aye, we do! How splendid, Ogier! What a wonderful coincidence! This would add another layer of festivity for our feast. Aye! It is Louis' birth celebration. And since we do not celebrate it with him in Aquitaine, this gives us even more reason to reunite these two friends. What steps do you suggest I take?"

"I think it best for you to bring them together, in your presence only, for the initial reunion. No one would want to stand looking at another in full view of court members, trying to place a person in the context of former years. After the morn's court cases are finished, meet them in the library. You may break any silence by a suggestive statement, such as 'I have heard some worrisome news about you Fulrad...from an old acquaintance.'" Ogier suggested.

"Be as dramatic as you can, Sire. Let us put them both on guard."

"Aye, let's do it!" The King delighted in the charade.

***

The morning hours crawled pass. Alcuin, Angilbert, and Rinaldo waited impatiently for the morning court to conclude. They had no other plan, should this one fail. If it did, they could only go to the King, describe their suspicions, and leave it to him to confront the Abbot.

"I dread this second resort," Angilbert voiced each man's feeling. "The Abbot may know the King better than he knows himself. Queen Hildegard does for certain. If that be the case, Fulrad will re-interpret everything-- despite any explanations, exhortations, or threats Jedediah makes. And we may be sure the Abbot will emerge victorious, not just exonerated of any wrongdoing."

"This is my concern exactly, Gil," admitted Alcuin. "But we have no proof of their scheme, no surety Jedediah was, indeed, involved in the attack on Rotrude. Neither can we prove the Abbot is behind all the previous threats. It's my conviction these attacks and their plans come from one person."

"We know King Desiderius would readily provide resources to implement any or all of them. I daresay Prince Adelchis, secure in Italy, might lend his support as well. He was happy here at court; but the Lombard war stripped him of all: his inheritance, his position, his kingdom. He gives up nothing, forfeits nothing, if King Charlemagne weakens.

"On the contrary, Charlemagne's fall would strengthen his claim overnight...especially if he and King Carloman's sons are of like mind. The frightening possibility is a collaboration between Adelchis and Gebnega. They might have used Pippin to further their dreams. If they approached Pippin with acceptance and warmth, they may have won his heart and his support."

"His lack of ambition is noteworthy." Angilbert commented.

***

Finally, the court was over for the morning. The three friends gathered in the small tent adjacent to the library where paper workers repaired and re-bound old parchments confiscated from conquered estates. They heard the guardsmen at the door of the tent.

"I was ordered to stand guard outside," one of them spoke. "Take the prisoner in and tie his hands behind his back. King Charlemagne ordered him to stand on the right side of the tent, there in the corner. We expect the King momentarily." At Rinaldo's suggestion, Ogier told the guardsmen the King wished to question the prisoner who was accused of stealing books.

"Good day to you, Karl." King Charlemagne greeted the outside guard. "Please wait. My questions of this prisoner will not take long." The King entered the tent.

"Good day to you, Brother Jedediah." Charlemagne

nodded to the monk. He frowned and looked quickly into the brother's face. "Have you been here in my court before?" Jedediah did not respond immediately. Fulrad told him repeatedly that he must deny acquaintance with anyone in the Church. Their acquaintance must not be suspected…not by anyone.

"Nay." Jedediah replied. "I seldom leave Lombard, Sire." Charlemagne still did not smile, though he thought the monk looked familiar.

"As you probably know, I'm a great lover of books and confiscate those discovered among my prisoners. I wish to know your own reasons for book thievery. Did you steal the books to sell them or…to read them yourself? Might you happen to be a rare member of the clergy who actually can read?" The King smiled.

"Damn it all to hell, I have no interest in books." Jedediah replied, his hands balled into fists, his face beet red. "I stole nothing! I'm a monk, by God. I don't steal! I was passing your camp when…"

"Wait. I hear someone approaching," the King interrupted. There was a shuffle at the door of the tent. Abbot Fulrad entered. He turned to the King, opened his mouth to speak, and, then recognized Jedediah. King Charlemagne watched the Abbot closely for signs of recognition; and, it must be added, delight. The flash of anger which crossed Fulrad's face surprised him. At the Abbot's stern look, Charlemagne understood the Abbot recognized the monk but attempted to cover his recognition. The King spoke.

"Look, Abbot Fulrad, one of your old friends has been inquiring about you." King Charlemagne beckoned to Jedediah who stood rooted in place. "He insisted you couldn't be in my court but…"

"I don't know this man." The Abbot responded quick-

446

ly, snapping his fingers in dismissal. "I never laid eyes on him. By the looks of him, he surely is not a monk. This man is too dirty, too unkempt, and too coarse to be about the Lord's work!" Fulrad stepped back, as if to distance himself from the monk. "Don't shame me by connecting this creature to me, Sire." Fulrad said to the King.

"You so judge me, do you?" Jedediah snarled back, his face dark with anger. "I do your bidding for 'nigh on twenty years and you judge me coarse? ...damn you to everlasting hell, you harlot-born scum!" Jedediah spit out.

"Ah, then, you know this man?" Charlemagne turned to the monk, confused by the denial but, even more, by the venom between the two men.

"Know him? ...for certain!" Jedediah shouted. "He's an ass, a hard-driving bastard, if there ever was one! See those cold, sneaky eyes? He betrays a friend in a heart-beat. Know him! How well I know and loathe him both!"

King Charlemagne was thunderstruck. This was not the "reunion" he envisioned between old friends. But, playing for the dramatic moment—just as Rinaldo hoped—Charlemagne said nothing more. He waited for the confrontation to build, instinctively knowing secrets were going to come out. What are these two men to each other, he wondered.

"Shut your mouth, you fool!" the Abbot snarled. "I don't know you! You mistake me for some other abbot. Where would I possibly meet the likes of you? I don't fre-quent brothels, drink in slime pits nor carouse with low life!" Jedediah stepped forward, out of the corner. Fulrad realized his mistake and stood with his palms out, his eyes pleading as he gazed at Jedediah.

"Your game's finished, Abbot." Jedediah's face was now deadly white. "All these years, all these plans, all this hate...I weary of you. Your hate directs my life no more. If I rot in hell, I'll know you're there with me. Your mind is the one to create these horrors. I? I was the hands! No more, Fulrad! No more." Abbot Fulrad was aghast. He stood frozen, mesmerized by the unnatural calm in Jedediah's eyes.

"I deny everything he says." the Abbot muttered softly. "I'm innocent."

The King was stupefied; he did not understand the men's accusations. He looked at Jedediah with a questioning stare, totally lost. Jedediah deliberately turned his back on the Abbot and spoke directly to King Charlemagne.

"Here is the source of your fear, Sire," he spoke. "Here stands the threat to your life, to your children, aye, to your very realm. I became the sword used to undo your rule—to murder you, to steal your babes. I with my misplaced loyalty--through my consort with the devil—labored to destroy you. Aye, I deserve to die! But I will not die alone! By God, I will not die alone!" The King leaned heavily against the library table, his face white, his hands trembling.

At that moment, Alcuin, Angilbert, and Rinaldo pushed through the door of the tent. Seeing them, Abbot Fulrad collapsed to the floor, weeping bitter tears and tearing at his face. The three men went to the King.

"Why, Fulrad? Why?" Master Alcuin whispered as he put his hand on the King's shoulder.

"You fool!" the Abbot shouted, snarling wildly at Alcuin. "You goddamn fool! The King's dreams and your skills do threaten everything I hold dear. This vision you share, this vision of educating the people...it is blasphemy! Educating the people will draw power from the clergy! Our guidance, our leadership, our interpretations of God's will -- all will be lost! The people look to the clergy for guidance; your education will encourage them to think, to defy God's holy men, to ignore the direction we supply. Such independent thinking, studying the scriptures themselves, interpreting as they will...such education weakens the Church."

"Church brothers will be puppets to this great King, the King who knows everything. He rewrites Church law; he appoints church leaders as he pleases, never consulting me or the bishops! He even thinks he can write music for the chants!" Abbot Fulrad pointed at Alcuin.

"In his pride, he reorganizes the Church, simplifies Church sacraments, assesses and judges clergy weaknesses. Your arrival here encouraged him, increased the speed of his efforts. This education for all, this vision of learning, thinking people--this is his last blasphemy in a life of barbarism." Fulrad pressed his hands to his lips in an effort to stop his speech. But he was so overwrought, he continued to scream at the four men.

"I dealt with the King's multiple marriages, two of them totally and completely against the will of God! What evil...to put away two lawful wives... to marry yet another! And, then, this third one — child after child she bears to this uncaring, lustful king! At least, King Pepin upheld the marriage bond. The Pope ever admired his restraint. King Charlemagne had a perfect model in his father. But did he note him? Did he value him? Nay! Nay! He and his evil mother mocked God's holy injunctions."

"And, then, this King who I made, who I made...! I who raised him from a child, I who taught him all he knew! He mocked my clergy--told me they were filthy, their morals had to be cleansed. But did he clean his own behavior? Nay! Did he slake his own lust? Nay, he was **the King** and above God's holy law!" Fulrad paused, exhausted from his own anger. He spoke again, more quietly this time.

"Then, I saw he did not die as other men, could not be felled by an arrow, by a knife, or by stealthy attack. Each of my efforts failed. I looked for another method and realized I would do best to destroy his spirit--destroy the living King and have a husk left! The best horror, the most awful punishment was to kill one...or more... of his children. It didn't matter which child! I would've killed them all, if I could. Then, God would be avenged. Our king would never thwart another holy law. I worked to destroy him. He and his hope, he and his vision for an educated people... I rejoiced in attempting to stop him at last!"

King Charlemagne cried out. He felt his knees weaken; he fell. From the floor, Charlemagne stared at Abbot Fulrad in disbelief. He watched the Abbot struggle and saw Alcuin and Angilbert physically restrain him.

Alcuin cried out. "Guards, come! Get in here!" The guards bound Fulrad's and Jedediah's hands and took them away."

Rinaldo sped to the herbalist's tent and returned with hot tea. All the while, King Charlemagne sat on the tent cushions, toying with the fringe of a pillow.

"Sire, drink this immediately." Rinaldo directed as he held the mug to the King's mouth. Without a sound, the King drank down the hot liquid. He clearly had no awareness of his surroundings or of his friends.

"Help him lie down, Rinaldo." Alcuin suggested. "The tea will hasten his sleep. We do all man can do for him now. I hope his mind is strong; this is a cruel blow." Alcuin covered the King with a heavy linen and sat.

"It does seem an impossibility, does it not?" asked Angilbert. "The man who taught him, who advised him, who loved him as a son. How do we explain such betrayal?"

450

"There's no black and white, my son," Alcuin answered. "There is always the extenuating circumstance. Some interpreters of religious belief refuse to accept that. They view the Father as a punisher: full of anger, favoring one believer above another, dictating strict laws which must be obeyed. Beware always those who are 'full of religion.' Their judgments damn us all, their lack of respect fuels horrible slaughter, and their love of power condemns all to suffering. Here, you see one of them before you. No matter his love for the King, the Abbot judged, damned and sought to hasten Charlemagne's punishment."

"The King...." Rinaldo murmured. "Will he survive this shock? Will he have the strength to go on?" He sat beside Alcuin on the bench and clasped the scholar's shoulder for strength.

"We can but wait." Alcuin replied as Angilbert sank slowly to the floor. The three men waited throughout the night for the King to waken. And, finally, King Charlemagne did wake, posing questions to them all.

"Why does God punish me?" He asked. "Firstly, it was Poppa whom I lost. My dear, wise Poppa who could have given me direction. Does the Father judge me evil? I lost Carloman and hoped his death was the end of the sadness. But it was not to be. Next, I lost my dear, little Adelhaid; and, following her, Lothar lived only a few months. Both my babes died overnight, it seemed. I had no way to save them!" The King fell to his knees, tears streaming down his face, soaking his tunic.

"But sorrow was not finished with me. I lost my dear brother, Roland. Never was there one so admirable as he, the epitome of a Peer. Who will be next? God help me!" He stopped speaking as the sobs filled his throat. "How can I go on? How can I name yet others I have lost? Dear, gentle Oliver took himself away from me--not as final as death, perhaps, but much more painful in the end." King Charlemagne ranted; he moaned; he wept.

"And, now, Abbot Fulrad: the guide of my childhood, the teacher of my youth, the friend of my maturing. How can he hate me so completely...that he tried to kill my children? What disgust and vehemence flowed from his mouth! Am I truly this lost, this far removed from God's holy laws, this deserving of His punishment! Oh, God, what shall I do?"

Rinaldo opened the tent flap to Gisela, to Queen Hildegard and to Charlemagne's children. They all clustered around the King. Rotrude and Bertha clasped his hands and wept with him. Charles stood by his father's side, stretching to hold his arm around the King's waist. Little Gisela grasped his left leg, unsteady on her toddler feet. Queen Hildegard hurried into the chamber from the corridor, coming directly to her husband, seeing no one else in the chamber.

"What can I do?" The King asked again, looking into Hilde's face.

"You must go on." Alcuin replied quietly, seeing Hildegard's pleading eyes.

"Look around you. Here are your children; here is your future...and the future of this realm. You must go on; create the world you envision for them. You must; there is no one else. There is no other choice." King Charlemagne looked into the scholar's intent face.

Rotrude pulled on her father's hand. She raised her eyes to his face.

"Poppa? You're strong. Help Ma-mam and Master Alc 'n." She whispered.

King Charlemagne stroked the side of his daughter's face; he hugged his little daughter to his chest. Rotrude's simple words opened his eyes. The King saw Alcuin's bafflement, Hildegard's shock and sorrow, the Peers' pain.

"If only Oliver were still among us, he would know exactly what I should do. But, alas, he is here no more. I'm relieved the Father spared him this sadness." He looked into the eyes of the men in the room; he gazed at his children.

"Aye." King Charlemagne nodded his head. "We must persevere; we have a new world to build. Let us begin." Alcuin came to his side.

"We will help you." Alcuin promised softly.

The End

Here ends volume 3 of The Carolingian Chronicles.

Lightning Source UK Ltd.
Milton Keynes UK
UKHW031125200922
409142UK00001B/25